Praise for
bestselling a

"Palmer demonstrates, yet again, why she's the queen of desperado quests for justice and true love."

—*Publishers Weekly*

"You just can't do better than a Diana Palmer story to make your heart lighter and smile brighter."

—*Fresh Fiction* on *Wyoming Rugged*

Dear Reader,

I've had Cal Hollister's story on a back burner for years, but it wasn't until I wrote *Wyoming Strong* that I finally connected Amelia with him. The problem was how to tell their story. The only way to do that was in flashbacks. You may think that it ends too abruptly. But it's an affirmation of a love that survived the worst efforts of twisted people to kill it. And when the truth came out, so did all the anger and pain.

It was while I was working on this novel that my German shepherd, Dietrich, was diagnosed with Lou Gehrig's disease. Yes, dogs get it, too. It's progressive. There is no cure. So I enjoy each day I have with him to the fullest, and I try not to look ahead. It's a reminder that life comes with no guarantees. And a reminder not to take one single hour of it for granted.

I send my warmest regards to the University of Georgia's Small Animal Clinic, where tests revealed Dietrich's disease. The personnel there, and our own Dr. Cecily Nieh, and my friend Chris especially, and the staff have been so kind to us both. I support research into this terrible disease. And I thank all of you for your kindness and patience if my books are a little more spread out while I care for my lovely fur child.

Diana Palmer

RANCHER'S LAW

NEW YORK TIMES BESTSELLING AUTHOR
DIANA PALMER

FREE STORY BY
TERI WILSON

SPECIAL RELEASE

ISBN-13: 978-1-335-00744-5

Rancher's Law
First published in 2024. This edition published in 2024.

Dog Days of Summer
First published in 2024. This edition published in 2024.

For questions and comments about the quality of this book, please contact us at CustomerService@Harlequin.com.

Harlequin Enterprises ULC
22 Adelaide St. West, 41st Floor
Toronto, Ontario M5H 4E3, Canada
www.Harlequin.com

Printed in U.S.A.

CONTENTS

RANCHER'S LAW 7
Diana Palmer

DOG DAYS OF SUMMER 221
Teri Wilson

Author of more than two hundred books, **Diana Palmer** lives with three Maine coon cats and a German shepherd in Habersham County, Georgia. She was married to James Kyle for forty-eight years, before losing him to Covid in 2021. They have one son, a daughter-in-law and two grandchildren. Her main hobby is gaming (PC and Xbox). She graduated summa cum laude with a BA in history in 1995. She loves hearing from her readers. She can be found online at Twitter (under cehntahr, her gamer handle), also on Facebook and at www.dianapalmer.com.

Also by Diana Palmer

Long, Tall Texans

Fearless
Heartless
Dangerous
Merciless
Courageous
Protector
Invincible
Untamed
Defender
Undaunted
Unbridled
Unleashed
Notorious
The Loner

The Wyoming Men

Wyoming Tough
Wyoming Fierce
Wyoming Bold
Wyoming Strong
Wyoming Rugged
Wyoming Brave
Wyoming Winter
Wyoming Legend
Wyoming Heart
Wyoming True
Wyoming Homecoming

Visit her Author Profile page
at Harlequin.com for more titles!

RANCHER'S LAW

Diana Palmer

To all the researchers trying valiantly to
find a cure for Lou Gehrig's disease. It is a
human disease, but it can also affect canines,
like my poor German shepherd, Dietrich. One day,
there will be a cure. I contribute to the cause.

Chapter One

Cal Hollister nursed his piña colada, only half watching the flamenco dancers on the dance floor at Fernando's in San Antonio. He wasn't sure why he kept coming here, except that she'd enjoyed the music back in the days when they were friends. Before the big blowup that had left him reeling with shock and fury.

He was drop-dead gorgeous. Tall, broad-shouldered, with thick blond hair and black eyes. Women noticed him. He never even looked up.

He sipped his drink, his mind far away. It had been seven years. All that time. He'd married a San Antonio socialite only two days after the woman from his past had brought the world down on his head. His socialite had herded him, drunk and in anguish, to a justice of the peace. And he'd texted the woman who betrayed him with bitter, shaming words and the news that he was now married. At the time, it had seemed exactly the right thing to do.

She, the socialite—Edie Prince by name—had always said that the other woman was too young and carefree to settle down. She'd convinced him that revenge was his best bet, and he'd said it was justified.

But the breakup was bad timing. He'd just come home from a devastating mission that had left him sick of his own hopeful new career and aching all over for Amelia. Her grief had led to an unforgettable night in bed, one that led to tragedy.

Guilt had ridden him hard afterward. At her grandfather's funeral, he'd taken Edie with him, just so he wouldn't have to face Amelia alone. He knew it had hurt and confused her. But then, he was confused, too. He'd thought mercenary work was right up his alley, with his background in police work. Well, it wasn't. He'd seen things, done things, that haunted him still.

He'd stayed away from Amelia for weeks while he got counseling, put his life back together, changed jobs and became settled. He'd finally come to terms with his feelings for her. He even had a set of rings in his pocket. He'd been looking forward to starting a new life. Then Amelia's great-aunt, in a fit of rage, had called him to say that Amelia had solved their little problem and now there were no complications, so he was free to seduce another innocent woman, wasn't he?

He took another swallow of the drink. That news had started him on the downward spiral that led him right into marriage with his worst nightmare. So long ago. So much pain. He'd given Amelia hell, not allowing her to even get a word in edgewise, not giving her a chance to defend herself, explain herself. And to complicate matters, a few days later, at the end of a drinking binge that had almost landed him in jail, he'd married Edie. Biggest mistake of his life.

It was a shame that he'd sobered up soon afterward.

Because Edie had faults that he hadn't known about when he'd put that ring on her finger. He hadn't known that she was a blatant alcoholic; that she used drugs; that she was a habitual liar. He'd found all those things out one by one.

She'd said they could have children, but that was before he found out that she'd had a hysterectomy some years before, and that she'd never wanted children.

They were a nuisance, she told him, and she wasn't risking her figure to add another squalling brat to the world.

It had only taken him a few days to realize that what he really felt for her, when he wasn't drunk, was contempt. He'd married her out of spite, to rub it in that Amelia meant nothing to him, that he'd never cared for her.

It had been a lie. His life had been hell for three long years before Edie finally drank too much one night and, after adding narcotics to the mix, had put herself in the morgue.

Cal, who'd given up mercenary work to hire on with the San Antonio Police Department, had climbed from patrolman to sergeant, then to lieutenant. He was now captain of the detective squad, a testament to his ability to manage cases and get along with politicians and protesters alike. Promotions that usually took years had taken him far less time, through a series of lucky breaks and ability.

But his job, although satisfying, was just a job. He went home to an empty house on his Jacobsville ranch, where he lived alone. He'd given Edie's house to a distant cousin of hers, who promptly sold it. Cal hadn't wanted it. The place held too many memories of his drunken wife making his life hell. He moved into an apartment and then, not long afterward, bought a small ranch in Jacobsville, where he and Amelia had first met.

People in his department noticed that he never dated. They assumed it was because he was still mourning his late wife. Nothing was further from the truth. He'd hated Edie with a passion. When he was finally cold sober, he slowly came to realize that he might not have had the whole story about what had happened in the past. But after he married Edie, he hadn't done any checking. He didn't want to know. Amelia was out of his life, and he could never trust her again, even if they met again someday.

He didn't know where she was, or what she was doing. He'd heard rumors that she was involved in some covert work, but that didn't sound like the young girl who'd listened, fascinated, to his stories about his mercenary years. She was soft and gentle, not at all the sort of person to involve herself in violence.

He grieved for the young girl she'd been when they'd first known each other. He never should have touched her in the first place, but he'd wanted her so desperately, for so long, until she was all he thought about. What happened was…inevitable, he supposed. But what came after had destroyed him.

Why hadn't she told him about the child? Didn't she realize that he'd have married her at once? He'd planned it even before he knew there was a child. He adored her. When he'd gone on that last mission, he'd almost ended up shot because he was thinking about her instead of the danger he was facing.

Only to be presented with evidence that she'd gotten rid of his child. She'd gone to a clinic. She hadn't wanted him, or the baby, and she hadn't even bothered to tell him. He'd been bitter. So bitter. He'd called her names, raged at her, damned her for what she'd done. But here he sat, after all these years, in Fernando's. Hoping she might walk in some day, because he'd brought her here at least twice to introduce her to the addictive tango. And he'd taught her to dance it.

It was stupid. She'd never come back. Her life was elsewhere, somewhere. Hell, she might even be married by now.

That thought depressed him even more. He finished his drink just as he spotted his friend Clancey sitting with her little brother, Tad, and her new husband, Colter Banks. Clancey had worked for him several years ago. He was fond of her and Tad. They were like the family he didn't have. He'd looked out for them until Banks came along. Well, he liked Banks, and it was good to see Clancey and Tad settled. But he was alone again. He didn't have friends, unless you included Father Eduardo, a fellow merc who'd taken the collar. He had a church in San Antonio smack dab in the middle of gang territory. But Los Serpientes had learned the hard way not to attack this priest. He'd put them in the hospital. Seven armed men, and he'd put them all down. Two had joined his church afterward. He chuckled silently. Father Eduardo was a local legend.

He paid the check and walked over to the table where Clancey was sitting with her family.

Clancey invited him to sit down after introducing her cousin from Chicago. The woman was nice-looking, but she was a brunette. Cal wouldn't have been interested even if she'd been a blond, though. He was still buried in thoughts of the past, in misery and anguish for what he'd lost.

Just as he started to excuse himself and go home, he saw her. There, at the counter, picking up an order. She hadn't aged a day! It had been years, and she was just the same as he remembered her.

He murmured something, unaware that his companions were staring at him. Amelia. His heart tried to climb into his throat. Same pretty figure, same pretty face, same blond hair in a bun atop her head. He'd have recognized her in a crowd of thousands.

She turned with her purchase, still smiling, until she spotted Cal. The smile was suddenly gone, wiped away like magic, to be replaced by a look of such anger that he felt those eyes making holes in him.

Amelia, he thought in anguish.

But if she felt anguish, it didn't show. She glared at him, turned and walked out of the restaurant. He murmured something to the people at the table and went out after her. He got to the sidewalk, and she was just gone, just like that.

He shoved his hands into his pockets and stared out at the misting rain with dark eyes that mirrored his misery. So many years without a sight of her, and here she was, back in San Antonio. But where? Doing what? He was going to have to do some digging. He had to find a way to talk to her. Somehow.

Amelia Grayson had darted around the corner of Fernando's and hailed a cab back to her new apartment.

Her heart was going like a fast watch, and she could barely catch her breath as she told the cab driver where to take her. She hadn't expected to see Cal. But, of course, she knew that he'd always gone there on Friday nights when he was in town to watch the flamenco dancers. And the tango.

He was a past master at tango, one of the few men she'd ever known who could dance it. In fact, he'd taught her, in the days when they were like one person, when the world began and ended with him in her life.

That was over. He'd never given her a chance to explain what had happened. It no longer mattered, anyway, she told herself. If somebody cared for you, they wanted an explanation. They wanted your side of the story. It wasn't like that with Cal. He'd attacked her verbally the minute he saw her. Accusations, blame, hatred, in the space of seconds, after they'd been so close that they almost breathed together.

He'd gone out of town on police business for two weeks. She'd been living with a hateful great-aunt here in the city, one now long dead and forgotten. After a tragic loss, and two days in the hospital, she'd left her great-aunt's house and gone straight to Eb Scott with her bags packed and her heart encased in ice. He'd always said he wouldn't train women, but she changed his mind. She told him what had happened. She lost her job, her home, her child… Cal. Everything. She had no place to go. So how about training her?

And he had.

Amelia hailed a taxi to her apartment. She just sat there, after giving the driver her address, in the back seat, staring into space. Seeing Cal so unexpectedly had opened gaping wounds.

The woman he'd married seven years ago was a socialite she knew. The woman had been a pest. She came down from the city on weekends to pester Cal, who seemed to find her amusing. At least, he never sent her away. Amelia had been furiously jealous, but he'd only laughed and said the woman was harmless; just bored and flamboyant. He'd known a dozen like her.

So Amelia hadn't fussed. But the woman, Edie Prince, didn't like her and made a point of trashing her clothes, her accent, anything she could find to pick on. Cal didn't seem to notice. He said she was just kidding, and Amelia shouldn't take her seriously.

That must have included not believing her when she said that Cal was just playing with Amelia because she was a novelty in his life, but he was going to marry Edie, so Amelia might as well enjoy Cal's company in the little bit of time left to her.

Amelia didn't believe her. The socialite had just laughed.

She'd see, she'd replied. And soon. Then, Amelia's grandfather had died. She and Cal had grown quickly intimate, but he'd backed off at once. She hadn't understood what had happened to him in Africa, not until she joined Eb Scott's counterterrorism unit. She did now, too late. Cal had been coping—rather, not coping—with trauma from what he'd seen and had to do in Ngawa. He'd been confused and upset, and she hadn't understood that it was just too much too soon.

But the baby was a fact. Her great-aunt, with whom she'd lived up in Victoria after her grandfather's sudden death, had been a fanatic about the family name never being soiled. And here was her great-niece, living with her, pregnant out of wedlock! Worse, Amelia was planning to keep the baby! Everyone in town would know. Great-Aunt Valeria was horrified. She'd acted out of that horror and caused a much worse tragedy.

When Amelia got out of the hospital, she had an aide go and pack her things and bring her suitcase to the hospital. The pain was too raw to allow her to even speak to the woman who'd done so much damage. From the hospital, she went to Eb.

So much pain. So much anguish.

And the worst was yet to come. Cal called her and she wasn't able to get one word in about what had really happened. He'd made his opinion of her known, railed at her, raged at her. He'd been drunk out of his mind, but she didn't know that. And he didn't know that Edie had phoned her earlier to thank her for getting rid of that little complication that Cal didn't want anyway.

Not three days after the accident, Cal married the flamboyant socialite. Everybody in town knew because Cal had put the announcement in the local newspaper. Amelia had lunched at Barbara's Café in Jacobsville on her way to Eb Scott's place, with sympathetic glances making her uncomfortable. It was a small town, and most people knew that she and Cal had been close. When couples broke up, it was food for gossip. Especially when one partner married someone else after the breakup. They thought of Amelia as family, and they were protective of her. It wasn't until much later, when she was doing jobs for Eb, that she'd learned Cal had bought a ranch in Jacobsville. But he had to shop for it in San Antonio. The owner of the feed store wouldn't trade with him. Through the anguish, it was one of the few things that amused Amelia in between jobs.

There wasn't much in-between time. She mostly worked as a bodyguard and traveled with her clients. Right now, she was between assignments, or she wouldn't have been around San Antonio. She had an apartment there because she wasn't living in the same town with Cal. She'd had enough of gossip. Even kindly gossip. She'd never forgotten that last day in the hospital. While she lay awake that night, she had a thought. Cal had worked for Eb Scott, who had a counterterrorism school in Jacobsville. He trained mercs and did jobs for many governments including, it was gossiped, ours. She'd heard that he'd trained at least one woman from overseas who was going to work for a foreign government. That meant that he might take on Amelia, if she could convince him. She wasn't afraid of much, and her grandfather had taught her to shoot a gun. It wasn't much, but it might get her foot in the door.

So the next morning, quaking inside, she'd phoned Eb and got an appointment to talk to him. She'd hitched a ride with an orderly at the hospital who lived in Jacobsville. He dropped her off at Eb's huge compound.

He'd given her a strange look when she told him why she was there.

"I can do it, Mr. Scott," she said quietly. "I may look like a wimp, but I'm not. And," she added quickly, "I have an undergraduate degree in chemistry."

That had raised both his eyebrows. "Chemistry?"

She nodded. "Plus, one of the guys auditing my class had done demolition work while he was in the service." She smiled slyly. "He taught us how to make deadly substances out of common household chemicals." She leaned forward. "I can make bombs," she added.

"Well, damn." He burst out laughing. "I have to confess, this is the most interesting interview I've conducted recently."

She grinned. "I learn fast, study hard, and I won't run under fire."

"Why do you want to do this sort of work?"

She sighed and sat back in the chair. "I've just been thrown over by the only man I ever cared about, because of something he thought I'd done that I didn't do. He wouldn't listen when I tried to tell him the truth."

"You might try to make him listen," he began.

"He got married two days ago," she said flatly.

Eb drew in a breath. He knew Cal Hollister, and his temper. The man was like a stone wall when he made up his mind. And if he'd married someone else, he was through with poor Amelia. Everybody already knew.

"It's not really a life for a woman," he began.

"I have nothing left to lose," she said simply and without self-pity. "There are lots of roofs. I only need to step off one of them."

He grimaced. He'd misjudged the level of her desperation. She kept her emotions under tight control, but she was in deep pain, and it showed.

"So it's you or Australia."

He stared at her. "Australia?"

"It's what the mob guys call it. Down under? Hint, hint?"

He got it and shook his head. "You're so young," he began.

"Misery doesn't have an age limit. I need to get out of Texas and do something with my life, while I still have one." Her dark eyes were quiet. "I know about the work you do. It's not only important—it saves lives. I know what your agents have done over the years. It's a record anyone would be proud of. I'd like to be a part of that. I'm good at chemistry, top of my class. I'll bet you've got somebody on staff who can teach me how to do demolition work for real."

"In fact, I do, part-time. I've got Cord Romero."

"I've heard about him," she recalled. "Stuff of legends."

"He is. He's with the FBI and gets antsy from time to time, but he's not risking his wife, Patricia, to try and slide back into merc work. So when he's climbing the walls, he comes down here to teach for a day or two a month."

She grinned. "I'd be a good student. I promise."

He shook his head and sighed. "Okay. But there will be lots of rules."

"I love rules," she said.

"And the work will be dangerous."

"I love dangerous, too."

"Are you sure?"

"I'm sure that if I don't find something challenging to do, that I'll mourn myself to death, Mr. Scott," she replied, and just for a few seconds, the depth of her anguish was visible.

He hesitated, but only for a minute. "All right."

She smiled. "Thanks. So, when do I start?"

"Tomorrow morning, at eight. You'll live in."

"Thank you. I was hoping I wouldn't have to pitch a tent on Victoria Road."

"You've got a house..."

She shook her head. "It's already on the market," she said, and her face hardened to stone. "I'd dig ditches before I'd live in a house with my great-aunt again, after what she did. And I was let go at my place of employment day before yesterday."

"Why?" he asked.

Her eyes met his. "Because I was in the hospital unconscious and didn't call to tell them that." She sighed "It's been a pretty harsh week."

"We all have those," he replied. "We get through them."

"That's what I'm counting on. A new job. A new life."

"It will be hard," he cautioned.

"Life is hard."

"Point taken." He stood up. "Welcome aboard, Amelia." And he smiled.

The first two weeks were the hardest. Amelia had never had to learn a martial art. She was out of shape, because the job she'd had in San Antonio was working in a warehouse doing inventory and putting up stock. That wasn't hard. Martial arts was.

Fortunately, she loved it at once, and excelled at it. Decked out in her new kit, she performed the katas with grace and energy, enjoying the feeling it gave her to learn something new and potentially lifesaving.

Guns came harder. She was a dead shot with a light pistol, but she couldn't cock the .45 auto she was given, so Eb switched her to a Glock. It was a lighter weight and fit her hands perfectly. She spent a lot of time on the firing range, using both hands, as she'd been taught, along with the different stances that were common to police department protocol.

"Not bad, Amelia," Eb said on her third week at it as he studied the placement of bullets in the target. All, every one, was dead center.

"I love it. Shooting is fun!"

He chuckled. "It is, here, because the targets don't shoot back!" he reminded her.

"Not to worry, sir, I can duck with the best of them!"

"Lies," a deep voice drawled from nearby.

She grinned at Ty Harding, who was also taking Eb's courses. He was tall and good-looking, with long dark hair, dark eyes and a handsome face. They'd graduated high school together. Ty had had a crush on her, but she never felt that way about him, so he'd settled for friendship.

"You think so?" she chided. "Okay, shoot at me. Go ahead. I'll show you how to duck and make it look graceful!"

"You do it and I'll send you to Guatemala to hunt narco lords," Eb threatened him.

Ty made a face. "You let her get away with murder."

"Not yet," Eb chuckled. "Okay. Back to work!"

She learned martial arts and gun safety. And within the first two months, Cord Romero showed up to teach her demolition.

"My wife made me give it up," he grumbled as he taught her how to assemble an IED—an improvised explosive device. "Just because a bomb went off once, only once!"

"A bomb…?" she exclaimed, all eyes.

Cord was gorgeous. He had a wife that he rarely talked about, but most people knew that he'd been a merc before he joined the FBI. Tall, dark-eyed, dark-haired, olive complexion. His foster sister, Maggie, was also gorgeous. Eb

Scott was engaged to her, although Ty Harding said that it was mostly just friendship. Maggie and Cord had been foster children, both adopted by the same woman. Maggie, so he said, went out of her way finding things to irritate the man she truly loved, which was Cord.

"I had my mind on something besides what I was doing," Cord explained. "So pay attention. When you defuse a bomb, there's nothing in the world except you and the bomb. Got it?"

"Got it," she promised.

"Okay. Now, this is how you connect the wires..."

She knew already how to combine chemicals to produce toxic substances, so adding that to ordnance in bomb-making was second nature. Cord had lots of experience at the art, and she paid close attention. As he explained to her, that knowledge might one day save her life, or someone in her group.

"Why chemistry?" he asked as they went on to a new project.

"I don't know," she said honestly. "I've always loved it. One of the first presents my parents ever gave me was a junior science chemistry set." She made a face. "I blew up the coffee table."

He chuckled. "I blew up a snake."

"A snake?"

"I improvised some fireworks. Mamie, my adopted mother, had no idea that I knew any such thing. One day while she and Maggie were out shopping, I bundled together some gunpowder and other substances in the outbuilding. I accidentally dropped the device right onto a rattlesnake." He grinned. "I didn't mourn much."

"Neither would I!"

He laughed. "When Mamie saw the damage to the yard, she started to fuss, but Maggie said that it was a great way to get poisonous snakes out of the way and she should encourage me to use my skills." His eyes sparkled. "Mamie gave in. I learned demolition mostly the hard way until much later, when I trained in it."

"Was your dad really a bullfighter?" she asked.

"Indeed he was, and very famous. So was my grandfather." He shook his head. "Bullfighting has a bad rep these days, but in the early nineteenth century, it was the mark of a man, to be able to walk into an arena armed with only a cape and fight a bull that could weigh half a ton. And you only had a cape and courage to do that. The bull had the advantage. They were huge, and their horns weren't blunted."

"I read about them," she said. "I got library books about Manolete."

"Yes, one of the most famous of them all. They called him El Monstrou, and it wasn't an insult. He was magnificent, they say. There's a monument to him, a statue, where he's buried."

"He got gored in the ring," she recalled.

"He did, but it wasn't the bull that killed him. It's said that he was given a blood transfusion with the wrong blood type." He shrugged. "There was a lot of gossip about his death."

"That's so sad."

He nodded. "The world was a different place in the late 1940s, just after the war. The bulls who killed matadors were as famous as the men who died in the ring," she added. She glanced at him. "They say it was that way with men who sang opera, back in the same period of time. They were treated like royalty in Italy, even in America!"

"Now, don't tell me you like opera," he teased.

"I love it. Anything Puccini wrote," she sighed. She glanced at him and chuckled. "I know. I'm a Texas girl.

I should love country-western music. And I do. But I've rarely met any sort of music I didn't like."

"That's good," he said. "There's nothing worse than a music bigot."

She burst out laughing.

"And don't you forget it," he added. "Now, back to work!"

She went to bed tired every night, but her new life was exciting, and she loved every facet of it. She still mourned Cal, though. It seemed some days that she'd dreamed the brief period of time she'd had with him when they'd been so close.

The cab driver spoke again as he pulled up at her apartment building. "Miss, we're here," he said, a little louder, interrupting her thoughts about the past.

She caught her breath. She'd been lost in flashbacks and hadn't heard him. "Oh. Sorry!"

He laughed. "I do the same thing. I drift off into the past. Sometimes it is good to look back and remember good times."

"These weren't so good," she said as she paid him. "But life is all lessons."

"Indeed it is. Have a good night."

"You, too."

Her apartment was one of the newer ones, very homey with all her little touches, and it had a great view of the River Walk. She had a small balcony. She liked sitting out on it and watching the boats go up and down with tourists on them while mariachis played nearby. San Antonio was a fascinating place to live. She never grew tired of it, although she'd been away for some time guarding ex-merc Wolf Patterson and his new wife.

Now that Wolf's enemies had given up or been killed, she wasn't really needed there anymore. She'd checked in with Eb Scott, but he had nothing at the moment, so she was taking a well-deserved vacation for a couple of weeks.

It had been going well, until tonight. She hadn't expected that she'd walk into a bad memory in Fernando's. A very bad memory.

She made herself a cup of coffee and ate her supper on the balcony, while her stubborn mind climbed back into the past in Jacobsville. She remembered the first time she'd seen Cal Hollister…

Chapter Two

Seven years ago, Amelia was in her last year of high school in Jacobsville. It was a hot summer and she and her maternal grandfather, Jacob Harris, had been sitting on the front porch, fanning with old-timey funeral home fans like they handed out in churches.

Her grandfather turned his head. A tall, blond strikingly handsome man was out in the front yard of his rental house watering flowering plants. "There's that man again," Jacob teased his grandchild, watching a faint flush come to her cheeks. "Why don't you ever talk to him?"

"Are you kidding?" she squeaked. She was painfully shy and there were rumors about their neighbor. He worked for Eb Scott, the former mercenary who'd founded an internationally known counterterrorism school. He and his educators taught all sorts of dangerous things, from defensive driving for chauffeurs to martial arts and weaponry to all sorts of people. Foreign governments kept his doors open.

But then, rumor said, so did our own government. Eb had the very best, experienced people teaching for him. He also had plenty of people he could send on missions when asked. It was rumored that Cal Hollister was one of them.

"He likes flowers," her grandfather remarked. "It's almost a character reference."

"He carries a gun and shoots people," she said under her breath.

"That would depend on why he shoots them," he said. "I heard that Eb Scott was loaning operatives he trained to a foreign government in Ngawa, an African country, to get the legitimate president back in office. There have been hundreds of murders of innocent people, including children."

"How do you know all this stuff?" she asked, trying not to feed on the sight of Hollister in khaki pants and a yellow pullover shirt. He was incredibly handsome.

"I go to the post office every day and sit on the bench outside while I go through the mail," he said simply, and grinned. "Sooner or later, every gossip in town sits beside me, anxious to share juicy news."

"I'm not living right," she murmured.

He chuckled. "Your day will come. Hollister there is formidable on the firing range, they say."

"It's still sort of an illegal occupation."

"Not so. He works for Eb Scott, and Eb never deals under the table. If he sends men to help fight, it's always for a good cause. In this case, it's a noble one. Ngawa has survived so many uprisings," he added sadly. "It's a beautiful place, with good, openhearted people. I hate seeing conflict there."

"How do you know so much about Ngawa?" she asked.

"I was stationed there years ago," he said, "in one of

the southern states. And don't ask why. A lot of operations that take place overseas are classified. Mine was, too."

She shook her head. "I'll never understand why we're always sending troops over to other countries, when our own is in such a mess."

"We call it patriotism," he said. "Our enemies call it imperialism. It's all politics, sugar. The rich guys in Congress declare wars and poor people die fighting them."

"There should be a law that any politician who votes for foreign wars that aren't a direct threat to us should be first in line to sign up for combat," she muttered. "That would sure limit the number of wars. It's easy to declare them when you don't have a personal interest in them."

"All too true," he agreed, rocking.

The blond man had spotted them on the porch. He set down his watering can and sauntered down the street toward them.

"Oh my gosh, he's coming here!" Amelia almost squeaked. "Is my hair combed? Do I look okay? Darn, I'm wearing a T-shirt with holes…!"

"He's not going to be trying to date you, sugar," he said under his breath, chuckling. "You're barely eighteen. He's in his midtwenties."

That stung, but she didn't take him up on it. She drew in a breath and forced a shaky smile.

"Hi, neighbor," she said, fanning for all she was worth.

"Morning," he replied. He had a nice voice, deep and smooth. His dark eyes studied them. "I'll bet you knew the guy who owns the house I'm renting," he told Harris.

He chuckled. "Yes, I did. He had a Friday night poker game. I was always the first one over."

"He said that. He's a sweet old guy. My sergeant at San Antonio PD introduced us before I quit and sighed on with Eb Scott. I didn't want to live in the city."

"You didn't want to be a career man?"

Hollister made a face as he perched on one of the wide stone balustrades leading down the steps. "Policing isn't what it was," he said. "And I'm notoriously politically incorrect. Eb Scott's operation is more my style."

"Eb's one of a kind," Harris replied. "I thought about asking him for a job. Then I got in a car wreck. Hurt my back. I can walk, after a fashion, but I'll never be agile again, I'm afraid." He chuckled. "I just became eligible for social security. It's made all the difference in the world."

"Tell me about it," Hollister sighed. "So many people would die without it."

"True. You used to live in Houston, didn't you?" he added.

Hollister nodded. "I grew up there. My mother was a nurse, and my dad was a cop."

"Was?" Harris asked gently while Amelia hung on every word.

He sighed. "She and Dad went on vacation. They stopped in at a fast-food joint to get a meal and there was a guy with an automatic weapon and a suicidal attitude."

The look in his eyes was terrible. "Such a pity that the perp took the easy way out. I'd have enjoyed being at every parole hearing. Assuming that it wouldn't have been the needle," he added with a taut expression.

"Amelia lost her parents in a car wreck," Harris told him. "Also, both at once."

"It's hard to get through that," Amelia said quietly. "At least I had my grandfather," she added, with a warm smile at the old man.

"And I had you," he replied, smiling back. "Doris and I only had one child, a girl—your mother, Mandy. And your dad was also an only child," he added.

"So was I," Hollister said, and smiled gently at Amelia.

"Families used to be larger when people lived on the land. These days, it's only one or two kids. And one is more common."

"Are you going to stay in Jacobsville?" Harris asked.

"I plan to. I don't have any relatives left and this is a nice place," he added, glancing around. "Notable citizens, as well," he said on a chuckle. "A population that seems to be half ex-mercs. It must be the safest town in America."

"We like to think so," the older man replied.

"What are you studying in college?" he asked Amelia. "I heard that you were enrolled at our local community college."

Her heart jumped. It was so fascinating that he'd even mention that. "I'm studying chemistry," she said.

Both eyebrows arched. "Chemistry?"

Her grandfather rolled his eyes and shook his head. "I encouraged her. She blew up half the dining room with a junior chemistry set Christmas present when she was ten. I bought her some books from a science website, and then she studied it in high school, as well. It seemed a natural choice. Besides," he added with a grin at Amelia, "she can blow up the school lab instead of my dining room!"

"I only blew it up a little," she protested. She laughed. "But I really have better insight now. And there's this old guy in our class. He's auditing one of my courses. He was demolition in the Middle East when he was stationed there." Her brown eyes sparkled with delight, making her look very pretty. "He's teaching us how to use ordinary household chemicals to make weapons!"

"He'll be expelled," her grandfather began.

"He does it before the professor walks in," she said with wicked glee. "I can make a flamethrower already!"

"Remind me to walk wide past your front door," Hollister chuckled.

"I wouldn't blow you up," she promised. "Just bad guys."

"And how do you know I'm not a bad guy?" he asked with an indulgent smile.

"You were watering your plants," she explained reasonably. "Bad people don't take care of plants."

Harris and Hollister exchanged amused glances.

"She's right, you know," Harris replied. "People who care for plants and gardens are nurturing people."

Hollister made a face. "Not always," he replied. "I knew a guy overseas who had this orchid plant that he carried everywhere he went. Another guy came in drunk and crushed it under his boot. Guy killed him, right there on the spot, without hesitation."

Amelia looked at her grandfather. "If we go by his house," she pointed to Hollister, "let's make sure we walk wide around the potted plants!"

Hollister chuckled with pure delight. He glanced at Harris. "Do you play chess, by any chance?"

"He's our local champ," Amelia said proudly. "He won a big competition a few years ago. We have the trophy on our mantel."

"Nice," Hollister said. "So, when you're free, how about a game?"

"I'd enjoy that," Harris replied. "Name a day."

"Friday night?"

"Perfect timing. I have to leave Saturday night on an assignment."

"My house or yours?" Harris asked. He added, "If we play here, you can have chocolate cake. Amelia's an amazing cook."

"Chocolate is my favorite," he replied, and smiled at Amelia, who blushed with unexpected delight.

"Then Friday it is. About seven?"

Hollister nodded and smiled. "Seven, it is."

* * *

The Friday night chess sessions were as exciting for Amelia as they were for her grandfather and Hollister. She made a point of cooking special desserts, things that Hollister would enjoy eating. In the meantime, she went to classes and learned more about chemistry than she'd ever dreamed she would. It was a hard subject, but she took to it like a duck to water.

Hollister wasn't a chemist, but he was an expert in some other areas, especially weapons.

One day in the autumn, he took her out to the target range at Eb Scott's school to teach her how to handle a gun. He had a .38 special that he let her borrow.

He was amazed that she put the first few shots within the smallest bull's-eye.

"You've been playing me," Hollister accused with mock anger. "You already knew how to shoot."

"Not a handgun," she said as she reloaded the automatic he'd loaned her. "I used to target shoot with a .22 rifle with some friends in high school."

"Well, you're pretty much a natural."

She grinned. "Thanks."

"Ever thought about going into police work?" he asked.

She shrugged. "I'm too squeamish. Shooting targets is one thing. Shooting people…" She glanced up at him. "I don't think I could."

"When bullets start flying in your direction, you'd be surprised how fast you could shoot people," he replied, and the smile he gave her was faint.

She wanted to ask if he'd shot people, but it wasn't something she felt comfortable talking to a relative stranger about.

"Now," he added. "Stance." He proceeded to instruct

her about the three stances that law enforcement people, notably the FBI, used.

"It gives you a centered balance," he said. "Doesn't do much good if you shoot straight and then fall over your own feet."

"Good point," she nodded. "I'm good at that, though. Falling over my own feet, I mean," she chuckled.

"Your grandfather plays a great game of chess," he said.

"He's smart. He did black ops when he was in the military. I've never been able to get him to tell me what sort. He's very secretive."

"Most people in covert ops are," he replied. "It's how we stay alive. One of the more formidable mobsters of the last century said that three people could keep a secret if two of them were dead."

She laughed. "That makes sense."

"It does. Now, another thing. Trigger pull," he said. "It's an art. If you can master it, you'll never miss a target. Although you seem to have that down pat already. As I said, you're a natural."

"I like guns," she said simply. "Even though I'd rather blow stuff up."

"Why?"

"I don't know, really," she confessed. "I'm not keen on noise and I've never wanted to overthrow a country. But there's just something short of magical about mixing various substances and having them utterly destroy objectives."

He shook his head. "You and Cord Romero," he murmured.

"Romero?"

"He teaches tactics at Eb's place, when he's not on assignment. He's FBI."

"Wow." She glanced up at him. "They say getting into the FBI is like trying to join the CIA. You apply and then they take months checking you out, everything from grammar school up and all in between."

"They're elite organizations," he said. "It pays to be cautious."

"Does Eb Scott do that? I mean, check out potential students?"

"Of course he does," he replied. "Especially foreign ones. There are some devious people in the world, and our country has enemies."

"I guess so."

"We'll go a few more rounds, then I have to go to San Antonio."

"Okay."

She wondered why he was going but she never pried. It seemed to be a character trait that he appreciated.

In fact, it was. He watched her covertly while she fired the pistol. She was a conundrum. Brilliant, but reserved and careful. She never asked prying questions or droned on about the latest reality television show or online talent competitions or even fashion shows. He knew a socialite in San Antonio—Edie Prince, one whom he dated infrequently—who bored him silly with such information. He couldn't have cared less. He watched the news and occasionally a movie. Nothing else.

"Do you watch television?" he asked absently.

"Not really," she confessed. "I'm taking algebra and Japanese along with chemistry. I don't have the free time."

"Japanese?" he exclaimed.

"I've always loved the culture," she explained. "I pig out on old Toshiro Mifune movies on the weekends. Granddad has several of them on DVD."

"Good Lord." He fired several shots dead center into the target without even aiming carefully. "I thought I was the only samurai fanatic in town."

She laughed, delighted to have something in common with him. "Not really. Granddaddy loves them, too."

"I grew up watching them. They were my dad's favorite films. It was samurai or Westerns all the time when he was off duty."

It was odd, the way he sounded when he spoke of his father. She couldn't quite place the tone. It wasn't one of remembered affection.

He saw her puzzled expression and noted that she didn't reply. He reloaded. "That's one thing about you that I really like."

"What is?" she asked, glancing toward him.

"You don't pry."

She smiled. "I don't like people who do. I've always been a private person. I could never go on a social media site and pour out all my problems to a group of total strangers. Although it seems to be the new national pastime," she added with a laugh.

"Social media has been the ruin of our civilization," he said darkly. "That, and the internet. People don't talk anymore. They go out to eat and spend the whole time staring at their cell phones."

"I've noticed that. It's sad."

"If I had a family—and don't hold your breath—there would be an ironclad rule that nobody was allowed to bring cell phones to the table at mealtimes."

"We already have that rule," she said, grinning at him. "My grandfather said I needed to know how to talk to real people."

"I like your granddad," he said. "He's got more common sense than most people I know. Most brainy folks don't have enough to come in out of a rainstorm."

"His grandparents were Mennonites," she said.

His eyebrows arched over twinkling brown eyes. "Really?"

"Yes. His grandfather founded a Mennonite church over in Comanche Wells, down the road from Jacobsville. By the time Granddaddy grew up, it had become a Methodist church, but it had that beginning."

"That must be a story and a half," he mused.

"It really is. There's still a Mennonite community in Jacobs County, but it's way out in the sticks now. They have a small church and stores that sell all sorts of lovely things like homemade butter and sausages and eggs." She looked up at him. "I shop there every week. I don't like grocery stores much."

"Neither do I, but it beats snake and rabbit," he said under his breath.

"Excuse me?" She was all eyes.

"When we're on a mission, sometimes we're so far back in woods or jungle that we run out of protein bars. Snake is pretty good. Rabbit's better."

She made a horrible face.

He laughed. "Staying alive is the thing, you know. When you're starving, you'll eat anything that won't eat you."

"I guess so," she agreed, but she shivered.

He glanced at his watch. "I'd better get you home. I'll be late."

"Thanks for the instruction," she said.

"Anytime. It never hurts to know how to handle a gun." He made a face. "Scares me to death when somebody comes into a gun shop and buys a gun for protection when they've never shot one in their lives. It isn't that easy to use one, especially in a desperate situation. There have been any number of innocent family members who were shot coming into their own homes unannounced."

"That would be awkward."

They climbed into his big SUV and put on their seat belts. "Of course, some of those accidental shootings aren't really accidental," he added as he cranked the truck and pulled out into the highway.

"They aren't?"

"Like the irate wife who accidentally shot her husband twenty-four times." He glanced at her with twinkling dark eyes. "She had to reload in between."

She burst out laughing. "That's not really funny, but it is," she said. "Did she go to jail?"

He nodded. "And for a very long time. The reloading is what got her. She wanted to make sure he was dead."

"I don't understand people. Why didn't she just divorce him?" she asked.

"It was revenge. He was running around with her best friend," he explained.

"Oh. Well, in that case…"

"Don't kill people if they don't want to stay with you," he interrupted. "It's that simple."

"Oh, I'd never do that," she agreed. "I just hope I never have to pull the trigger on anything except a deadly snake or a rabid animal."

"I hope that for you," he replied, and he was momentarily somber.

She looked out the window. "We need rain," she said. "Everything's parched. Our few little tomato plants are wilting."

"Shade," he suggested.

"I've got them in the shade," she replied, "but ninety-degree weather wilts most everything, including me!"

He glanced at her and chuckled. She was wearing a tank top with jeans and sneakers, and her long blond hair was up in a bun. He wondered idly how long it was when she let it down. She was good company, and he liked having her around. Of course, she was just a kid. So it wasn't a good idea to toss covert glances at those pert, firm little breasts under her top. He cleared his throat and looked back out the windshield, and he kept his eyes there the rest of the way home.

Amelia loved being with Cal. She knew that he didn't see her as anything except a young friend, but her heart sang when he came for the weekly chess match with her grandfather. She always had a special dessert for him. And while he and her grandfather were focused on their game, she could sneak glances at him. He was so handsome. She wondered that he was able to stay single. He must get hunted by women, even gorgeous women.

He was seeing somebody in San Antonio, her grandfather said. Cal hadn't told him, but it was gossip. The woman was wealthy, a socialite with a biting tongue who seemed hell-bent on landing Cal. So far, they were just friends, to her irritation.

Amelia knew that Cal was a grown man, and subject to male appetites. She'd never really felt desire, so she didn't understand it, but other women had said that most men couldn't go a long time without a woman.

It was painful to think that Cal would never belong to her. She thought of him constantly, loved being near him, ached to have him hold her, kiss her. But she had to hide those hopeless longings. If Cal ever knew about them, she'd never see him again. She knew that without being told.

She did wonder about his woman friend in San Antonio. But she never asked. One day when Cal was out of town, doing some job for Eb Scott, Amelia watched a luxury car park in Cal's driveway. A tall, willowy woman got out at the steps.

She was brunette. Very pretty even at a distance, with

short hair and a knockout figure. She was wearing silk slacks and a silk shirt, and she looked rich. Very rich.

She spotted Amelia watering her tomato plants and walked over.

"Hi," she said lazily. "Have you seen Cal?"

"Hi," Amelia replied, and forced a smile. "No. We don't know where he is. Sorry."

The woman's eyes narrowed, and she studied Amelia closely. "You must be Amelia."

She laughed. "That's me."

"He said you like to blow things up?" she added warily.

Amelia grinned. "Only bad things. Honest. I'm a chemistry major."

"In high school, right?" she asked.

"Well, no, I graduated this year. I'm going to our community college now."

"Then you'd be, what, eighteen or so?"

"Eighteen and three months and ten days and," Amelia looked at her watch, "twenty minutes." She grinned brightly.

The woman laughed in spite of herself. "I'm Edie Prince," she introduced herself. "Cal and I go out together."

"Oh." Amelia just nodded. She didn't ask questions.

Edie gave her a going-over with her pale blue eyes. Eighteen. And she'd been afraid of the competition. She laughed at her own folly. Cal talked about this girl a lot, and she'd been jealous. But the girl was a kid, barely out of high school. Definitely not Cal Hollister's sort. He liked experience.

She relaxed. "Well, I'm sorry I missed him. Will you tell him I was here, please?"

"Of course," Amelia said. "Nice to meet you."

Edie nodded. "Same."

She sauntered back to her car, got in and sped away.

Amelia let out the breath she'd been holding. So that was the sort of woman Cal liked? She wasn't impressed. Too much perfume, too much makeup, too much…everything. And the woman had to be the wrong side of thirty. Makeup only covered up so much.

She finished watering the plants and went back inside.

Cal was home two days later. It was Friday and he came over for the chess match.

"Want some chocolate cake?" Amelia asked him as he and her grandfather sat down.

"Yes," her grandfather said. "And coffee. Black. Strong!"

"Double that," Cal chuckled.

"Coming right up," she assured them.

"Oh, and you had a visitor," her grandfather told Cal. "Some woman in a black luxury car. She spoke to Amelia."

Cal's dark eyes flashed. "Edie."

"I don't know," Harris replied. "I didn't speak to her."

"She's an acquaintance," Cal said, and didn't add anything to that. But it irritated the hell out of him that the woman had come down here to nose around the town where he lived. She was possessive already. He didn't like it.

Amelia didn't say anything, but she saw that irritation in his expression before he concealed it. He must like the woman, or he wouldn't spend time with her. But it was obvious that he also didn't like having people pry into his life.

She fixed coffee, poured it into two mugs, sliced cake and presented it all to the men.

"You should learn to play chess," her grandfather commented.

"Never," Amelia said. "I've been slaughtered too many times on that board by you," she added darkly.

Her grandfather chuckled. "It's because you don't stop to think about your moves. You rush in and attack."

"So did Pancho Villa!"

His eyes widened. "He played chess?"

"He fought in the Mexican Revolution," she corrected. "And he only knew one method of fighting. Attack!"

"Well, that's definitely you, sugar," her grandfather chuckled.

"One day I might beat you," she retorted.

"Fat chance."

"Chess can be taught, just like shooting a gun," Cal interjected.

"I like shooting guns. I hate chess."

"Excuses, excuses," Cal teased.

"You two can have chess. I'll take mahjong."

"That's just memorization," Cal pointed out.

"Yes, well, I remember things better than I think them out," she replied. "Besides, mahjong is fun!"

"So is chess," Cal told her. "It's a magnificent relic of the past. They used to call it the game of kings, because they studied the use of tactics playing it."

"I hate tactics, too. But I like cake." She grinned and took her cake and coffee into the kitchen, to enjoy while she made rolls for tomorrow's meals. Meanwhile, she was able to angle the occasional unconscious glance toward gorgeous Cal, while he and her grandfather battled across the chess board.

Cal was going out the door with Amelia when he turned suddenly on the porch.

"Did Edie say why she came down here?" he asked abruptly.

"Not really," she replied with a hopefully disinterested smile. "She just said she was looking for you, and to tell you she'd been here."

"I see."

His hands were shoved deep in his pockets and the dark eyes she couldn't quite see were narrow and angry.

"She's really pretty," Amelia said.

He glanced down at her and seemed to relax a little. He studied her face. It wasn't beautiful, but it had character—like its owner. He smiled. "So are you, Amelia," he replied quietly. "It's not what's outside that matters. It's what's inside."

Before she colored too rapidly and gave herself away, she grinned and said, in mock horror, "You mean, my guts?"

He thought about that for a minute, threw back his head and roared with laughter. "Good grief," he muttered. He flapped a hand at her. "I'm going to bed." He was still shaking his head as he walked down the driveway.

Amelia was grinning when she went back inside. Her grandfather, who'd been eavesdropping, was also laughing.

"Your guts," Jacob Harris said, shaking his head. "Honestly!"

"He's somber a lot," she explained. "I like making him laugh."

"Well, Eb Scott said the guy has a reputation with his men, and it doesn't include laughter. In fact, he says he hardly ever smiled before he started coming over here. He was fishing," he added with some amusement, "about whether or not Cal had a case on you."

Her heart jumped into her throat.

"Of course not, I told him," he added without looking at her, which was a good thing. "After all, you're just eighteen, sugar. Hardly old enough to get mixed up with a professional soldier. You'd need to be street smart and a lot more sophisticated."

She nodded, averting her eyes. "Like that pretty lady who came to see him," she agreed.

"Exactly. She looked hard as nails, and she'd need to be!"

She raised both eyebrows in a silent question.

"Think about it, Amy," he said softly, using the nickname that only he had ever called her. "A man like that keeps his emotions under lock and key. It's a matter of survival, to be stoic and levelheaded. He's hard as nails—no sentiment in him. He'd never settle with a woman who wasn't his equal in temperament."

"In other words, he'd walk all over somebody less hardheaded."

"Exactly." He smiled at her. "Even if you were older, it would be a very bad mix." He shook his head. "You don't know what these men are really like until you've served beside them. Something you'll never know about," he added firmly.

"Absolutely not," she agreed at once. "I'm going to learn how to blow up stuff instead!"

"Amy…!"

"Controlled demolition," she interrupted with a grin. "It's how they take down buildings in big cities. It's fascinating! Just last week, we learned how to do timed charges…"

"Oh, no, not again!" he said in mock anguish.

"You know it fascinates you," she teased. "I could tell you all about it," she added.

"I'm really sleepy," he said with a mock yawn. "I have to go to sleep right now. So lock up, sugar, okay?"

"Retreat is like surrendering!" she called after him.

He threw up a hand and kept walking.

Chapter Three

"What were you doing in Jacobsville?" Cal asked Edie later in the week, while they had cocktails at her fancy apartment in downtown San Antonio.

"I was looking for you, of course," she replied in her softly accented voice. She threw down her cocktail and poured herself another. She drank more than he did, but he didn't pay it much attention. People in her social class drank more than most people.

"You met Amelia."

"Well, yes." She looked at him from under her lids. She was wearing a sketchy green outfit that left her midriff bare and outlined her pretty breasts. "I was curious."

He just stared at her.

"I thought she was competition," she purred. "But she's just a schoolgirl. I didn't know she was so young."

He sipped his own drink. "I don't like being checked up on," he said flatly.

"Oh, don't be mad, Cal," she chided softly, dropping

down onto the arm of the chair he was sitting in. "I wasn't prying. I really did go down there just to see you," she lied. It wouldn't do to let him know how possessive she really was.

"Don't do it again," he cautioned, and the threat was in his dark eyes.

"I won't," she said at once. "I promise."

"I'm a free agent," he added. "And I have no plans to involve myself with anyone at the moment. I'm in a high-risk profession. I can't afford personal complications."

She sighed. "In other words, no sex?" she probed delicately.

"That's more blunt than I would have put it, but yes." He finished his drink. "The missions I'm on lately are intricate and involved. I don't want distractions."

"But that won't last forever, right?" she asked, toying with a thick strand of his pale blond hair.

"I don't know. I'm not sure what I want to do with the rest of my life."

"I could suggest some things," she said, about to move down into his lap.

He stood up. "Don't push," he cautioned quietly.

She made a face and filled another glass. "Well, it's hard not to," she said. "You're very attractive."

"So are you. But we're friends. That's all."

He was making a point. And she didn't want to lose him, so she agreed.

"I'm going out to the firing range. Want to come along?"

She made a horrible face. "Of course not! I hate guns!"

He raised an eyebrow and she flushed. She was feeling the alcohol and antsy because she needed something more than alcohol, needed it badly. She didn't dare let him see that.

"Sorry," she said at once. "I know they're important to your profession. I'm afraid of them, that's all."

"Okay. No problem."

"There's a fashion show at the civic center Saturday," she began.

"I'll be out of town."

"Ah, well, I'll go alone, then," she said.

"I don't do fashion shows," he chuckled. "We could go fishing when I get back…?"

She made a worse face. "Honestly, that's the most disgusting hobby of all. Nasty worms." She shuddered.

"You are not an outdoor person."

"Of course not," she replied. "I spent my youth in boarding schools, learning how to be graceful and fit into society."

Which emphasized the gulf between them. She was upper class, he was middle class. Besides that, he suspected that she was already in her midthirties, while he was just twenty-seven. He didn't think much about the age or social differences, however, because he had no intention of getting serious about her. She was just somebody to take around town when he was in the mood.

"How about Fernando's Friday night?" he asked as he got ready to leave.

"Oh, Cal, that's such a common place," she muttered.

"I'm a common man," he replied, and he wasn't smiling.

She went to him, smiling apologetically. "I didn't mean it like that. I just don't like Spanish music, or dancing, that's all. The symphony orchestra is performing next week, though. Debussy."

"I could stomach Debussy, I suppose," he said.

"It will do you good. Culture is important."

He made a face. "Culture."

"Yes. It's what makes us all civilized," she teased. "So. Go with me? I'll get tickets."

"When?"

"A week from Saturday night."

He thought about it. "I should be back by then. All right."

"You'll text me, yes?"

"I'll text you," he said easily.

She reached up to kiss him softly. She drew back at once, not wanting to push her luck. He'd been really irritated. "Have a safe trip home."

"Sure. Good night."

She watched him go. He never returned her caresses. But then, he was in a dangerous profession. He was also loaded. He hadn't told her, but she had friends who knew the sort of work he did and what it paid. She had social background, but she'd blown most of her inherited fortune gambling. She had an expensive habit, and although she'd tried to quit, it had become harder. She needed bankrolling.

Of course, Cal was also attractive, there was that. But it was as easy to care about a rich man as a poor one, and she was good at pretending. She finished the cocktail and went to her room to get what she needed to add a jolt to the liquor.

Cal, meanwhile, was still irritated at Edie's obvious possessive attitude toward him. He didn't want a woman hanging on him, trying to own him. He liked his own space.

He thought about how different Amelia was. She never pried or stalked him. She was funny and gentle, and she loved the outdoors. He wondered if she liked to fish. He'd have to remember to ask.

Fishing, Amelia thought, was one of the most relaxing sports there was. Especially when it was shared with a drop-dead gorgeous man who also loved it. They'd found a deep, wide stream, almost a river, under a bridge on a little-traveled dirt road that was known locally for bigmouth bass.

Amelia sighed. "This is great fun."

"Yeah, and the yellow flies just adore it," he muttered as he slapped another one.

"Your hair is yellow. They think you're a relative," she teased.

He chuckled. He laughed more with her than he'd ever laughed in his life. She made life seem uncomplicated. His had never been that, especially not now.

"They don't bite you, I notice," he pointed out.

"That's because I know simple, secret homemade solutions to keep them away."

"Such as?" he asked.

"I told you. They're secret ones."

"Might you share them with a friend who loaned you his spinning reel?"

She glowered at him. "A cane pole is just better for these things," she said with a sigh. She got up and handed him back the spinning reel. She then picked up her old cane pole with its hook, line and lead sinkers. She baited the hook and threw it in.

"Primitive," he pointed out.

She felt a tug on the line, but she let it run until the nice fish hooked himself. Then the battle began. She pulled and let the line slack, pulled again, slacked again, going up and down the bank.

"Wow, what a fighting fish!" she exclaimed happily.

"Can you tell what it is?"

"It's a fish. I told you…oh!" She drew back and jerked. The fish soared out of the water and landed at Cal's feet.

He picked it up with a finger through the gill. "A big-mouthed bass. About three pounds unless I miss my guess," he chuckled.

"Supper," she said, smacking her lips. She took the fish and put him in the bucket. Then she baited her hook again. "I'll catch one for you, too," she teased.

He sighed, looking at his spinning reel with disdain. "I think I'm losing my touch," he said.

"It's just that the fish in this creek are sort of primitive," she chuckled. "I don't think they like fancy equipment."

"So next time we come here, I'll bring a cane pole," he said with resignation.

"Might save that spinning reel for a trout stream," she said.

"Good idea. And where would we find one, in this heat?"

"Canada."

He glared at her. "I'm not going to Canada to catch a fish."

"Then get a cane pole and fish for… Oh, I've got another one!"

Cal let out a word that her grandfather often used if he hit his thumb with a hammer. Amelia burst out laughing. Cal just shook his head.

When they got back to her house, they had five big bass. Hers were four of them.

"I think I'll give up fishing and go in for surfing," Cal told her grandfather.

Harris laughed. "You can't ever compete with her at fishing, trust me," he told the other man. "It's an ego-smasher."

"I noticed."

"There, there, you were just fishing for trout instead of bass," Amelia said soothingly.

"Way too hot for trout fishing," her grandfather said. "Going to stay for fish? She makes homemade french fries."

"Wow," Cal said. He looked at Amelia. "Can I?"

"Sure," she chuckled. "There's plenty to go around. And I cooked some butterbeans with fatback last night, right out of the garden. I made fresh rolls, too."

Cal just sighed. "I really did the smartest thing in my life, moving across the street from you two."

"I'll bet you can cook," Amelia said cagily.

"I can," he replied. "Snake, turtle, crocodile..."

"I mean regular food," she laughed.

"I can if I have to," he conceded. "But no way can I make fresh rolls, and I love them."

"In that case, I'll make extra so you can take some home."

"If we only had real butter," he mused.

"But we do," she said, grinning. "I went to the Mennonite store early this week. We have real butter to go on them."

Cal sat down on the sofa near her grandfather's recliner. "I'll have to be dragged out," he threatened with a laugh.

"We won't do that," Amelia promised and went to work.

They walked him out to the steps after supper, which included an apple pie with homemade ice cream.

"I've never eaten better in my whole life," Cal told Amelia. "Thank you."

"Thanks for going fishing with me," she replied. "Granddaddy hates fishing."

"Yes, I know it sounds odd, but I really do. I used to hunt when I was younger, but I was never a fisherman."

"There's a good reason," Amelia volunteered.

Her grandfather looked sheepish. "I threw my line out too hard in a rowboat, capsized it and almost drowned my father. That was after I'd hooked his pants with another bad throw. He said that the only safe way to fish was to tie me to a chair and leave me at home. I took him at his word. I've never gone fishing since!"

They all laughed.

Amelia walked back inside with her grandfather. He was giving her strange looks.

"Something wrong?" she asked gently.

He went into the living room with her and sat down. So did she.

"There are men who are suited to small-town life," he said gently. "To picket fences and babies. That man across the street isn't one of them. He feeds on danger. He likes it. He won't settle, not for years. And quite frankly, if he does, it will be for somebody like that fancy woman who turned up at his house. She's the kind of woman who attracts such men."

She flushed. "I didn't realize it showed," she said sadly.

"It won't, to him. Only to somebody who knows you. But you can't afford to let him see it, not if you want him to keep coming here for friendship. If he sees it, he'll not come back, for pitying you."

She ground her teeth together. "I guess I knew that."

"It's harsh to say it, but always better to face an unpleasant fact than to ignore it. He's a handsome man, and he's got a way with him. But you're not his sort of woman, and there's that age difference. He's twenty-seven. You're eighteen. It wouldn't matter so much if you were in your twenties. But now it would."

She nodded. "I knew that."

"I'm sorry. I like him, too. But you have to keep those longings under control. He's at ease here. If you're careful, someday…"

She grinned. "Someday."

"Now go study those chemistry books," he said, waving her away. "You have to learn to blow up stuff if there's ever a war down the road."

She laughed out loud. "Roll on the day. I'm dangerous!"

"Yes, you are. And my treasure," he added with a warm smile. "I'm so lucky to have you for company."

"I'm the lucky one," she replied. She kissed him on the head and went on to her room.

But she didn't study. She brooded. She was very attracted to Cal. She ached when she looked at him. Her grandfather was right, it would never do to let him see it. She would have to play a waiting game, be careful and secretive, and never let Cal see how much she cared for him. But could she?

Yes, she could, she thought doggedly. Because as hard as it was to pretend not to care, it would be harder to never see him again. Or, worse, to have him pity her for the feelings she couldn't help. That would smother her pride.

So she would keep her secret hidden and never let Cal know that she treasured him. Even if the fancy lady came calling again, and she might. She opened her chemistry book and turned to the page her lessons were on.

The summer went by slowly. Cal was home on and off, but mostly off on hush-hush assignments overseas for Eb. Autumn came, with colored leaves and harvest festivals and hayrides and turkey shoots.

One of the ongoing events in Jacobsville was a turkey shoot with frozen turkey prizes. The competition was stiff, but Amelia went every year. This year, a recently returned, and very surprised Cal, went with her.

"I can't believe that you shoot a shotgun," he said again as they stood waiting for their turns. "I've never known a woman who'd even pick up one."

She shrugged. "I've always loved weapons," she said.

"Yes, and she can shoot!" one of the other contestants added, glaring at her. "And much too well!"

"Sour grapes, Andy, you had the same chances I did," she replied with a grin.

The old man wrinkled his nose. "First, we had old man Turner, and he won every year. Then it was Rick Marquez, who's a detective in San Antonio. Now, it's you," he muttered. "A good man hasn't got a chance around here!"

"Yes, you do, Andy, you just have to outshoot me!" she replied. "And him," she added, jerking her thumb toward Cal, who grinned.

"Who's he?" he asked.

"He works for Eb Scott…"

"Oh, damn the luck!" Andy exclaimed and threw his hat on the ground.

"Eb sort of wins any shooting competition going, or his men do," she explained to Cal. "So most people know what's going to happen when one of them competes."

"Cheer up," Cal told the man brushing off his hat, "I do miss. Sometimes."

"Name the last time you missed," Amelia asked him.

He frowned. "Let's see, I was ten, and my uncle had taken me to a turkey shoot."

"And you missed?"

"I missed dead center in the bull's-eye," he explained. "It was just a hair off."

"I am never going to win a turkey," Andy muttered.

"The grocery store has lots of them," she pointed out. "And there's a contest downtown for six of them that are giveaways. It's a raffle."

"Got a better chance of being carried off by one of them UFOs than I have of winning a contest. And I hate buying turkeys!"

"Then send Blanche," she suggested.

Andy sighed. "Well, that's not a bad idea, I suppose." He grinned at her. "If I'd known you were coming this year, I'd have stayed home."

She laughed. "That's sweet."

"Nope. Just the truth. I'd wish you good luck, but the other people are going to need that," he said, nodding toward the assembly of hopefuls. "See you, honey."

"See you."

"Nice old guy," Cal said. "I hope he won't go hungry," he added suddenly.

"Andy drives a new Jaguar," she pointed out. "Every year," she added.

"Oh." He scowled. "Then why was he here?"

"Because he's cheap," she said, and grinned.

He chuckled. "Okay. I get the idea. I didn't want to think we were going to hustle some poor guy out of Thanksgiving dinner."

"That would never happen here. We have two charities that do nothing except feed the poor, especially at holidays. There are rumors that one of our local citizens pays to bus poor homeless people down here from San Antonio, so they get a good hot meal. We had several whole families last year," she added quietly, and her voice almost broke.

He patted her on the shoulder. "It's good that you care that much," he said, and he smiled at her. "I've become cynical about people. I'm always wary of being played."

"I'm hard to play," she replied, looking up. "And whole families, Cal," she added softly. "Just imagine how that must feel. You lose your job, your home, your car..." She ground her teeth together. "What a nightmare that would be, especially if you had children."

He just stared at her thoughtfully. It hadn't occurred to him. But then, she had no idea what his background really was, how he'd been brought up. He hoped she'd never know. It wasn't a pretty tale.

"Maybe I'm too cynical," he said after a minute.

She smiled. "It's the job you do," she said simply. "I know guys from high school who went to work for Eb. It changes you, changes the way you look at the world."

"I suppose it does." He glanced down at her. "Who do you know that works for Eb, besides me?" he asked suddenly, shocking himself and her, because it wasn't a question he had any right to ask. She was eighteen, for God's sake!

"Ty," she blurted out.

His eyebrows arched. "Ty Harding?"

She nodded.

He averted his gaze. "He's Native American. Different culture, language, religion, the works."

"I know. He and a girl I knew almost got engaged. Her people found out and actually came down here from the Northwest to talk him out of it. They even talked to his parents. They said that not only would it not work, but that he'd be an outcast in their family. There had never been a mixed marriage in the family, you see," she added.

"Not you?" he asked, frowning.

"Heavens, no," she laughed. "Ty and I are just friends."

"Oh."

It was hard to hide the joy welling up inside her, but she managed. Before Cal could notice the sudden glow, her name was called, and she stepped up to face the target.

She and Cal took home a turkey.

Cal was out of the country until the day before Thanksgiving. He came over for dinner the next day, having been invited by Amelia's grandfather. Amelia had been working nonstop in the kitchen for two days, which is what it took to bring all the food together, and she couldn't leave the stove. So Jacob Harris had to go over with the invitation.

He found a man who was worn to the bone and limping just a little.

"You're not in the easiest profession," he told the younger man.

Cal shrugged. "Sometimes we don't duck fast enough," he said with a forced grin.

Harris put a hand on his shoulder. "I'm an interfering

old coot, and I should keep my mouth shut. But eventually, you're going to see something or be forced to do something that will shatter your life," he added quietly. "And when that happens, you'll have to live with the nightmares for the rest of the days you're on this earth."

Cal was quietly belligerent. "And you know this for a fact?"

"Didn't Amelia tell you? I was spec ops overseas," he added.

Cal felt his face tauten. He hadn't known that.

"And the nightmares," Harris concluded softly, "are horrendous." His eyes as he spoke were almost black with pain.

"I didn't know," he said.

"I lived and came home," he said. "But my poor granddaughter had to listen to me when I was bursting with the need to tell somebody, anybody, what I'd been through. I was almost crazy," he added. "They wanted to send me to a shrink at the VA, but I'd heard all about that from a buddy of mine." His expression was eloquent. "It was a guy who'd never shot a gun, never been in combat and knew nothing about war. He said it was all he could do not to deck the guy on his way out."

Cal drew in a breath. "You might get luckier than he did."

"I might not." He searched the other man's dark eyes. "I don't know what demons are driving you, but I suspect they're pretty formidable. It takes that to send a man into wet work."

Cal scowled.

"Yes, I know. Most of what you do is classified, and you aren't officially attached to any government. Plausible deniability. But the people who hire you don't have to live with what you do to accomplish a mission." He studied the other man's face. "For you to go into this," he added quietly, "you must have a pretty raw background to start with—something that you don't want to face, that you put yourself at risk so that you don't have to deal with it."

"You see too much," Cal bit off.

He sighed. "I've been where you are," he replied. "I don't talk about my past, either. Even my late wife, Doris, God rest her soul, wasn't told. I thought doing special assignments in the service would be exciting enough to put the bad things away, so that I didn't see them." He drew in a breath. "But what happened was that the exciting things were a hundred times worse than what I'd already had to live through. When I came home, I was a mental basket case."

"How did you cope?"

"I had a friend who'd been in combat for half his life, a mercenary. He talked me down. You remember that," he added. "If you don't want to go to a shrink, even though there are some really good ones, have somebody close who'll just listen and let you pour it all out. It might save you from trying to eat a bullet. In my case, it did just that."

"It's early days yet, but I don't think I'll run into anything I can't handle," Cal said quietly. "I'm not the type to commit suicide."

"Nobody thinks they are, until there's a good reason."

Cal was unconvinced, but he didn't say so. "Thanks for the pep talk," he said quietly.

"You're welcome. Now. How about a huge Thanksgiving dinner tomorrow that promises to throw your cholesterol so high that your doctor will feel it even before you get to his office?"

Cal chuckled. "I'd love it."

"Fine. You're invited. Oh, and it's informal. You can leave off the tuxedo," he joked.

Cal made a face. "Spoilsport."

Harris just laughed.

So Cal came for Thanksgiving dinner, and produced a perfectly cooked apple pie to go with all of Amelia's efforts.

"Nice pie," she commented, noting the way it was made with a fancy fluted crust all around. "Did you go all the way to San Antonio to find a bakery?"

Cal glared at her. "I made it myself, I'll have you know," he said with mock indignation. "Snake isn't the only thing I can cook!"

She burst out laughing. "Oh. Well, it's beautiful," she said, admiring it. "I can't even do a crust like that. It's elegant."

"I'll teach you how. It's not hard. That," he indicated the perfect homemade rolls she'd just taken out of the oven, "is hard!"

"It's not," she said. "Only a handful of ingredients, and the mixer does most of the kneading. It doesn't even take long."

"Fine. You can teach me to make rolls, and I'll share my pie decorating tips with you," he said with sparkling black eyes.

She chuckled. "It's a deal."

"But meanwhile, when do we eat?" he asked, admiring all the food she'd dished up on the big table that was used for cooking.

"In about ten minutes," she said.

"Can I help?" Jacob asked.

"Yes! If you'll start carrying things into the dining room," she told him, "I'll finish carving the turkey."

"You should let me do that," Cal protested. "I'm great with knives."

"You're hired," she said, handing him a sharp butcher's knife. "Go for it!"

He grinned. “Do you want boring flat slices of turkey, or something artistic, like leaves or unicorns?” he asked, deadpan.

The other two just shook their heads.

Chapter Four

Amelia noticed that Cal was unusually quiet while they ate. He wasn't a boisterous man by nature, but he seemed reserved.

"How did you do grade-wise this semester?" he asked her suddenly.

She grinned. "Straight As."

He shook his head. "I should have known. You're bright."

She laughed. "Not so much. I study hard, though."

"Chemistry, of all things," he remarked as he started on the apple pie, with a steaming cup of black coffee at his side. "I've never known a woman who studied chemistry."

"I love it," she said. "It's the most fascinating thing I've ever studied."

"You haven't blown up the lab yet?" he teased.

"They won't let us near the really dangerous stuff," she muttered.

"I hope they have good insurance," her grandfather mentioned dryly.

"I'm a very good student," she protested. "Even my professor says so. I will not blow up the lab."

"If you say so," he chuckled.

"Now, Fred Briggs, he did blow up the lab," she added. "All because Maria Simms walked by him in a low-cut dress and smiled at him. He mixed in the wrong chemical and the table blew up."

"My goodness," her grandfather said. "Was anybody hurt?"

"Fred got a little singed. But when Maria realized that he liked her that much, she started dating him. So I guess he blew up the lab for a good cause."

Cal chuckled. "Dangerous way to make an impression."

"Yes, and he almost made an impression right through the wall!" Amelia said with glee.

Cal shook his head. "And I thought I was in a dangerous profession," he said, chuckling.

"You really are, though," Amelia said, growing solemn. "Doesn't it bother you?"

He gave her a quiet appraisal. "Yes, from time to time. But then I think about what I'm doing, and why I'm doing it, and it doesn't bother me as much." He smiled. "We're protecting a group of people who are under the rule of a madman, who kills women and children of anyone who questions his authority."

"Oh, good grief!" she exclaimed, shocked. "Why doesn't the government do something to stop him?"

"Because he is the government," he replied. "He chased out the legitimately elected president and took his place. We contract with the legitimate president, who wants his country back."

She gave him a long look. "That's a noble cause," she said finally.

That comment, from her, touched something deep inside

him. He felt a rush of affection that he quickly stifled. She wasn't fair game. She wouldn't be, for years, and he was a bad risk. He'd grown fond of her and her grandfather. He didn't want to do anything to jeopardize that friendship.

"Thanks," he said softly, and his eyes were quiet. "That means a lot."

"I feel the same way," Harris seconded. "It truly is a noble cause. But you can be killed even for doing something noble, if you're caught on the ground doing it in another country. I'm sure you realize that any authority would immediately disavow knowledge of your actions." He leaned forward. "And don't ever harbor a thought that our government doesn't know what you're up to. They may decide to turn a blind eye to it, if they agree with the purpose. Or they may not. In which case, you and your colleagues will be courting disaster."

Cal laughed. "We have backing from the people who count," he replied. "Eb has contacts high up in government."

"I hope they're people who wouldn't run to the exits if your exploits get exposed."

"Unlikely," Cal told him. "At least two of them would go down with us if we called a press conference to tell what we'd done, and why."

"A lot of people call press conferences, and nobody shows up except people with channels on the internet," Amelia interjected. "The legacy media is owned, and I mean owned, by corporations. They decide what you'll see and hear, and nobody stands up to them."

"All too true," Harris said sadly. "In my youth, journalism was held to a higher standard, and it wasn't controlled by any corporations. Not to mention that journalism in my parents' day was almost a sacred trust. In fact, my grandmother said that in her younger days, Walter Cronkite was known as the most trusted man in America. He was a newsman. She said he cried on live television when he announced the Kennedy assassination on the news." He paused. "She said everybody cried, regardless of their political parties, and that the whole nation was in utter shock."

"I guess so," Amelia said. "I remember Granny talking about it, too, things her father told her. There were conspiracy theories at the time, but a lot of new information is coming out all the time."

"I hope and pray that we'll never see another presidential assassination," Harris said solemnly.

"Well, not in this country," Cal remarked. "But in some countries, it's the only way to get rid of a vicious leader."

"Don't you get killed," Amelia said firmly, and she glared at him. "I mean it."

He laughed in spite of himself. She looked so fierce. "I promise you that I'll do my best to stay alive," he replied with a warm smile.

Her insides lit up at that smile, but she didn't let it show. She didn't want him to know how crazy about him she really was.

The conversation changed to local politics and charity dances.

"There's a dance for the animal shelter Friday night," Amelia told Cal at the beginning of the next week. "Granddad and I are going. I love animals."

"And yet you don't have any," he replied.

She smiled sadly. "Granddaddy's allergic to fur, which rules out cats and dogs, and I'm afraid of snakes. That just leaves frogs or lizards or fish, and they're all a lot of trouble. So I just pet other people's fuzzy companions."

"You should have a dog," he said. "Even a small one is good to warn you if there's an intruder. Come to think of it, geese are even better."

She blinked. “Excuse me?”

He grinned at her. “One of our guys lives on an island, and he has a flock of them. He swears that they're better even than dogs, because they start up at the first sound of footsteps. They're also dangerous. A goose is fairly large, and they can be very aggressive.”

“I like geese.”

He sighed. “Most men don't.”

“Why?” she asked.

“Because if a goose comes after a man, it's with only one target in mind, if you get my drift.”

She did and flushed.

He chuckled. “That's exactly why I don't have a goose.”

“Good thinking.”

He cocked his head. “If I'm here and I go to the animal rescue charity dance, are you going to dance with me?”

She had delicious chills up her spine. “I might,” she said, hiding her delight in teasing.

“Can you dance?” he probed.

She shifted. “Sort of.”

“Sort of?”

“Well, I know how to do a box step. It's just that my feet don't connect with my brain. So most people don't really want to dance with me,” she confided.

“We'll work on that,” he said, hating his own attraction. It was getting quickly out of hand. Fortunately, he had a mission the week after the dance. It would give him a breather, while he tried to get Amelia out of his mind. She was becoming essential to his happiness.

Amelia smiled. “Okay!” she said.

Meanwhile, Cal went up to San Antonio to talk to a man he knew at the police department. He'd been trying to persuade Cal to come back to the force and give up on merc work.

"You loved the job when you were a patrolman here," Jess reminded him. "You'd love it if you came back. We save the world, too, you know, just in a more legal sort of way and you're less likely to die in an explosion. Mostly."

Cal chuckled. "You're pretty persuasive."

"You're my pal," he replied easily. "Trust me, this is a really great opportunity. There's always plenty of room for advancement. The pay's still not bad. Not as good as you're making now, but the work is a little less traumatic."

And he'd know, Cal thought, because Jess himself had been spec ops in the military at one time.

"Do you ever miss the life?" he asked the other man.

Jess paused for a minute, thinking, and then one side of his mouth drew down. "Honestly, yes. But I'm married and I have two kids. What would happen to them if I got myself blown up in some country they couldn't even find on a map?"

"Good point. But I don't have that problem."

"I know. I was like you, once. But there's always the woman who'll make you settle down, even if you don't want to," he replied with a grin. "You'll see."

"It's unlikely. I don't want to get married. Ever."

The look on Cal's face when he said it made Jess change the subject.

"Well, anyway, think about what I told you," he said.

Cal smiled. "I will."

He went by Edie's apartment while he was in town. She opened the door, and he was surprised at the way she looked.

She was usually immaculately dressed, even at home, makeup on, hair combed. This woman was disheveled and looked as if she hadn't slept in weeks.

"What's the matter with you?" he asked worriedly.

"Just a few drinks too many," she replied with a hollow smile. "Come see me another time, okay?"

"Will you be all right?"

She waved a hand at him. "I'm okay, just hungover. I'll call you."

"All right. If you need me, I'll come," he said, genuinely concerned. He didn't have friends, but Edie was one. Sort of.

"Thanks," she replied softly. "Thanks a lot. See you."

She closed the door quickly.

He wondered how alcohol could leave a person looking like that. He knew she had no issues with street drugs, but maybe she was only saying that. She wasn't the sort of person to get hooked on drugs. Although alcohol was bad enough.

He knew about alcohol. He was the child of abusive alcoholics, both parents. His childhood had been a nightmare of yelling and pushing and sometimes beatings, if they were drunk enough. Of course, he could have called family services and he would have been taken out of that environment. But he knew foster care could be hit-or-miss, because three of his classmates were being fostered. None of them raved about it, and he was warned that as bad as things were at home, they could be worse. A lot worse.

So as he grew, Cal learned how to get around his parents. He became canny and insightful. He read books on alcoholism and learned about the reasons people drank. He also read about programs for detox. He actually tried to get at least his mother into one of the programs, but she backed out. And there was no hope with his father, who was mixed up with the local criminal crowd in Houston, just as he'd been in Cleveland, Ohio, before his father had moved the small family to Texas. Half the stuff in their home wouldn't pass a stolen item check by the police.

He thought that one day he'd be a policeman and clean up the neighborhood where he lived. But those thoughts were few and far between as he hovered between homework and horror. Eventually he graduated, and the first place he went was to the police department, to sign up. But not in Houston. A tragedy there, the death of both parents, had left him reeling. Even alcoholic parents were better than none, he thought sadly. It was a bleak time in his life. He needed a change. The army looked like a good fit at the time. Free college and all sorts of benefits. And his grandfather, the man he'd respected most of all in his young life, had been an army man. So he signed up.

When he got out of the service, after seeing some action overseas, he resettled in San Antonio and joined the police force there.

He went through the preliminary training, scored highest in his class on the firing range—because he spent half his time practicing—and then was placed on patrol duty.

It was the best two years of his life. He loved the work. But then he heard about Eb Scott and his group. They were advertising covertly for people to join, and Cal loved the idea of adventure. He was still young enough to long for foreign places and excitement, although he never drank or gambled. So he went to see Eb Scott. And he signed on. He felt bad leaving the department, but one superior officer was sympathetic, and told him there would always be a place for him. It was like a safety net. It gave him the confidence to go ahead with what he most wanted to do, at that stage of his life.

The move to a rental house in Jacobsville felt almost premeditated, because that was where Eb Scott had his base. Cal had worked out of San Antonio for several years, but when he signed on with Eb, living in Jacobsville made the commute a little easier.

Eb's group was into a hot situation right now in Africa, with the corrupt leader of a small nation there. The former president, a good man and a caring one, had been ousted by a lunatic with a ragtag army. The lunatic was destroying the communities under his control. The former president, backed secretly by several other nations, had contracted with Eb to oust the idiot in control. Eb had agreed at once.

They were getting organized right now to go in again, and this time they had the manpower to accomplish regime change.

But in the meanwhile, there was the dance at the community center, which Cal was looking forward to.

He hadn't told Edie about it when she called and asked if he wouldn't like to come up Saturday night and go out to dinner. He made an excuse and told her he'd see her the next day. She whined, but finally agreed that it would be fine. She'd probably be hungover, she added, but that was her problem.

He hung up, feeling guilty, as she meant him to. He knew alcoholics all too well. He hoped that he might be able to help Edie somehow get out of alcohol's grasp. He was optimistic that he could do it.

He almost didn't recognize Amelia when he moved through the throng of local citizens at the dance. He was wearing a gray suit, which highlighted his pale, thick blond hair and his nice tan. He was a striking man. Women eyed him as he moved around, looking for Amelia and her grandfather.

He'd passed over her twice while thinking privately what a glorious head of blond hair that woman had, shining and clean and hanging almost to her waist in back. He had a real weakness for blond hair.

And then, on the third pass, the woman turned around, and it was Amelia.

He stopped, laughing. "I didn't know you," he chuckled, moving closer. "You always wear your hair up in a bun." He admired it. "I didn't know it was so long."

She laughed, too. "It's a nuisance to wash, but I love long hair," she confessed.

"So do I," he said softly, and he reached out to touch its thick silkiness. "It's glorious."

"Thank you," she said shyly.

"Where's your grandfather?" he asked.

She shook her head, and nodded toward the back of the room where her grandfather and one of his friends were sitting on either side of a chess set.

"Chess, chess, chess," she moaned. "He never dances. He gets in the back with whichever chess fanatic friend of his who shows up, and they play chess until the last dance."

He laughed. "Well, whatever floats your boat," he mused.

"Exactly!"

"So why are you sitting here all alone?" he asked, indicating all the other people.

"Oh, I'm always on my own at these things," she said simply. "I don't mix well." She looked up at him. It was a long way, because she was wearing low-heeled shoes. "Most people aren't interested in how to blow up stuff," she whispered.

"I'm very interested," he replied, and slid his hand down to catch hers. "You can tell me all about it while we're dancing."

"I'll trip over my own feet and kill somebody," she objected as he led her to the dance floor. Her whole body tingled at the feel of that big, warm hand closed around her own.

"I'll save you," he promised, and drew her close.

It was the first time she'd ever been so close to a man, and it was shocking how much she liked it. She could feel the fabric of his suit jacket under her fingers and, deeper, his breathing. She could smell the spicy cologne he used and some sort of masculine soap, as well. He was always immaculate, even in regular clothing.

But it was the effect it had on her that caught her attention. She felt tight all over, as if every muscle in her body was tensing. She couldn't quite breathe normally.

And her heartbeat was doing a hula. It was very disconcerting, especially to a woman who spent most of her time with men in a lab at college, where she was just one of the guys. Now she felt like a woman felt with a man—at least, like the women in the historical novels she liked to read.

Cal was feeling something similar and fighting it. Why hadn't he realized that this was a very bad idea, and found a way to keep out of it? He hadn't thought past sitting with Amelia and Jacob Harris and having one of their usual conversations. He certainly hadn't thought about dancing.

It was sheer heaven, dancing with Amelia. Feeling her close in his arms, one hand at her waist, the other tangling gently in that glorious fall of thick, soft hair that smelled of roses.

"Your hair is incredible," he said in a hushed tone.

She smiled. It was nice, that he liked something about her. "Thanks. I wish it was the color of yours," she added.

"Why?"

"Because your hair shines like gold in the light," she replied. "Mine is dull."

"Not so. It's beautiful. I'm glad you wore it down, this once."

She laughed. "I wasn't going to, and then Granddad asked why I was hiding my light under a bushel. So I let it down."

"Good for him. I hope he wins his match," he added.

"You're kidding, right? He's playing with old man Ridgeway. He takes half an hour to make a single move. They'll be here till midnight, and when the cleaners get ready to lock up, Mr. Ridgeway will complain about being rushed out of a winning move."

He burst out laughing. "I never knew this town had so many interesting people," he said.

"Eccentrics," she corrected. "We're infested with them," she laughed. "But they're all nice people and we protect them from outsiders. Like Fred, who can find water with a forked stick, and Miss Betty, who can talk out fire and talk off warts, and old Bill, who can predict the weather without TV or radio."

"The things I missed growing up in the city," he said, shaking his head.

"San Antonio?"

His face tautened. "Cleveland, Ohio." He glanced down at her. "Now don't you say one word about my being from up north," he cautioned firmly. "Just because I'm not a native in Jacobsville doesn't mean I'm not a true Texan. I've lived here since I was six. That's more than enough time to be considered a native."

She burst out laughing. "That's the best defense I've heard yet."

"Ha! A likely story. You think we talk funny."

She was chuckling. "I think you talk just fine. And I hold no grudges. Honest."

"Fair enough, but it's our secret, got that?" he asked, looking around with mock unease. "And don't you tell a soul where I'm really from!"

"I won't tell," she promised under her breath. "I swear! I'll take your secret to my grave!"

He laughed, too, and suddenly pulled her close in an obvious hug, making her head spin with joy. "You light up all the dark places in me," he whispered. "I never laughed so much in my life as I do with you."

"I don't have dark places, but you light up my life, too. And Granddaddy's," she added quickly, so that she didn't sound too forward.

He perceived that. He was glad that she understood he wasn't hitting on her. He wanted to, of course. She made his heart skip. But she was far too young for a man of his experience. He liked sophistication. Besides that, she was innocent, and he still had some sense of honor, left over from his own grandfather. He barely remembered the old man, who was devastated when his only son decided to move to Texas. He'd been the babysitter for Cal all his life, and he said that it was like losing two sons instead of one. He said that a man had to be responsible for his actions and willing to accept the consequences of them. If it sounded like a soldier talking, it was because the old man had retired with the rank of lieutenant colonel in the army. He'd been in combat overseas, and he was military to his bones. He'd been Cal's hero. It had broken his young heart to leave the old man, who'd died not a year later. Cal's father hadn't even taken the family to the burial. He said he didn't want to lose his job with the city's sanitation department. But he really just plain didn't care. He had his father cremated and a friend buried the ashes beside his mother's grave, in the same church cemetery.

"You're really quiet tonight," Amelia said softly.

He looked down at her. "I was remembering my grandfather," he said simply. "He was a good man. We moved to Houston when I was six and left him behind. He died the very next year. He was in the army. A combat veteran." He smiled sadly. "He was my hero, when I was little."

That was odd. Shouldn't his dad have been his hero? But she never pried. She accepted what he decided to tell her and didn't ask for more. He thought it was because she didn't really care. But it was because she cared a lot and didn't want him to know it.

"When do you leave on your next assignment?" she asked.

"Monday, before daylight."

She looked up at him, dreamy with delight, smiling. "You come back, now. You hear?"

He chuckled because she'd drawled it like characters on a TV show. "I'll come back," he said, and hoped he could. He had a feeling about this trip, a bad one. He wasn't psychic or anything like that, but he had feelings, premonitions, intuitive insights. They'd already saved his life at least twice. He didn't talk about them.

"You dance beautifully," she remarked.

"And you haven't tripped once," he pointed out with a grin.

She shrugged. "I didn't want to tell you that I won a dance contest my last year of high school," she said, peering up at him with twinkling dark eyes. "I did the tango with one of my friends. He's from South America. He married my best friend." She grinned from ear to ear.

"You little devil," he said, and jerked her close to leave a playful bite on her earlobe. "That wasn't fair!"

She giggled with pure joy. "Yes, it was. It was so cute, listening to you persuade me to dance."

"I get even," he threatened.

"Oooh," she teased. "I can't wait!"

He laughed, shook his head and pulled her close for a minute. "I go to this place in San Antonio on Friday nights—Fernando's. They're famous for flamenco and the tango. We'll show the audience how the tango is done."

"Is that a promise?"

He drew back enough to see her face. She could feel his black eyes probing hers, feel his breath on her lips. "It's a promise," he said in a deep, husky tone, and he didn't smile.

It was a moment out of time, one of those moments when things are so sweet, so poignant, that it seems they can last forever. Of course, they don't. Ever.

He averted his gaze to someone he knew and waved, and then the music and the magic ended.

But she'd had her perfect evening. She held it to her like a security blanket, and every night, she relived it before she slept. And she worried. Because Cal was now overseas, not dancing, but fighting for his life most likely. She kept him in her prayers and lived for the day when he came home.

Cal, meanwhile, was on a flight to an airport in the middle of an African nation, Ngawa, that was being destroyed by two sides of a war for control. Along with his friends from Eb Scott's group, there were some older and more knowledgeable mercs on hand to help with strategy and tactics.

He'd heard of the three who turned up from nowhere. Laremos and a man called Archer, and one called Dutch. The three were legendary. The younger men stood in awe of them, despite their own well-honed skills.

Three of the older men found that adulation amusing.

Cy Parks was a marvel with Bowie knives. It was an education to watch him throw them. He never missed. He had black hair and green eyes and a mean attitude. He was the sort of man who could walk down a back alley with twenty-dollar bills hanging out of his pockets and he'd never be approached by a criminal.

Rodrigo Ramirez was a maverick. He worked for the federal government in drug interdiction from time to time, when he wasn't off with Eb Scott's group on missions. He spoke several languages, which made him invaluable in undercover work. He was also the wealthiest employee Eb had. He had the equivalent of the annual budget of a small nation in a bank somewhere in Denmark, where his father, a minor royal, had lived before his death. His mother was a titled Spanish noblewoman, and both parents had been wealthy beyond the dreams of avarice. There was a sister, as well. Ramirez spoke of her rarely, but with affection. They were the only two survivors of their family.

The third member of the small, tight group was Micah Steele. He'd trained to be a doctor, even had his medical license, but he'd taken exception to some of the rules he was expected to obey. And he'd jettisoned a potential career for merc work, which paid much better. He was blond and handsome, a ladies' man for real, and a deadly man with an automatic weapon. He had a father and a stepsister, but no other relatives. Rumor was that he hated the stepsister and made her life miserable.

Cal was fascinated by the men around him. He hadn't really lived long enough or worked in the field long enough to gain a reputation that anyone would take notice of. But he was going to change that. He was going to be as well known in merc circles as these men were one day.

He was intelligent enough to know how to listen and pay attention to details, which stood him in good stead with Cy Parks, who was the de facto leader of the bunch.

As they planned the incursion, and worked out the details, a demolition man, who was another legend, came on board. Cord Romero was the son and grandson of famous bullfighters in Spain. He'd been orphaned at a young age, but adopted by a kindhearted Texas woman, who raised him and a little girl who was his foster sister by adoption. After a brief career in the FBI and, rumor said, a wife who died by suicide, he'd gone into merc work more or less full-time.

Watching him work, Cal was forcibly reminded of Amelia and her capability with deadly chemicals. He mentioned it to Cord, as he put together small IEDs for use in the incursion.

"Does she want to do merc work?" Cord asked with twinkling dark eyes.

Cal sighed. "I hope not."

He was shocked at what he'd let slip. It was none of his business what Amelia did, but the thought of her in a camp like this, overseas, in constant danger, made his blood run cold. And that hit him in the gut like a fist.

Chapter Five

Cord Romero gave Cal a pointed smile. "You don't want her to do this sort of thing?"

"She's only nineteen," Cal said, pushing back his own feelings. "Her grandfather would be outraged."

"Then why does she study chemistry?" he persisted.

Cal scowled. "I don't know. I should have asked."

"Plenty of time," the other man said lazily. "If she's that young, she's got years to decide on a profession. She might teach." He chuckled as he said it.

"What's funny?"

"I tried that. Teaching," he added. He shook his head. "It's not for everyone."

"What was your field of study?"

"Chemistry," Cord said. His eyes twinkled. "I taught high school chemistry for a year fresh out of college. Even then, I was drawn to demolition. It got me into trouble with the principal and the school board."

"Why?"

"They objected to my slight deviations from the curriculum," he replied.

"He was teaching the children how to blow things up," Cy Parks interjected with a chuckle.

"Only little things," Cord argued. "My God, it was just one little desk, not a building. I even offered to replace the desk!"

"So your principal was ordered to replace you," Micah Steele added with a grin.

"And that was our good fortune, because this man is a genius with explosives," Ramirez said with a dramatic sigh. "There should be a prize for such things."

"There is. I think it's called prison," Cal told them.

"Ex-cop," Cy Parks said, jerking a thumb at him. "Ignore him. It might be contagious."

"Ignore him," Ramirez said, indicating Cy. "I've been DEA on and off."

"The 'heat,'" Cord muttered, jerking a thumb at Ramirez. "You can't even escape it here!"

"You were never arrested," Steele chuckled. "And you're FBI when you're not here, so don't crow so loud."

Cord gave him an international symbol of distaste.

Steele gave him one right back.

"And just imagine, nobody here has a straitjacket," Cal said under his breath.

Somebody threw a towel at him.

There was a young local boy named Juba who'd become a sort of mascot to the small group. He knew the area, having been brought up there, and he was a walking library on plants and animals.

Cy Parks was particularly fond of him. He had a young son and loved to show off photos of him on his cell phone. Of course, the phone stayed on the plane when the group was ready to go into combat. There, only satellite phones were of any use in the jungle.

It never ceased to amaze Cal that huge modern cities could cohabit with small rural villages. And the strangest thing was that the people in the villages were always laughing, always happy, in what seemed like inescapable poverty. While in the cities, people walked past each other without even a nod, frowning, lost in their own worries.

"This is an amazing place," Cal mused while they were waiting for a local militia leader to give them a situation report.

"It is?" Laremos asked.

"Look," Cal said, indicating laughing children amusing laughing adults. "Do you see anybody scowling and muttering about how hard life is?"

Laremos grinned. "Just us."

Cal laughed. "I live in a small town in Texas," he mused. "It's sort of like this. A lot of people are poor, but they always seem to find reasons to smile. In cities, you just don't really see that much."

"True," Laremos agreed. "I live in Guatemala. It's largely rural, in my area. Palm trees, sand, drug dealers..." He laughed. He glanced at one of the younger men in the group. "Still, at least we have groundwater, Gomez," he called to the man.

"Rub it in," Gomez called back. "But we have ancient Mayan ruins, as well!"

"So do we," Laremos countered. "And lovely streams and waterfalls..."

"Quintana Roo is abundantly blessed with water, thank you. It's just underground!"

"What, there's no surface water in the Yucatan Peninsula?" Cal asked. "Like our rivers in Texas that only run at certain times of the year?"

"I mean there aren't any rivers," Laremos corrected. "None at all."

"Good Lord! Why?"

"There was an impact thousands of years ago, a meteor called Chicxulub. It hit in the Gulf of Mexico and destroyed pretty much the surrounding area. I think that's why. Everybody has a theory. That's mine."

"I couldn't live in a place with no running water," Cy Parks murmured. "My place in Wyoming has plenty of it."

"He has a ranch the size of New Jersey," Dutch commented.

"You should move next door," Cy chuckled. "It's a great place to raise kids."

"Kids!" Dutch shivered. "Never in a million years! I break out in hives just thinking about it!"

"Woman-hater," Laremos said in a mock whisper.

"It goes beyond hate," Dutch said, and he didn't smile. He finished what he was doing. "Okay, there's our second IED. God, I hope we don't have to use any of them here," he added, looking around at the villagers.

"That I can't promise," Cy replied. "But we'll do our best." He smiled at Juba, who came running with an AK-47, a weapon that was old but still serviceable. Many of the young fighters still carried them.

"I need bullets!" Juba said with his big toothy smile. "And a candy bar…?"

Cy chuckled and got one out of his pack. "You're bankrupting me," he murmured as he handed it over.

"You have many. You are a rich American," Juba laughed, pulling the wrapper open. "The United States must be such a rich country to have so many sweet and wonderful things! I would like to go there!"

"And so you might, one day," Cy said, rubbing the boy's thick hair. He'd become very fond of Juba, who had been orphaned by the turmoil going on around him. He had a cousin in a distant village, but the cousin had five sons and didn't want him. So Juba hung around the village with his American friends, and some other nice soldiers who had come from overseas to help win the fight for liberation of his country.

"This is so good of you," Juba said, suddenly serious. "To help us, I mean."

"It helps us, too," Cy replied solemnly. "When we help to fight an evil that affects many lives, it gives us a feeling of, well, of purpose. Of doing something worthwhile."

Juba nodded. "Yes. It is what I would like to do also. Perhaps when I grow up, I will be a politician like our poor president who is in exile."

"If you do, we'll have your back."

Juba frowned, his black eyes questioning.

"We'll help protect you," he clarified.

"Ah." He grinned. "Just so!"

"Juba, can you take this to the French army over there?" Laremos called, raising a hand at one of the foreign fighters he knew.

"Legion-etrangere!" came the mocking reply.

"French Foreign Legion!" Laremos yelled back.

The Frenchman put a finger to his lips and went "Shh! Say ex-Legion, or I can't go home!"

Everybody laughed.

Cy Parks watched Juba run to do the errand. "I'd love to take Juba home with me," he said quietly. "This is no place for a child of promise, in a perpetual combat zone."

"Could you do it?" Laremos asked.

He nodded. "I have contacts. I'll use them."

Cal, listening, nodded, too. He liked being part of this incursion. He liked it a lot.

The group stayed a week, long enough to get a better

picture of what would be needed for the upcoming offensive, including more weapons, more ammunition, the works. They'd worked out a battle plan with the other insurgents, all of them hoping to end this miserable standoff and get the country back to normal.

They flew home, just for a couple of weeks. Then it would be back into the fires of hell.

When Amelia saw Cal pull into his driveway, her heart flew. She had to grit her teeth to stop herself from running across the street and throwing herself into his arms. But that way lay disaster. He didn't know how she felt about him, and she didn't dare let it show. He'd already put up caution signs. No followers. He was free and he liked it that way.

He might change his mind one day. If he did, Amelia was going to be right there, waiting.

She cooked a huge dinner that night, anticipating that Cal would come over to visit. And he did.

She walked to the kitchen door as her grandfather let him in. "The prodigal returns!" she said dramatically.

He made a face at her and grinned. "Something smells nice."

"I saw your car pull in, so I made extra. You're welcome," she added pertly, and grinned before she went back to the stove.

At least, she saw no bullet holes or bandages, so he must not have been in any heavy fighting. Not yet, anyway. She sent up a mental thanks.

Supper was riotous. Cal had a dozen stories about his companions. Without giving anything tactical away, he described his friends.

"They're all pretty much misfits," he mused, "even though some of them came to merc work from law enforcement."

"Spec ops takes a different mindset," Harris commented.

"It's a known fact that no man who can pass a standard psych profile is spec ops material." He chuckled.

"Is that true for you?" Cal asked.

He nodded. "I can't talk about it. Most of our missions were classified." He looked up. "But, believe me, I know the life. I'd be willing to bet that most of your crew is confirmed bachelors."

Cal nodded. "Only one has a family. That I know of. They don't talk about personal things much."

"I was the odd one out in my group, as well. It doesn't mix with family life." He glanced covertly at his granddaughter as he spoke, noting her lowered head, although he was certain she was hanging on every word.

"Still," Cal sighed, "it feels good to come home, even just for a couple of weeks. That reminds me. How about Fernando's Friday night?" he asked Amelia with a grin.

She looked up, her face flushing prettily. "Fernando's?" She was still hanging on what he'd said about most of the men being confirmed bachelors.

"The tango?" he reminded her. "Flan? Flamenco dancers…?"

"Oh!" She laughed self-consciously. "Yes. I'd like that."

"Me, too. I don't do much dancing in Africa," he added, tongue-in-cheek.

"Do you have to do martial arts, too?" she wanted to know. "Besides, you know, blowing up stuff?"

"Definitely," he replied. "Eb Scott has experts in every field. He's going to have the finest counterterrorism school on the planet before he's done. It will put Jacobsville on the map—even if it's just a small map." He finished his cake. "That was delicious," he told her with a smile.

She grinned. "Thanks. It's just basic chemistry," she added with a wicked grin.

They all laughed.

"How about coming out to the school with me tomorrow?" he asked Amelia. "Do you have early morning classes at college?"

She nodded. "One at eight that's two hours, and one at ten that's an hour. I'm not taking a full courseload this semester."

"So, how about one o'clock tomorrow? We'll go out to Eb's place and I'll teach you some basic self-defense."

Her eyes lit up. "That would be great! But won't you be too tired? I mean, you've just got home after a really long trip..."

He drew in a breath and laughed. "You're always one step ahead of me. Yes, I am tired, and I have to see a man in San Antonio in the morning. Maybe day after tomorrow? What's your class schedule?"

"It's the same, every Tuesday and Thursday."

"Day after tomorrow, then."

"Does Eb go with you on these missions?" she wondered.

He shook his head. "He's got too much responsibility here right now. He used to, though," he added, smiling.

"Probably too many injuries to be an asset on a fast-moving mission," Amelia's grandfather added with twinkling eyes. "That was why I had to give it up."

"Well, you got married, too," she pointed out.

He grimaced. "Your grandmother wasn't too enthusiastic about seeing me lining up to be a battle casualty," he confessed. "And I was too crazy about her to make a fuss. By and large," he added, finishing his coffee, "the decision I made was the right one."

"Not one I'll have to make," Cal said with a weary smile. "I've got enough excitement in my life without adding complications."

"Wise man," Amelia said, smiling at him. And she was lying through her teeth, but Cal didn't realize it.

He shoved back his chair and got up. "Thank you both for the lovely supper," he nodded at Amelia, "and the conversation. But I'm ready for bed." He stifled a yawn. "It's a long ride home from where we were."

"Get some rest," Harris said as they walked him to the door.

"Planning to," he replied. He smiled at Amelia. "Day after tomorrow. At one. Okay?"

"Okay!" She was beaming.

He threw up his hand and went home.

Amelia's grandfather closed and locked the door.

"You're setting yourself up for some heartache, you know," he said very gently. "He's not a settling sort of man."

"Neither were you," she pointed out.

"I agree. There's always the woman who can turn a man's priorities on their head. But you're very young and our friend across the street is savvy in a sophisticated way."

"You mean he knows his way around women, and I'm stuck in double dating," she translated, but with a grin.

"Exactly my point. So you watch your step. He's the sort of man who can enjoy a day and walk away from it with no regrets. That's not you, sugar. You're a forever sort of girl."

She felt the heaviness of sorrow as she listened. "You're right," she agreed. "But hope is the last thing we lose." Her eyes met his. "He's…the whole world," she faltered, and flushed.

He put his arms around her and hugged her tight. "I know that. It's why I warned you. I can't live your life for you but have a care. I know a train wreck when I see one."

"Maybe it will be just a small train wreck with no casualties."

"Sugar," he sighed, "all wrecks have casualties. Just… be careful."

She nodded against his shoulder. "I will. I promise."

* * *

Cal woke to the ringing of his cell phone playing the theme from a popular action film. He reached for it, knocked it off the table and almost fell out of bed retrieving it.

"Damn," he muttered as he fumbled it open. "Hello!" he said belligerently.

"Well," Edie's voice came over the phone. "If that isn't a happy welcome!"

"Sorry. I dropped the damned thing," he muttered. "What time is it?"

"Eleven o'clock. Where are you? Weren't we supposed to have lunch today?"

"Lunch." He scowled. Now he remembered. He'd almost stood her up by offering to take Amelia to Eb Scott's place today, until she'd remarked that he must need rest. Something Edie was never concerned about. She didn't like illness or hospitals and avoided both.

"Yes, lunch! How soon can you be here?" she wanted to know.

He blinked his eyes. Food had no place in his thoughts at the moment. "About an hour, I guess."

"I made the reservations for eleven thirty," she said tersely. "It will be an inconvenience if I have to cancel them and sweet-talk the maître d' into holding our table."

"I don't frankly give a damn," he shot back. "Eat it yourself!" He hung up.

Edie was adversarial when she wanted something, and she made his life miserable if he didn't fall in with her wishes. He was getting tired of it. He didn't like having a woman try to lead him around by the nose.

He showered and shaved. The phone had been ringing constantly. He finally answered it.

"I'm sorry," Edie said in a wheedling tone. "I'm really

sorry. I didn't mean to sound so horrible, and when you're only just back in the States."

He relented, a little. "One more time, and you can find another friend to take you out," he said coldly. "Understand?"

Her indrawn breath was audible. He could almost hear her teeth grinding.

"Okay," she choked. "I get it."

"Fine. I'll be there in thirty minutes. We can get a hamburger someplace."

"I changed the reservation. Half an hour will be fine. Really."

"All right."

He hung up. She was becoming a liability. He felt sorry for her, because she didn't mix well, and she had a drinking problem. But pity only carried a man so far. He preferred Amelia, who was gentle and kindhearted and fun to be around. She wasn't as sophisticated as Edie, or as pretty, but she was a far better companion, despite her age. Not that he had any serious thoughts about Amelia. She, like Edie, had to be just a friend. He had plans, and they didn't involve white picket fences.

"I really am sorry that I was so brash," Edie told him while they ate their way through late lunch at one of San Antonio's finest restaurants.

"We all have bad days," he remarked.

"I have lots of those," she said with a sigh. She was picking at a salmon salad without much enthusiasm.

"Why do you spend so much time alone?" he asked her. "Don't you have friends besides me?"

"Loads of them. Rich people with connections," she said, laughing. "The best kind."

He frowned. "Money doesn't buy character."

She made a gesture with her fork. "It pays bills, though,

and gets you where you want to be in life. I wouldn't be poor for anything!"

He was remembering Juba in the Ngawan village, a kid who had nothing but who was always smiling.

Edie, never observant, still noted his changed expression. "What did I say?" she wanted to know.

He shrugged. "There's this kid. Juba," he added with a nostalgic smile. "His parents were killed in one of the incursions, and he has nobody of his own except a distant cousin. One of our group is thinking about bringing him over here..."

"Good God, what for?" she exploded, wide-eyed. "As if we don't already have so many parasitic poor people pouring in here!"

The waiter, who'd just stopped by to ask about dessert, had a closed and locked expression.

"Nada mas, gracias," Cal told him. He added in a low tone, *"Lo siento. Mi amiga sabe nada sobre el gente quien tiene nada sin que El Dios. Entiende?"*

The waiter smiled at him. He nodded. *"Mil gracias."*

"La comida es muy sabroso," he added, smiling. *"Pero no nos gusta tener los pasteles. Pues, mas café, por favor?"*

"At once," the waiter said in perfect English and went away.

"You speak that awful language?" Edie asked curtly. She was fidgeting in her chair, nervous and getting more unsettled by the minute. "People who work in this country should speak English!"

"The waiter is from the Yucatan," Cal said icily. "His first language is Mayan. His second language is Spanish. His third language is English."

She blinked. It wasn't registering. She had beads of sweat on her forehead. "Why is it so hot in here?" she muttered. "They need to fix the air-conditioning."

"It's cool," he said, puzzled. She was wearing a short-sleeved dress. There was no reason that she should be complaining about the heat.

She wiped her forehead. "Easy for you to say," she muttered.

The waiter was back with the coffee. He served it, took Cal's credit card back to pay the bill and returned promptly, leaving the ticket in its little book on the table with a smile at Cal and ignoring Edie entirely.

"No manners," she grumbled as the waiter left. "He didn't even wish me a good afternoon."

"You're the one with no manners," Cal snapped as he finished his coffee. "And this is very likely our last lunch together."

He got up, leaving her to follow.

Once they were outside, he was almost vibrating with anger. She'd shamed him with her behavior. It wasn't something he'd seen in her before. He didn't like it.

"I'm sorry," she mumbled as she joined him on the sidewalk. "I don't feel well. I need to go home."

He took a long breath. He led her to the car, drove her home, saw her to her door and started to leave.

"Don't you want to come in?" she asked. "And have a drink?"

He turned and looked at her with an expression that could have started fires. "I do not," he said coldly. "Goodbye."

"Cal, I'm sorry," she wailed. "I'm really sorry!"

"You're always sorry," he said icily. "But you never change."

She shifted restlessly. "I have problems."

"Everybody has damned problems," he shot back curtly. "But most people just endure and get on with their lives. You make everybody around you miserable because you can't live with yourself!"

She glared at him. "I'm going in now."

"Then go."

He went back to his car and drove away. He didn't even spin gravel getting onto the road.

Edie picked up a vase on a table beside the door and slammed it into the carpet, shattering it. She hated Cal. She hated people who weren't in her social class. She hated the world.

She poured herself a large whiskey and sat down to drink it. She hated herself, she thought miserably. But drinking helped. It helped a lot. When she drank enough, she could forget her problems.

Cal would come back, she told herself. He always did, no matter how mad she made him. He was just tired. Sure. That was it. She had another swallow of her drink. She was already feeling much better.

Cal picked up Amelia at her house the next day. She was wearing sweats, neat gray ones.

He chuckled. "You dressed the part, I see," he teased.

"Well, I don't have a karate kit or anything," she replied, smiling. "This was the next best thing. Will it be okay, you think?"

He sighed. "It will be fine," he assured her, mentally comparing her behavior with Edie's. They were polar opposites.

"Is it karate or tae kwon do or tai chi that we'll do?" she asked. "I've been reading up," she added with a grin.

He chuckled. "Eb teaches all three. But mostly it's tae kwon do." He glanced at her. "What we learn for combat is pretty different."

"Different how?" she wanted to know.

"What Eb teaches at the school is defensive martial arts.

In the military, or in merc work, you learn killing techniques."

"Oh."

"Don't tell me, you're squeamish," he teased.

She shrugged. "I can't even kill a mouse," she confessed sheepishly. "I caught one in the kitchen once, in a mason jar. Granddaddy said to kill it. I just couldn't. When he went to take his nap, I took it out to the back garden and let it go."

"It probably made its way right back into the house," he pointed out.

She laughed. "There were all sorts of delicious vegetables in the garden that year," she recalled. "Plus, I kept sneaking crackers and guinea pig pellets out to him."

"Amelia, you're hopeless," he groaned.

She chuckled. "I like animals. What can I say? I'd have loved a cat or a dog. I wish Granddaddy wasn't allergic. But I'd rather have him than a dozen pets."

"He's a sweet man," he agreed.

She sighed. "I wish his sister was," she groaned. "There aren't enough bad words to describe her."

"Where does she live?"

"Victoria, thank goodness, but she's coming to visit next week for a few days. She'll complain about her room and the food and the temperature in the house and then she'll mention all the things I need to correct about my looks and my behavior…"

"What's wrong with your looks?" he asked curtly, glancing at her. "And your behavior is great."

She flushed. "Wow. Thanks."

He shrugged. "You're not like a lot of women, who think they should have every wish granted, every complaint seen to at once."

"That sounds as if you know one," she fished.

"I do. She embarrassed the hell out of me at a restaurant, making nasty remarks about immigrants."

Her face softened as she looked at him. "We have this couple down the street, the Gomezes. They have three kids. They're some of the nicest people you'd ever want to know. Mrs. Gomez has been teaching me Spanish. I babysit her kids when she has to take her husband to the doctor. He's diabetic and he won't eat right, so he goes into comas periodically."

His heart melted. He compared that behavior with Edie's and just shook his head. "We have some Hispanic operatives in our group. Fine men." His face tautened. "That friend of mine remarked about how everyone living here should speak our language. I talked to our waiter, who was Mayan. He spoke three languages."

"That's impressive," she said softly. "People who put them down just don't know them, Cal," she added quietly. "A lot of the problem is they only learn about immigrants from what they hear on the so-called news."

He chuckled. "So-called news?"

"Try getting any real news out of them," she grumbled. "They're so busy not offending anyone that they're scared to tell the real news. They're an entertainment, not a source of information. Granddaddy says that reporters he used to know would refuse to work for any of the TV news stations, because they had integrity, and the TV news has none."

"I have to confess that I feel exactly that way." He pulled into a huge compound near a towering Victorian house, surrounded by quonset huts. "And we're here," he said, as a tall, rangy man in boots and jeans and a Stetson noted their arrival and started toward them as they got out of the car.

"Hi, Eb," Cal greeted him, shaking hands. "Remember Amelia?" he asked wickedly. He leaned forward. "She knows how to blow up stuff!"

Chapter Six

Eb Scott's green eyes laughed as he grinned at Amelia. "Oh, yes, I remember you. I've never seen anybody hit a bull's-eye dead center the way you do. Except him." He jerked his thumb at Cal. "Never misses." He just shook his head.

"I'd rather blow up stuff, though," she replied, laughing.

"If you get good at blowing up stuff, you may be asked to hire on one day soon," he told her.

She laughed, too. "I'd be delighted!" she said, and meant it. "But first I have to learn some more deadly recipes."

"You go to college?" Eb asked.

She nodded. "I'm a sophomore. Well, I'm in a degree program that I graduate from at the end of the year. Then I have to decide if I want to go the whole way to a BS in science or settle for an AS."

"Big decision," Eb agreed. "But you're young."

"Not so much," she laughed.

"Young," Cal said firmly and grinned at her.

"Come along and I'll give you the grand tour," Eb said as he led the way into the compound. "I've just added defensive driving for chauffeurs. Our courses are growing by leaps and bounds. So is our student population. I'd like to be with you guys in Africa," Eb added with a glance at Cal. "Maybe in a couple of weeks, if I can settle things here and get a competent manager on the place."

"You'd be welcome," Cal replied. "The more, the merrier, in this case."

"In any case," the older man replied somberly.

He took them through all the classes, although he didn't interrupt the instructors. Some of his teachers had been in elite forces. There was even a retired SAS guy teaching sniper tactics.

"We draw from all over the planet," Eb said as they continued over to the huge martial arts complex. "A good deal of ex-military can't settle. So teaching keeps them close to the action without risking the success of an incursion by adding them to it. You slow down as you age and collect battle wounds." He grimaced. "I'm carrying a few extra grams in my carcass from bullets the surgeons couldn't remove."

That was something Amelia hadn't considered—that modern men got shot and the bullets had to stay in them.

"They say that Doc Holliday had a lot of them in him that they didn't take out, back in the late 1800s," she remarked.

"Absolutely true," Eb agreed. "They had no antibiotics back in the day. Any surgeon probing for a bullet could cause a fatal infection. Bullets ricochet on bone. Sometimes they travel in unpredicted ways, depending on the caliber of the gun, the velocity of the bullet and the distance from the victim."

Amelia was hanging on every word. "Wow," she said.

Eb chuckled. "I should give you a place in my operation. You just soak up knowledge. And you know a lot already," he pointed out.

"She's going to finish college and teach other people how to blow up stuff," Cal said firmly. "Ask her granddad."

Amelia made a face. "I guess so," she agreed. "He'd never approve of me going off to war, no matter how much I'd like to."

Eb stopped and turned to look down at her. "War is hell, Sherman said, and he's right. Until you've been in a battle where you lose favorite comrades and have bullets flying right at you, you have no idea what war actually is." His eyes were dull and sad. "Every man has to learn that the hard way."

Cal hadn't, yet. His stint overseas in the military had been mostly mop-up operations, not front-line stuff. He just smiled. "I'm sure we all cope in different ways," he said.

"Oh, we cope." Eb sighed. "To a point. Let's find you a free mat."

Amelia learned to fall. She groaned and glared at Cal after the tenth back breakfall.

"When am I going to learn tae kwon do?" she asked with a little heat. "All I'm learning is how to fall down!"

"Falling down the right way is what will spare you many injuries," Cal told her with a smile. "This is always taught first."

She groaned again. "Okay," she said. "Maybe if a guy comes at me with a gun, I can just fall on him and win the fight."

"You'd need to gain a lot of weight first," he chuckled. "Okay. Side breakfalls…"

She sighed and followed his instructions.

From side breakfalls, on both sides, they progressed

to front breakfalls. But she couldn't do it. She just stared down at the mat and then at Cal with misery written all over her flushed features, her blond hair wisping around her sweaty face as it threatened to escape the tight bun high on her head.

"It's too far down," she wailed. "I'll break my nose!"

"And it's such a pretty nose, too," he teased, tapping it with his finger. "That's why you do this," and he demonstrated falling to land squarely on his forearms, slapping the mat just before the impact.

"I'll break my nose," she repeated.

"No. You won't. Come on. Give it a try."

She hesitated. She glanced around her at the other students in various stages of training. Several of them were also doing breakfalls.

She took a deep breath, leaned forward and fell. She slapped the mat and landed on her forearms, her nose inches from the mat. She burst out laughing. "Hey, that's not hard at all!" she said breathlessly as Cal reached down and pulled her up in front of him.

"Nice fall," he said softly, pushing back the wisps of hair from her face. His dark eyes were quiet and curious as he studied her. She was game. She complained, but never meant it. She was fun to be around. She made him laugh. He hardly ever had, until she came into his life.

"Thanks," she whispered huskily, lost in his eyes, trembling inside with raging emotions that she could only barely control.

He came back to himself almost immediately and stepped back. "Okay, now that you know how," he said, and grinned, "back to it!"

She made a face at him, but she obliged.

Before they left the camp, Eb took them out to the shooting range.

He handed Amelia a .45 Ruger Vaquero double-action revolver, loaded, but with the cylinder pushed out. "Do your worst," he invited, indicating a man-shaped target in front of them on the range.

"Wow," she whispered. "I love this thing! It's like being in the last century, fighting outlaws!" She glanced at Cal. "I know, you prefer your .38, and I like shooting it. But I've never shot one of these!"

"Pretend the target is a highwayman and give him hell," Cal told her.

She laughed. She slapped the cylinder back in, aimed and sent six shots right dead center into the target without hesitation.

"Damn!" Eb exploded. "That pistol is heavy, too!"

"Double damn!" Cal seconded. "How did you do that?"

"I really don't know," she said simply. "It seems so easy to me, even with unfamiliar guns." She grinned at her companions. "This one is super!" she added, admiring it.

"If you ever want a job," Eb said, "you've got one here. I'd hire you in a minute to teach or to go on missions…"

"Never," Cal said firmly, and glared at her, because she was already caught up in the excitement and eager. "It's no life for a woman. And I'd bet real money that you've never had a woman on the place, as far as instruction goes."

"That's true," Eb admitted. "But then, I've never seen anybody do what Amelia just did," he continued. "Or what she did last time she was here, on this same range with the .32. Except you," he added, as he glanced at Cal. "Well, maybe you slipped once. But, almost never."

"What does he mean?" she asked Cal.

"I shoot a hundred times, I hit the bull's-eye a hundred times," Cal said simply. "Except this one time when, for God knows what reason, a bee landed on my nose when I fired."

"True story," Eb seconded. "Damnedest thing, I didn't know we had a bee on the place. Turns out, there was a whole hive of them in the wall of one of my outbuildings. We got a beekeeper to come over with a smoker and a hive. He found the queen, put her in the hive, all the workers followed, and he took the hive home with him." He laughed. "The fringe benefit is that I get a jar of honey whenever I want one. I love honey."

"I do, too, but I'm not a fan of bees on the shooting range," Cal replied.

"No kidding?" Eb just chuckled.

"I would love to work for Eb Scott," Amelia said on the way home. "That place of his is out of this world!"

"When you get through school, go talk to him," he counseled. "But your granddad will probably have something to say about it."

She sighed. "I think I can bring him around," she said. "I had fun!"

"I did, too," he replied with a warm smile. "You're good company, Amelia," he added quietly.

"Thanks. So are you," she replied softly.

He checked his watch. He'd agreed to take Edie to a concert she wanted to see in San Antonio.

"I'm keeping you from something," she said in an apologetic tone.

"Just a concert," he said. "But I've got plenty of time to get there."

"Okay, then." She smiled, but inside she was feeling abandoned. She'd have bet that his concert was being attended by another woman also. Probably that fancy city woman who'd been loitering around his yard sometime back. But she had no strings on Cal, who was determined to retain his freedom. She brightened a little. If he felt like that, then his fancy woman wouldn't have strings on him, either. It made her feel better. And, after all, she was young. She could wait for any happiness that might come her way.

Cal felt a strange surge of relief that she wasn't jealous. She must suspect that he had a date. But on the heels of that sensation came one of vague disappointment. It disturbed him that she wasn't bothered. He sighed inwardly. He was overthinking this. They were friends. He'd told her already that he had no plans to involve himself in a relationship. If she'd taken him at his word, and she seemed to, then she had no need to be jealous. He felt vindicated. He smiled to himself. Of course she wasn't jealous.

He glanced at her and smiled. She smiled back. Then she knew she'd done the right thing, by not reacting. She didn't dare let him know how she really felt. It would drive him away. That was the last thing she wanted.

He left her at her door.

"Thanks," she said, grinning up at him from a face surrounded by disheveled hair. "It was great fun!"

He chuckled, trying to imagine Edie in her place. The woman was always immaculate when they went out together. Involving herself in martial arts was the last thing Edie would have done. But Amelia loved it.

"Martial arts and blowing up things and guns." He shook his head. "I'd never have believed it when I first met you."

"I look like a wimp?" she asked with mock horror.

He laughed. "No. But you seemed so sedate and unflappable," he explained. "I didn't think you had a wild streak."

"Oh, is that what it's called?" she asked, amused.

"There's probably a better name for it," he replied. He brushed back strands of her golden hair. "You're pretty good on the mat."

She was trembling inside at the proximity and doing her

best not to let it show. "Good at falling?" she asked, and rolled her eyes. "When I tell Granddaddy that I've spent the day falling on my face, he'll laugh himself to death!"

"No, he won't," he promised. "Don't forget. Fernando's tomorrow night." He gave her a long look. "Wear a dress," he added.

Her eyebrows shot up.

"So I'm sexist," he replied with a long sigh. "I just love the way women look in dresses, especially when we dance something as elegant as the tango."

"I'll find something appropriate, then," she teased.

He smiled. "Okay. I'll pick you up about six. We'll have dinner first."

"That sounds nice."

"They have great food. But the dancing's not bad, either. See you later."

"Okay. Thanks again."

"My pleasure," he said, and meant it. She was unique. He'd never known anyone quite like her.

She went inside. Her grandfather looked up from his news program. "Good Lord," he said. "Have you been caught in a car wash?"

She glared at him. "I've been falling. Just falling. I did nothing but fall for two hours!"

"Breakfalls," he said, nodding.

"Front breakfalls," she added.

He chuckled. "I tried to get your grandmother to do one of those. She ran out the back door and hid until I promised to stop hounding her about it."

She grinned. "Smart woman. Oh, and when I got through falling, Cal took me out to Mr. Scott's firing range and Mr. Scott handed me a .45 Ruger Vaquero!"

"Wow," he said softly. "That's one fine pistol."

"Yes, it is."

"Did you shoot well?"

"Six shots, all dead center," she replied.

He sighed and smiled. "You always were a natural with a gun. Well, with a pistol," he added. "But a .45 is a lot heavier than that .38 Cal carries."

"It didn't feel much different," she said. She smiled. "I wish I had one," she sighed.

"I offered to let you use my .12 gauge. It's heavy."

She glared at him. "It weighs more than I do, and it kicks like a mule. I'll shoot my .28 gauge, thanks very much."

"The .12 gauge is better. But you won't touch it."

She shifted. "I could shoot it if I wanted to," she protested.

"If you could learn how to pull the trigger on it," he retorted. "The stock is specially padded to cushion the recoil. But even with that .28 gauge, I never could get you to actually hit the damned skeet targets."

"I did try," she apologized. "Several times. It's hard for normal people to hit something going sixty miles an hour," she added. "Skeet targets are too fast."

"Well, we all have things we can't do. Speaking of which, I couldn't talk Valeria out of coming next week," he added miserably. "But she'll only be here for two days."

"Only two days. Gosh. I wish I had an appointment out of town," she muttered.

"It won't be so bad," he tried to encourage her.

"She'll start complaining when she walks in the door," she replied. "The temperature will be too cold. Her bed won't be made right. The food will be too greasy or too sweet or too something. And then she'll complain that the carpet isn't clean enough."

"I'm truly sorry that I couldn't head her off," he said gently.

"Maybe if she'd ever married, she'd have mellowed," she grumbled. "Honestly, though, I can't imagine a man brave enough to put a ring on her finger. Of course, she'd be putting one through his nose at the same time…!"

"Now, Amelia, she is your only surviving great-aunt," he reminded her.

"And your only sibling," she said, nodding. "I'm sorry. It's just…"

He smiled. "She's a pain in the butt. Yes. I know. But she's family, so we'll both grit our teeth and pretend we're glad to see her."

"If I can pull that off, I'll be ready to sign up for theater at school," she sighed.

"I know," he teased. "You're no good at getting up in front of people."

"True. I'd rather blow things up." Her eyes gleamed and she grinned. "I'm going to have a quick shower, then I'll start supper. How about a burger with homemade fries?"

"Delicious!"

"Coming right up, after I've cleaned up," she said.

"Might invite Cal to help us eat it," he suggested.

She shook her head. "He's got a date," she said, and smiled to let him know she didn't mind. "I'll be down in a jiffy!"

He watched her go with quiet, loving eyes, and when she was out of sight, he grimaced. She was smitten with their neighbor, who was far too worldly for a girl of her years—a green girl, at that. He hoped she wouldn't get her heart broken, but he had no control over that. All he could do was stand and watch and pick up the pieces, if her crush ended badly.

He knew men like Cal. They didn't settle down and

raise kids. They were the sort of people who hacked a living out of the wilderness or sailed wooden ships across the sea to fight in wars, or founded settlements in dangerous places. They were adventurers, explorers, warriors.

Amelia wouldn't understand that, because she was a homebody. Despite her interests, she had no idea what such a life would actually be like. And she was too soft to adapt to it. So Cal would go on with his lifestyle and Amelia would end in tears, because there was no way she could cope with loving a man like that, a man who would live for adventure and immerse himself in it, regardless of the danger.

Edie was dressed like a debutante. She was wearing a sexy black cocktail dress with lacy inserts, spiky high heels and a shimmering wrap that accentuated her pretty complexion and short, dark hair. She looked good. Really good.

"Thanks for offering to take me," she said as they got into his car. "I've been looking forward to this for weeks!"

"What's playing tonight?" he asked.

"It's Mozart." She looked at herself in the mirror. "It was Debussy, but they changed it."

He managed not to react. He was fond of Debussy and Respighi and Dvorak. He hated Mozart with a passion. But he smiled at her. "That sounds good," he lied.

"How was Africa?" she asked idly.

"Ngawa. Dangerous," he replied.

"You're making a lot of money, though."

"Tons," he said easily. "Most of it, I've invested. Even in a low market, my investment counselor is making me money."

She sighed. "I've lost most of mine because I trusted a business manager who ran off with it. More fool, me."

"Sorry about that."

"I've still got some assets from what my father left me," she replied. Actually, she didn't, but she didn't want Cal to think she was stalking him for the fortune he'd already made signing on to fight in a foreign war. But that was what she was doing. Oh, he was handsome, and personable. That was dressing on top. His value was in his holdings. She was going broke, and she couldn't support her habit. If she could land him, she'd be on easy street. No more money worries.

"How's your little friend?" she asked suddenly. "The one who blows up stuff."

"Amelia?" He laughed. "I had her doing breakfalls all afternoon."

"Breakfalls!" She made a mock shiver.

"Then I took her out to the pistol range. She hit the bull's-eye six times in a row. With a .45 wheel gun."

"I hate guns," she muttered.

"They're my stock in trade," he reminded her.

"Nasty things. They make too much noise." She dismissed them. "The conductor is a friend of mine," she changed the subject. "He's friends with the mayor, so he got me an introduction. I know lots of important people in the city now," she purred.

He didn't know a single one, and he wasn't impressed. Why was she such a social climber? he wondered. But he didn't question her, because he really didn't care. She started talking about the program and he just listened.

They sat through the program with Cal growing more restless by the minute. When it finally ended, he was out of his seat with visible haste, escorting Edie out of the auditorium.

"Honestly, do we have to hurry so much?" she complained. "The president of the city's biggest bank was in the row behind us. I wanted to talk to him."

"You have money there?" he asked idly.

"No, but it's a good idea to speak to important people."

He stopped and looked down at her. "Why?" he asked with honest curiosity.

She gaped at him. "Because it's how you move up in elite society," she said, exasperated. "It gets you privileges."

"Why do you need them?" he persisted.

She drew in a loud sigh. "Honestly, Cal, you're such a dolt sometimes!"

He just grinned and led her to the car.

She hesitated at her front door and went close to him. "Don't you want to come in for a while and have a few drinks?" she purred.

"Not really, thanks," he said. "I'm tired, and I have to be up early tomorrow for a conference."

"You always have an excuse," she muttered as she moved away.

He just stared at her. "It's my life. I don't answer to anyone. Ever."

It was pleasantly spoken, but firm.

She grimaced. "Okay. I get it. Nothing interferes with the mission."

"Exactly," he returned.

"I'll see you again before you go back?" she asked.

"Certainly," he replied.

She smiled. "All right, then. Take care."

"You, too."

He walked to the car and drove away. He didn't look back. Not once.

Edie saw that and cursed and cursed. She picked up a vase and started to throw it when she realized its value.

She put it back down, gingerly. No sense in costing herself money over a man who refused to get serious.

But he liked her, and he kept coming around. So she wasn't giving up. She had plenty of time.

When the big day came, Amelia was all thumbs getting ready for her night on the town with Cal. She'd only been on dates a handful of times, and never with a man she was crazy about. She had on her best dress. It wasn't really fancy, just a white off-the-shoulder Mexican-style dress, but when she paired it with white high heels and a lacy white mantilla and her mother's pearls, she looked elegant enough. Especially with her hair down, clean and gleaming pale gold in the halo of the overhead lights.

"Will I do?" she asked her grandfather.

He looked up from his paper and his eyes grew misty. He smiled. "You're the image of your grandmother. I swear you look just like her."

She smiled. "Thanks. I was worried that I wouldn't look elegant enough."

"You'll do," he said. "It's not a gala affair. You're going to Fernando's. Yes, it's high-class, but most people who turn up there on Friday nights wear jeans and boots," he chuckled.

She grinned at him. "I was going to, but Cal said you just can't dance a tango in jeans."

"He's probably right. You have a good time."

"I hope so," she said.

Cal was right on time. He wasn't overdressed, either, although he had on beige slacks with a yellow polo shirt and a stylish jacket. He looked handsome.

"Nice," he said, eyeing Amelia.

"She looks like her grandmother," Harris chuckled. "I used to take her dancing, but that was back in the dark ages."

"Can you do a tango?" Cal asked him.

"Not to save my own life," came the dry reply. "So you two go up to San Antonio and wow the crowds. I'll stay here with the dragon drama."

"The new season doesn't start tonight, does it?" Cal asked, because he was a fan, too.

"Last season. I bought it on Amazon," he said with twinkling eyes. "The whole season, so I can watch it whenever I like."

"That's one way to do it. I love the show."

"Me, too. You two have fun."

"We will," Amelia promised him.

"So will I. Joy before grief," he groaned.

"What was that about?" Cal asked her when they were on the highway.

"Great-Aunt Valeria," she muttered. "She's descending on her broomstick next week to visit for two horrible days. We'll go mad!"

"Is she that bad?"

"Worse," she glowered.

"Only two days, though," he said sympathetically.

"When she leaves, I'll be running through town howling like a wolf with sheer glee. And Granddaddy will probably set off fireworks."

"The things I miss, not having relatives." He shook his head.

"Nobody at all?" she asked gently.

He didn't reply. He was remembering things. Terrible things.

"They have flan at Fernando's," she interrupted his thoughts with a lilt in her voice, to distract him. "Right?"

"What? Oh. Yes, they do. The best flan in town."

"I didn't eat lunch," she said. "So I'd have room for it!"

He laughed. "Well!"

"I can make a flan," she added. "But I'm not good enough to compete with the kitchen staff at Fernando's. Their food is just out of this world."

"I think so, too. I used to hang out there every Friday night when I was on the police force."

"You were a policeman?" she exclaimed.

He laughed. "Yes, I was. For three years. Then I heard about the group Eb was forming. I'd grown restless. I wanted a change, a chance to make money, an adventure." He smiled. "It's been that, all right."

"Adventure is dangerous."

"Which makes it enticing," he replied, and wiggled his eyebrows.

She laughed at the twinkle in his eyes. "Is that it?" she teased.

"You like blowing up things. I like going to foreign places and helping change the world."

"Now I feel like a slacker," she said with a grin.

"Not you," he replied easily. He sighed. "I relax when I'm with you. It's a new feeling. I like it."

She wondered if it was a compliment. You relaxed with people who were familiar, who didn't excite you or challenge you.

"Thanks. I think?"

He chuckled. "It's a compliment. I'm not good with people," he added solemnly. "I don't…fit."

She sighed. "Me, neither."

He glanced at her and smiled. "Well, you stick with me, kid. We'll hold off the world."

"That's a deal!"

Chapter Seven

Fernando's was packed. They had to wait for ten minutes even though Cal had made a reservation.

"So sorry you had to wait," the waitress apologized as she led them to a booth near the pretty fountain in the center of the huge room.

"The food here is worth waiting for," Cal assured her with a smile.

She smiled back. "Your waiter will be right with you," she promised, and left.

Amelia was looking around. The restaurant was in a converted theater. It had a live band, exquisite woodwork, velvet curtains, red tables and chairs with real linen tablecloths and napkins and the staff dressed in red. The fountain in the center of the room dominated. It contained live Chinese goldfish and pretty floating lights.

"This place is awesome," she said, fascinated.

He smiled at her. "Everybody thinks so. I know it impressed me, the first time I saw it." He looked around.

"He spent a fortune remodeling it, but he made back every penny. He's still making a profit, too. Amazing eye for detail."

"Who is he?"

"Fernando Reyes," he told her. "He was a former governor of some province down in Mexico. He came to this country a few years ago with a bankroll and decided to open a restaurant. The rest is history."

"He must be a fascinating person."

"Believe me, he is. He plays guitar and his wife dances the flamenco. It's the highlight of the evening. Before, and after, there's dancing. But first," he told her with twinkling black eyes, "there's food!" He indicated the approaching waiter.

"Good evening," the man said with a smile, handing them both menus. "What can I bring you to drink?"

"Sweetened iced tea," Amelia said at once.

"Piña colada," Cal said.

"Coming right up."

Cal laughed at her expression. "We'll be here for a while. If you eat while you drink alcohol, it doesn't have as much effect on you. I won't land you in jail."

"Well, okay. But if you do, you're coming along," she promised him.

He smiled affectionately. "Done. What would you like to eat?" he added, turning his eyes to his own menu.

She looked at hers. She was scanning it for the cheapest thing she could find, which was chicken.

He watched her. He had the measure of her by now, and he knew what she was doing. He pulled the menu down and met her shocked eyes. "Amelia, I could afford lobster every night if I wanted it, so stop looking at chicken dishes and order what you want."

She flushed. How had he read her so well?

"I was a cop," he reminded her. "We get good at reading people."

"Oh." She grimaced. "Well..."

"Besides, how many meals have you cooked for me?" he pointed out. "If you have to call it something, how about the repaying of a favor? And you're a great cook, by the way," he added with a gentle smile.

She let out a sigh. "I must wear signs," she murmured. "Okay. I love fish. And then there's flan..."

He chuckled. "Done. No wine?"

She shook her head. "It upsets my stomach. Or should I admit that?" she added.

"Figures," he said, smiling. "You aren't like any woman I've ever known. Not that you're..."

"If you say I'm not a woman, I'll hit you," she promised, because at nineteen, she certainly was a woman.

"I was going to say that you're not odd," he countered, grinning. "But you truly are unique."

She cleared her throat. "Thanks." She managed a nervous smile.

"And will you relax?" he chided. "It's the same thing as sitting at your table at home, except the surroundings are different. We're the same people in both places."

She let out a breath and laughed self-consciously. "Sorry. It's just that I haven't been on many dates. Even with friends," she added.

He toyed with his napkin. "I don't date that much myself." He didn't add that he'd been out with Edie and her behavior had embarrassed and irritated him. It hadn't encouraged him to escort other women.

Amelia, however, was the exception to the rule. She was polite and friendly to the waiter, grateful for the most minor services like coffee refills, and generally pleasant company.

They were finishing the flans when he stopped eating and just looked at her.

She lifted her eyes to his with her fork in midair and raised her eyebrows.

"Manners," he said.

She put down the fork. "Excuse me?"

"You have exquisite manners."

She laughed. "My mother was a stickler for them," she said softly, remembering. "Always say please and thank you, always be polite to people, even people you dislike. Never be sarcastic or abusive in your language. Never, never discuss politics or religion in public. And always treat people the way you'd like to be treated. That was Mama."

He sipped the last of his piña colada. "My grandfather was very much the same."

Her eyes fell to her plate. He never spoke of his parents; only his grandfather. There must have been a solid reason for that. Usually people were left out of conversations because they weren't liked.

"You never ask questions," he remarked.

She just smiled. "I hate that. I mean, I hate having people ask me questions about things that make me uncomfortable. So I don't do it myself."

He turned his glass on the table idly. "Such as?"

Her eyebrows arched again.

He chuckled. "What makes you uncomfortable?"

"Other women who think I'm backward because I don't do bedroom tours with strange men," she said curtly.

Now his eyebrows arched.

"My mother said a man will treat a woman the way she asks to be treated. These days, it's…it's…like Rome in its last days! They had orgies…!"

The waiter had just stopped at their table. Amelia's eyes

widened in horror and her face turned beet red. And Cal, darn him, sat there laughing until tears came into his eyes.

"I meant, I was only talking about, I mean..." She reddened even more.

The waiter, a very hip-looking young man with his hair in a ponytail and wicked eyes, leaned down. "Ma'am, your secret is safe with me! Those nasty old Romans!"

Now she was laughing, too. So was Cal.

"Nice. You'll be able to retire on the tip," Cal told him, grinning.

The waiter grinned back. "Can I get you anything else?" he asked.

"Coffee?" he asked Amelia, who nodded enthusiastically. "Make that two," he told the waiter.

The waiter clicked his heels and bowed. *"Statim domine,"* was the crisp reply.

Cal inclined his head. *"Mille gratias!"* he replied.

The other man, blindsided, picked up Amelia's white napkin, with an apology, and waved it in surrender. "I'm a fraud," he said. "That's the only Latin I know!" he chuckled.

Amelia was gaping at both of them.

"I can read a little of it. My grandmother taught languages at university," he added with a smile. "She spoke several. Latin was one."

"Brainy people." The waiter put down the napkin. "I envy you, sir," he added. He smiled. "Back in a jiffy." He paused. "I, uh, can't say that in Latin, though." He wiggled his eyebrows and went toward the kitchen.

Amelia and Cal chuckled together.

"What are the odds?" she asked. "Honestly, I didn't know you spoke any other languages than English!"

"You speak Spanish," he pointed out, having experienced her almost flawless accent when she used it.

"Oh, so do you, and much better than I do," she replied gently. "But Latin! Gosh!"

"Only a few phrases, mostly famous sayings," he said. "My grandmother tried to get me interested, but I wouldn't listen. At least, not until my grandfather taught me that last phrase—a thousand thanks." He smiled sadly. "He was brilliant. I read a lot about him when I grew up. He's in one or two books on military theory. He could speak several languages, like his wife, my grandmother, and play piano. I took it up when I was grown."

"You can play?" she asked.

He shrugged. His eyes went to the band. "Matter of debate," he mused. He drifted away, his face locked and cold.

She leaned forward. "The waiter is loopy," she whispered. "I like him!"

It brought him out of the past, laughing. "Me, too. I wasn't kidding about the tip, either. Waiters don't make much. Tips are how they pay the bills when they get their checks."

"Think he's a student?" she asked.

His eyes were on the waiter, approaching with a coffeepot. "Let's find out."

"Almost instant refills. Sorry, we're busy tonight!" the waiter apologized.

"Not a problem." Cal fixed him with black eyes. "Okay, come clean. We've got a bet going. Are you a student?"

The waiter's eyes bulged. "How in the world…!"

"Latin," Cal said. "Latin. How many people do you run across in the course of a year who can speak even one word of it?"

"I can count them on one finger," the waiter chuckled. "Yes, I'm at university, majoring in Norwegian."

They both gaped at him.

He cleared his throat. "Listen, it's not nuts. Norwegian

is a great language. Especially if you're marrying someone whose whole family speaks it!"

"Ah, the light breaks," Cal chuckled. "Are you planning to live in Norway?"

He nodded and smiled as he refilled their coffee cups with a flourish. "I'm a senior this year. So is she. But she's majoring in history, and I help her study for exams. This past month she had essays written by some of the classic authors. In Latin," he added with a chuckle.

"Congratulations," Cal said. Amelia seconded him.

"Thanks. We started going together as freshmen. I never thought I'd find anyone so kind." He saw their expressions. "Kindness and a gentle heart are far more important than wealth or beauty or power. Kindness lasts."

"You should have majored in philosophy," Cal said with a warm smile. "You'd be a natural."

"Thanks. Can I get you anything else?" he asked.

"Not now. We're just going to wait until dinner settles, then we're going to shock the establishment with a tango," Amelia said mischievously. "He'll be dancing magnificently, while I fall over my feet into someone's table and create a tragic scene. There will be ambulances and rubberneckers."

The waiter leaned closer. "I'll keep a mop handy, so do your worst," he chuckled.

After the waiter left, Cal sipped coffee and studied Amelia with soft eyes. "You are one of the nicest people I've ever known, Amelia," he said quietly.

"Awwww," she said, treating it as a joke.

"I mean it," he corrected. "I've watched you when we're around other people. You're natural and open, and you genuinely like people. It's such a refreshing attitude."

She wondered if he was comparing her with his lady friend. If he was, she felt flattered. "I do like people, mostly," she said. "Not everybody. Some few members of the human race are just mean!"

"Yes, and you can find them in chat rooms under every single YouTube video and gaming forum," he agreed at once.

"I know!" She rolled her eyes. "Keyboard warriors! They're the same people who slink around and never look you in the eye in person." Her eyes narrowed. "Backstabbers."

"Nice analogy."

"You'd know about those, I'll bet, from your days on the force."

"I would, indeed. There was this one time," he recalled, "when we got called to a café where a victim of social media had tracked down the man who said hateful and very threatening things to him on his mother's funeral website."

"You're kidding!" she exclaimed. "Nobody could be that heartless…!"

"Somebody could, and was. He learned a valuable lesson about hate speech, litigation and possible arrest, all at the same time. His parents, who were contacted subsequently, were shocked, to say the least. They thought he was a quiet, studious boy who just liked being by himself. That was before they found the guns and pipe bombs in his closet, however," he added.

Her lips fell apart.

"Yes, people can be that mean, also. He hated one of his teachers and two or three classmates. He even had a battle plan and a camera shoulder mount. He was going to film it all."

"Mental issues?" she asked softly.

He was stunned.

"Well, normal people don't really do those things, do they?" she wondered aloud. "And if his parents didn't know what he was doing online, did they pay him much attention?"

"As little as possible. They had very responsible jobs. They told the prosecutor and the judge that, many times during the course of the trial. The boy was sixteen, which meant that he got sent to juvie. But he did get a psych evaluation. And medicine to treat a condition that his parents also didn't know that he had." He grimaced. "There are so many kids in homes where they're either neglected or abused. Too many."

She knew without being told that Cal had been one of those.

And when he looked up, he saw that knowledge in her odd, intent look. "Are you reading my mind?"

She didn't speak. It was the strangest sensation. Like falling a great distance. Like a firm, solid connection at the same time. "Most policemen are cops for a reason," she said quietly. "My friend Bobby was one. He had terrible scars. His father used a quirt on him. He never told anybody. His grandmother accidentally saw the wounds, called the police herself and had her own son arrested. He went to jail. He's still there."

"And Bobby…?"

She smiled sadly. "Joined the police force in town the day he graduated high school. They say he's going to be a great addition. He talks to grammar school classes about drugs."

"That's a nice success story. Many aren't."

"Life is hard."

"Very." He put down his cup. "So. Nice and full and comfy? Ready to shame those people who think they can dance?" His head jerked toward the dance floor, which was filling up fast.

She grinned. "Oh yes."

He laughed and led her to the dance floor.

The music was slow and dreamy when they started. Cal's arm contracted around her waist, and she shivered inside with feelings she'd never had with anyone else. It was always like this when she was close to him. Like bubbles coming up out of her body, like joy dancing in colored lights in her bloodstream. Like…being in love.

She bit down hard on that last sensation. She couldn't afford to give way to such thoughts. Cal wanted a friend, not a life partner, and she'd better remember it or there wouldn't be any more friendly dates. He would avoid her, to keep from hurting her, if he knew. He was basically a kind man.

But she didn't want that. So she laughed instead, disguising her unsteady nerves. "This is fun," she said.

His cheek brushed hers. "Fun," he agreed. His voice was deeper, softer than it usually was, and the hand on her back was idly caressing. The hand holding hers had it pressed to his chest against his shirt. Under it she felt muscle and thick hair. It was very sensuous, to dance like this.

He could feel her heart beating faster, hear her breath rustle under his chin. This was a very bad idea, but he loved the feel of Amelia in his arms. She made him feel different. Younger. More alive. Joyful.

"You're tangling me up," he murmured aloud, when he hadn't meant to.

"Oh. Sorry," she said, misunderstanding. "My big feet…"

He laughed, relieved. "No, that's not what I meant. You dance very well."

She forced a smile. "Thanks. So do you."

He started to speak just as the music ended, and then began again. The tango. A couple nearby groaned and left the floor. Two more followed. Only Cal and Amelia and two couples were left.

"And a one, and a two," he teased in her ear.

He drew her into the rhythm, delighted at the way her small feet followed his big ones perfectly as they drew together, moved apart, drew together again, all with a series of slow sliding steps and quick darting ones.

"This is awesome," she whispered, caught up in the excitement.

"Awesome." He could barely get the words out. He felt her firm breasts pressing hard into his chest, felt them harden at the tips. He felt her heart like a wild thing, beating into his. He smelled the faint floral perfume she wore and the fresh womanly smell of her.

His hand tightened at her back, bringing her even closer. Now his breath was also coming quickly, like his heartbeat. This was dangerous. He should stop. He should take her back to their table and drink something heavy enough to calm his nerves.

Except that it felt so damned good to be this close to her. He was trapped in the sheer sensuality of the tango, bound to her by more than a dance, more than a shared pleasure of movement.

She almost groaned aloud. His body was muscular without it being obvious, and his strength was as apparent even in dance as it was on the gym floor doing martial arts.

If only the dance would never end, she thought recklessly as she forced her gaze to remain at his collar. She couldn't look up. He mustn't see what she felt. It would be as plain as a whisper in her eyes.

They moved as one person, smoothly, seductively, interpreting the music with such grace that the two other couples attempting the tango actually moved to the sidelines just to watch.

The two people themselves were oblivious to their spectators. They were lost in the music and each other, caught in a web of growing hunger, need, exquisite pleasure.

His hand contracted around hers. "This is a bad idea," he ground out, feeling the passion rise abruptly.

"Very bad," she choked.

He thought that if the music lasted one minute longer, the dinner crowd was going to be shocked…

And just as he thought it, the music cooed to an end. And sudden applause from the sidelines saved Cal from an embarrassing interlude.

He laughed. So did Amelia. They made bows and went quickly back to their table, avoiding any more stares.

Cal was happy to sit down with his feet under the table and be only visible from the waist up. It had been a near thing. He didn't like his loss of control. It was disturbing. Amelia was far too young for any sudden approaches on his part. And he didn't want attachments. He couldn't afford them.

"Don't look now, but I think we won," she said in a stage whisper.

He chuckled. "Apparently."

She let out a breath and sipped quickly cooling coffee to help still her nerves. Thank goodness her hands didn't shake!

"I'm out of breath," she exclaimed, stating the obvious. "I don't get in much practice."

"Neither do I. I love tango," he added as his own pulse slowed.

"I do, too, but I haven't had anybody to practice with since Ty left town."

Ty Harding, she meant, and he felt his neck hairs stand on end. He wasn't jealous, of course. That would be absurd. He took another sip of coffee. He wanted to leave, but he didn't know how to put it across without sounding as if he was tired of her company. He wasn't. He was trying to avoid complications. Big ones.

She whistled softly. "I'm sorry, but do you think we could go home?" she asked, surprising him. "I have a big test coming up Monday and there's all the housework to get done, as well. Weekends are busy," she added, hoping that she wasn't making him feel that she hated his company.

"I was just thinking that I have to see some people tomorrow," he laughed, relieved. "Yes, I need to go, too."

She smiled her relief.

He left her at her front door. He looked down at her quietly. His whole being was in turmoil. She wasn't absurdly pretty. Her figure, while nice, wasn't extraordinary. She was young and sweet and not at all sensuous. Except that she stirred him up more than any woman in recent years. It was unwelcome. He wasn't ready to become obsessed over a woman.

She looked up at him, perceptive to his emotions. That tango had done something to both of them. Best not to allude to it, she thought.

"I had a great time," she said, grinning. "Thanks. For supper and the dancing."

"I had a good time myself," he said.

"Well..."

His head jerked to one side. "Well."

She drew in a breath. "You go back overseas soon, don't you?"

He nodded. "You may not see me for a few days. I have things to do before I leave."

She nodded, too. She understood what he was saying. He was going to keep his distance because that dance had moved him as it moved her.

"Don't get killed," she said firmly.

He shrugged.

"Okay, don't get shot," she emphasized.

He smiled involuntarily. "Worried about me?"

"That would make me sound proprietary," she said with a smile back. "And we both know you can't be appropriated."

He pursed his lips and chuckled. "Nice perception."

She held out a hand, palm up, and frowned. "There isn't any perception. It's too dry!"

He burst out laughing and suddenly gathered her close and hugged the breath out of her. "Damn, you're fun to be with, Amelia," he said at her ear. He drew in a breath, which brought them even closer. "But I'm going to back off, and you know why."

"Of course I know why," she said softly. "I won't sulk."

"I know that, too." He didn't add that it hurt him to do it, because he had a pretty good idea that she was hiding more than she realized.

"Just come home."

He drew back and kissed her hair. "I will." He let her go and forced a smile. "Tell your granddad that when I get back, we'll have that chess match he's been promising me."

"I'll tell him," she said, and grinned. Her face was going to freeze in that position, but it sure beat bawling.

"Okay, then. See you," he added.

"See you, Cal."

She turned and went inside quickly, before he could see that she was acting for all she was worth.

Cal went home and had a full glass of whiskey with one ice cube. And he slept until almost noon.

Amelia groaned when she saw her great-aunt Valeria pull up at the front of the house in her ancient Mercedes. She could have afforded ten new ones, but this one suited her and she refused to give it up.

She was tall and willowy at sixty-six, dark-haired and dark-eyed and always looked as if she was sucking on a lemon. She was wearing a black dress that came to just under her knees with a sweater. It was in the eighties, but she wore a sweater when it was ten degrees warmer. She always felt cold. Amelia had wondered sometimes, wickedly, if the woman had ice where her heart should have been.

"Hello, Amelia," she said curtly, eyeing her great-niece with a disapproving glance. "Still going around in those horrible dungarees and T-shirts. Can't you dress more appropriately?"

"This is appropriately for a college student, Aunt Val," Amelia replied.

"Aunt Valeria," she corrected coldly. "I detest abbreviated names."

"Sorry," she replied, and didn't mean it.

Just as Valeria opened her mouth to speak, Amelia's grandfather came out on the porch.

"Valeria," he greeted his sister. "It's nice to have you here for a few days."

"Two days," he was corrected, and she tolerated a hug from him. "My luggage is in the trunk. I hope you don't have car thieves around here," she added.

"We aren't San Antonio," Amelia said without thinking, because in some areas of the city, that had been a problem. "Or even Victoria," she added mischievously.

"San Antonio has a symphony orchestra and a ballet company. Even an opera company," she informed Amelia haughtily. "And there are no common thieves where I live in Victoria!"

"Excuse me," Amelia apologized. But she didn't mean it.

"Stop being such a sourpuss," Harris chided.

She glared at her brother. "I know about these small towns. You're overrun with immigrants and criminals!"

Amelia started to speak, and it wouldn't have been happy words.

Her grandfather cut her off. "Let me show you to your room," he said quickly.

"You only have one guest room, and I know where it is," she snapped.

She went down the hall. Amelia and her grandfather exchanged resigned glances. Well, it was only for a couple of days. Surely, they could survive it!

Two days later, Amelia was praying for aliens to come down and kidnap the older woman and take her anywhere except here.

When she mentioned it to her grandfather, he had to stifle laughter. Both of them tiptoed around Valeria, who was the most demanding house guest anyone had ever had to put up with.

With pure mischief, Amelia introduced her great-aunt to an episode of *Fawlty Towers*, an old British situation comedy that featured a woman who was the living fictional image of Valeria Harris.

Her grandfather gave her such a glare that she felt scorched. She gave him an angelic smile. And pushed Play.

To her surprise, Valeria roared with laughter as the elderly woman on the screen refused to turn on her hearing aid to save the batteries, so that anyone trying to communicate with her had to shout.

Amelia and her grandfather exchanged amused and surprised glances.

When the show ended, Valeria was fanning herself. "What an amazing program! Where can I find it on TV?" she asked.

"It's rather old," Amelia replied. "And you have to get it on disc. Or on one of the streaming channels."

"Disc? Streaming channels?" Valeria was all at sea.

"I'll explain," Amelia said softly, and she did.

Valeria just let out a sigh. "I don't watch television, as a rule. Most of it is so outrageous! I only watch old movies on the classics channel, when people had to act with all their clothes on. I'm sure it was much harder then," she added with a snarky smile.

She glanced at them. "I think I might stay another few days," she said, glancing around. "But you will have to cook with less grease, Amelia. I simply can't tolerate it!"

Amelia swallowed. "Yes, Aunt Valeria." A few more days. A few more days! Hell must feel like this…

"And some tea would be nice now, don't you think?" Valeria added.

Chapter Eight

A few more days. A few more days! Amelia was frozen in place in absolute horror.

Valeria didn't notice. She was leaning back with her eyes closed. "And Jasmine tea, none of that silly modern concoction. With one packet—only one—of that sweetener I like." She sighed.

Amelia almost choked. "Yes. I'll just...go make it." She walked away stiff-legged, thinking hell must feel like this.

Her grandfather, reading her very well, sat with twinkling eyes, watching his sister. "It's nice of you to extend your visit, especially considering the circumstances," he said pleasantly.

Her eyes flew open. "Circumstances? What circumstances?"

"Our neighbor, the one who takes Amelia dancing, just came down with a nasty fever. And he was just over here the day before you came. Did you notice how flushed Amelia looks?" He frowned. "She was exposed. She might even have it..."

Valeria rocketed out of her chair. "How dare you both expose me to something infectious! You know how fragile I am! The very nerve...and that man is a hired killer. What is Amelia thinking? You let her go places with such a person? Think of the scandal if it ever gets out that my great-niece is dating a...a...hit man!"

"Valeria, he's a soldier..."

"A hired killer!" she persisted. "The stain on our family name would never come off. People, common people, would gossip about us! The shame of it. Jacob, how could you?"

Amelia poked her head out of the kitchen door. "What's going on?"

Valeria wheeled, her face red with rage. "You're dating a hired killer. You'll put the family name in the toilet, Amelia. You'll shame us all over south Texas! And besides that, you've exposed me to a disease! How could you! How could both of you do this to me...? I am leaving!"

Valeria stomped down the hall to her room, still muttering.

Amelia looked at her grandfather with wide eyes.

He grinned and put his forefinger to his lips. She just nodded and smiled.

Fifteen minutes later, Valeria was headed back to Victoria.

"Brilliant," Amelia applauded him. "Just brilliant." She laughed. "I thought I'd go nuts. Sorry, Granddaddy, I know she's your only living relative besides me. But she's such a pain!"

"She's always been a pain. She erupts," he added. "She has rages. She lashes out. She pushed a waiter over a table one time and broke his arm. Her late husband had to pay damages in a civil suit, and she was lucky they didn't prosecute it as attempted homicide." He shook his head. "She's always sorry later, but that doesn't help much. She's capable of anything in those moods."

"I know. That's why I bit my tongue." She sighed. "She has issues."

"Many." He chuckled. "But she's gone."

"I'll throw confetti. And I'm not giving up my lovely olive oil, whatever she says. Grease!" She threw up her hands. "It's the best cooking oil in the world!"

"And tastes great," he added.

"Thank you for braving the dragon," she said. "If I had a medal, I'd give you one."

"Thank you."

"That was a nasty remark she made about Cal," she muttered. "She's very…" She waved her hand.

"Straitlaced?" He nodded. "Yes, she is. She has an overworked sense of family honor. The family name must never be besmirched!" He shook his head and laughed. "I wrote something naughty on the side of the principal's car our senior year in high school. She pushed me down that sheer wall behind the school building. I broke my arm."

"What?"

"She was very sorry afterward," he said. "I've always thought she had some undiscovered mental issues, to be honest," he told Amelia.

"What did your parents say?" she asked.

"They had a long talk with her about controlling her temper, but she was crying and apologizing and swearing she'd never do anything like it again. They just accepted that it was bad temper."

"It doesn't sound like bad temper," she pointed out.

"I know." He sighed. "They didn't believe in mental

health issues, you see. Back when they were growing up, it was a taboo subject in a small, rural town like Jacobsville."

"She could have killed you!" Amelia pointed out.

"I did mention that."

"And?"

"She cried harder and hugged me half to death."

She sighed. "Still, they should have taken her to the nearest mental health clinic."

"Bite your tongue, girl," he teased. "And besmirch the family name by accusing her of being nuts?"

"It isn't nuts if you have behavioral problems."

"You're preaching to the choir. But not to Valeria. She was horrified that anyone would think she wasn't mentally sound!"

"At least she doesn't have to worry about it now, right? She was married..."

"She kept the family name and didn't take her husband's, have you forgotten?"

She pursed her lips and whistled.

"She said it was too much work to change all those documents, so she kept her family name. Her husband was an only child, and his father and mother were already dead. He was sort of a wimp," he added, chuckling.

She smiled. "I barely remember him. He was funny."

"Yes, he was, but Valeria told him how to do everything. He left her a fortune. Which I'm often reminded that she plans to leave to her dog, or her favorite charity of the week."

"We do very well without a lot of money," she pointed out.

"I saved when I was young and invested wisely," he agreed. "So now the dividends keep us in grocery money and incidentals."

"I could get a part-time job," she began.

"What for? You've seen a fur coat you want to buy?" he teased.

She hugged him. "I feel like I'm not carrying my weight," she said. "And besides, there's college…"

"College is a public one, so no exorbitant fees," she was reminded. "Books are the only real expense."

"I only have two, and I got used ones," she said. "And I get my degree next month."

"So you do," he said, smiling. "Then, on to school in San Antonio."

She hesitated. "I don't know," she said. She was thinking of the expense. She couldn't afford a car and there was barely enough money to manage as it was.

"Valeria values education," he reminded her. "She'd probably be happy to pay for your expenses."

"I think she might draw the line at helping fund me in learning how to blow up stuff," she pointed out.

"We wouldn't tell her that part," he teased.

She laughed. "I've been looking into scholarships. My grades are good. It's the transportation part of it," she added on a sigh. "And I don't want to live on campus. You don't get to pick your roommate and I'm not living with some strange boy!"

He ground his teeth together. "Valeria would never go for that, modern times or not."

"Exactly."

"We might arrange for you to ride with someone," he said.

She sighed. "There aren't that many people who work in San Antonio and live here," she said.

"Well, we'll worry about it after you graduate. Did you invite our neighbor?" he added.

She smiled. "Cal's going off on a mission in a couple of weeks. He won't be here, so I didn't ask."

He cocked his head and studied her. "And…?"

He knew her too well. She shrugged. "Things got a little…complicated…while we were doing the tango at Fernando's. So he said we needed a cooling-off period. Like he's not coming around for a while, until we both forget it."

He grew solemn. He nodded. "Considering his line of work, that was a wise decision. And I applaud his consideration for you."

"Me, too, but…"

"He's not ready to settle down," he interrupted. "Don't push. If you're patient, things will work out."

"Do you think so?" she asked.

He drew in a breath. "He was a policeman, which means he's seen some pretty awful things. But combat is another thing altogether. Most men who survive it never want to go back."

"But he was in the military," she pointed out.

"He was in the unit that more or less cleared away the debris, not the one that did the hard fighting. I don't think he's yet seen the madness that overcomes men in killing situations."

"You mean, he might give it up voluntarily one day?"

He nodded. "Time will tell."

"I hope you're right," she said on a sigh. She forced a smile. "Meanwhile, I'm going to graduate and start working on scholarships and transportation."

"That's the spirit!"

She missed Cal. It was amazing that she missed him so much. She graduated, with her grandfather in the audience, cheering when she received her diploma and turned her tassel. She worked hard on scholarship requests.

"I'm so tired of filling out forms," she wailed as they finished supper one night.

"It will be worth it," he promised. He grimaced. "Sugar, will you get me a couple of those acid reflux tablets?"

"Heartburn again?" she asked, fetching the bottle. "You need to talk to your doctor. He might have a preventative that would help."

"I go next month," he reminded her. "Meanwhile, these work. Sort of," he added as he chewed the tablets and swallowed them. The pain was pretty bad. He took deep breaths. Odd, how nauseated he felt. He was sweating. Of course, it was late summer. Even with air-conditioning, the house was hot.

"We haven't talked about the house," he said after the pain passed.

Her eyebrows arched.

"I haven't been quite honest with you. I guess I need to be."

"What do you mean?"

"You know those reverse mortgages you hear about on television? Well, I did that. I mean, I do have some investments, but they wouldn't keep us for a week." He shrugged. "It seemed the best thing to do, so that we didn't have to worry about money, you know?"

Her sense of security took a nosedive. "They aren't going to repossess the house or anything?"

"Of course not," he said, and patted her hand where it lay on the tablecloth. "But when I kick the bucket, they'll take possession, is what I mean."

"You're not doing that until I'm old, too," she said firmly.

He chuckled. "Well, I'm not planning to go, you know," he told her. "I'm just mentioning it. You'll get the stocks and bonds. They aren't worth much, I'm afraid."

"I'd rather have you than any of it," she said, and she smiled.

He smiled back. "You've been a joy to live with, sugar," he said. "I'm sorry you lost your parents, but I'm happy that I still have you."

"I've loved living here," she said. "And you're not leaving. Got that?" she asked firmly.

He chuckled. "Yes. I've got it."

It worried her, that her grandfather was sharing financial stuff with her. He'd never done that before. And he was eating that acid reflux medicine like candy. It couldn't be good for him. At least he did have an appointment to see his doctor. Maybe there was a stronger medicine. Meanwhile, she cooked nothing that was spicy.

Cal had stopped by just long enough to say goodbye, on his way overseas, a few days before she'd graduated. He wouldn't tell them where he was going, but he said it wouldn't be a lengthy stay.

"Take care of my friend, here," he told Jacob, shaking hands as he nodded toward Amelia. "Keep her out of mischief."

"Not to worry, she doesn't have anything explosive around here," her grandfather assured him.

He grinned. "See that you behave," he told her firmly, and hugged her just for a few seconds. "I'll be back before you know it."

She nodded, choking back tears with a big smile. "You be careful."

"I'm always careful," he drawled. He stared at her for just a few seconds longer than he should have and then dragged his eyes away. "I'll see you both."

They waved him off. Amelia swiped at a tear that escaped.

"He's fighting it, but he feels something," her grandfather said softly. "It shows."

"Really?" She turned to him, her eyes brimming with hope and anguish.

He nodded. He smiled. "Patience."

She swallowed. "Patience," she agreed.

"And day after tomorrow is graduation," he pointed out with a grin. "Got everything laid out?"

"Oh, yes. I forgot to tell Cal," she added with a grimace. "Well, he was leaving anyway, so he couldn't have come."

"He realized that. He left you something."

"What?" she asked excitedly.

"After graduation, he said, and that's when you'll get it," he replied with a smug look.

"Granddaddy!"

"Threats and intimidation won't work. You'll have to wait."

She sighed. "I know. Patience."

He grinned from ear to ear. "Exactly!"

Cal got off the plane with the rest of his small group. Eb was with them on this mission, because it was the most important one of all. This battle would decide the future of the small country they were trying to save.

Cy Parks was bending over a radiant Juba, handing him a Bowie knife in a beautiful, beaded rawhide sheath dripping fringe.

"That's some knife," Cal remarked to Eb Scott.

He chuckled. "Nobody knows more about knives than Cy."

"I noticed. He's deadly."

"One of my oldest friends," Eb added. He glanced at Micah Steele, who was broody. "Micah's having some family issues," he said. "I hope he'll keep his mind on what we're doing."

"He usually does. Or seems to," Cal added, because he

still didn't know the group that well. "There's Eduardo," he said, waving to a big, smiling man with long black hair unbound. "I met him a few years ago. He likes to go to Fernando's in San Antonio and watch the dancers."

"He's a good man."

"One of the best. But those," he indicated Laremos, Archer and Dutch, "are the real legends."

"Headed for retirement after this," Eb confided. "They have other interests now." He studied the other man. "Are you sure this is the kind of life you want to live?" he asked abruptly.

Cal frowned. "Well, yes…"

"You were a cop. That's conventional. This," he said, indicating their surroundings, "isn't." His eyes bored into Cal's. "So far, you've seen logistics. You've never seen war the way it's waged here."

Cal just smiled. "You see a lot in police work. And I was in the military."

"You weren't a front-line soldier, were you?" he asked wisely.

Cal grimaced. "Well, no."

"You don't see this kind of warfare other places," Eb replied. "It's not too late to turn back."

Cal's eyebrows arched.

Eb knew a lost cause when he saw one. He laughed shortly. "Okay. I'm convinced. Just keep close to us when the shooting starts, all right? It's easy to lose track of where your comrades are. Ngawa isn't like other places, other wars."

Cal nodded. "I've read about that."

Yes, read about it, not experienced it, Eb was thinking. This kind of warfare had left many a man either drowning the memories in alcohol or, sometimes, eating bullets. Cal had a soft heart, and that could be a liability. He'd do what he could to shield him. But it might not be enough.

"And here we are again," Rodrigo Ramirez said with a grin as he joined them.

"How can the DEA spare you?" Eb teased, shaking hands.

"Because they don't know I'm here, compadre," he whispered loudly. "Surveillance is a misery I try to avoid. Six days in a parked car, trying to look unobtrusive," he groaned.

"At least I hope the cars were changed daily."

"Twice daily, and it did not help," Ramirez muttered.

"Well, this will make you long for it."

"You think?" Ramirez flashed him a grin and went to speak to the others.

Cal had seen horrible things. He thought they were horrible. In retrospect, after he returned to the States much later, he realized that those things in the past were only minor disturbances.

Juba, the Ngawan child the group of Americans had adopted as part of their contingent, ran toward a nearby building for cover, just as the worst of the firefight began. A ragged soldier behind a machine gun had just thrown a small pack into the doorway. He aimed and shot it the instant Juba jumped over it. Cy Parks had yelled and yelled, but Juba hadn't stopped. Not until the explosion. Not until Juba screamed and the world went up in a rain of straw and pieces of lumber and pieces of Juba.

"Oh, God," Cy groaned when they managed to get to what was left of the little boy. The band of AK ammo around his thin body was lying in pieces around him. He was missing an arm and a leg and there was a huge gash in his small belly from which matter exuded.

They knew there was no power on earth that would save him.

They used pain medication from their packs to stop

the screaming. Then Cy sat with the agonized child in his arms, held close, wrapped in the woven blanket Juba wore, talking softly to him in a broken voice, until he, mercifully, died. While the soldiers who had set the trap lounged in a nearby machine-gun nest that held the whole unit at bay, catcalling that the kid was a waste of skin and soon they'd do the same thing to his so-called friends.

Nobody spoke. Cy gently laid the little boy down, closed his eyes. When he looked up, his green eyes were like emerald flames. The fury inside him was visible. He got up, his .45 cocked and ready, his attention fixed on the machine-gun nest from which the explosives had been thrown. From where the catcalls were still coming.

"Cy, no!" Eb Scott yelled above the gunfire.

But they were pinned down. There was almost no cover. They lay flat in the dirt of the small village, bullets hitting around them like hail.

Cy didn't hear, didn't answer. His furious gaze was fixed on the machine gunner who'd made, and set, the explosive that had killed Juba. The man had been bragging loudly about his talent while Juba died in Cy's arms.

Cy plowed right toward the nest, cursing every step of the way, ignoring the shouts of his comrades.

The gunner laughed as he turned the machine gun on the man approaching. Cy walked right into the gunfire, oblivious to the bullets that, amazingly, mostly missed, until he reached the gunner and emptied the .45 into him at point-blank range.

"Look out!" Cal yelled as two men started toward him from behind.

Cy reacted immediately, whirling. Two knives flew from under the loose sleeves of his jacket, burying themselves up to the hilt in the approaching insurgents. Cal had never seen anything like it.

Cy whirled, bleeding, and started toward the rest of the men firing at them from cover where the dead machine gunner lay.

"Bring him down!" Eb yelled over the gunfire.

Laremos and Dutch and Archer tackled him, and it took all three of them to stop him. They managed it just as three other insurgents opened fire directly at their grieving, furious comrade.

Cal was firing for all he was worth. He was usually one of the most accurate shooters. But all around him, men were screaming in pain. Insurgents on both sides were bleeding from wounds, everything from lost limbs to fatal hits in the body. It was a nightmare of sounds and smells. He was shaking. He hadn't realized it. He was firing, firing, and the gun was empty, but he couldn't stop. Despite his service on the police force, his time in the military, this was a type of gore he'd never experienced in his life.

Eb was yelling at him, but he was deaf to his comrade's voice. All he could hear were the screams. All he could see was blood, blood, more blood…!

"Fall back!" Eb yelled again.

Eduardo grabbed him by his pant leg and dragged him backward with the retreating group. At the edge of his vision, he saw what was left of Juba. The little boy had been laughing with them, begging chocolate as they massed for the attack, carrying an AK that weighed almost as much as he did. The bullets were still flying as both sides tried to gain ground. But Cal was so disoriented that he wasn't sure where his lines even were, and still Eduardo dragged him backward, flat on the ground, with dust filling his mouth, his vision, with bullets hitting all around them.

And even as reinforcements arrived, he was still lost in the horror of it.

Cal realized what Eb Scott had tried to spare him. This

was unlike police work. Commando war was down and dirty, bloody, full of mangled, bleeding bodies, of people screaming from wounds that left them without arms or legs or both. It was a war where children carrying AKs and pistols and rocket launchers, hyped up on drugs, came at them in droves and were cut down. Children the age of Juba, who had known nothing except war.

They'd reloaded their weapons during a lull, and they were waiting for the signal to attack again. As they moved forward, Cal spotted one of the child combatants lying on the ground with his leg half off, screaming. Cal turned toward him, despite the fact that the child was with the enemy forces. He needed help.

Eb was yelling at him, yelling for all he was worth. Cal couldn't make out the words buried in gunfire.

As he approached the child, the boy's hand went to a .45 automatic that had been lying under him. He laughed as he shot at Cal, just one shot, before the loss of blood led him to unconsciousness and then death.

Cal felt the blow against his upper thigh, as if someone had beaten it with a fist. He was suddenly weak, and he couldn't get up. How odd, he thought. Nothing was wrong with him. Why couldn't he get to his feet?

Eb was standing over him, calling for medical supplies, his eyes wild.

He tried to ask why Eb looked so worried. He felt wetness under him. He looked down. He was bleeding. He was bleeding badly. Had he been shot? He was only trying to help the boy.

His eyes went to the child who'd shot him. The pistol was lying beside him. His eyes were open. His leg was in a pool of blood.

"The…child…" Cal could barely speak. How odd.

"Dead," Eb said coldly.

"Still...bleeding," he added. The boy couldn't be dead because blood was still pumping out of him.

"You can't save someone with a wound like that," Eb said calmly as he started to apply bandages. "He's dead. His body hasn't realized it yet. He only has a minute or two left."

Micah Steele was beside him now with a hypodermic needle. He shot it right into the vein at the crook of Cal's elbow.

"What...?" he started to ask. Then the pain hit him. All at once. Fire. Blood. Anguish. He'd never felt anything so horrible. He wasn't going to start yelling. Men didn't do that. Except they did. He groaned aloud.

"Peace, compadre," his friend Eduardo said from somewhere close by. "Be still. Let the medicine work."

There was another shot. The pain began to recede, bit by bit. He was staring around at all the bodies. There were so many. Some were children, boys of grammar school age who would never grow up to be doctors or lawyers or even soldiers. Boys. Little boys. Torn to pieces by bullets, by bombs, by people, well-meaning people, who only wanted to save their government so that they could grow up in a safe place, with hope for the future. Bright ideals. Swimming in blood. So much blood...

"They're bringing Cal home today," Amelia's grandfather told her when he came home from the post office.

She brightened. Until she chewed on the words he'd chosen. Not Cal's coming home. Somebody was bringing him home. Whole other connotation.

"Bringing him...?" Her heart stopped in her chest.

He sat down at the table, dropping the few pieces of mail onto the tablecloth. "He was badly wounded," he told her. "It's going to be a long recuperation."

"Oh, no!" She sat down, heavily. "But, he's alive?" she added quickly.

He nodded. "Alive. Eb and his men, some of them, got back last night." His face was hard. "I think it was a battle that none of them will ever forget. And some of them will never be the same. Cal, especially."

"That bad?" she asked in a husky tone.

He nodded. "That bad."

She drew in a long breath. "I can take care of him," she said.

"Let's wait and see if they send some of their own people," her grandfather told her.

"You're worried about gossip," she said.

He smiled. "Really?"

She grimaced. "Sorry. I knew better."

"Valeria, now, that's another story."

"What she doesn't know won't bother her," she reminded him with a grin.

"I suppose so," he conceded. He reached again for the bottle of acid reflux medicine.

"When is that doctor's appointment?" she asked.

"Three weeks," he said. "Not that long a wait."

"You could see somebody sooner, at one of those walk-in clinics," she suggested.

He shrugged. "I'd rather see my own doctor."

"You can't bully the people in the walk-in clinic," she translated.

He chuckled. "I'm okay. Just heartburn. Now stop worrying!"

She gave in. "Okay."

He patted her on the back on his way to get a Coke out of the fridge. "I'm glad you worry about me. Now stop doing it."

She laughed, as she was meant to.

* * *

Cal came home in an ambulance. Eb Scott drove up just as Amelia came running from across the street.

She was terrified and unable to hide it. She followed the men with the gurney, and Eb, into Cal's house and waited while they settled him on his bed.

"I'll see about a private duty nurse," Eb began.

"I don't need a nurse," Cal said through his teeth. "I'll be fine. I can walk!"

"No, actually, you can't," Eb said, aware of Amelia hovering.

"I'll take care of him," she said quietly. "What do I need to do?"

"Get a rope," Eb said curtly. "A strong one. We'll tie him to the bed!"

"I said, I can walk!" Cal tried to get up.

"Aaaaaaah!" Amelia said, using the tone her grandmother had always used with her when she tried to do something stupid. She put her hands against his broad chest where his shirt was parted in front and pushed gently until he was horizontal. His eyes were wild. She'd never seen such an expression. "You aren't going anywhere," she said shortly.

"Thank God," Eb said under his breath as Cal made one small effort to resist her and abruptly gave in and lay back down—not without a harsh glare.

"You have prescriptions," Eb said. "I'll go get them filled. You'll need groceries. I'll see if I can find somebody to cook for you…"

"I can cook," Amelia said. "I even know how to bribe him with his favorite food," she added.

Eb managed a short laugh. "Okay. Are you sure?" he added. "It's not a pretty wound and it will need to be watched for signs of infection."

"I can blow stuff up," she said, and wondered why both men looked so traumatized when she said that. "I'm not squeamish."

"All right, then," Eb said gently. "I'll go to the pharmacy and the grocery store."

"Petty cash is in a jar on the kitchen table," Cal said heavily.

"Not a problem." Eb went out behind the ambulance guys and closed the door.

Amelia looked down at him, thankful that he was still alive, even if he was wounded. But the way he looked was troubling. She'd never seen that expression on his face in all the time she'd known him.

"It was bad, wasn't it?" she asked.

His dark eyes were shimmery with pain. "You have no idea."

"Well, you're home and safe now," she said. "I'll take care of you," she added quietly. "It's all right."

He was fighting horrible memories. Hearing things, seeing things he could never share except with a comrade who'd been there. He looked at Amelia, but he didn't see her. He saw Juba, in pieces on the killing ground. It was a picture he was never going to get out of his mind.

His life was never going to be the same again. And this was just the beginning of the nightmare as he tried to adjust to life as it would be from now on. Eb had been right. He had no idea what he was letting himself in for. Now he had to try to live with it.

Chapter Nine

Amelia cooked for him and kept the house clean. Her grandfather came and sat by Cal's bedside sometimes. He and the younger man spoke with the door closed, shutting Amelia out. It was a conversation she wasn't allowed to participate in.

"You guys shut me out," she complained to her grandfather the week Cal came home, while she was fixing supper. She carried plates across to Cal for each meal, even breakfast.

"You're not ready to hear these kinds of stories, sugar," he said gently.

"I'm no wimp," she teased.

"No. But this isn't polite conversation, either," he said solemnly. "Cal needs to talk to somebody who's been where he is right now. Amelia," he added quietly, "this is going to be a long haul. He isn't ever going to be the man you knew again."

She finished frying chicken, took it up and moved the pan off the burner as she clicked it off.

"You're scaring me," she said.

"Cal was a policeman," he said. "You see terrible things when you do police work. But this kind of war that he's seen, it's not something he can share with you."

She sighed. "I want to help."

"Be his friend," he said simply. "You never push, which is just what he needs. I can listen to him and advise. But what you can do to help is just keep him fed and quiet, while he tries to get past it."

She grimaced. "Was it really bad?"

He nodded. "I did spec ops," he said. "But even I didn't see the kind of combat he was exposed to."

"Did they accomplish what they meant to do, at least?"

"Yes. They put the legitimate government back in power," he replied. "And it was a noble thing. They saved thousands of lives." He smiled. "There were people from all over Africa, all over the world, helping. Combatants and support people, all of whom volunteered and risked their lives to support the cause."

"It must be nice, to make a difference like that," she said.

"It is. But there's a terrible cost. Cal is paying it right now."

She grimaced. "He'll get over it, though, right?"

He hesitated. "He'll learn to live with it," he said. Which wasn't the same thing. Not at all.

She became Cal's unofficial home health unit. He didn't want her to see what was under the big bandage on his thigh, but he was running a fever by the fourth day, and she insisted.

His leg was in bad shape. There was a small hole in the

front of his thigh, and a much bigger one in the back of it. The flesh around it was red and hot.

"I'm calling Eb," she said.

"It's just healing," he argued.

"It's just rotting off," she replied, and kept dialing.

Eb came over with a tall, husky blond man who looked more like a wrestler than a doctor. He probed and cleaned the wound and dressed it again.

"I'm changing the antibiotic," he told Cal. "And you need probiotics, as well." He looked up at a worried Amelia. "Do you…?"

"Yes," she said, nodding. "I have to cook for my grandfather and keep him healthy. I don't feed him or Cal anything fried except an occasional chicken, and I cook mostly veggies and fish dishes. With probiotics."

He smiled. "Good."

"How's Colby?" Cal asked, because during that two-day firefight, Micah Steele had been forced to amputate a fellow combatant's arm in the field.

"Not adjusting well at all," Micah replied. "I'm sending him to a psychologist I know in Houston. Good doctor. Keeps snakes." He shuddered.

"Nothing wrong with boa constrictors," Cal said. "I used to have one."

"I like big lizards," Amelia said.

They both stared at her.

She shrugged and grinned.

"Okay," Micah said as he got up. "Here." He handed Amelia a prescription. "Lucky for you I didn't quit medicine until after I got my license. I keep it. Comes in handy."

"He'll be okay?" Amelia asked as he stood up.

"If he does what he's told," the big blond man replied.

"I'll make sure he does," Amelia said. "Thanks."

He smiled. "If it doesn't improve in three or four days,

have Eb call me. I live in Nassau, but I'm up this way pretty often on business."

"Okay."

"He's nice," Amelia told Cal.

He drew in a long breath. "The whole unit's like that. I think…" He picked up his cell phone from the bedside table. "Hello?"

There was a pause. He glanced at Amelia and away. "No, I've got all I need. Yes, I know how you feel about sick people. No problem. Sure. Bye."

He hung up. It was a woman, Amelia was certain of it. But she just smiled. "I'll go get your prescription filled."

"They've got my credit card on file," he said. "I'll call and have the medicine charged."

"Okay."

Amelia went out and he watched her with concern. She was too involved with him. He was going to have to work through this bad time, and he didn't know how he was going to cope with the trauma. Edie had phoned to tell him she was glad he was alive but, of course, she wasn't coming near him. She couldn't bear sickness. It was just a failing she couldn't help.

He thought about how nurturing Amelia was, and he felt guilty. He wanted her. It was a growing problem. He wasn't certain how to cope. He didn't want to get tangled up with a girl her age, and especially with an innocent. She was getting to him.

Combined with the problems he already had, Amelia was one he didn't want to have to tackle. He was going to have to step very carefully. He didn't want to hurt her.

Meanwhile, he was dealing with a trauma he'd never experienced. It had sounded like such a great line of work. Loads of money, excitement, adventure. Eb had tried to warn him. He hadn't listened. Now he was going to pay the price.

Of course he'd seen bad things while he was doing police work. Life on patrol was never boring, you worked wrecks, you worked domestic disturbances, gang warfare, escaping criminals, all sorts of things. But you didn't generally see people blown apart.

Like the rest of the unit, he'd become fond of Juba, the orphan they looked after when they were on the ground. He was just a kid, but already he could field strip the old AK-47 he'd been given by a comrade, and he knew how to clean it. It was his most prized possession.

Cy Parks had taken the loss harder than any of the rest. He had a young son back home in the States, and he had naturally gravitated toward the young boy. They became close. Cy was always bringing him presents, things he'd probably never seen, like Game Boys and drones.

Then, in a space of seconds, Juba had disobeyed a yelled order to stop. He'd gone into a building and hadn't seen the explosive that Cy had spotted. Body parts rained down along with part of the building the bomb had been set in. Not too far away, a cheer was heard and then unrelenting taunts and catcalling. The men in the machine-gun nest who'd given the cheer would pay a hard price for it.

But that was to come later. In the meantime, Cy had cradled the boy in his arms—what was left of him. Amazing, that Juba was still conscious. They'd doped him as much as they dared, hoping the pain would recede just enough. Because he'd lost too much blood to live. Micah Steele had just shaken his head when the men watching asked about Juba's chances. The injuries were too great, the blood loss too much.

So Cy rocked him in his arms until he died. It was a memory that haunted all of them. But it wasn't the only one.

When Juba died, Cy went looking for the men who'd cheered when the building went up, the group that had bragged about setting the bomb.

Nobody had ever seen anything like it. Cy walked right into the bullets, firing as he went. The nest was in a pivotal area, and it had been stonewalling the foreign troops, making it impossible for them to relieve the company up ahead.

Cy changed all that. He took out three men in the space of a heartbeat. There was a fourth man who'd been sitting among the parts of an IED he was constructing. Cy dropped the automatic rifle and started throwing knives. There wasn't a lot left of the bomb maker when he was through.

Micah patched Cy up while he sat and smoldered, furious that the men who'd killed Juba had been granted such an easy death. He looked like death warmed up himself, but, God he was game! He got to his feet, patched wounds and all, refusing any pain meds, grabbed an automatic rifle and fell in with the company. Together, they marched into the thick of the battle.

The bomb that killed Juba wasn't the only one they encountered. There were others. Too many others. They were concealed in hidden spots, in cunning ways, the way you'd set a trap to catch a wild animal. Except that these devices didn't catch anything. They blew men to component parts.

They say you can get used to anything, Cal thought blandly, but it was a lie. You never got used to seeing things that he'd seen in combat. He would never forget it. Maybe it would dim, as a memory, as years went by. But despite the lure of big money and adventure, nothing would get him back into the field. Even police work would seem tame by comparison. He had every intention of going back to work for San Antonio PD when he was healed enough.

One of his comrades, Eduardo Perez, was the morale

booster of the bunch. He had a bloodthirsty past, but something about the tone of this campaign had changed him. He became religious. He wasn't aggressive about it, but he did pray with any of the men who needed it, and because of his own ferocious past, the men respected him, even those who weren't religious. After the worst of the combat, when all the men were bandaging wounds and looking for extraction and trying to cope with even more horrible memories, Eduardo announced that he was going to study for the priesthood. In fact, another of their group, Jake Blair, was also questioning his own lifestyle. And Jake spooked even some of the worst men in the group. They called him "snake," because he could get into places most of them couldn't. The men with the best hearing couldn't detect even a footfall when he went out to scout for them. All he carried was a Bowie knife and a .45 auto. And he was never wounded. Not even once.

They'd started out with many sympathetic comrades. But they came back with only a handful. And most of them, oddly, ended up in Jacobsville. Because of Eb Scott's new anti-terrorism training camp, the town was becoming a name that people remembered. And the sting of battle memories was easier when shared.

Cal had wanted to talk over his experiences with the other members of the group, but they were all coping in their own ways. It had been a godsend that Amelia's grandfather had been in special ops during the Mideast wars. He hadn't seen quite the things that Cal had. But his own experiences were not much less bloody, and they wore on his conscience. Cal looked to him more and more for guidance as he worked his way through the horror to some semblance of a normal life.

The fever was burning him alive. He felt sick to his stomach, as well. Amelia was taking such good care of him. She was so unlike Edie, who liked his company but wouldn't go near him while he was sick. He wondered why he even took the woman on dates. He felt no desire for her, none at all. That part of him that was sensual had gone into eclipse since Amelia came into his life. He thought about how innocent she was, how careful of her reputation here, in this very small rural community. She'd laughed when he mentioned it once. She said she didn't want to be that woman that everybody pointed out in stores. It sounded odd to him, who'd lived mostly in impersonal places, in cities. But as he spent more time in Jacobsville, he began to understand.

It wasn't really that people were judgmental. It was that they had certain standards that went back two centuries. They didn't apologize for them, or try to explain them. They were just part of the community. If you stepped outside the bounds of what was considered decent and right, you were looked at. No pressure. No censure. Just eyes, staring. Nonverbal restraint.

Before social media, that silent restraint had been responsible for keeping morality in check, for holding families together, for discouraging things that used divisions and tears. Here in Jacobsville, some people still felt that way, felt that tradition had a place at the table. People in very small towns were clannish. They were many generations of people who knew each other well, who thought and acted alike, who didn't easily accept radical viewpoints of any sort. And because Jacobsville hadn't really moved with the times, some transplanted city dwellers who'd tried to live here had moved right back into their former homes in cities. Not everybody could fit in. Not everybody wanted to.

Cal wanted to. He hoped he could. He loved Jacobsville. He loved the people, the customs, the feeling of belonging to a family. And it was. A family. A small community where most people shared relatives, who had a long history in this part of Texas. To Cal, who'd lived impersonally and anonymously for so long, it was a revelation.

And especially now, it felt very comfortable, while he tried to get back on his feet. Without Amelia and her grandfather, his recovery might not be as easy, and certainly not as nurturing. He'd never known any of his neighbors in apartments where he'd lived in the past. In Jacobsville, he quickly learned his surroundings, and the people who lived in them.

He moved restlessly in the bed. He didn't want to sleep. The nightmares came again and again. He hoped they might stop one day. He'd asked Amelia's grandfather about them. The older man had just said that they diminished. He didn't know if that meant in frequency or in vivid detail. He hoped it was both.

The front door opened. It had a familiar squeak, like in a haunted house movie. He loved the old place.

"I'm back," Amelia said, as she dropped her purse and jacket off on his sofa and made her way to the bedroom. "Two things," she said, holding up the bag. "A new antibiotic, and pain meds."

"I hate pain meds," he began.

She just sighed. "The pharmacist said that if you have to fight the pain along with the infection, you won't heal as fast," she said, and stared him down.

He made a face.

"That's what he said," she repeated. She cocked her head and smiled faintly. "Then he mentioned how you pill a cat, by rolling it up in a towel."

He sighed. "Okay. Pest," he added.

She grinned and went to get him something to drink with the pills.

He was too sick to eat supper. The medicine would work, she was sure, she was hopefully sure, but his fever was pretty high. Micah had said to give him Tylenol for the fever, which she did.

She took his temperature again. It was still high. "You need to be sponged down," she began.

"No." He said it very firmly for a sick man. He glowered at her. "I'm not having you bathe me in bed!"

"Oh, for God's sake, Cal," she began, throwing up her hands.

"When you've been married for a year, come back and we'll talk," he replied.

She made a face. "All right. But if the fever doesn't come down soon, I'm calling Eb Scott, and he can sponge you until the fever's down!"

He shifted. "Okay," he said after a minute.

"You are a prude," she accused as she started to leave.

"And you're bluffing," he said, with a knowing look that made her flush. "You know as much about men as I know about theoretical physics."

"Well, that may be, but I'm never going to learn it here."

He chuckled in spite of himself and groaned because any movement hurt his leg.

"The pain meds should kick in soon," she said encouragingly. "I wish you felt like eating. I made potato soup."

"My favorite," he sighed. His eyes closed. "Maybe later."

"Maybe later."

She pulled the covers over him. "I'll be in the living room reading if you need me…"

"You'll be at home taking care of your grandfather if I need you." He picked up his cell phone from the bedside table and showed it to her. "My phone has your number on speed dial. If I get into trouble, all I have to do is push one button."

She was reluctant, but he was in one of his stubborn moods, so she knew it would do no good to argue. "Okay," she said on a sigh. "I'll leave. But I'll be back at suppertime."

"Bring soup," he said, and forced a smile. "Hopefully, my stomach will settle by then."

She beamed. "Optimism! I approve wholeheartedly!"

He smiled back. "And thank you, for all the kind care," he added.

She shrugged. "It's no more than you'd do for us, Cal," she replied with a smile. "See you later."

He reflected on that when she'd gone. Yes, he thought. If their situations were reversed, he'd be a fixture in their home. It was a revelation. He'd never been overly generous with his time in the past. But he was getting lessons in sacrifice both from Amelia and her grandfather. He hoped there would come a time when he could repay their kindness.

Amelia was back at suppertime, along with her grandfather. She carried in a bowl of potato soup, which Cal was now able to eat.

First, she checked his fever, and found that it was much reduced. "Thank goodness!" she said heartily.

"The meds are working," he replied. "I feel just a bit better."

"Bullet wounds take time to heal," Amelia's grandfather said as he dropped down into the easy chair they'd placed at Cal's bedside.

"You'd know," Amelia said. "Granny said you had more than one."

He chuckled. "I did, none of them drastic, thank God.

And you got off lucky," he added to Cal. "An in-and-out wound without hitting bone. I won't go into how rare that is."

"Steele told me already," he chuckled as he ate. "Amelia, this is the best potato soup I've ever had, and I'm not exaggerating."

"I'm glad you like it."

"Now go home and let us talk," her grandfather said, but with a grin. "And yes, the soup was delicious. As usual. How about dessert, in about an hour?"

"Dessert?" Cal's eyebrows lifted.

"Chocolate cake with vanilla frosting," she said.

"My favorite," Cal sighed.

"Mine, too," the older man chuckled.

"I'll bring slices when I come back," she said. "Don't forget to take the antibiotic," she added to Cal. "It's three times a day, not two. And Tylenol for the fever in," she checked her watch, "two more hours."

Cal rolled his eyes. "Shades of Nurse Jane," he mused.

She laughed. "I'm better at blowing things up, but I can do nursing when needed," she said, and then wondered why he seemed paler. "You okay?" she asked quickly.

"I'm fine," he lied, and forced a smile.

"All right. Back in an hour," she said, and breezed out.

The older man waited until he heard the front door close before he spoke. "She doesn't know about IEDs, except how to make them," he pointed out. "And she'd never have said a word if she knew what you'd been through."

"I know that." He finished his soup and put the bowl down with a sigh. "I thought I was tough enough for any sort of military action," he said. "I was an MP when I was in the service, though, and I never got into any of the real fighting. When I came out, it was San Antonio PD. I thought I'd seen everything." His eyes closed. "Dear God, what human beings can do to one another!"

"Yes, I do understand," he replied. "It will take time for you to get past this, I won't lie to you. But eventually it will fade to just a bad memory."

"What about the nightmares?" Cal asked, tight-lipped.

The older man sighed and gave him a sad smile. "Well, that's the other thing. They don't stop. They just come less frequently."

"That's something, I guess," Cal replied.

"Take time to heal. Don't rush back into anything. You'll be laid up for a while. You'll be able to get around better, but you have to be careful about that wound and watch for any sign of infection. Like the one you've got right now."

"Amelia insisted on calling Eb because I had a fever," he said curtly, and didn't mention that she'd looked at the wound, because it was in a rather intimate place.

"She was right," he replied. "You don't want to wait until red lines appear and it starts to turn green," he added with pursed lips and twinkling eyes.

Cal managed a laugh. "No, I don't want that. It may be mangled but it's still a leg."

"It's not the only wound, I imagine?" the older man said slyly.

Cal drew in a breath. "No. I took two bullets in the chest. Fortunately, they were fired from a distance and barely penetrated the muscle. Micah patched me up while we were regrouping. I'd just gotten back to a comfortable level when we went back into offensive missions, and I was wounded again." He shook his head. "I didn't know I was so careless."

"Has nothing to do with it," the elderly man said. "I took three bullets in the chest when I was just walking from one tent to another. Laid me up for almost two months."

He smiled. "I never told my wife, but she found out for herself when I came home." He burst out laughing. "I'll never forget what she said."

Cal's eyebrows lifted.

"She said she hoped all the meanness in me leaked out those bullet holes before they got plugged up!"

Cal laughed and grimaced when it hurt.

"She was a tiger, my wife," he said warmly. "I miss her every day. Amelia's so much like her. She's got guts. I haven't found anything yet that she's afraid of."

"I thought I hadn't, too. Life teaches hard lessons."

"Life is all about lessons," was the reply. "We don't know why we're put here, or what purpose we serve. But we all have our own ideas about that," he added. "The problem is that some people aren't satisfied until they force you to believe the way they do. And that's how wars start."

"I'm learning about that."

"Tell me about Juba," the older man began.

Cal's eyes were terrible to look into.

"I know. It's an open wound and I'm rubbing salt into it. But until you talk about it, it's just going to fester until it causes real damage. You have to get it out."

Cal closed his eyes. Then he sighed. He looked at the old man. "I've been hiding my head in the sand."

"Won't help. And I should know."

Cal smiled. "Okay."

So he told Amelia's grandfather what had happened. His voice broke a couple of times, because he'd been fond of the boy. But he got through it.

"I didn't have to see such things," the old man told him, "but I know men who did. Some of them turned to alcohol and drugs to forget. Two committed suicide. Those were the ones who couldn't, or wouldn't, face it and come to terms with it." He leaned forward intently. "I don't mean you to be one of those. That's why I was insistent."

Cal looked at him with new respect. "I see."

"Not just yet. But one day, you will. We're all terrified when we go into combat in the first place. One of the things we learn quickly is how to lean into the fear, instead of avoiding it, and use it to help us do desperate things when we have to. Any man who tells you he's never felt fear is either a liar or a serial killer," he added ruefully.

"That's a hard thing to admit," Cal replied.

"Of course. We're men. We're strong. We can face down armies with a knife between our teeth and an auto rifle. That works fine in video games, by the way, but it's a killer in real life. I was shaking all over when I went into my first incursion. One of the older men in the group took me to one side and taught me how to deal with it. It worked. After that, I owned the fear, and I used it. I think it's one of the reasons why I came home, and many of my comrades didn't."

"I guess a lot of myths go up in smoke when we see combat for the first time."

"All of them do," he said.

Cal stared at him. "I'll never be able to thank you enough for this," he said. "I haven't been dealing with it well. In fact, I haven't been dealing with it at all."

"It's not easy. It helps to talk to other people who've been in your situation. Eb Scott would listen anytime you needed him to. He's a good man. I know several of his students. He's teaching them the right way, using experts in every field as instructors. He's going to put Jacobsville on the map."

"I'm glad he's doing well. I wish I'd asked more questions, done more research, before I threw my hat into the merc ring, however."

"Universal feeling. Me, too."

"To his credit, Eb did try to talk me out of it. I wanted in more for the feeling of purpose than quick cash, to know that I was doing a noble thing by helping the right people back into power." He sighed. "Nobility has a lot of definitions these days. Not all of them laudable ones."

"War is hell," came the reply. "Sherman said so and made it so. People in some states back east still use his name as a curse."

"So do some of the Plains tribes that he fought."

"Still, he was effective, in a burned-earth way."

"When you're hit, hit back hard."

"It usually works, too."

The front door opened. "I have cake!"

"Come right in," Cal called back, and both men laughed.

Cal was fed cake and given meds. Then a reluctant Amelia followed her grandfather out the front door.

"I feel mean, leaving him. He's a long way from well," she told her companion.

"Yes, but it's a very small town," he pointed out with a grin. "And do you want to be that woman who's always pointed to?"

"Now you sound like your sister," she chided, laughing.

"I do. She'd have a fit at what you've already done, if she knew." He paused when they were back in their own house. "What about that woman who came to see him?" he asked suddenly.

"Edie?" She shrugged. "She called him while I was there. Apparently, she can't abide being around anybody sick or wounded. Lovely woman." She rolled her eyes.

"I don't imagine it's her nursing skills that interested him in the first place, sugar," he said gently. "Just…don't let yourself get too involved. You know what I mean?"

She smiled. "Of course. He's my friend," she added,

hiding the fact that her heart was already in jeopardy and that the thought of his leaving Jacobsville terrorized her at night. She knew he wasn't likely to continue with merc work, and that was a blessing. But he was surely going back to the city. There were rumors that he wanted to sign back on with San Antonio PD. She hadn't asked him yet. She didn't have the nerve. Plus, she didn't want it to be true.

Life without Cal would be no life at all. And she'd only just realized it since he'd been wounded.

She didn't know what to do. He wasn't a man who'd settle down to life in a small town, marriage and kids. He was too freedom-loving, too adventurous. Any woman who tried to trap him would regret it for the rest of her life.

Maybe Edie would do that and get kicked to the curb. That was the nicest thought Amelia had all night.

Chapter Ten

Amelia went every day to take meals to Cal and make sure he took his meds on time. He was getting better. The antibiotics worked fast. Too fast. He got up and tried to walk and the wound started suppurating. So Amelia called the doctor.

But Micah Steele was out of the country. So she called Eb, and was told to try a local doctor, Copper Coltrain. She thanked him, hung up and had a panic attack. Copper was known in Jacobsville. Very well known. For his temper and his attitude.

On the other hand, she had to do something. Cal refused to go to the emergency room, so it was call the doctor or trust to luck.

"Don't worry," her grandfather said when told about Cal's stubbornness. "I've got this." He picked up the phone and punched in numbers.

Amelia was amazed at how easy he was with the man on the other end of the line. Obviously, he wasn't scared of the redheaded doctor.

He hung up. "He'll swing by after he makes rounds at the hospital. About one," he added. He grinned. "I had to bribe him, though."

"I heard. Two slices of chocolate cake…?"

"Oh, I thought we might give him three. After all, you've got the ingredients to make more…?"

She just laughed.

She let her grandfather go over to Cal's when the doctor arrived, carrying several slices of cake in plastic wrap in a grocery bag. It wasn't that she was afraid, of course.

She chided herself for her cowardice. If she couldn't face down one doctor, how was she going to face down people in college in San Antonio when she started classes in two months? And how was she going to deal with the public if she got a job using her new skills?

That was in the future, she reminded herself. She'd worry about that problem when she had to. Being shy was a lifelong issue. It had kept her free of boyfriends—well, except for Ty Hardin, who'd been in her high school graduating class. He'd signed on with Eb Scott's group as a merc. She'd only seen him once since then. He had a crush on her that wasn't returned. He was a nice guy. Clean-cut, smart, a gentleman. But her heart was pointed in another direction, despite the hopelessness of it.

A few minutes later, her grandfather came up the steps. The doctor was just driving away.

"He said it's not anything to worry about unless it starts pumping out blood or…well, Cal's okay. He put on a temporary bandage, just while it's closing. He'll be fine."

"Thank goodness! I'd have driven him to the emergency room—assuming the truck would crank—but he refused to go. It's beyond my powers to forcibly dress a tall man and carry him bodily to our precarious method of transportation," she added with a grin.

He chuckled. "I see your point. You did the right thing. Although," he added slowly, "you might wait a couple of hours before you go over to check on Cal."

She stared at him. "Any particular reason?"

"Well, until he stops cussing would be one."

She pursed her lips. "Okay. I'll go make something edible."

"Good idea."

She went into the kitchen and didn't see her grandfather smothering laughter.

It was late when she went back to check on Cal. Her grandfather had been doubled over with acid reflux. He had medicine for it, but it wasn't working. Finally, he mixed up some baking soda in water and drank it, and he said it worked. But he looked bad. He was pale and his shirt was palpitating where his heart was.

"You need to go back to the doctor," she said firmly.

"It's just heartburn," he assured her. "I had a physical only last month. That's when he recommended these tablets for the reflux. You take them for ten days and they work. But not on the first day. You have to use the chewable tablets until they do work."

"Oh. Okay," she said, relieved.

He grinned. "I'm fine. A lot of people have this problem. It's why I can't eat spicy foods or drink alcohol. Maybe that's for the best."

"About the alcohol, sure, but give up spicy foods?" she moaned. "I can't live without the occasional taco or fajita or chimichanga!"

"I know. I miss them."

"I'm sorry. I'll try to enjoy mine enough for you, Granddaddy," she promised.

He just smiled.

Cal was sitting up in bed reading a book on his cell phone when she walked in. He gave her a glare that could have set fire to kindling.

"Now, now," she said before he could speak, "let's not jeopardize our potato soup and chocolate cake over a little matter of the doctor coming out to see you."

The glare didn't subside. "You didn't even come over while he was here, you chicken."

"I know his reputation," she said. "Nobody ever said I had to sacrifice myself for a friend. And I am keeping one nicely fed and medicated." She smiled.

He drew in a breath. "Honest to God, I thought I was back in grammar school. That man…!"

"He's a very good doctor. Everybody says so."

"His bedside manner would do a cobra proud!"

"I like cobras," she said. "They're really cool to look at."

"You wouldn't like to be bitten by one," he pointed out.

She looked around the floor. "I hope you aren't planning to drive that point home…?"

"I don't keep cobras!"

"Our deputy sheriff has an albino python," she said. "It weighs a hundred and ten pounds and it's absolutely gorgeous! It has yellow-and-white-patterned skin and red eyes!"

He rolled his eyes. "I never would have figured you for a woman who liked snakes."

"Well, I don't. I mean I don't like all of them. Especially rattlesnakes. I almost got bitten by them twice." She shivered. "But black snakes and king snakes are okay."

"Why?"

She made a face. "Because black snakes aren't dangerous and king snakes eat poisonous ones."

"How do you know all that?" he wondered.

"Ty Hardin. He was in my graduating class." She made another face. "He had this awful crush on me. I laid awake nights finding ways to avoid him. I mean, he's nice and all, but he just isn't my type."

He cocked his head. "What is your type?"

She sighed. "That gorgeous man who played in *Game of Thrones*," she said. "The blond one who lost his hand."

"He was a…!"

"Please." She stopped him. "There are ladies present."

"Oh, yeah? Where?"

Now she was glaring.

"Okay. Sorry." He sighed. "And I guess you were right about calling the doctor. He said it wasn't an emergency, but I needed to slow down trying to get back on my feet. Rome wasn't built in a day."

"It really wasn't," she pointed out. "The more you try to rush recovery, the more you'll set it back."

"Were you eavesdropping?" he asked, "because that's exactly what he said." He laid his head back on the pillow. "I guess you're both right. I just feel useless lying here. I've got a hundred books, and I don't want to read any of them."

She held out her hand for his phone. Her eyes popped. "What do you do with this thing, just call people and read books? There are no weather apps, no earthquake apps, no news apps, no mahjong, no solitaire… This is just pathetic!"

He was staring at her. "What?"

"Mahjong. It's my favorite game. And I love solitaire."

"I used to play that with a deck of cards."

"Now you can play it online."

He grimaced. "I guess a few apps wouldn't kill me," he said. "And I like games. Go ahead. Load it up."

"You mean it?"

"I mean it."

She grinned and pulled up the Apps app.

She'd created a monster. Now all he wanted to do was play solitaire. He played it between bites of supper and while he was supposed to be sleeping. He played mah-jong, too, and loved it once he got the hang of it. He added other games, as well. It kept his mind occupied while his body was healing, and Amelia didn't have to fuss so much.

Meanwhile, Amelia's grandfather's heartburn seemed to be getting more frequent, despite the medicines he was taking for it. With a little coaxing, she convinced him to phone his doctor's office and make an appointment. There were plenty of medicines that worked for that condition. He just needed the right one.

Cal improved day by day once he was convinced that trying to rush his recovery was doing his body no favors.

The wounds healed enough that he could stand to wear sweatpants, which meant he could get around the house and out onto the porch. He mentioned driving and Amelia went through the roof.

"I'll check with the doctor first," he promised. And muttered, "Anything to keep peace," under his breath.

She grinned. "I'm a pest, I am."

He laughed. "You are. But a nice pest. And you really can cook!"

"Thanks. It's just basic chemistry, though." She didn't mention making bombs. Her grandfather, while giving away no secrets, had told her in confidence that certain things shouldn't be discussed around their neighbor.

A stranger came to see Cal one day, loaded him into the car and drove him away. He was gone until almost dark. When Amelia went over to take his supper, after his visitor left, he told her what was going on. Not all of it. Just what he was comfortable confiding. It was going to upset her, and he didn't want to do that. Not now.

"I'm thinking about going back into police work," he explained at the table while he ate the delicious spaghetti and garlic bread she'd carted over. "In San Antonio, where I worked before," he added.

She almost sighed aloud with relief. "You're not going to try to go back out with Eb's group?" she asked.

Her tone told him things she wouldn't. He smiled gently. "No. Other peoples' wars should be left to their citizens."

"Good for you." She smiled. It hadn't occurred to her that he might want to live where he worked, and he wasn't going to burst any bubbles. Not yet. When he was ready to leave the rented house and move into the apartment he'd already put down a deposit on—then, he'd tell her.

He was able to get around very well. Amelia was ready to sign up for her college classes and get on with her future. She was reluctant, of course, because it was going to take her right out of Cal's future. She had to work harder by the day to hide her growing love for him. He didn't want it. He'd even made vague references to not wanting to be tied down for a long time yet.

So, she told herself, she'd go along and hope that he'd keep in touch with her and her grandfather. It wasn't hopeless. There was always hope.

Life, at the moment, was going along at a nice, easy pace. Which meant, of course, that disaster was hiding around the corner.

One morning, two days before her grandfather's doctor appointment, he complained of heartburn at the breakfast table. While she was getting the baking soda he'd asked for, he keeled over out of his chair and hit the floor, stone dead.

It was amazing, she thought, how numb and cold you felt when a crisis happened to you. It was like going on autopilot. She phoned 911, thought about the process she'd need to go through—everything from the clothes she'd need to take to the funeral home, to arranging the funeral, to phoning her great-aunt, seeing a lawyer about probate, even checking the status of the house's equity. She thought about all that while she sat on the floor beside her still grandfather and talked to him, telling him how much she loved him, how much he'd meant to her, how she was going to miss him.

She choked up and the tears came about the time the ambulance arrived. They examined him, started CPR, tried the paddles. Then, after a long and futile effort, they loaded him up in the ambulance, and called in for orders. Amelia told them she'd follow them to the hospital. They just looked at her with pity. They all knew the end of this tragedy.

"I know," she told them, and managed a smile. "I'll call the funeral home."

The female EMT just nodded and smiled at her before the door closed.

Cal's car was gone. Now that he could drive again, he often took off just to look around. He said he needed to get his mind off things.

She managed to get the truck cranked and drove to the hospital. They told her, of course, what had happened. It was a massive heart attack. If her grandfather had been in a room in the hospital, they couldn't have saved him. She thanked the EMT for trying—because they were getting ready to go on another call when she passed them on the way in—and the EMT hugged her.

"I lost my dad last year," she told Amelia. "I know how it is."

"Thanks," she whispered, and managed a smile.

That night she'd already phoned the lawyer's office for an appointment and called her great-aunt with the news and been told that she'd be down the following afternoon to help. *Oh, joy,* she thought, *I'll never escape her.*

She'd be pressed to go home with her great-aunt, she knew that already. The house had been reverse-mortgaged, but unknown to her, her grandfather had sold it months ago to keep finances going. Worse, his bank accounts were almost empty. She cursed herself for not realizing how things were, and not getting a job after her graduation from community college.

She wouldn't be able to afford the rest of her education now, not unless she inherited a fortune—fat chance—or was lucky enough to have people at admissions overlook her dismal SAT scores. She knew the material, but tests shook her. She never did well on them.

So here she sat at the table, too sick at heart to cook, with no money, no home and, worst of all, no Granddaddy to tell her, "Sugar, it's going to be all right."

The thought just dissolved her in tears.

While she was crying her eyes out, she didn't hear the front door open. She felt a pair of strong arms pull her out of the chair and hold her close, rocking her while she cried.

"I only just heard. I'm sorry I wasn't here," he said tightly. "The one time you really needed me, and I let you down."

"It's all right," she said, swallowing grief. "I got everything done. I have to take Granddaddy's clothes over to the funeral home, but I'll do that tomorrow."

"Have you eaten anything?"

"I can't," she said in a whisper. She drew in a breath. "My great-aunt's coming down tomorrow from Victoria. I wish she was here now…!"

"You don't want to be alone."

"Isn't it silly? I don't believe in ghosts, and I know Granddaddy would never hurt me. It's just..."

"I know. It's that there might be ghosts."

She nodded and nuzzled her cheek against his warm strength.

"I'll stay with you tonight."

She looked up.

"Nobody will know," he teased. "The lights are still on in my house and they're on an automatic timer. My car's in the driveway. Unless you're expecting company at this hour, it will be our secret."

"Nobody's coming. They'll come tomorrow with food. The church always does that when somebody dies."

He scowled. "They bring food?"

"Yes. Everybody brings something, even if it's just biscuits or a vegetable dish or fruit or a roast." She smiled. "It's for the family, so everybody can eat without having to cook."

"What a nice custom."

"It is."

"How about digging me out a pair of your granddad's sweatpants for the night? We were the same build. And I know he wouldn't mind," he added gently.

She smiled. "No, he wouldn't. He was fond of you."

"I was fond of him. He got me through a rough patch of my own."

"He said it helped him, too." She pulled back reluctantly. "I'll find you something." She paused. "Thanks, Cal."

He shrugged. "Small town, big family," he said gently.

She smiled.

It was comforting, having Cal in Granddaddy's bedroom next door. She thought she'd sleep without any effort. She couldn't. She worried about the future. She cried silently at her loss. She tossed and turned, and still the tears came.

The door opened and closed. Cal eased into bed beside her and pulled her against his bare chest. "I thought it would be like this," he said quietly. "I couldn't sleep, the night after...well, before I got shot."

She pressed close, aware that her thin cotton gown was letting her feel far too much of his warm, hair-roughened muscular chest. It made her feel shivery all over, and it wasn't with fear. She caught her breath.

He heard that. He felt something, too—the sudden hardness of her nipples against him, even through the cloth. His big, warm hands spread on her back and became caressing.

He had to keep his head. He told himself that while he felt all of him go rigid with the most intense desire he'd ever felt in his life. She was innocent. She was a virgin. He'd come in to comfort her, not to seduce her.

But he'd wanted her for, oh, so long, and here she was, warm and tender and clinging, and he was only human.

She felt him turn her, felt his weight on her. She was going to protest until his mouth gently covered hers and explored it in a slow, expert manner that made her into a limp cloth. His hands smoothed away the gown, and it was wonderful, the feel of them on her bare skin. She caught her breath as they moved slowly from her silken back onto her rib cage, with just his thumbs smoothing over the underside of her breasts.

She'd never done anything intimate with a man. She had no experience at all that would help her save herself. The feelings were too new, too explosively passionate. She hadn't known that she was passionate until she felt his leg easing between both of hers, and his mouth deepening the kisses until they were invasive and hungry and overpowering.

It had been cool in her bedroom, but now it was hot. She moved under him, her leg sliding over his, her mouth answering the passion she felt in his. Her short nails dug into his back as his mouth shifted down onto her breasts and smoothed over them, causing sensations that arched her back and brought helpless moans out of her throat.

After that, it was impossible for him to stop. It had been a long time between women, and Amelia was the most delicious morsel he'd ever tasted. She was butter and cream, exquisite.

He ate her like candy, from head to foot and back again. By the time she finally felt his body against hers without the intrusion of fabric, she was his willing partner. She moved with him, lifted for him, clung and arched and held him even when the flash of pain stiffened her against him.

She recalled vaguely that he'd asked if she was okay, if she wanted him to stop, and she'd put her mouth on his and lifted again and again to the slow, hard thrust of him in a nonverbal answer.

It was a feast of passion. They went from one position to another, all over the bed, almost onto the floor, clinging to each other, drowning in kisses, feeling ecstasy build until it exploded in both of them, and they cried out together as the sweet, sweet anguish of fulfillment left them shuddering in each other's arms.

For lazy minutes they lay together, gently touching, without recriminations, without regrets. Until inevitably, he turned to her and kissed her again. And she turned into his body and welcomed him as if it was the first time, all over again. Until they, finally, slept.

She was under the covers, back in her gown, when the door opened, and Cal came in with a cup of coffee.

"I can only cook snake, at the moment," he said gently.

He sat down beside her, putting the cup on the bedside table. He brushed the long, soft blond hair back from her face and just stared at her.

She stared back, robbed of words. It had been the sweetest experience of her life, although she was very uncomfortable in unmentionable places, and too shy to say so.

"I want you to promise me something," he said quietly.

"Okay."

"I want you to go to the pharmacy and get the morning-after pill," he said. "I was reckless, and I'm sorry. It's been a long time, and I wasn't prepared."

"I can do that," she said, trying to sound sophisticated.

He drew in a sigh as he looked at her. She was beautiful, he thought, without makeup, without artifice, and it wasn't purely physical beauty. She was unique in his whole life. He smiled gently.

"I'm not ready for undoable things," he began.

She reached up and put her fingers softly against his mouth. "I know all that. It's okay."

It wasn't, but she was a good actress.

He looked relieved. "All right, then. I'm going to go home and start getting things together..."

"Together?" She felt the shock all the way to her feet.

He grimaced. "I wasn't going to tell you yet. I'm sorry, it slipped out." He took a breath. "I'm signing back on with San Antonio PD. They have an opening. I put a deposit on an apartment there. I'm moving to the city. I'm sorry, Amelia. I wasn't trying to hide it. I just thought..."

She could see what he'd thought. It was all over his face. She had a crush on him, and he didn't want to hurt her. He still didn't. But he wasn't a forever-after man, and he wasn't ready to settle down.

"It's all right," she said. "You'll be okay. And San Antonio is a nice city."

He raised an eyebrow. "It's nice if you don't do police work there," he replied.

She shrugged.

He frowned. "I didn't mean for this to happen," he said, struggling for the right words. In fact, he was confused and uncertain, and trying to understand why. He felt guilt as well, because she'd been innocent, and he'd taken something that she'd most likely saved for marriage—if women even did that sort of thing these days.

"It takes two people to make mistakes like this one," she said simply and didn't notice the flicker in his eyes. "No worries. I'll take care of everything."

The words hurt. He wasn't sure why. He got to his feet. "If you ever need me," he began.

"Thanks," she said. "But I'm moving, too. The house was only Granddaddy's for his lifetime. It goes to a Realtor now. I'll probably stay with my great-aunt until I get signed up for college."

"That's right. Your major is going to be chemistry, right?"

"Yes." It was a lie. She couldn't afford college. There were grants, of course. She'd have to start late or wait until spring. But that wasn't his problem.

"Well, thank you for taking care of me, when I needed it." He drew in a breath. "I've got a big bankroll..."

"If you offer me money, I'll hit you," she said, and her dark eyes flashed.

"I wasn't going to. Not the way you mean. But if you need help with college..."

"That's nice of you. But I have scholarships," she lied, and smiled.

"Oh. Well." He drew in another breath. "You take care of yourself. I'll see you at the funeral."

"Okay."

He paused at the door, his back to her. “I had good intentions, Amelia. I really did.”

“I know that.”

He paused again, half turned. Then went out and closed the door. She waited until she heard the front door close before the tears fell.

Her great-aunt arrived in great glory the next afternoon. By then, Amelia had washed the bed linen and her gown. She wished it was as easy to wash away the shame. She’d meant to go to the pharmacy. In fact, she did go. Old Mrs. Smith was at the counter, and she just couldn’t work up enough nerve to ask her grandmother’s best friend for a morning-after pill.

So she went home and the truck wouldn’t crank, so she couldn’t drive to San Antonio to get one, either. She called the local shop and had them take it in, only to be told it would be a couple of days at least before they could even get to it, but the mechanic thought she’d blown up the engine—there was an oil leak that she hadn’t discovered, and the oil pan was empty. He said gently that it would be cheaper to buy another vehicle than to fix it. She said she’d think about it.

Then her great-aunt walked in, and there was no more time to try and do anything about her reckless night. She’d worry about it when she had time, although she didn’t think it was the right time for anything to happen. She hoped it wouldn’t. Even if it did, she could never tell a man who didn’t want her something like that. She had too much pride. She’d messed up her life royally, but it had been because she loved him so much that she couldn’t help herself.

The funeral was well attended. The house was full of food, which she’d invited friends in to help them eat. Her great-aunt, not the most social of people, was touched by the kindness, and by the friendly people who found her interesting. She didn't dress rich, so they took her for a relative in bad financial shape, like Amelia. It made her beam, to find out that people could like her when they thought she was poor. It amused Amelia, who saw a whole new side of her rambunctious relative.

Cal did come to the funeral, but he had a woman with him. Amelia recognized her at once. It was the woman who didn't like sick people, who'd come looking for Cal that one time.

It made her sick to her stomach to see how quickly he'd tossed her aside for the city woman. But she put on a good show. She greeted them after the graveside service and introduced her great-aunt and her plans to move to Victoria. Edie, condescending until she saw the great-aunt's chauffeured limousine, was suddenly all smiles and charm when Amelia finished hugging friends and joined the older woman at the car.

"All the best, Amelia," Cal said, forcing a smile.

She forced one, too. "I wish the same for you...both," she said, including Edie. She avoided his eyes as she slid into the limousine just ahead of her great-aunt.

Cal was feeling more guilt than he'd expected. Amelia had been closer to him than anyone in his whole life. He'd seduced her and then ignored her, and now he'd paraded Edie in front of her. He didn't know why. He hadn't meant to hurt her so much, and at such a time. He knew she loved him. It was blatant.

He also knew that he was a bad risk. Maybe it was best to make her regret what they'd done during that long, sweet night, so that she could move on. He just hadn't known that it would hurt so much.

Chapter Eleven

Probate was a little easier because in his will, Amelia's grandfather had left what little there was to Amelia. It was a long-standing will, which he'd never changed. It was just as well, because there was very little that anyone could inherit. It did, however, give Amelia a break from having to deal with the legal aspects. Her great-aunt had her own fine attorney and he handled everything.

Amelia moved in with Valeria in Victoria, although it was a wrench to leave Jacobsville where she was born. She found a job as secretary to an attorney, through her great-aunt's attorney, which made life a little easier. It didn't pay a lot, but it allowed her to pay rent—which she insisted on doing—and buy a few new pieces of clothing.

She forced herself not to think about Cal. She didn't know anybody who had ties to him, and that helped a lot. Absence, she thought, might just do the trick. It was a lie. She thought about him all the time, missed him, relived that night over and over in her thoughts. She wasn't going to be able to stop loving him. But at least she wouldn't have Edie rubbed in her face over here with her great-aunt.

Life went on, in a dull, everyday way. Amelia went to work, came home, cooked, watched the news with Valeria and went to bed.

Valeria couldn't understand why her great-niece went to bed with the chickens, and said so.

"I'm just tired," Amelia replied with a smile. "I think it's aftereffects of losing Granddaddy."

Valeria sighed. "I know, child. I miss him, too. Except for you, he was the last family I had."

"What was he like, when he was young?"

She shook her head. "The black sheep of the family! Honestly, he embarrassed Mama so much that she threatened to give him away. You know, family names are handed down for generations. Black marks are handed down with them. So far, there's never been a blight on ours. It's quite an accomplishment, in this day and time." She shook her finger at Amelia. "You make sure you never disgrace us, either, young lady. That's an order."

Amelia just grinned and said, "Yes, ma'am."

But it grew harder and harder to do much of anything when she got off work, and she was feeling nauseous. Her clothes were growing too small, and it wasn't because she turned the dryer heat up too high. Her breasts and her waistline were expanding.

With something like panic, she bought a home pregnancy kit after she got off work the next Friday and took it home, sneaking it into the bathroom. She could tuck the used kit in the tote she carried to work and dispose of it someplace Valeria wouldn't see it.

But all her plans flew away when she actually used the kit. It was positive. She was pregnant.

She sat down on the commode lid and felt the shock all the way to her feet. She had no contact with Cal, who'd already said he didn't want ties. She had a job, but she lived in a smallish city with a reputation-conscious elderly woman who would never adjust to a pregnant out-of-wedlock great-niece. So what did she do now?

Dazed, she dropped the kit into the trash can without thinking and went to her room and sat on the bed. Panic would surely set in soon. She had to figure out what to do next.

Not that she had any intention of getting rid of her child. She could move back east or west, someplace where Cal would never know she was still alive. He'd think she'd used the morning-after pill, so he had no need to check on her anyway. She could go away, invent a fictional husband...

She looked up to find her great-aunt in the doorway, holding the box and the used pregnancy test in her hands.

"You little slut!" she hissed.

Amelia got off the bed. "It's okay. I'm going to move out. Nobody will know. I can go back east..."

"Disgraceful! It was that mercenary who lived across the street, wasn't it? Oh, yes, my brother told me all about how close you were. He did this and just left you?"

"It's not like that," Amelia began.

"You tramp! You pack your things and get out of my house right now!" she almost screamed at the younger woman.

There were many replies that Amelia could have used, but none of them would have worked. "Okay," she said softly, because her volatile relative was about to lose control. "I'll just go downstairs and get my suitcase out of the closet," she added, and walked toward the staircase.

"Of all the evil, despicable things women do to themselves these days, they're no better than...!"

Amelia wasn't listening. She got to the staircase and the first step.

"How could you, Amelia?" Valeria wailed. "How could you do this!"

"Aunt Valeria," she began.

"You…traitor!"

In a fever of rage, Valeria reached out and pushed her, violently.

Her horrified face was the last thing Amelia saw. The last thing she heard was, "No! Oh, no, I didn't mean it!"

She came to in the hospital with a concussion and she'd lost the baby. The doctor, an older man, was apparently her great-aunt's physician.

"Valeria is very sorry," he said at her bedside. "She has these rages. You may not know that she's diabetic and she cheats on her diet with candy and sweets. It's landed her in the hospital twice. I know," he added gently, "it doesn't excuse what she's done to you. But it explains it."

"I won't go back there," Amelia said solemnly. "And I won't see her." She looked at the doctor with sad brown eyes. "I wanted my baby. I loved his father, so much."

The doctor winced. "I am truly sorry. Is there any way I can help?"

"If someone would go to my great-aunt's house and pack my things," she said, "I'd be much obliged. I had my cell phone in my pocket…"

He opened the drawer beside her bed, took it out and handed it to her. "Good thing you have a charging case," he added.

She turned the charge on. "It is. I'll call my employer and explain. Or sort of explain. God knows, I wouldn't want to embarrass my snow-white aunt for any reason," she added bitterly.

He didn't answer that. "I'll ask one of the aides to do that for you after she gets off work. She can bring your stuff in with her tomorrow."

"Thanks very much," she said.

"It's little enough to do. And I am sorry."

Her bags were packed and brought to her hospital room, along with her notebook computer.

Valeria, still in the heat of anger after having been up all night, and hearing from her physician that Amelia had lost the baby, remembered hearing that Cal had gone back to work for the police in San Antonio. It was his fault, all of this. Her great-niece would never speak to her again, all because of him. He'd ruined the girl, dirtied her reputation. Valeria had regrettably lost her temper and done something unforgiveable. The guilt about the baby ate at her until she realized that it was all Cal's fault. None of this would have happened if he hadn't seduced her innocent great-niece. Then he'd just walked away, with no consequences, leaving the girl to take care of herself. Well, he wasn't getting away with it, either! She tracked him down.

He answered the phone, puzzled because only a handful of people knew him well enough to call him.

"I'm Amelia's great-aunt, Valeria," she introduced herself with sugary sweetness.

"Amelia!" He groaned. "How is she? Is she okay? I was going to call her last night and check on her. I should have done it sooner, but things have been hectic around here..."

"That's why I phoned. To tell you how she is. I just wanted to tell you not to worry about the baby," she said in a tone dripping with sarcasm. "Amelia went to a clinic yesterday, and had the baby removed. So you're all set now, aren't you? You can go on your merry way with no consequences whatsoever and seduce someone else's innocent relative!"

And she hung up.

Cal just sat for a moment, shocked out of his mind. He'd assumed that Amelia had taken the morning-after pill, so he hadn't been concerned. He'd missed her terribly, but he'd been dealing with the aftermath of Ngawa, and his mind had been on much more horrible things than poor Amelia and how she'd managed after her grandfather died. It shamed him that he'd just walked away, without telling her how he really felt. Not that he'd realized how he felt, until very recent days. He'd known where Amelia was, and he had every intention of getting her back into his life. Until right now, when he knew how little emotion she felt for him. She hadn't bothered to tell him about their child. She didn't want it. The thought tortured him. He thought she loved him. It was the one certainty in his miserable life. Had she thought he wouldn't want the baby? That he'd cut her out of his life? Or had she just never loved him in the first place?

He still had Amelia's phone number. He tried to call her, but the call went to her voice mail. Since she'd never set it up, she never got it. She didn't recognize the number in her missed-call file and assumed it was a telemarketer and erased it.

That night a very drunk Cal showed up at Edie's apartment. She was feeling good, high as a kite, and delighted to see him—in any condition. "Why, come in! You look like something the dog brought in, darling," she laughed.

"She got rid of it."

"Excuse me?"

He sat down heavily, his head in his hands. "I lost my head. I swear to God I thought she got the damned morning-after pill, but she didn't. She was pregnant. She went to a damned clinic!"

"Well, sweetheart, if you wanted her to take the pill, why is getting rid of the child so shocking? It's the same thing."

"It's not." His dark eyes were blazing. "She should have told me. She should have given me a choice!"

"Her body, her choice," she replied.

"Fathers have no rights?" he asked belligerently.

"Boy, are you high," she murmured. "Listen, most women don't want kids. They ruin your figure and your life, and you never look the same. I never wanted any. I still don't."

He'd thought of nothing but Amelia for days. Missed her. Ached to see her. Guilt had kept him away. He'd just walked away from her, without a word of explanation. Now he was in a fog of misery. He'd meant to go after her, now that he'd finally reconciled himself with the anguish of Ngawa. In fact, he'd gone to a jewelry store and bought a set of rings. Amber diamonds, unique, like Amelia with her blond hair and dark, dark eyes. He'd been thinking about marriage. He knew she loved him. And he was only just discovering the anguish of a life that she wasn't part of. He'd had plans, to go and see her in Victoria. As he'd told her aunt, he'd meant to phone her that night and try to explain. And now, this. Proof that she wanted nothing more to do with him. If she'd loved him, she'd have wanted the child.

"She betrayed me," he said furiously. "She sold me down the river!"

"That's right," she agreed. "She truly did. So," she added, cocking her head, "why don't we pay her back? Let's get married. That will show her how little she means to you!"

"Married." He blinked. He was having trouble concentrating.

"Sure! Let's go get a marriage license!"

"I'm drunk."

"No problem. I have strong coffee. I'll fix you right up."

So three days later, he married Edie in the office of the justice of the peace. And immediately afterward, he sent Amelia a text message, having remembered belatedly that she hadn't ever set up voice mail on her phone. It was one of the things he'd promised to help her do.

But he tried calling again, and this time he got through.

"You miserable excuse for a human being!" he raged the minute he heard her voice. "You didn't want the baby, so you just got rid of it? I had no right to know, to be told what you planned to do?"

"Cal, please listen…"

"To what, more lies? Damn you! Damn you to hell! I thought you were different, that you valued life, that you cared about me, that you…" He broke off. He couldn't even say the word. "Well, great, you're free now, no need to disturb your perfect life with any complications, right?"

"It's not…!" she tried again, horrified at what he was thinking.

"I never wanted you for keeps in the first place," he said in an icy tone. "One night was more than enough. Edie and I just got married, by the way, so thanks for helping us out by making sure I wouldn't be hit with child support. And you have a terrific life, Amelia. Just don't ever get in touch with me again. I hope you burn in hell!"

He hung up, wishing he could have slammed the receiver down. He was still cursing ten minutes later, and he'd made inroads into a new bottle of rum he found in

Edie's liquor cabinet. By the time she came back from her shopping trip, he was passed out on the sofa.

Amelia had answered her cell phone just as they were getting things ready to release her from the hospital. She just stared at her phone blindly. How had he known about the baby? Maybe one of the hospital staff knew him and had phoned him. He must be in and out of the hospital a lot in his line of work, talking to victims of violent crime. But this was Houston, not San Antonio, so how would he have known?

The furious tirade had broken her heart. She'd still loved him, despite everything. But his harsh condemnation ended that part of her life very neatly. Cal thought she'd deliberately gotten rid of the baby. He wanted nothing to do with her. He was married. He wished Amelia in hell. And her only crime had been to love him.

Now she had no ties, nothing to hold her to Texas or Jacobsville, even less to her great-aunt. With the small amount of money she had left, she hired a car to take her down to Jacobsville and wait for her while she spoke to Eb Scott. On the off chance, she had her belongings with her.

She could lie to the world, but not to Eb. She told him the whole miserable story, from the beginning to the painful end.

"He didn't seem like that kind of man," Eb said when she finished. "But then, we never really know people, do we?"

She smiled sadly. "I guess not." She cocked her head. "I have no place to go. I lost my job because I couldn't contact them for two days to tell them where I was—and I wouldn't have dared tell them why I was in the hospital, or my great-aunt would have murdered me. You said once that you'd give me a job if I asked. I'm asking."

He studied her. He'd never trained a female operative, but she was good material to work with. She was smart, and a dead shot—something he'd tease her about for years, that he trained her to shoot—and she could follow instructions.

"Okay," he said. "But you're on trial temporarily. That work? Either one of us isn't satisfied at the end of a month, we'll make decisions."

She smiled. "Okay. Thanks. And you won't mention any of this to Cal, if you ever see him? Promise me, please."

"Easy promise," he replied. "And his loss."

"He's married."

"What?" Eb asked, shocked.

"This fancy woman he knows in the city. I guess she was more his style than I was. He called me…" She didn't add what else he'd said.

"Did you answer him?"

"Blocked his number." She smiled sadly.

He chuckled. "Nice move. Okay." He got up from the table. "Let's get you settled."

She hadn't told him about the rest of the furious one-sided conversation, that Cal hated her guts and accused her of getting rid of her child. She still wondered how Cal knew.

There was one attempt by her great-aunt, in the years that followed, to contact her, to apologize.

She didn't answer the text. In fact, she blocked Great-Aunt Valeria's number. She could forgive an old woman who had a dangerous medical condition. But wanting to be around her was another thing altogether. It was too much a reminder of the anguish.

She could have gone back to college and studied chemistry, but learning the skills of demolition from a real-life expert—Cord Romero—was so much better than sitting at a desk. She was a good student.

And not only in demolition. Time after time she won competitions on the firing range.

"I taught her everything she knows," Eb would lie glibly.

Everybody laughed. They knew better.

She learned all the dark skills of a mercenary, and learned them well. Within months, Eb was sending her on missions. He was careful to exclude her from anything especially dangerous, without her knowledge. He didn't want her death on his hands. But she made him proud.

There was only one slip, although it was a bad one. She set the time just a few seconds off on an explosive device, and a man died. She took the heat for it from his friends, one of whom later went to work briefly as a foreman for one of her clients. She never denied her part in the man's death. She went to his funeral and let his relatives get all the anguish out of their systems. She knew how they felt. Her lost baby was never far from her thoughts. But at the end of the funeral, she was forgiven, because that was how Texans lived their faith. Without forgiveness, faith was a poor thing.

Ty Harding showed up once in Wyoming when she was working as a bodyguard for Wolf Patterson's future wife. She was polite but cool to him. She wanted no more involvement with men. She listened to her comrades talk about women they'd been involved with, because they treated her as just one of the guys, and she learned how few of them ever really cared about a woman they took out. It was a painful lesson, but she learned it well.

She became, in her turn, a person of faith, because it was all she had to hold on to in some of the desperate situations her work took her to.

The men teased her about it, but they stopped using profanity and obscenity around her, and talking about their conquests. They saved that for bar crawling, something in which Amelia never indulged.

The years passed slowly. She heard about Cal from time to time from people who didn't know about her involvement with him. He was now a captain in the San Antonio Police Department. Someone mentioned that strings had to have been pulled because that was a meteoric rise. She knew better. Cal was just conscientious and careful, and compassionate. Well, he had compassion on the job. None for the mother of his lost child.

His wife had died, she heard. It didn't interest her. That was the past. She lived from day to day, mission to mission. Life had made her tough as nails.

Or so she thought.

Until one Friday evening she went into Fernando's in San Antonio when she was between missions to get takeout. And she walked right into Cal Hollister.

She gave him a look that would have fried bread and went straight out the front door and hailed a taxi. She didn't even look his way as the car pulled out into traffic.

A day later, she found him behind her as she exited her apartment and started down the street to the restaurant where she was to meet a clandestine contact for Eb.

She whirled and glared at him from eyes like hot flames. "What do you want?" she asked icily.

"I want to talk to you," he said shortly.

"What would you like to say that you didn't say six years ago just after your wedding?" she asked with venom.

He closed his eyes. "I was drunk when I married her."

"It takes three days to get a marriage license," she said sweetly. "Were you drunk for three days?"

His own dark eyes burned. "What if I was?"

"Not my problem," she said. "And I'm working, if you don't mind."

"Working? At what?"

She turned, pulling back her jacket to reveal the gun at her hip.

He looked shocked. "You're in police work?"

"I work for Eb Scott," she said quietly. "I'm one of his top operatives."

She could have sworn he lost two shades of color from his tanned face. "Operative...and he hired you?"

"He trained me." She gave him a cold look. "When I got out of the hospital, I had nowhere to go. I couldn't stay with my great-aunt and I lost my job. I went to see Eb and he hired me."

"Wait, what do you mean, when you got out of the hospital? I thought it was a clinic."

"A clinic?"

He was really glaring now. "The clinic where you had the baby, removed, I believe your great-aunt said when she called me?"

She looked at him with horror. Great-Aunt Valeria had done that to her, lied to Cal? "She called you," she said, as if in a fog.

"Yes, she called me, to make sure I knew that I didn't have anything to worry about..." He was hesitating because of the look on her face. "Hospital?" He was still trying to make sense of it.

She drew in a long breath. So now she knew why Valeria had tried to apologize. It wasn't enough to push her down the staircase. She'd ruined any hope that Cal might care about her. Not that he had. He'd married that woman, hadn't he?

She looked up at him with sad eyes. "Some things are

better just left in the past," she said. "I'm sorry about your wife. Someone told me, I don't even remember who, that she'd died."

He'd hated his wife. He stared at Amelia, idly wondering why she looked no older than she had when they were close. She hadn't aged. "What hospital?" he persisted.

She just smiled. "It was a long time ago. We're different people now. Strangers. And I'm working. Goodbye, Cal."

"Working on what?" he asked before she could turn away.

"Nothing that concerns you. A project of Eb's overseas."

His blood ran cold. "Overseas, where?" he asked curtly.

"Cal, this doesn't concern you. It's Eb's business. I'm not breaking any laws here. I even have a concealed-carry permit for the pistol, okay?"

He was still just staring at her. "You haven't aged," he said, almost in a daze.

She laughed shortly. "Thanks. But it's not true. Harding said just the other day that I was going gray."

"Harding? That guy who had the crush on you?" he asked.

She nodded. "He's working for Lassiter's detective agency again. He left it, but he went back. The money was too good. He works out of Houston, but he helps us out sometimes."

He hated the idea of Harding. He was still jealous of her, after all the long years in between, all the anguish.

"Why didn't you tell me?" he asked harshly.

She raised both eyebrows. "About what?"

"You know damned well about what!"

"When it would have mattered, you didn't want to know," she said simply. "I tried to get the pill, but my grandmother's best friend was at the pharmacy counter. I couldn't do it. Then the truck broke down so I couldn't get to San Antonio and then Great-Aunt Valeria came."

He saw the pattern, all too well. "You had my phone number."

"You walked away at my grandfather's funeral and never said another word to me."

Reminding him, subtly, that Edie had been with him. Another in a long line of mistakes he'd made along the way.

He shoved his hands into his pockets. "I was dealing with things I could barely face. My whole life was in flux. I made…bad decisions."

"You made the ones you needed to make," she said simply. "Edie was gorgeous," she recalled with a sad smile. "I'm just ordinary, but she would have drawn eyes everywhere. Isn't that what men want? A wife that makes other men envious?"

He was shocked speechless. She thought he'd thrown her over for Edie because she wasn't pretty enough for him. It was an absolute lie, and it made him even more ashamed, that he'd given her that impression.

"It was a great gesture, though, bringing her to the funeral. Making sure I couldn't say anything that might embarrass you."

"That wasn't why," he said heavily.

She looked at her watch. "I'm really late. Just chalk the whole thing up to misplaced lust and don't worry about it… Cal!" she exclaimed, because he had her by the shoulders and he looked devastated. Anguished.

"It wasn't," he bit off.

She laughed. It had a hollow sound. She drew back from his hands, and he let go. "I work with men. They talk, all about their conquests, how they talk a woman into doing what they want and how they get rid of her afterward. I've been educated. I know all the tricks."

He winced. "It wasn't like that."

She just sighed. "It was exactly like that. You said it yourself. You'd gone for a long time without a woman, and I was very obviously besotted."

"I never said that about you," he said curtly.

"Really? Edie did. She said you laughed about it, that you were both very grateful that I, how did she put it, removed the problem baby from the equation." She even smiled.

Edie had called her. He hadn't known. What in the world had she said? On the other hand, Amelia had gone to a clinic. A clinic!

"Women are treacherous," he said coldly.

"And men are weasels," she shot back. "I'm going."

She turned and walked off toward the restaurant.

"Will you stop threatening to pull a gun on me and listen to me?" he yelled, losing his temper.

She had her hand on her pistol without thinking. "I am not trying to shoot you!" she raged.

He was suddenly aware that two of his own officers were standing by a patrol car, along with a very pregnant Clancey Banks and her husband, along with a tall, Italian-looking man who held a pretty brunette in his arms. They were all suppressing laughter. Cal was never flustered or out of control. The gossips would feed on this for weeks, he thought irritably.

He cleared his throat. This wasn't going to be easy to explain. And, worse, the object of his hunt had escaped. He didn't even see which way she went.

The rest of the day was taken up with Clancey giving birth to her first child. Banks, a Texas Ranger and the proud father, was absolutely strutting. The baby was precious. He hated wishing it was his. He'd almost had one. Thanks to Amelia, that had never happened.

He got through the rest of the day and went home, to the Santa Gertrudis ranch he'd bought years ago with some of the proceeds of his brief mercenary career. His wife had hated the place, preferring to drink herself to death at her apartment in San Antonio. All those years married, and he'd never touched her. She threw Amelia up to him all the time. He didn't care. He hated Amelia for what she'd done.

But he couldn't get out of his mind what she'd said, about being in the hospital. Why would they put her in the hospital after she'd gone to the clinic? Had there been complications?

And what sort of mission was Eb sending her overseas on? He thought of two possible areas of interest in the news and his blood went cold.

He made a pot of coffee, sat down with a cup of strong black Colombian and called Eb Scott.

Chapter Twelve

"Well!" Eb exclaimed. "It's been an age since I've heard from you. How've you been?"

"Better," Cal said heavily. "Listen, I know it's none of my business. But where are you sending Amelia?"

There was a brief pause. "That's not your concern," he said quietly.

Eb was like himself, there were limits to how far you could go with him, even in conversation.

"She won't talk to me," Cal said.

"I'm not surprised."

"Did she tell you what she did six years ago?" Cal asked, irritated at the other man's tone.

"Before or after she got out of the hospital?" Eb asked.

"Why would they take her to the hospital to get rid of a baby?" he asked, all at sea.

Now there was a pregnant pause. "She didn't tell you?"

"I...didn't give her much of a chance to speak. I was

angry and hurt. I said a lot of things. She blocked my number so I couldn't call her again."

"Your wife did."

"I didn't know that, until Amelia told me, today. My wife and I didn't speak often. She was usually too high to notice whether I was around or not," he added bitterly.

"I see." Eb was stunned.

"Amelia said she'd been in the hospital. I thought there were clinics for that sort of thing."

"Her great-aunt pushed her down the staircase," Eb interrupted. "That was why she was in the hospital," Eb said. "That was what happened to the baby, too. Amelia isn't the sort of person who goes to a clinic. How can you say you know her, but you don't know that about her?" he added.

"Her great-aunt…what?"

"Pushed her down the staircase. She said Amelia had disgraced the family."

"Surely, that wouldn't have been enough to provoke such a response," Cal said, accustomed to such incidents from years of listening to tragedies in his job.

"It would if Amelia had refused to get rid of the child, Cal. I imagine that's why. And that's not all. She lost her job, her home, her baby. She had no money and no place to go. That's why she came to me."

Cal's eyes closed. He'd made assumptions. He'd been certain that Amelia didn't want his child. He hadn't checked on her after the passion they'd shared. He'd even taken Edie to the funeral as armor. He'd done every damned thing in the world to show Amelia how little he cared. And there she was, pregnant, her grandfather dead, no place to live except with her prejudiced great-aunt. Afterward, she lost the baby and Cal told her that he was married, that he blamed her, that she could go to hell…

Amelia, with the world shattered at her feet, so desperate that she signed on with a bunch of mercs and went to war because she had nothing left. Nothing. Nobody. Least of all, a man who cared about her. He felt the sting of moisture in his eyes.

"Then your wife called her, and she probably had a few things to say about how you felt, if you told her the story you thought was the truth." Eb added his own measure of salt to the wound.

"I didn't know that Edie had done that," he said on a heavy breath. "Even when she was sober, she was the kind of person who enjoyed rubbing salt in open wounds," Cal added bitterly.

"So Amelia lost everything and she had nothing left to lose. So she came to me and asked for work. I didn't have the heart to refuse her."

Cal's heart was breaking. After what he'd done to Amelia, it was no wonder that she wouldn't speak to him. He'd accused her with no evidence except a snarky phone call from her great-aunt, and he knew Valeria was a fanatic about the family name. Why hadn't he tried harder to talk to Amelia? Why had he hesitated? Because, to his shame, he'd believed Valeria. He was never going to get over the pain of doing that. He'd have to live with it for the rest of his life, along with the nightmares that never ceased.

"Cal?"

"What? Oh. Sorry. I was just…thinking. Eb, if you can, please don't send her someplace where she's likely to be killed. I have no right to interfere with her life, but I can't…" He stopped, just before his voice broke with emotion. He collected himself. "It's my fault. All of it. What happened. I don't want her to run away from me and into something she can't handle."

"You could go and talk to her."

"I followed her all over San Antonio, trying to do that. She listened to me and smiled and just kept walking."

"She's very bitter about what happened. I think your wife has a lot to answer for. And Amelia's great-aunt, as well."

"They were accessories. I was the devil in the mix. It's so funny, how you can go looking for something your whole life, only to realize that you had it under your nose, and you threw it away."

"Life's like that."

"Life sucks."

Eb chuckled. "Yes. Sometimes. You should get married and have kids."

"No chance of that. Not anymore. Take care of my girl, will you?"

"I've always done that. Come out and see us sometime. The facility's expanded. We're teaching all sorts of new stuff, including computer hacking. In fact, I think we have a couple of card-carrying Feds here checking us out undercover."

"I might do that one day. Thanks for the information. I won't mention where I got it."

"Good thing. She can still outshoot me."

"Take care."

"Sure. You, too."

After a few minutes, during which he relived every bitter word he'd said to Amelia, every stupid thing he'd done to her, Cal got up from the table, poured out his coffee, grabbed a tea glass and filled it to the brim with rum. He opened the refrigerator to look for ice. His cell phone dropped but he didn't see it. He closed the door and opened the freezer unit on top. He opened the ice tray and added one ice cube to his drink. Then he sat back down at the table.

This was a stupid thing to do, his brain told him. Shut up, said his aching heart.

* * *

Two days later, one of his officers came looking for him. Lt. Rick Marquez was a favorite of the captain's. It was Rick who usually got sent to talk him down when he drowned his problems. It had only been a couple of times. The last one had been bad. The captain had happened upon a bank robbery and stepped out of his car with his pistol drawn right into the path of one of the robbers pointing a loaded shotgun at him. He fired and threw the shotgun up. The criminal died. The captain stayed drunk for days.

Clancey Banks, who was the closest thing to a relative he had—he'd more or less adopted her little brother and her years ago when she'd been his secretary—got him to the phone. But he was totally incoherent except to say that he was sick of life.

Which spooked her, and she called his office and told them they'd better get somebody out to Cal's ranch, pronto. She would have gone, but the new baby had a cold and she wasn't leaving him.

Word got around, just in the department, that the captain was on a bender. Nobody was brave enough to wander out to his ranch and try to talk him down this time until Marquez volunteered.

It became obvious very soon that intervention was going to become a job. The front door of Cal's ranch house was unlocked. When nobody answered several knocks, Rick walked in. The captain was lying facedown on the living room floor. Snoring. Yep, he thought. It was going to be a job. If not a career.

Rick got the captain as far as the sofa—he was a big guy and dead weight. He left the unconscious man long enough to find a blanket in the bedroom that he brought to cover his superior with. Then he went into the kitchen and made coffee.

"I don't want any more of this!" Cal raged, red eyes blazing as he finished the third cup that Rick had almost forced down his throat.

"I don't blame you. What the hell kind of coffee is this, anyway?" he added, sniffing it.

"Vanilla. I think. The wrong kind. I bought it and thought I'd take it back and exchange it for Colombian, but I never did." He made a face. "It tastes like a pastry."

"I think it's supposed to."

The captain drew in a long breath and sat back on the sofa. It all came rushing into his head, now that he was sober—halfway at least. Amelia. The staircase. The baby. The concussion. Edie. The rushed marriage. The nightmares. It all conglomerated in his head like Jell-O in a fridge.

He bent over, with his hands on his knees propping up his throbbing head. "I was happier drunk," he muttered.

"Everybody is happier drunk, but it would be a terrible scandal if they had to fire you for it, sir," Rick pointed out.

Cal sighed. "Yeah."

Rick had no idea what had set the captain off, but other officers had mentioned seeing the captain following a blond woman around town. The woman wouldn't listen to him. There had to be a history there, but it was obviously something personal and Rick didn't like to pry.

"Is there anything I can do?" he asked finally, his tone concerned.

Cal took a deep breath. "Yes. Get me a priest."

Rick gaped at him. "Sir, suicide is a very bad way to handle personal problems…!"

He glared at his subordinate. "I don't want to commit suicide! I want to talk to Father Eduardo Perez. He's at the Catedral de Santa Maria. I think his number's on my cell phone. If I can find my cell phone…" he mumbled, still not quite sober.

"I'll look for it," Rick said, and got to his feet. "When did you see it last?"

"I was pouring a drink and looking for an ice cube," the older man mumbled.

Rick finally found the missing phone after searching through every drawer in the room. After the conventional places, he looked in the unconventional ones. The phone was in the refrigerator. He took it out. Fortunately, it warmed up quickly and there was a dial tone. He just shook his head.

He carried it back into the living room. Cal still hadn't stirred. "It was, uh, in the fridge?"

Cal looked up, deadpan. "Don't you keep yours in the fridge, Lieutenant?" he asked blandly. "Does a hell of a job keeping them from overheating."

Rick smothered a laugh.

Cal didn't. He chuckled out loud as he took it from Rick. "I went to get an ice cube for my drink. I looked in the fridge for it." He looked up at Rick. "No comments," he said firmly.

"Sir, I swear, I never meant to say a word," Rick assured him. "Where you keep your phone is nobody's business."

"Yeah? Well, I'd better not hear any gossip about it when I'm back in the office tomorrow."

"You won't, sir. I can guarantee it," Rick said with a carefully placid expression.

"Good enough. Go home, Marquez. I'm all right now." He hesitated. "And…thanks."

"No problem, sir. Glad to help."

Cal waited until Rick's car started up. Then he dialed. A deep voice answered. "Can you come over for a few minutes?" he asked. "I think I really need to talk to somebody."

There was a deep chuckle. "Ten minutes."

* * *

Father Eduardo was something of a legend in San Antonio. He lived and worked in a section of San Antonio that had belonged to the Little Devil Wolves gang—mostly teenagers, responsible for some of the bloodiest murders in the history of the city. When Father Eduardo had first become rector of the parish, seven heavily armed members of the gang decided to get rid of him.

The guns weren't enough to save them. After calling an ambulance for the most injured two, the priest went with the rest of them to the hospital and waited patiently while they were treated. Two of them converted on the spot. The rest left him strictly alone—especially when they discovered that he was best friends with the leader of the rival, and more deadly, gang, Los Serpientes. Over a period of months, the Little Devil Wolves had been prosecuted into oblivion, and good riddance. The Serpientes, while still deadly, were kindness itself to children and the elderly. So was Father Eduardo.

Eduardo had been with Cal and Eb and the others in the African conflict. All of them were scarred from the experience. When Cal was really down and tormented by memories, Eduardo was the man he called for help.

"This time it isn't Ngawa, is it, compadre?" Eduardo asked over yet more cups of the detested vanilla coffee.

Cal shook his head. "I was infatuated with a girl I knew in Jacobsville when I got home from Ngawa. Things happened. She lost her grandfather and her home and had to move in with a great-aunt in Victoria." He took a deep breath. "She was pregnant. Her great-aunt pushed her down a staircase. She lost the baby."

"I am truly sorry," Eduardo said. He scowled. "She wanted it?"

He nodded. He drew in a breath. "I was told that she

went to a clinic. Her great-aunt phoned me to say that. Then my late wife also called her to thank her for getting rid of an encumbrance." He looked up. "So helpful, both of them. I hated Amelia for what I thought she did. I called her and cussed her out, without giving her even a chance to explain. Then, a few days ago, Eb told me what really happened." He drew a breath and winced. "Amelia's great-aunt pushed her down the staircase. She lost the baby, got a concussion and was in the hospital. Lost her job. She'd already lost her grandfather." He shook his head. "And I just found out what Amelia has been doing for a living for the past few years. She's working for Eb Scott." He lowered his head and sipped coffee to hide the anguish he felt. "She won't even talk to me."

"I assume you said something to her all those years ago?" Eduardo probed.

He drew in a breath. "Some terrible things," he replied. "Plus, I got married at once, to show her how little I cared." He looked at Eduardo. "You know how that worked out. Living with Edie was hell on earth. Not that I didn't deserve that, and more, considering what I did to Amelia's life."

"So that is the past," Eduardo replied. "What about the future?"

He grimaced. "Eb's sending her on some mission overseas. He won't tell me what."

"I can only imagine where," Eduardo replied.

"Exactly." He looked up. "I can't live if she gets herself killed. She's all I've thought about for years. Even when I blamed her, when I thought she didn't want the baby, I couldn't stop caring." He looked away. "I detested my wife. I couldn't touch her."

Eduardo didn't reply. He'd once been married, before

he took the collar, and lost his wife and child in a horrible way. He'd never thought of having women since then.

"I remember what she was like."

"I was very drunk when I married her." He looked up. "I don't drink, usually."

"I know that, too."

He finished his coffee. "I don't know what to do. She won't listen."

"You could pick her up for jaywalking."

Cal gave him a speaking look.

"Flowers? Candy? A mariachi band?"

"She'd throw away the flowers, stomp on the candy and probably shoot the mariachis," Cal said gloomily.

"Then take her dancing at Fernando's," Eduardo said gently, smiling.

"Optimist."

"I believe in miracles. I see them every day."

"That's your business. You deal in miracles. I deal in the lowest common denominator of humanity, crime."

"If you never expect miracles, you never see them," Eduardo continued gently. "First, you must believe."

He met the priest's warm dark eyes. There was such kindness there, such compassion. He felt his doubts slowly melt. He smiled. "Okay," he said. "I'll try."

"And that is the first step," Eduardo replied. "Now, I have a question."

"Of course. What is it?"

"Where in the world did you buy this truly detestable coffee?" Eduardo asked, making a face at the coffee cup.

Amelia was sitting all alone in her apartment, sipping black coffee and waiting for Eb to send over a man with details of her new assignment. Phones could be hacked. It was better to do it in person.

Her mind kept going back six years. She'd been young and in love for the first, and last, time. And life had tortured her. Everything that could possibly go wrong in her life, had. She missed her grandfather terribly. Valeria was the only relative she had left. Despite the woman's apologies, Amelia wanted nothing to do with her. The loss of her child was a torment. Cal had thrown her away like a used napkin. But she hadn't been able to stop loving him, even then. She'd wanted her baby.

She sipped coffee and thought of the lonely, bitter years in front of her. If she caught a bullet on this assignment, who cared?

The knock at the door startled her. Finally, she thought, the messenger.

She opened the door. "No," she bit off. "He wouldn't have sent you…!"

Cal edged his way inside, gently but firmly, and closed the door behind him. "We have to talk. You know that."

She glared at him. "There's no need. We're not the same people we were six years ago. I don't look back. Ever."

"That was me, six years ago," he said. His black eyes searched her pale ones. "I threw you aside and walked away. I need you to understand why."

"We won't see each other again," she emphasized. "I'm not coming back after this assignment. Not to Texas."

He looked worn. "I smell coffee."

She hesitated. "All right. But I'm expecting someone."

His heart fell. Another man. Why hadn't he expected that? She was young and she had an allure that had nothing to do with physical assets. She was a nurturing person. They were rare in Cal's life.

He followed her into the kitchen. "Father Eduardo and I had to drink vanilla coffee. I bought the wrong kind and didn't return it."

She glanced at him. "Vanilla?"

He made a face. "Yes."

"I'd rather drink muddy water," she said simply. She poured him a cup of hot black coffee and handed it to him as he sat down at her kitchen table.

She warmed her own cup and sat down with him. It was going to be an ordeal, but maybe he was right. Maybe they had to talk it out before he could let go of the past.

"Six years ago," he began, "you wouldn't have been able to understand what I'm going to tell you." He leaned back on her sofa with his coffee. "In fact, I wouldn't have told you six years ago. You were so incredibly innocent. About men. About life."

She frowned. She didn't understand.

He saw that. He laughed hollowly. "Ngawa was a nightmare, even for the more experienced mercs." He took a sip of coffee. "We had this kid that we sort of adopted in our unit. We had plans to bring him to the states after the mission was through." He drew in a long breath, hating the image that popped in 3D, in full color, into his mind. "His name was Juba. One day we moved into an enemy position. There was a house. In the doorway, an explosive. Juba ran ahead of us to check it out, with his AK-47 shouldered. They shot the explosive while he was taking cover." He shivered. "Have you ever seen a man blown up, Amelia?" he asked quietly.

She hesitated. Nodded. She swallowed down the nausea. "I set a charge a few minutes too soon. A man died." Her eyes closed. "I've had to live with it, and with the survivors who were his friends. None of us can forget it."

He was shocked. He hadn't yet connected her expertise in demolition with her actual job for Eb. "You do demolition work for Eb," he said suddenly, and fear carved a cold place in his heart.

"Yes," she replied. Her eyes were cold as they met his. "I'm good at it now."

He sipped coffee. He had to talk her out of going overseas. He didn't know how. "Cy Parks sat with Juba in his arms and rocked him until he died," he continued quietly. "It was just the beginning of the horror. I saw things, participated in things, that I wish I could forget. Sometimes the memories get really bad, and I drink." He sat up, putting his empty cup on the coffee table. "Marquez, who works in my office, just came over to talk me down. This is the first time I've been completely sober in several days."

"The memories…" she began.

"I didn't know your great-aunt pushed you down a damned staircase," he said, his black eyes flashing. "I didn't know that Edie had called you."

The information sat on her like a hundred bricks. She just looked at him, her eyes wide.

"I stayed away from you after that night because I knew I wouldn't be able to stop if we were together again," he bit off. "It was why I took Edie to your grandfather's funeral. I wanted you all the time." He looked up at her. "Besides that, I was trying to deal with the aftermath of what happened to us in Ngawa, and I wasn't able to cope with it. I couldn't tell you about it because you wouldn't have understood. Not like you can now," he added.

She took a breath. "I've had my own feet in the fire," she said quietly. "I know what it's like. Well, sort of. Eb always has me behind the lines doing demo work."

God bless Eb, he thought fervently.

"So you can understand some of what I was going through. I was an emotional train wreck," he continued. "I had to deal with the memories, get back into the world. That meant going back to police work and moving to San Antonio. Edie was always around. I didn't encourage her.

My mind was on you most of the time, but guilt and mental anguish kept me away. I had no idea about the baby…" He bit off the rest and his eyes were on the carpet.

She felt his misery. It was a devastating blow, to realize that what she'd been hating him for was the result of outside interference from two hateful women.

"I thought that, because you stayed away, you didn't want anything else to do with me," she said quietly. "But I was going to keep my baby. I wanted him so much! I left the pregnancy kit in the bathroom, I was so shocked by the results, and Valeria found it. She insisted on a termination, but I told her I wouldn't do that. I told her I'd move out, I already even had a job…" She stopped. Her eyes closed on the memory. "She pushed me. I came to in the hospital. The concussion was the least of my sorrow."

"And then I called you and cussed you out, after all that." He stopped, fighting for control. He felt sick to his soul.

She saw the anguish in his face. It seemed so strange, to be sitting here with Cal after all they'd been through, to realize how much he still cared. He'd wanted the child. He'd wanted her. Only now could she understand what he'd been going through six years ago, the terror, the confusion, probably some guilt into the mix.

"At least you had someone to help you through all the trauma," she said.

"If you mean Edie," he said heavily, "her only purpose was to avenge you."

"Excuse me?"

"Rubbing salt into open wounds?" he replied, lifting his head. "She made my life hell. I couldn't touch her. She was physically repulsive to me, and she knew it, but only after she'd coaxed me in a drunken haze to marry her. After that, it was men and booze and drugs for the rest of her life. When she died, it was a relief for both of us. Hell on earth, Amelia," he added softly.

She gaped at him. "Couldn't...touch...her," she stammered.

"She wasn't you," he said simply. He reached into his pocket and pulled out a jeweler's box. He put it on the coffee table and opened it. It was a wedding set of diamond rings. Amber diamonds.

He stared at her. "I bought those six years ago," he said quietly. "Hid them in my travel kit. I was going back to get you. I'd planned to call you the day Valeria called me."

It was too much. Just too much. She started crying. Sobbing. If it hadn't been for Valeria...!

She felt arms around her, holding her, arms that were still familiar after all the years between.

"Don't cry," he whispered at her ear. "Don't. It's over. We found each other again."

Her arms tightened around his neck. "Damn her!" she sobbed. "And damn Edie!"

"And damn me, too, but we can't go back and change a thing. We can only go forward, Amelia." His hands were caressing on her back, slow and tender, like the voice at her temple. He drew in a long, shuddering breath. "I would give an arm to take back what I said to you, what I did. It was my fault, more than anyone's. I refused to listen. If I'd just kept my damned temper...!" He groaned out loud and held her closer. "I'm sorry, honey. I'm so...sorry!"

She felt a wetness at her throat where his face was buried. Tears stung her own eyes. Six long years of agony because of two miserable people who liked to cause trouble. "Me, too," she choked.

He just held her, rocking her, in a silence that finally calmed them both.

* * *

He lifted his head and searched her dark eyes with his. “We can’t go back,” he said sadly. “But we can go forward. We can start over. Just you and me, Amelia, the way we were meant to start over six years ago. And this time, there won’t be any interference.”

Her face nestled into his throat, and she snuggled close as he lifted her and sat back down with her in his lap. His arms tightened and he sighed with pure delight. He hadn’t expected this reaction from her. Not even in his dreams.

“I love you, Amelia,” he whispered huskily. “I think I loved you the first time I saw you. But I only knew it when it was too late.”

She nuzzled closer. “I loved you, too. It was why I would never have given up my baby.”

“I should have known that.”

She stilled. “How did you know, about how I lost the baby?”

“Eb told me.” He sighed. “I’ve been drunk for three days. Marquez came this morning and shoved that disgusting vanilla coffee into me to sober me up. I hated being sober. I relived what happened all over again. I was going to buy a new bottle of rum. But I thought maybe I could get you to listen to me if I just came over and stood at your door until you let me in.”

She laughed softly. “I didn’t mean to.”

He kissed her hair. “I know you didn’t. Father Eduardo told me just a few hours ago that miracles happen when you expect them. So I expected this one. I’ll have to phone him and tell him it worked.”

She lifted her head. “Father Eduardo? The priest who faced down seven armed attackers and sent them all to the emergency room, empty-handed?”

“The very one,” he said, smiling.

"He's something of a legend in San Antonio."

"He was a legend in Ngawa, as well."

She drew in a long breath and wiped her eyes on a paper towel from her pocket. He caught her hand and kissed it.

"We can get a license at city hall," he suggested. "I already have the rings. We can buy you a really pretty dress. Then we can have a honeymoon. Afterward we can go to Fernando's every Friday night and do the tango!"

She laughed. "I haven't danced in years."

"Dancing is something you never forget how to do. Along with something else that we did very well together," he said, bending to kiss her very gently. "But this time, we wait until after the wedding," he added firmly. His eyes searched hers. "That is, if you'll marry me."

She searched his eyes and saw the years of anguish, of hopeless, helpless love that she'd seen in her mirror for the same length of time.

"Take a chance on me," he said quietly. "Believe in miracles."

She took a long breath. He was absolutely gorgeous. The ice inside her that had kept her going for so long was slowly melting under the warmth of his hunger for her. And not just physical hunger. The love in his eyes was like brown velvet.

But he was tense, waiting. Hoping. Not pressuring. She saw all that, in a flash. Her own love had never wavered, even when she thought he hated her. It never would.

She smiled, finally, and wrinkled her nose at him. "Okay."

"Thank God," he ground out, and bent and kissed her, tentatively at first, and then with such hunger and passion that she moaned aloud.

A long time later, he lifted his head. He took deep breaths. "First, we get married," he said tightly. "We do it right, this time."

She smiled dreamily and reached up to kiss him softly. "Yes." She laid her head on his chest with a sigh.

"And you stop carrying a gun," he added in a teasing tone.

"I will if you will."

"I'm a law enforcement officer. I'm required to carry a gun," he said smugly.

She lifted her head and started to speak.

"Show me your concealed-carry permit," he challenged.

"It's in my wallet."

"Is it?" he purred. "You can't watch it every minute."

"I what?"

He gave her a blithe smile. "One of my officers ate the license of a man who verbally abused him during a traffic stop in town," he pointed out.

She began to see the light. "You wouldn't dare," she exclaimed, reading between the lines, her eyes like saucers.

"I can arrest people, too," he pointed out.

She gaped at him.

"I have handcuffs," he added.

He just stared at her. Until they both burst out laughing.

"You're going to be a lot of trouble," she said.

He nodded and smiled. "Count on it."

Chapter Thirteen

They were married in the Methodist Church in Jacobsville by Pastor Jake Blair, with a building full of friends of both bride and groom. Eb and his family were in the front row as Cal and Amelia said their vows.

There was a huge reception in the fellowship hall with, sadly, no riot, as lamented by Police Chief Cash Grier, who had warm memories of one when local DA Blake Kemp married his secretary, Violet. Liquor had been allowed, and the ensuing mayhem was remembered with humor by most of the participants. Grier, especially.

They honeymooned in Jamaica, in a hotel in Montego Bay. Their room opened onto the beach, where they took a midnight stroll before finally ending the day in the appropriate manner.

It was like six years ago. Amelia was shy at first, but Cal knew how to cope with that. A few kisses later, she was helping him get the fabric out of the way.

"I never forgot…how it felt," she whispered as his mouth lowered to her breasts.

"Neither did I," he groaned. "Not once. Oh, God, this is so…sweet!"

"Sweet," she moaned, holding on tight as she felt him move between her parted legs. "Sweet!"

He wanted to take ages with her, but it had been a long time between women. "I'm truly sorry," he began to apologize as his movements became insistent.

"You don't need to be sorry," she whispered back, shifting as their positions became suddenly intimate and hectic. "Just…hurry!" she said on a laugh and a groan, all at once.

She closed her eyes as the fever burned high and bright, almost incandescent as it brought waves of pleasure, each one taking them higher and higher, until finally, at the culmination, they both cried out at the intensity of fulfillment.

For a long time they stayed like that, just holding each other as the sound of the waves crashing on the shore became audible.

"Was it that sweet before?" he whispered huskily.

"I'm not sure." Her long leg slid against his. "Can we do it again and make sure it was?"

"With pleasure…!"

They stayed for a week, bringing home memories of moonlit nights and feverish passion interspersed with sightseeing and souvenirs.

The ranch house was laden with food the day they came home, courtesy of neighbors and friends.

Rick Marquez and his wife and daughters, and baby son, came to greet them, along with his mother, Barbara, who owned Barbara's Café, and her friend, the ex-mobster and now policeman Fred Baldwin.

"And if that's not enough, you just let me know," Barbara added, hugging them both before they left.

They surveyed the kitchen table with its huge platters of food.

"We can last until Christmas at least," Cal remarked.

"Maybe New Year's," she seconded.

They laughed and started putting away food.

The captain's new wife fascinated his officers. Every time she visited, she was whisked into the canteen to be quizzed about her former job.

A lot of the questions came from Clancey Banks, who had at one time been Cal's secretary and was still like a young sister to him. Clancey and Amelia got on famously. So did she and Clancey's baby brother, Tad.

Clancey had a new baby boy. She and her husband, Colter, were frequent visitors at Cal's ranch, which gave Amelia a chance to hold the baby. Cal did his share of that, too.

One afternoon, when the Banks had gone home, Amelia sat in Cal's lap on the porch in the rocking chair reminiscing about the baby.

"Babies are nice," he commented.

She smiled. "Yes, and holding Clancey's is good practice for you."

"It is?" he asked, his eyes on one of his prize Santa Gertrudis cattle grazing in the nearby pasture.

She held a plastic stick under his nose.

He looked at it. He looked at her, his eyebrows raised.

"It's the right color," she said mischievously.

"The right..." His brain clicked. One and one made two. "You're pregnant?" he exclaimed, so loudly that the cow raised her head and stared at him.

"Oh, yes, very pregnant," she said, grinning.

He got up with her in his arms, rocking her, fighting

tears. "Miracles," he whispered as he bent to kiss her hungrily. "Everyday miracles."

"Yes," she agreed and nuzzled close. "Love doesn't die. No matter how hard you hit it."

He chuckled. "Truly. But we aren't hitting it anymore."

"Never again." She reached her arms around his neck. "I hope you don't mind that I sometimes remember how much fun it was to blow up stuff before I did it for a living?"

"Not if you don't mind if I occasionally remember how much fun it was to dream about being a mercenary."

"The reality is less fulfilling than the anticipation," she agreed. "Except when it comes to having babies."

He grinned. "I agree wholeheartedly." He kissed her warmly. "I'll love you until I die. And then some."

She searched his black eyes. "And I'll love you until I die. And then some. Aren't we the two luckiest people in the whole world?"

He nodded. He kissed her. "And then some," he teased.

* * * * *

A Q&A with Diana Palmer

Who or what inspired you to write?
I was a working newspaper reporter when I sold my first book to a company called MacFadden Paperback Romances in New York. I wrote for a living at the time, but only with facts. Creating books is just a step forward from that, but one that I love!

Who are your favorite authors?
I read mostly factual books for research, including forensics, criminal investigation, stuff like that. When I read for pleasure it's either the Alien Vs. Predator books, graphic novels, and comics. My favorite historical author is Frank Yerby (I used to write him fan letters, which he actually answered!). I also love Brian Anderson's *Dog Eat Doug* comics (they're great!), Craig Johnson's Longmire novel series (awesome!), Harlequin Romances by Betty Neels (delicious light love stories with very happy endings), and

language books (currently I can speak Chinese, Japanese, Spanish, French, and Russian. I plan to try to learn English when I finish the others, lol).

Where do your story ideas come from?
I don't know, and that's the honest truth. I sit down at the computer and start typing and there are people! Sadly, sometimes there are people who don't want to follow my nice plot and go off on their own. Those are usually my best books.

What is your most treasured possession?
My late husband's skeet shooting medals. He went to competitions all over the US and he won a lot of them. My second favorite would be my 10k gold wedding band, which has been on my finger for over fifty years now. My third favorite possession is my grandfather's cane. He used to kill rattlesnakes with it. It's almost a hundred years old, and I still use it to help me get around. It gets buried with me. (Not planning to go just yet, however, I have too many books to finish!)

Do you have a favorite travel destination?
Yes. Japan. I went there in 2001 and toured Osaka, Kyoto and Tokyo. I was already in love with Japan. I don't think Jim and I missed a single movie that featured samurai. Our favorites starred Toshiro Mifune. The Harlequin people in Japan took such wonderful care of me, and my son Blayne and my best friend Ann, who went with me. I have never felt so treasured.

What is your favorite movie?
Alien vs Predator! Followed by the 2018 *Predator* movie. (There's also a terrific *Predator* movie from 2022, but I haven't watched it yet—saving it for a special occasion).

Honorable mention: *Captain Marvel*! I've watched it a dozen times and I never get tired of it. Plus, Jude Law is a dish!

When did you read your first Harlequin romance? Do you remember its title?
You bet I do! It was Margaret Way's *Red Cliffs of Malpara* (I hope I spelled it right; I have the book, but it's tucked in with about eight hundred other Harlequin titles and I don't have time to search for it). I wrote Margaret fan letters for years, and we were featured together in a double novel called *Husbands on Horseback*. Margaret has since passed away, and I miss hearing from her. She became a friend as well as my favorite romance author.

How did you meet your love?
I met James when I went to work for a local manufacturing company, keeping books for the warehouse. He was spreading cloth outside my office and he stopped by at lunchtime to talk to me and the other girls in the office. My mother dared me to invite him to supper, so I did. I served him unsalted macaroni and some other awful dish because I was so nervous. He was unbelievably handsome! We started dating on a Wednesday, got engaged two days later, and got married the following Monday. That was fifty years ago last October. I lost him in August of 2021 to Covid. The other part of me still lives here and writes books.

How did you celebrate when you sold your first book?
I was working in the newspaper office when I got the call. I said thank you, and went to our local drugstore and bought myself and my friend Ann a chicken salad sandwich with potato chips. I was too poor at the time to afford anything fancier, lol. Jim and I had about $2 a week left over after we paid bills. Those were hard times. Good, but hard.

Other than author, what job would you like to have?
Colonist on the first ship to Mars. Or pilot. Or medical officer. Anything that would get me there. I love Elon Musk and I still think Starship will get us to Mars. Maybe not in my lifetime, though. I'm 77 this year. However, my husband is already on the other side of this dark veil, and I would bet money that *he's* been to Mars! I look forward to sharing God's universe with him and my family, most of whom are already there except for my sister and son and my extended family. Jim's family is the most wonderful collection of people I've ever known. Mine isn't bad, either, including my reader family all over the world. Love you all.

USA TODAY bestselling author **Teri Wilson** writes heartwarming romance for Harlequin Special Edition. Three of Teri's books have been adapted into Hallmark Channel Original Movies, most notably *Unleashing Mr. Darcy*. She is also a recipient of the prestigious RITA® Award for excellence in romantic fiction and a recent inductee into the San Antonio Women's Hall of Fame.

Teri has a special fondness for cute dogs and pretty dresses, and she loves following the British royal family. Visit her at www.teriwilson.net.

Also by Teri Wilson

The Fortunes of Texas: Digging for Secrets

Fortune's Lone Star Twins

Harlequin Special Edition

Comfort Paws

Dog Days of Summer

Love, Unveiled

Her Man of Honor
Faking a Fairy Tale

Lovestruck, Vermont

Baby Lessons
Firehouse Christmas Baby
The Trouble with Picket Fences

Montana Mavericks: Six Brides for Six Brothers

The Maverick's Secret Baby

Visit her Author Profile page
at Harlequin.com for more titles!

DOG DAYS OF SUMMER

Teri Wilson

For our special friends at
Juniper Village Lincoln Heights and
Northwood Elementary School

xoxo Teri and Charm

Chapter One

So this was Texas.

Maple Leighton wobbled in her Kate Spade stilettos as she stood on a patch of gravel across the street from the Bluebonnet Pet Clinic and fought the urge to hotfoot it straight back to New York City. What was she even doing here?

You're here because you sold your soul to pay for veterinary school.

A doctor-of-veterinary-medicine degree from a top-rated university in Manhattan didn't come cheap, especially when it was accompanied by a board-certified specialty in veterinary cardiology. Maple's parents—who were both high-powered divorce attorneys at competing uptown law firms—had presented a rare, united front and refused to fund Maple's advanced degree unless she followed in their footsteps and enrolled in law school. Considering that her mom and dad were two of the most miserable humans she'd ever encountered, Maple would've rather died. Also, she loved animals. She loved them even more than she loathed the idea of law school. Case in point: Maple had never once heard of animals clawing each other's eyes out over visitation rights or who got to keep the good wedding china.

Especially dogs. Dogs were always faithful. Always loyal. And unlike people, dogs loved unconditionally.

Consequently, Maple had been all set to plunge herself into tens of thousands of dollars of student-loan debt to fulfill her dream of becoming a canine heart surgeon. But then, like a miracle, she'd been offered a full-ride grant from a tiny veterinary practice in Bluebonnet, Texas. Maple had never heard of the clinic. She'd never heard of Bluebonnet, either. A lifelong Manhattanite, she'd barely heard of Texas.

The only catch? Upon graduation, she'd have to work at the pet clinic for a term of twelve months before moving on to do whatever her little puppy-loving heart desired. That was it. No actual financial repayment required.

Accepting the grant had seemed like a no-brainer at the time. Now, it felt more like a prison sentence.

One year.

She inhaled a lungful of barbecue-scented air, which she assumed was coming from the silver, Airstream-style food truck parked on the town square—a *literal* square, just like the one in *Gilmore Girls*, complete with a gazebo right smack in its center. Although Bluebonnet's gazebo was in serious need of a paint job. And possibly a good scrubbing.

I can do anything for a year, right?

Maple didn't even *like* barbecue, but surely there were other things to eat around here. Everything was going to be fine.

She squared her shoulders, pulled her wheeled suitcase behind her and headed straight toward the pet clinic. The sooner she got this extended exercise in humiliation started, the sooner it would be over with.

Her new place of employment was located in an old house decorated with swirly gingerbread trim. It looked like a wedding cake. Cute, but definitely not the same vibe as the sleek glass-and-steel building that housed the prestigious veterinary cardiology practice where Maple was *supposed* to be working, on the Upper West Side.

She swung the door open, heaved her bag over the threshold and took a glance around. There wasn't a single person, dog, cat, or gerbil sitting in the waiting room. The seats lining the walls were all mismatched dining chairs, like the ones in Monica Geller's apartment on *Friends*, but somehow a lot less cute without the lilac walls and quirky knickknacks, and Joey Tribbiani shoveling lasagna into his mouth nearby. The celebrity gossip magazines littering the oversize coffee table in the center of the room were so old that Maple was certain the couple on the cover of one of them had been divorced for almost a year. Her mother had represented the wife in the high-profile split.

I turned down my dream job to come here. A knot lodged in Maple's throat. *Could this* be *any more of a disaster?*

"Howdy, there."

Maple glanced up with a start. A woman with gray corkscrew curls piled on her head and a pair of reading glasses hanging from a long pearl chain around her neck eyed Maple from behind the half door of the receptionist area.

"Can I help you, sweetheart?" the woman said, gaze snagging on Maple's shoes. A furrow formed in her brow, as if the sight of a patron in patent-leather stilettos was somehow more out of place than the woefully outdated copies of *People*.

Maple charged ahead, offering her hand for a shake. "I'm Dr. Maple Leighton."

A golden retriever's tawny head popped up on the other side of the half door, tongue lolling out of the side of its mouth.

"Down, Lady Bird," the woman said, and the dog reluctantly dropped back down to all fours. "Don't mind her. She thinks she's the welcome committee."

The golden panted and wagged her thick tail until it beat a happy rhythm against the reception desk on the other side of the counter. She gazed up at Maple with melting brown eyes. Her coat was a deep, rich gold, as shiny as a copper penny, with the feathering on her legs and underside of her body that goldens were so famous for.

Maple relaxed ever so slightly. She could do this. Dogs were dogs, everywhere.

"I'm June. What can I do for you, Maple?" the receptionist asked, smiling as benignly as if she'd never heard Maple's name before.

It threw Maple for a moment. She hadn't exactly expected a welcome parade, but she'd assumed the staff would at least be aware of her existence.

"Dr. Leighton," she corrected and pasted on a polite smile. "I'm here for my first day of work."

"I don't understand." June looked her up and down again, and the furrow in her brow deepened.

Lady Bird's gold head swiveled back and forth between them.

"Just one second." Maple held up a finger and then dug through the vast confines of her favorite leather tote—a novelty bag designed to look like the outside of a New York pizza parlor, complete with pigeons pecking at the sidewalk—for her cell phone. While June and Lady Bird cocked their heads in unison to study the purse, Maple scrolled quickly through her email app until she found the most recent communication from the grant committee.

"See?" She thrust the phone toward the older woman. The message was dated just over a week ago and, like every other bit of paperwork she'd received about her grant, it had been signed by Dr. Percy Walker, DVM. "Right here. Technically, my start date is tomorrow. But I'd love to start seeing patients right away."

What else was she going to do in this one-horse town?

June squinted at Maple's cell phone until she slid her reading glasses in place. Then her eyes went wide. "Oh, my."

This was getting weird. Then again, what wasn't? She'd been in Bluebonnet for all of ten minutes, and already Maple felt like she'd landed on a distant planet. A wave of homesickness washed over her in the form of a sudden craving for a street pretzel with extra mustard.

She sighed and slid her phone back into her bag. "Perhaps I should speak with Dr. Walker. Is he here?"

June went pale. "No, actually. I'm afraid Dr. Walker is...unavailable."

"What about the other veterinarian?" Maple asked, gaze shifting to the old-fashioned felt letter board hanging on the wall to her right. Two veterinarians were listed, names situated side by side—the familiar Dr. Percy Walker and someone named Dr. Grover Hayes. "Dr. Hayes? Is he here?"

"Grover?" June shook her head. "He's not in yet. He should be here right shortly, but he's already got a patient waiting in one of the exam rooms. And I really think you need to talk to—"

Maple cut her off. "Wait a minute. We've got a client and their pet just sitting in an exam room, and there's no one here to see them. How long have they been waiting?"

June glanced at an ancient-looking clock that hung next to the letter board.

"You know what. Never mind," Maple said. If June had to look at the clock, the patient had already been waiting too long. Besides, there was a vet in the building now. No need to extend the delay. "I'll do it."

"Oh, I don't think—" June began, but then just stood slack-jawed as Maple swung open the half door and wheeled her luggage behind the counter.

Lady Bird reacted with far more enthusiasm, wagging her tail so hard that her entire back end swung from side to side. She hip-checked June and nearly wiped the older woman out.

Someone needs to train this dog, Maple thought. But, hey, at least that wasn't her problem, was it? Goldens were sweet as pie, but they typically acted like puppies until they were fully grown adult dogs.

"Where's the exam room?" Maple glanced around.

June remained mum, but her gaze flitted to a door at the far end of the hall.

Aha!

Maple strode toward the door, stilettos clicking on the tile floor as Lady Bird followed hot on her heels.

June sidestepped the rolling suitcase and chased after them. "Maple, this really isn't such a good idea."

"Dr. Leighton," Maple corrected. Again. She grabbed a manila folder from the file rack hanging on the back of the exam-room door.

Paper files? Really? Maybe she really could make a difference here. There were loads of digital office-management systems specifically designed for veterinary medicine. Maybe by the time her year was up, she could successfully drag this practice into the current century.

She glanced at the note written beside today's date on

the chart. *Dog seems tired.* Well, that really narrowed things down, didn't it?

There were countless reasons why a dog might be lethargic. Some serious, some not so worrisome at all. She'd need more information to know where to begin, but she wasn't going to stand there in the hall and read the entire file folder when she could simply go inside, look at the dog in question and talk to the client face-to-face.

A ripple of anxiety skittered through her. She had zero problem with the dog part of the equation. The part about talking to the human pet owner, on the other hand…

"Dr. Leighton, it would really be best if we wait until Grover gets here. This particular patient is—" June lowered her voice to a near whisper "—rather unusual."

During her surgical course at her veterinary college in Manhattan, Maple had once operated on a two-headed diamondback terrapin turtle. She truly doubted that whatever lay behind the exam-room door was something that could shock her. How "unusual" could the dog possibly be? At minimum, she could get the appointment started until one of the other vets decided to roll in to work.

"Trust me, June. I've got this." Maple tucked the file folder under her arm and grabbed hold of the doorknob. "In the meantime, would you mind looking into my accommodations? Dr. Walker said they'd be taken care of, but I didn't see a hotel on my way in from the airport."

She hadn't seen much of anything from the back seat of her hired car during the ride to Bluebonnet from the airport in Austin, other than wide-open spaces dotted with bales of hay.

And cows.

Lots and *lots* of cows.

"Dr. Walker…" June echoed, looking slightly green

around the gills. She opened her mouth, as if to say more, but it was too late.

Maple was already swinging the door open and barreling into the exam room. Lady Bird strutted alongside her like a four-legged veterinary assistant.

"Hi there, I'm Dr. Leighton," Maple said, gaze shifting from an elderly woman sitting in one of the exam-room chairs with an aluminum walker parked in front of her to a much younger, shockingly handsome man wearing a faded denim work shirt with the sleeves rolled up to his elbows. Her attention snagged on his forearms for a beat. So muscular. How did that even happen? Swinging a lasso around? Roping cattle?

Maple's stomach gave an annoying flutter.

She forced her gaze away from the forearms and focused on his eyes instead. So blue. So *intense.* She swallowed hard. "I hear your dog isn't feeling well this morning."

There. Human introductions out of the way, Maple could do what she did best and turn her attention to her doggy patient. She breathed a little easier and glanced down at the animal, lying as still as stone on the exam table and, thus far, visible only in Maple's periphery.

She blinked.

And blinked again.

Even Lady Bird, who'd muscled her way into the exam room behind Maple, cocked her head and knit her furry brow.

"I, um, don't understand," Maple said.

Was this a joke? Had her entire interaction at this hole-in-the-wall practice been some sort of weird initiation prank? Is this how they welcomed outsiders in a small town?

Maybe she should've listened to June. How had she put it, exactly?

This particular patient is rather unusual.

A giant, Texas-size understatement, if Maple had ever heard one. The dog on the exam table wasn't just a little odd. It wasn't even a dog. It was a stuffed animal—a child's plush toy.

And Cowboy Blue Eyes was looming over it, arms crossed and expression dead-serious while he waited for Maple to examine it as if it was real.

Don't say it.

Ford Bishop glared at the new veterinarian and did his best to send her a telepathic message, even though telepathy wasn't exactly his specialty. Nor did it rank anywhere on his list of abilities.

Do not *say it.*

Dr. Maple Leighton—she'd been sure to throw that *doctor* title around—was definitely going to say it. Ford could practically see the words forming on her bow-shaped, cherry-red lips.

"I don't understand," she repeated. "This is a—"

And there it was.

Ford held up a hand to stop her from uttering the words *stuffed animal*. "My grandmother and I prefer to see Grover. Is he here?"

"No." She lifted her chin a fraction, and her cheeks went as pink as the blossoms on the dogwood trees that surrounded the gazebo in Bluebonnet's town square. "Unfortunately for both of us, Grover is out of the office at the moment."

"That's okay. We'll wait," Ford said through gritted teeth and tipped his head toward the door, indicating she should leave, whoever she was.

Instead, she narrowed her eyes at him and didn't budge. "I'm the new veterinarian here. I'm happy to help."

She cleared her throat. "*If* there's an actual animal that needs—"

"Coco isn't eating," Ford's grandmother blurted from the chair situated behind where he stood at the exam table. "And she sleeps all day long."

As if on cue, the battery-operated stuffed animal opened its mouth and then froze, exposing a lone green bean sitting on its fluffy pink tongue. There was zero doubt in Ford's mind that the bean had come straight off his grandmother's plate during lunch at her retirement home.

Dr. Maple Leighton's eyes widened at the sight of the vegetable.

Lady Bird rose up onto her back legs and planted her paws on the exam table, clearly angling to snatch the green bean for herself.

"Down, Lady Bird," Ford and Maple both said in unison.

The corners of Maple's mouth twitched, almost like she wanted to smile…until she thought better of it and pursed her lips again, as if Ford was something she wanted to scrape off the bottom of one of those ridiculous high-heeled shoes she was wearing. She'd best not try walking across the cobblestone town square in those things.

Her forehead crinkled. "You know Lady Bird?"

"Everyone in town knows Lady Bird," Ford countered.

Delighted to be the topic of conversation, the golden retriever opened her mouth in a wide doggy grin. This time, Maple genuinely relaxed for a beat. The tension in her shoulders appeared to loosen as she rested her hand on top of Lady Bird's head.

She was clearly a dog lover, which made perfect sense. She was a vet. Still, Ford couldn't help but wonder what it would take for a human being to get her to light up like that.

Not that he cared, he reminded himself. Ford was just

curious, that's all. Newcomers were somewhat of a rarity in Bluebonnet.

"Can I speak to you in private?" he said quietly.

Maple lifted her gaze to meet his and her flush immediately intensified. She stiffened. Yeah, Maple Leighton definitely preferred the company of dogs to people. For a second, Ford thought she was going to say no.

"Fine," she answered flatly.

Where on earth had Grover found this woman? She had the bedside manner of a serial killer.

Ford scooped Coco in his arms and laid the toy dog into his grandmother's lap. She cradled it as gently as if it was a newborn baby, and Ford's chest went tight.

"I'm going to go talk to the vet for just a minute, Gram. I'll be right back. You take good care of Coco while I'm gone," he said.

"I will." Gram stroked the top of the dog's head with shaky fingertips.

"This will only take a second." Ford's jaw clenched. *Just long enough to tell the new vet to either get on board or get lost.*

He turned, and Maple had already vacated the exam room. Lady Bird, on the other hand, was still waiting politely for him.

"Thanks, girl," Ford muttered and gave the dog a scratch behind the ears. "Keep an eye on Gram for me, okay?"

Lady Bird woofed. Then the dog shuffled over to Ford's grandmother and collapsed into a huge pile of golden fur at her feet.

"Good girl." Ford shot the dog a wink and then stepped out into the hall, where Maple stood waiting for him, looking as tense as a cat in a roomful of rocking chairs.

It was almost cute—her odd combination of confidence mixed with an aching vulnerability that Ford could somehow feel deep inside his chest. A ripple of…something wound its way through him. If Ford hadn't known better, he might have mistaken it for attraction.

He crossed his arms. "You okay, Doc?"

"What?" She blinked again, as if someone asking after her was even more shocking than finding a fake dog in one of her exam rooms. Her eyes met his and then she gave her head a little shake. "I'm perfectly fine, Mr.…"

"Ford."

She nodded. "Mr. Ford, your dog—"

"Just Ford," he corrected.

Her gaze strayed to his faded denim work shirt, a stark contrast to the prim black dress she was wearing, complete with a matching black bow that held her dark hair in a thick ponytail. "As in the truck?"

He arched an eyebrow. "Dr. *Maple* Leighton, as in the syrup?"

Her nose crinkled, as if being named after something sweet left a bad taste in her mouth. "Back to your 'dog'…"

Ford took a step closer to her and lowered his voice so Gram wouldn't hear. "The dog isn't real. Obviously, I'm aware of that fact. Coco belongs to my grandmother. She's a robotic companion animal."

Maple took a few steps backward, teetering on her fancy shoes in her haste to maintain the invisible barrier between them. "You brought a robot dog to the vet because it seems tired. Got it."

"No." Ford's temples ached. She didn't get it, because of course she didn't. That hint of vulnerability he'd spied in her soulful eyes didn't mean squat. "I brought my grandmother's robotic companion animal here because my gram asked me to make the dog an appointment."

"So you're saying your gram thinks Coco is real?"

"I'm not one-hundred-percent sure whether she truly

believes or if she just *wants* to believe. Either way, I'm going with it. Pets reduce feelings of isolation and loneliness in older adults. You're a vet. Surely you know all about that." Ford raked a hand through his hair, tugging at the ends. He couldn't believe he had to explain all of this to a medical professional.

"But Coco isn't a pet." Maple's gaze darted to the exam-room door. "She's battery-operated."

At least she'd had the decency to speak in a hushed tone this time.

"Right, which is why Grover usually tells Gram he needs to take Coco to the back room for a quick exam and a blood test and then he brings the dog back with fresh batteries." He threw up his hands. "And we all live happily ever after."

"Until the batteries run out of juice again." Maple rolled her eyes.

Ford just stared at her, incredulous. "Tell me—does this pass as compassion wherever you're from?"

"I'm from New York City," she said, enunciating each syllable as if the place was a foreign land Ford had never heard of before. "But I live here now. *Temporarily.*"

Ford's annoyance flared. He wasn't in the mood to play country mouse to her city mouse. "As much as I'd love to take a deep dive into your backstory, I need to get back to Gram. Can you just play along, or do we need to wait for Grover?"

"Why can't you just replace the batteries when she's not looking? Like, say, sometime before the dog gets its mouth stuck open with a green bean inside of it?"

"Because Gram has been a big dog lover her entire life and it makes her feel good to bring her pet into the vet. She wants to take good care of Coco, and I'm not going to deny her that." He let out a harsh breath. "No one is."

Maple just looked at him as if he was some sort of puzzle she was trying to assemble in her head.

"Are you going to help us or not?" he finally asked.

"I'll do it, but you should know that I'm really not great at this sort of thing." She pulled a face, and Ford had to stop himself from asking what she meant. Batteries weren't all that complicated. "I'm not what you would call a people person."

He bit back a smile. Her brutal honesty was refreshing, he'd give her that. "Could've fooled me."

"There are generally two types of doctors in this world—general practice physicians, who are driven by their innate need to help people, and specialists, who relate more to the scientific part of medicine," Maple said, again sounding an awful lot like she was talking to someone who'd just fallen off a turnip truck.

If she only knew.

"Let me guess. You're the latter," Ford said.

Maple nodded. "I have a specialty in veterinary cardiology."

"Got it. You love dogs." It was a statement, not a question. "People, not so much."

She tilted her head. "Are we talking about actual dogs or the robot kind?"

Ford ignored her question. He suspected it was rhetorical, and anyway, he was done with this conversation. "June can show you where Grover keeps the batteries. I'll go get Coco."

"Fine," Maple said.

"I think the words you're looking for are *thank* and *you*." He flashed her a fake smile, and there it was again—that flush that reminded Ford of pink dogwood blossoms swirling against a clear, blue Texas sky.

"Thank you." She swallowed, and something about the

look in her big, brown doe eyes made Ford think she actually meant it.

Maple and her big-city attitude may have gotten themselves clear across the country from New York to Texas, but when she looked at him, *really* looked, he could see the truth. She was lost. And he suspected it didn't have much to do with geography.

She turned and click-clacked toward the lobby on her high heels.

"One more thing, Doc," Ford called after her.

Maple swiveled back toward him. "Yes? Is there a teeny tiny robotic mouse in your pocket that also needs new batteries?"

Cute. Aggravating as hell, but cute.

"Welcome to Bluebonnet."

Chapter Two

If Maple had been the type to get teary-eyed, the way Ford's Gram reacted once Coco was back up and running might've made her crack. The older woman was as thrilled as if Maple had breathed literal life into her ailing little dog, and she promptly ordered Ford to get Maple a pie from someplace called Cherry on Top as a thank-you gift.

But Maple wasn't the type to cry at work, not even when his gram called her "an angel sent straight from heaven." So she averted her gaze and focused on the jar of dog treats sitting on the counter in the exam room until her eyes stopped stinging. All the while, Lady Bird nudged her big head under Maple's right hand, insisting on a pat. The dog was relentless.

As for the pie, Maple wasn't holding her breath.

"So long, Doc." Ford held the door open for his grandmother and escorted her out of the clinic without so much as a backward glance.

Maple sagged with relief once they were gone. She wasn't sure why the pang in her chest felt so much like disappointment.

She rubbed the heel of her hand against her breastbone, ignoring the way Lady Bird's soft gaze bore into her as if the dog could hear Maple's thoughts. Still, it was unsettling.

She turned her back on the dog to home in on June, still stationed behind the reception desk. "Do we have any more patients waiting to be seen? *Live* ones, that is?"

"I tried to warn you," June insisted as she replaced a jumbo-size pack of size C batteries in one of the overhead cabinets above her desk. "And no, we don't have any more patients waiting. But it looks like someone is here to see you."

June's gaze darted over Maple's left shoulder, toward the tempered glass window in the front door. Maple's heart thumped in her chest as visions of pie danced in her head.

Stop it, she told herself. *What is wrong with you?*

Bluebonnet was small, but not small enough for Ford to have already procured a baked good and made his way back to the clinic. Also, she didn't want to see him again. Ever, if she could help it.

She followed June's gaze and caught sight of a red-faced man marching up the front step of the building's quaint covered porch. Again, no animal in sight—just a middle-aged human with salt-and-pepper hair and an angry frown that Maple felt all the way down to her toes.

Before she could ask June who the man was, he burst through the door and stalked toward Maple. He looked her up and down, jammed his hands on his hips and glanced at June. "Is this her?"

"Yes, sir," June said.

Lady Bird, clearly unable to read the room, wagged her

tail and panted as she danced circles around the cranky visitor.

Actually, he wasn't technically a visitor, as Maple realized when she spotted the monogrammed initials stitched onto his shirt collar—*GH*, as in Grover Hayes. Oh, joy.

"You must be Dr. Hayes." Maple stuck her hand out for a shake. "I'm Dr. Leighton."

"So I gathered." He narrowed his gaze at her. "Unfortunately, the first I'd heard of you was when June called me a little while ago to tell me that a complete and total stranger had insisted on treating Coco in my absence."

In Maple's defense, the only reason she'd taken over the appointment was because he'd been late. Still, this didn't seem like the time to point out his breach in professional etiquette.

She'd come all this way. Today had been *years* in the making. How was it possible that Percy Walker, DVM, hadn't informed a single other person at this practice that she was starting work this week? It just didn't make sense. The practice had paid tens of thousands of dollars for her education, and not a single other person here knew who she was?

"I don't understand." Maple shook her head.

"That makes two of us," Grover huffed.

"I have years' worth of emails, some as recent as a week ago. If we could just talk to Dr. Walker, I'm sure we can clear all of this up." Maple took a deep breath. The sooner Percy Walker materialized, the better. "Do you know when he's going to be in? Technically, my start date isn't until tomorrow. I came by the office because I just got to town, and I was ready to hit the ground running."

She glanced toward her suitcase, still sitting behind the reception desk like a fly floating belly-up in someone's soup. "Plus, I'm not sure where I'm staying. Dr. Walker said my accommodations in Bluebonnet would be taken care of by my grant."

Now that Maple was saying all of this out loud, she realized it sounded a little off. She'd just flown across the country to a strange town in a strange state with no idea where she might be staying. For all she knew, Percy Walker was an internet catfish.

Except catfish didn't ordinarily fund someone's higher education, did they? Didn't catfishing usually work the other way around? Even so, either of Maple's lawyer parents probably would've been delighted to point out a dozen red flags after looking over the simple one-page contract she'd signed when she'd accepted the grant.

Which was precisely why she'd never shown it to them.

"I'm afraid Dr. Walker won't be coming in." Grover went even stonier faced, a feat that Maple wouldn't have thought possible if she hadn't witnessed his near transformation into an actual gargoyle with her own two eyes. "Ever."

Maple blinked, even more alarmed than when she'd walked into the exam room to find a fake dog on the table. "Ever?"

"Ever," Grover repeated.

What was going on? Had her one and only contact at Bluebonnet Pet Clinic gotten fired? Resigned?

In either case, did this she mean she could go back to New York now? Could she really be that lucky? Maple felt a smile tugging at the corners of her lips.

"Dr. Percy Walker passed away eight days ago. The funeral was yesterday morning," Grover said.

And just like that, the smile wobbled off Maple's face. "What?"

Passed away, as in *dead*. Now what? Was she free to grab her suitcase and get on the next plane back to New York? As heavenly as that sounded, it just didn't seem right.

Of course. June chose that moment to oh-so-helpfully chime in, "For the record, I tried to tell you that too, Maple."

Dr. Leighton. Maple swallowed. She didn't bother correcting the receptionist this time. What was the point?

"Wait a minute." Every last drop of color drained from Grover's face as he regarded her with a new wariness. "Your first name is Maple?"

She nodded. "Yes. Maple Leighton, DVM."

"Why didn't you tell me this?" Grover's gaze flitted toward June. Lady Bird's followed, as if the golden was trying to keep up with the conversation.

Good luck, Maple thought. She could barely keep up with it herself.

"She *really* prefers to be called Dr. Leighton," June said, peering at Maple over the top of her reading glasses.

Maple had worked long and hard for that degree. Of course, she wanted to be called "Doctor," although perhaps she shouldn't have been so eager to correct June. Clearly, no one here cared a whit about her veterinary degree. Inexplicably, all Grover seemed interested in was her first name.

"Does my first name really matter all that much?" Maple asked. This day was getting more bizarre by the minute. Had she traveled to Texas, or fallen down a rabbit hole, Alice in Wonderland-style?

"In this case, it just might," Grover said, looking distinctly unhappy about it. "We need to talk. Follow me."

He swept past her without waiting for a response.

Maple glanced at June, who simply shrugged. Clearly, she didn't know what was going on any more than Maple did.

Lady Bird trotted gleefully after Grover, which frankly, felt like an enormous betrayal. Completely unreasonable, since Maple had known the dog for all of twenty minutes.

Still, it was nice having someone on her side in the middle of all this chaos. Even if that someone was a dog.

Then, just as Maple's heart began to sink to new depths, Lady Bird stopped in her tracks and turned around. The golden fixed her soft brown eyes on Maple and cocked her head, as if to say, "What are you waiting for?"

Hope fluttered inside Maple, like a butterfly searching for a safe place to land.

"I'm coming."

Dr. Grover Hayes's office was located just off the reception area, behind the very first door on the right. By the time Lady Bird led Maple there, Grover was already seated at his desk and shuffling through a pile of papers.

"It's around here somewhere. Just give me a second," he said. Then he nodded toward a chair on the other side of his desk, piled high with file folders. "Sit."

Maple assumed he was talking to her rather than Lady Bird, although in all honesty, it was difficult to tell. She had a feeling if he'd been addressing the dog, he would've been more polite. So she scooped the stack of patient files into her arms, deposited them on a nearby end table and sat down. Once Maple was settled, Lady Bird plopped on the ground and planted her chin on the tip of one of her stilettos.

Perhaps it was that tiny show of affection that gave Maple the confidence to assume she was actually employed at the clinic, despite all current evidence to the contrary.

"I was thinking that while I'm here, I could help us get started on a digital office system. Having patient files on a cloud-based platform would save loads of time."

Grover glanced up from the stack of papers in front of him and snorted. "Our system works just fine."

Maple's gaze swiveled from the mountain of files she'd just removed from her chair to the mishmash of documents on Grover's desk. "I can see that. Efficiency at its finest."

"And let's not forget that you don't even work here, missy," Grover added, although he seemed to have lost a fair bit of his bluster.

What *was* the man looking for, anyway? Had the mention of her first name somehow reminded him that he did, indeed, have a copy of her grant paperwork lying around somewhere?

"Ah, here it is." He grabbed hold of a slim manila envelope and frowned at the words written neatly across the front of it before shoving it toward Maple.

Last Will and Testament of Percy Walker

"Take it." Grover shook the envelope until Maple begrudgingly accepted it.

She placed it in her lap, unopened, where it sat like a bomb waiting to detonate. Her mouth went dry. *Something about this feels woefully inappropriate.* Maple didn't really know Percy Walker. They'd exchanged little more than a handful of emails over the past four years. Why would his business partner just hand her his last will and testament?

Maple shook her head. "I'm sorry? Why do you want me to have this?"

"Go on." Grover waved a hand at her. First impressions were rarely one-hundred-percent accurate, but he didn't seem at all like the type of person who'd have the patience to deal with an elderly woman and her beloved robotic companion animal. Wonders never ceased, apparently. "Open it."

She lifted the flap of the envelope and slid the legal document from inside.

The pages of the will were slightly yellowed with age. Maple's eyes scanned the legalese, and familiar words popped out at her—phrases that had been part of her parents' vocabulary for as long as she could remember. She still had no idea what any of it had to do with her.

"Would you care to give me a hint as to what I'm looking…for?" she asked, but her voice drifted off as her gaze snagged on the first paragraph of the second page.

> I have never been married. As of the date of this will, the following child has been born to me:
>
> Maple Maribelle Walker

Maple's heart immediately began to pound so hard and fast that Lady Bird lifted her head and whined in alarm.

"This isn't me." Maple shook her head. If she shook it any harder, it probably would've snapped right off and tumbled to the floor. "It can't be. My last name is Leighton."

But her first name was obviously Maple, and her middle name, which she'd hadn't mentioned to anyone in Bluebonnet, was indeed Maribelle.

What were the odds this was all some crazy coincidence? Maple had never met another living soul who shared her first name. In Manhattan, she'd grown up among a sea of Blairs, Serenas, and Waverlys, acutely aware that she hadn't fit in. Maybe it was a more common name down here in Texas?

"My parents are both divorce lawyers," she said, as if that fact was relevant in any way. "In *Manhattan*. I'm not even from here."

"Clearly." Grover let out a laugh.

Finally, they agreed on something.

"What's your middle name?" he asked, frowning like he already knew the answer.

Maple reached down to rest a hand on Lady Bird's head. The dog licked her with a swipe of her warm pink tongue. Maple took a deep breath. "It's Maribelle."

If the furrow in Grover's forehead grew any deeper, Maple could've crawled inside of it and disappeared.

"Surely there's another Maple Maribelle who lives right here in Bluebonnet," she said, but she was grasping at straws, and she knew it. If there'd been anyone else who remotely fit the bill, Grover wouldn't have gone pale the moment he'd heard her first name.

"I'm afraid not," Grover said. "I think it might be time for you to call your lawyer parents up in New York to try and get to the bottom of this. In the meantime, I'll give Percy's attorney a call and see if he can come right over."

"But why?" The last thing Maple wanted to do was call her mother and father. When she'd told them she was starting a new job this week, she'd conveniently left out the part about the practice being located in Texas. They didn't know about the grant, either. For all they knew, she was still living in her little studio apartment in the city, ready to launch her new career as a veterinary cardiologist.

As she *should* be.

In hindsight, Maple clearly should've gotten their advice before signing on the dotted line.

"With all due respect, Percy Walker is dead. Why would I need to get my family involved?" She picked up the last will and testament by the very tip of the corner of its stapled pages. Maple hadn't wanted to rid herself of an item so badly since the last time she'd played a game of hot potato. She would've thrown the document across the desk if she hadn't suspected that Grover would toss it right back at her. "What difference does any of this make?"

Couldn't they simply pretend none of this had happened? No one else needed to know that her first and middle name matched the one listed on Percy's will. Maple wasn't his daughter, full stop. She knew it, and now Grover knew it. Case closed.

Maple didn't know why there was a voice screaming in the back of her head that things couldn't possibly be that simple. She almost wanted to clamp her hands over her ears to try and drown it out. Even the comforting weight of Lady Bird's warm body as the dog heaved herself into a sit position and leaned against Maple's legs failed to calm the frantic beating of her heart.

"I'm afraid it makes a very big difference, young lady." Grover sighed, and Maple was so thrown by this entire conversation that she forgot to get offended at being referred to in such a condescending manner. "If you're the Maple Maribelle listed in that document, that means you're Percy's sole beneficiary and you've inherited everything—his house, his half of this veterinary practice..."

Lady Bird let out a sharp bark.

Grover's gaze drifted toward the golden retriever. "*And* his dog."

Chapter Three

Maple tried her mother first, but the call rolled straight to voice mail, so she left a message that was as vague and chipper as possible. Other than a brief mention of Texas, she in no way hinted at her current existential crisis. No need to panic anyone. This was all just some huge misunderstanding. As soon as she met with Percy's attorney—the only one in town, apparently—Maple could get on with her new life in Bluebonnet.

She was assuming Grover would let her stay, of course. Whether or not Percy left behind any paperwork documenting her grant didn't really matter. Maple owed the clinic a year of work and, as unpleasant as it seemed, she intended to fulfill that obligation. If Grover wouldn't let her stay…

Well, she'd simply deal with that later. Right after she managed to convince Grover she was in no way related to his recently deceased business partner.

"It's not true," she said aloud, as if the crammed bookshelves and clutter scattered atop Percy Walker's desk could hear her. Grover had banished her to Percy's office to make her phone calls, against Maple's fervent protests.

Lady Bird, who'd sauntered into the office on Maple's heels and promptly arranged herself on a faded flannel dog bed in a corner by the window, lifted her head from her paws. She cocked her head and eyed Maple with obvious skepticism. Or maybe Maple was just anthropomorphizing. She had a tendency to do that on occasion.

"I'm not his daughter." Maple fixed her gaze on the dog. "Seriously, I'm not. I don't belong here."

Lady Bird's tail *thump-thumped* against her dog bed. The golden clearly wasn't listening.

"A simple phone call will prove it." Maple turned her cell phone over in her palm and scrolled through her contacts for her dad's information. If her mom wasn't answering, maybe he could help. She couldn't keep sitting here in a strange man's office in a strange town, trying to convince a strange dog that she really was who she said she was—Maple Maribelle Leighton of New York City.

Before she could tap her father's number, her phone rang with an incoming call and Maple jumped. She really needed to get a grip.

It's Mom. She pressed a hand to her abdomen as her mother's name scrolled across the top of the phone's small screen. *Thank goodness.*

"Hi, Mom," she said as she answered, going for bright and confident, but managing to sound slightly manic instead.

"Hi, honey."

Wait. That wasn't her mother's voice. It almost sounded like her father.

Maple frowned down at her phone. "Dad?"

"It's both of us, Maple," her mother said.

"*Both* of you?" Maple glanced at Lady Bird in a panic. The last time her parents had joined forces, it had been to try and talk her into going to law school. If they were willing to put aside their many, *many* differences to join forces, things must be far more dire than Maple imagined.

But wait—Maple hadn't even mentioned Percy or his will in her voice mail. How could they possibly know she'd been calling about something as delicate as her parentage?

"You mother said you're calling from Texas," Dad said.

And there it was.

Maple's heart sank all the way to her stilettos, which seemed to be covered in a layer of barbecue-scented dust. One brief mention of Texas had been enough to get her parents back on speaking terms?

This couldn't be good.

"I'm here for work. Remember when I told you about my vet school scholarship?" Maple swallowed. Lady Bird, sensing her distress, came to stand and lean against her legs, and Maple felt a sudden swell of affection for Percy Walker. Whoever he'd really been, he'd raised a lovely, lovely dog, and that alone spoke volumes about his character. "There was a small technicality I might not have mentioned."

"What kind of technicality?" her dad asked. Maple could hear the frown in his voice clear across the country.

"In exchange for a full ride, I agreed to spend a year working at a pet clinic here in Texas." Maple took a deep breath. "I guess you could say I live here now. *Temporarily.* Something strange has come up, though, so I wanted to call and—"

"Where in Texas?" Mom asked in a voice so high and thin that Maple barely recognized it.

"It's just a small town. You've probably never heard

of it." Maple bit down so hard on her bottom lip that she tasted blood.

Maybe if she didn't say it, she could stop this conversation before it really started. She could keep on believing that she knew exactly who she was and where she'd come from. She could swallow the name of this crazy place and pretend she'd never set eyes on Percy Walker's last will and testament.

In the end, it was her dad who broke the silence. And the moment he did, Maple couldn't pretend anymore. There was more to her educational grant than she'd thought. Had there ever even *been* a grant? Or had it simply been Percy's way of getting Maple to Texas? To *home*?

Maple shook her head. She'd never felt farther from home in her entire life.

Dad cleared his throat. "Tell us the truth. You're in Bluebonnet, aren't you?"

An hour later, Maple stared in disbelief at a version of her birth certificate she'd never set eyes on before.

It had been sent via fax from her mother's office in Manhattan, straight to the dinosaur of a fax machine at June's workstation in the pet clinic's reception area. Maple wouldn't have believed it if she hadn't seen it herself—not even after her mom and dad had calmly explained they weren't actually her birth parents. Maple had been adopted at only two days old. Charles and Meredith Leighton had flown down to Bluebonnet and collected her themselves.

It had been an open adoption, arranged by one of their attorney friends. Maple's birth mother had only been seventeen years old, and she'd died in childbirth. The grief-stricken father had been so overwhelmed that he'd agreed to give the baby up, under one condition: the adoptive parents had to promise to keep the baby's first and middle names. Maple Maribelle. Once Maple held the faxed birth certificate in her trembling hands, she understood why.

Mother's Name: Maple Maribelle Walker

The words went blurry as Maple's eyes swam with tears. She'd been named after her birth mother. Everything she'd read in Percy's last will and testament had been true. The man who'd paid for her education and brought her to Bluebonnet had been her *father.*

And now he was gone.

They both were.

"Let's see that, missy." Grover snatched the birth certificate from her hands.

At some point, Maple was going to have to school this man on how to speak to his female colleagues. But, alas, that moment wasn't now. She was far too tired to argue with the likes of Grover Hayes. All she wanted to do right now was crawl into bed and pull the covers over her head. Too bad she still had no idea where she was staying.

"Believe me, no one is as surprised by this crazy turn of events as I am," Maple said as Grover studied the document.

Grover made a noise somewhere between a huff and a growl. Lady Bird's ears pricked forward and she cocked her head.

"We need to talk," Maple said, even though she had no idea what she was going to say. Up was down, down was up and nothing make sense anymore.

"Just come home," her mother had said.

"I've booked you on the first flight out of Austin tomorrow morning," her dad had added. "First class."

It had been decided. Maple had never belonged in Bluebonnet. As far as her parents were concerned, she should just come back to New York and forget her ill-fated trip to Texas had ever taken place. They'd fallen all over themselves apologizing for never telling her the truth about her birth. Maple couldn't remember either of her parents ever uttering the word *sorry* before. It was almost as disorienting as learning she'd been born right here in Bluebonnet.

"Indeed, we do." Grover stalked toward his office, fully expecting Maple to follow.

What choice did she have?

At least June shot her a sympathetic glance this time. Maple gave the receptionist a wan smile and fell in step behind Grover as Lady Bird nudged her gold head beneath Maple's hand.

The dog was growing on Maple. Technically, the golden was hers now, right? She could pack the dog up and sweep her off to New York if she wanted to. Not that Maple would do such a thing. New York City was made for purse dogs. Life in Manhattan would be a major adjustment for a dog accustomed to living in the wide-open spaces of Texas. It wouldn't be fair.

But that didn't stop Maple from dreaming about it.

"I've been thinking things over, and I've decided to let you off the hook," Grover said as soon as the office door shut behind them.

Maple heaved another pile of file folders out of the office chair she'd occupied earlier and plopped down on the worn leather. "I'm not following."

"For the grant. You and Percy had an agreement, did you not? A fully funded veterinary education in exchange for one year of employment here at Bluebonnet Pet Clinic?" Grover leaned back in his chair.

Maple nodded. "Yes, but…"

"But I'm letting you off the hook. Percy's gone now. I think we both know the real reason he wanted you to come here." Grover shrugged. "I see no reason to make you fulfill your obligation. I think this morning proved you're not a good fit here. Wouldn't you agree?"

Ooof. He was one-hundred-percent right. There was no reason why his words should've felt like a blow to the chest, but they did.

"Agreed." Maple gave a curt nod and tried her best not to think about the way she'd spoken to Ford Bishop earlier. The appointment had been a total disaster. Yet another reason to put this town in her rearview mirror as quickly as possible.

Lady Bird sighed and dropped her chin onto Maple's knee.

"So." Grover shrugged. "You're free to go."

Maple gripped the arms of her chair so hard that her knuckles turned white. The effort it took not to sprint out of the building, roadrunner-style, was almost too much to bear. "I'm leaving on the six a.m. flight out of Austin tomorrow morning. My ticket is already booked."

Her dad had even managed to pull some strings and gotten Maple another shot at her dream job. The veterinary cardiology practice that had made her such a generous offer after graduation still wanted her to come to work for them. When Maple had asked how that was possible, since she knew for a fact that the position had been filled after she'd turned it down, her father had simply said that veterinary cardiologists got divorced, just like everyone else did. He'd apparently represented Maple's new boss in a nasty split and was now calling in a favor.

"Good." Grover nodded. *"Excellent."*

Maple knew she should ask about Percy's estate. Didn't she need to sign some papers or something? There was the veterinary practice to think about… Percy's personal effects…and his dog.

She could deal with all of that from New York, though. Her parents were lawyers. Maple probably wouldn't have to lift a finger. They could make it all disappear, just like they'd promised on the phone.

None of this is really your responsibility. You can walk away. Grover just said so himself. Maple buried her hand in the warm scruff of Lady Bird's neck.

Charles and Meredith Leighton had been divorced since Maple was in first grade. The separation had been monumentally ugly—ugly enough that she could remember hiding in her closet with her stuffed dog, Rover, clamping her hands over her ears to try and muffle the sound of dishes smashing against the marble floors. They were two of the city's highest paid divorce attorneys, after all. Fighting dirty practically came naturally to them.

The fact that they seemed to have to put aside their many, *many* differences to help Maple deal with Percy's estate and get her back to New York was nothing short of surreal. In the ultimate irony of ironies, she'd managed to fulfill her childhood dream of stitching her broken family back together. All it had taken was the accidental discovery of a whole *other* family that she never knew existed.

"Where am I supposed to stay tonight?" Maple said, willing her voice not to crack.

Grover opened the top drawer of his desk and pulled out an old-fashioned skeleton key, tied with a red string. He set it down and slid it toward Maple.

She eyed it dubiously. "What is that for?"

"It's the key to Percy's place." Grover paused, and the lines on his face seemed to grow deeper. "Although technically it's your house now."

Not for long.

She reached for the strange key and balled it into her fist. Percy's house was the absolute last place she wanted to go for her few remaining hours in Bluebonnet. She longed for a sterile beige hotel room—somewhere she could hide herself away and feel absolutely nothing. Unfortunately, the closest place that fit the bill was nearly fifty miles away. Maple had already done a search on her cell phone.

She slapped the key back down on the desk.

"I'm not sure staying at Percy's house is the best idea. I don't even know how I'd get there. I don't have a car." With any luck, Uber hadn't made it all the way to rural Texas. "Didn't I see a sign for a bed-and-breakfast near the town square? I'm sure that's much closer."

"Closer than next door?" Grover stood, reached for his white vet coat and slid his arms into its sleeves. "I think not."

"Percy's house is right next door?" Maple squeaked.

Of course, it was. The population of this place was probably in the double digits.

"Yes, he lived in one of the Sunday houses. He owned this one, too, until he sold it to the practice." Grover cast a sentimental glance at their surroundings. Then his gaze landed on Maple and his expression hardened again.

"What's a Sunday house?" she asked before she could stop herself. Why spend any more time in Grover's presence than absolutely necessary? The wording made her curious, though. She'd never heard of such a thing in New York.

"A Sunday house is a small home that was once used by ranchers or farmers who lived in the outlying area when they came into town on the weekends for social events and church. Sunday houses date back to the 1800s. There are still quite a few standing in the Texas Hill Country. A lot of them are historical landmarks." He glowered. "You might want to brush up on some local history before you think about selling the place."

"I'll get right on that," she muttered under her breath.

"Percy's home is the pink house just to the right of this one." He fumbled around in the pocket of his white coat and pulled out a banged-up pocket watch that looked like something from an antique store. He squinted at it, nodded and slid it out of view again. "I'd walk you over there, but I've got an appointment with a turtle who has a head cold."

Sure he did.

Maple didn't believe him for a minute. Grover just wanted her gone. At least they'd finally agreed on something.

"You can leave the key under the front mat when you head out in the morning. Have a safe trip back home," Grover said, and then he strode out of his office with a tight smile.

Nice to meet you, too, Maple thought wryly.

Lady Bird peered up at her with a softness in her warm brown eyes that made Maple's heart feel like it was being squeezed in a vise. Was she moving too fast? Maybe she should slow down a take a breath.

She closed her eyes, leaned forward and rested her cheek against Lady Bird's head. A voice in the back of her head assured her she was doing the right thing.

This was never what you wanted. Now you have an out. You'd be a fool not to take it.

Maple sat up and blew out a breath. Lady Bird's tail beat against the hard wood floor. *Thump, thump, thump.*

"Come on." Maple said, and the dog's big pink tongue lolled out of the side of her mouth. "Let's get out of here."

She sure as heck wasn't going to spend the night in Percy's house alone, and Lady Bird seemed more than willing to accompany her.

June was clearly more conflicted about Maple's decision

to fly back to Manhattan. She at least had the decency to look somewhat sorry to see Maple go.

"You don't have to be in such a hurry, you know," the older woman said as Maple took hold of her wheeled suitcase. "Don't mind Grover. I know he seems madder than an old wet hen, but he's not that bad once you get to know him. He and Percy were really close. He's taking the loss hard."

So hard that he basically ordered his dead friend's long-lost daughter to leave town immediately. Do not pass GO. Do not collect 200 dollars.

Maple fought back an eye roll. "I'm going to have to take your word on that, June."

June nodded and fidgeted with her hands. "You let me know if you need anything tonight, Dr. Leighton. I'll be 'round to collect Lady Bird first thing in the morning. She's been staying with me since Percy's passing, but you take her tonight. That dog has a way with people who need a little TLC. She's actually sort of famous for it around these parts."

Maple suspected there might be more to that story, but before she could ask June to elaborate, a client walked into the clinic holding a cat carrier containing a fluffy black cat howling at the top of its lungs.

"I think that's my cue to go." Maple tightened her grip on the handle of her suitcase. "Thanks for everything. And June…?"

June regarded her over the top of her reading glasses. "Yes, Dr. Leighton?"

"You can call me Maple." Maple's throat went thick. She *really* needed to make herself scarce. It wasn't like her to get emotional around strangers. Then again, it wasn't every day that she learned something about herself that made her question her place in the world.

June's face split into a wide grin, and before Maple knew what was happening, the older woman threw her arms around Maple's shoulders and wrapped her in a tight hug.

It had been a long time since someone had embraced Maple with that sort of enthusiasm. As much as she hated to admit it, it felt nice.

"I really should go now," she mumbled into June's shoulder.

June released her and gave her shoulders a gentle squeeze. "Goodbye now, Maple Maribelle Walker."

Leighton, Maple wanted to say. *My name is Maple Leighton.* But the words stuck in her throat.

She dipped her head and dragged her luggage toward the door, carefully sidestepping the cat who was now meowing loud enough to peel the paint off the walls. Lady Bird trotted alongside Maple as if the cat didn't exist. Golden retrievers were known for their unflappable temperament, but this really took the cake.

If Grover hadn't told Maple which house in the neat row of half-dozen homes with gingerbread trim had been Percy's, she still would've located it easily. Lady Bird led the way, trotting straight toward the little pink house with her tail wagging to and fro.

A nonsensical lump lodged in Maple's throat at the sight of it. It looked like a dollhouse and was painted a pale blush-pink that reminded her of ballet slippers. Everything about the structure oozed charm, from the twin rocking chairs on the porch to the white picket fence that surrounded the small front yard. Maple couldn't help but wonder what it might've been like growing up in this sort of home, tailor-made for a little girl.

Tears pricked the backs of her eyes. There must be something in the water in this town. Maple never cried, and this was the third time today that she'd found herself on the verge of weeping.

She took a deep inhale and pushed open the gabled gate in the white picket fence. Lady Bird zipped past her, bounding toward the tiny covered porch. The dog nudged at something sitting on the welcome mat while Maple hauled her bag up the front step.

"What have you got there, Lady Bird?" Maple muttered as she rummaged around her NYC pizza-parlor handbag for the ridiculous skeleton key Grover had given her earlier. Was there *anything* in Bluebonnet that didn't look like it had come straight out of a time capsule?

The key felt heavy in her hand, weighted down by yesteryear. Maple's fingers wrapped around it, and she held it tight as she bent down to see what had captured Lady Bird's attention.

Once she managed to nudge the golden out of the way, Maple saw it—a large pink bakery box with the words *Cherry on Top* printed across it in a whimsical font.

Her breath caught in her throat. Ford Bishop had really done it. He'd done as his grandmother had asked and brought her a pie. Maple had been so busy with her identity crisis that she hadn't eaten a bite all day. She hadn't even thought about food. But the heavenly smell drifting up from the bakery box made her mouth water.

She picked it up, closed her eyes and took a long inhale. The heady aroma of sugar, cinnamon and buttery pastry crust nearly caused her knees to buckle. Then her eyelashes fluttered open, and she spotted the brief note Ford had scrawled on the cardboard in thick strokes from a magic marker.

The man had terrible handwriting—nearly as indecipherable as that of a doctor. Maple had to read it a few times to make out what it said.

Doc,
I wasn't sure what kind of pie you liked, so I went with Texas peach. The peaches were homegrown here in Bluebonnet. There's more to love about this place than just dogs, although our canines are admittedly stellar. Just ask Lady Bird.
Regards,
Ford Bishop

Maple's heart gave a little twist. She couldn't even say why, except that she'd spent the entire day trying to hold herself together while her life—past, present, and future—had been fracturing apart. She didn't belong here in Texas. That much was clear.

But the secret truth that Maple kept buried deep down inside was that she'd never fully felt like she'd belonged anywhere. Not even New York. She'd always felt like she was on the outside looking in, with her face pressed against the tempered glass of her own life.

Maple had always blamed her social anxiety on her parents' divorce and a lifetime of learning that love was never permanent, and marriages were meant to be broken. Her mom and dad had never said as much aloud, but they didn't have to. It had happened in their very own family. Then Maple had quietly watched as her parents battled on behalf of other heartbroken husbands and wives.

She'd avoided dating all through high school, afraid to lose her head and her heart to someone who might crush it to pieces. Then in vet school, she'd decided to prove her parents wrong. She'd thrown herself into love with all the naivete of a girl who hadn't actually learned what the words *prenuptial agreement* meant before her tenth birthday. When she fell, she fell hard.

Justin had been a student in her study group. He was

fiercely competitive, just like Maple. She'd foolishly believed that meant they had other things in common, too. Two peas in the pressure cooker of a pod that was veterinary school.

For an entire semester they did everything together. Then, near the end of the term, on the night before they both had a final research project due in their animal pathology class, he disappeared…

Along with Maple's term paper.

At first, she'd thought it had to be some weird coincidence. He'd been in an accident or something, and she'd simply misplaced her research paper or left it at the copy place, where she'd had all one hundred pages of it bound like a book for a professional aesthetic. But Maple knew she'd never make a mistake like that. Instead, she'd made one far more heartbreaking. She'd trusted a boy who'd used her for months, biding his time until he could swoop in and steal her research project so he could turn it in as his own.

By the time Maple flew into her professor's office the following morning to report the theft, Justin had already switched out the cover page and presented the work as his own. The professor insisted there was no way to tell who'd copied whom, and Maple had been left with nothing to turn in. It had been the one and only time in her life she'd received an F on a report card.

Lesson learned. Her parents had been right all along.

But maybe there was more to the detached feeling inside of Maple than her messed up childhood and her ill-fated attempt at romance. Maybe the reason she'd never felt like she fit in was because she'd been in the wrong place. The wrong *life*.

If Maple hadn't known better, she would've thought the wistful feeling that tugged at her heart as she read and reread Ford's note might have been homesickness. Nostalgia for a place she'd never really been but longed for, all the same.

Homegrown here in Bluebonnet. Her gaze kept straying back to that phrase, over and over again, as she stood on the threshold of Percy Walker's home, clutching a pie that had been a reluctant thank-you gift from a perfect stranger. Somewhere in the distance, a horse whinnied. Lady Bird whimpered, angling for a bite of peach pie.

It wasn't until Maple felt the wetness on her face that she realized she'd finally given up the fight and let herself cry.

Chapter Four

Percy's landline rang in the dead of night, jolting Maple from a deep sleep.

At first, she thought she must be dreaming. It had been years since she'd even *heard* the shrill ring of a landline. She scarcely recognized the sound. Then, once she dragged her eyes open, she realized she was in a strange bed in a strange house with a strange dog sprawled next to her.

Yep. She plopped her head back down on her pillow and threw her arm over her face. *Definitely a dream.*

But then she caught a whiff of cinnamon on her forearm, and everything came flooding back to her at once. She was in Bluebonnet, Texas. Percy Walker, DVM, was her father, and Maple had found out the truth too late to do anything about it. No wonder she'd eaten an entire peach pie straight from the box for dinner while Lady Bird chowed down on a bowl of premium dog food.

That pie had also been *delicious*. Hands down, the best

she'd ever tasted. Maybe Ford had been right about the virtues of homegrown produce. In any case, Maple had zero regrets about the pie.

She let her swollen eyes drift shut again. She'd wept throughout the entire peach-pie episode, and subsequently had the puffy face and blotchy skin to show for it. Lovely. Her mother would no doubt book Maple a facial the second she deplaned at JFK.

At least the landline had stopped ringing. A quick glance at her cell phone told her it was after two in the morning. If she fell back asleep in the next fifteen minutes, she could still get a good three hours of shut-eye before her hired car showed up to take her to the airport in Austin. As she'd suspected, Uber wasn't a thing in Bluebonnet. It was going to cost her an arm and a leg to get to the airport on time because she'd had to book a service all the way from the city.

Worth every freaking penny, she told herself while Lady Bird snuffled and wheezed beside her. The dog snored louder than a freight train. Alas, not quite loud enough to drown out the landline as it began to ring again.

Maple sat up and tossed the covers aside. "Seriously?"

Who called a dead man's house at this hour?

She stumbled toward the kitchen, where the phone—a vintage rotary classic with a cord approximately ten thousand feet long—hung just to the left of the refrigerator.

Maple plucked the handset from its hook. "Whoever this is, you've got the wrong number."

"Oh." The woman on the other end sounded startled. Again, *seriously*? Couldn't people in Bluebonnet tell time? "I was looking for Lady Bird. Is she not there?"

Maple felt herself frown. "Lady Bird is a dog."

"Of course, she is. Is she available?"

Maybe Maple really *was* dreaming. "You want to speak to Lady Bird on the phone?"

She glanced around, but for once, the golden wasn't glued to her side. No doubt she was still splayed diagonally across the bed, belly-up.

"That's cute, but no. This is Pam Hudson. You can call me Nurse Pam. Everyone does. I work at County General Hospital, and we were hoping Lady Bird could come in to visit with a patient."

Maple blinked as something June said in passing earlier came back to her.

That dog has a way with people who need a little TLC. She's actually sort of famous for it around these parts.

Lady Bird must be a therapy dog. Therapy dogs were specially trained to provide comfort, support, and affection to people in health-care settings. Why hadn't anyone said anything?

Probably because it was none of Maple's business, considering she already had one stylishly clad foot out the door and she hadn't planned on taking the golden with her.

"I apologize for the late hour, but we have a little boy here who's had quite a difficult night, and he's been asking for Lady Bird for the past half hour. It would mean the world to him if she could come visit, even for a few minutes," Nurse Pam said.

"Right now?" Maple asked in a panic.

No. Just…no.

Therapy dogs didn't visit patients all on their own. They worked as a team in conjunction with their owners. And as of today, Lady Bird's owner was Maple.

But Maple wasn't cut out for that type of work, as evidenced by the epic disaster at the pet clinic. She was the absolute last person who should be visiting someone sick and vulnerable. Therapy dog handlers were compassionate. They were active listeners and knew how to engage with people experiencing all sorts of challenges or trauma. They were confident in social situations.

Maple was none of those things.

"I know it's late. I'm so sorry for the interruption, but Oliver always lights up when Lady Bird is here. Percy was always so good about bringing the dog around whenever we called, no matter the hour. I know this is none of my business, but I heard you're his daughter." Pam's voice cracked. "We're really going to miss him around here."

Maple's throat clogged.

Not again. She was done with crying. She'd had her pie-fueled moment of weakness. There was no reason whatsoever to get emotional over a person she'd never met before.

"Do you think you'll be able to bring Lady Bird by?"

The nurse was relentless. Fortunately, Maple had the perfect excuse. "I'm sorry, but even if I wanted to—" *which I don't* "—I can't. I don't have any way to get there. I don't have a car. In fact, I'm leaving early in the morning, and—"

"That's an easy fix!" Pam gushed. "Don't you worry. Someone will be by Percy's house to pick you up shortly."

Maple froze, a deer in headlights. This couldn't be happening. "Wait, no. That's really not—"

Pam interjected, cutting her off. "No need to thank me. We help one another out here. It's the Bluebonnet way."

Of course, it was. Maple couldn't wait to get out of this place and back to New York, where she was hemmed in by people on every side and none of them knew her name or cared a whit about her.

She opened her mouth to protest again, but it was too late. There was a click on the other end of the line as Pam hung up the phone.

Maple gaped at the receiver. She tried pressing the silver

hook where the handset usually rested, but no amount of jabbing at the ancient device would make Pam reappear.

"Nope," Maple said aloud. "Nope, nope, nope."

She wasn't going to do it. Pam couldn't make her. Maple would just call the hospital back and refuse.

But Maple had been half-asleep when she'd taken the call and couldn't remember the name of the hospital the nurse had mentioned. Nor did she know what floor or department Pam had been calling from. All she remembered was that the patient was a little boy named Oliver and that Oliver was having a tough night.

Join the club, Oliver.

Maple dropped her forehead to the phone and concentrated on taking deep breaths. As out of it as she'd been a few minutes ago, she was wide-awake now. Any minute, a stranger intent on dragging her to the hospital was going to knock on the door and they were going to find Maple on the verge of a panic attack, dressed in her favorite cupcake-themed pajamas with pie crumbs in her hair.

This town was the *worst.* How did introverts survive here?

The dreaded knock at the door came in just under twenty minutes. Maple had barely had time to pull on her softest pair of jeans and a J.Crew T-shirt with sketches of dogs of various breeds drinking cocktails from martini glasses. Comfort clothes. Clothes that said she was staying in for the night, no matter what Nurse Pam had to say about it.

She swung Percy's front door open, ready to dig in her heels.

"Look, I—" Maple's tongue tripped over itself as she took in the sight of the man standing on her porch dressed in hospital scrubs. She swallowed hard. "It's you."

Ford Bishop.

Just how small was the population of this town? The man was everywhere—bringing his grandmother into the pet clinic, buying pies, delivering therapy dogs to the hospital in the dead of night. Maple apparently couldn't swing a stick in Bluebonnet without it smacking into one of his nicely toned forearms.

Oh, no. She was staring at his forearms again, wasn't she?

She blinked hard and refocused on his face…on those eyes of his that somehow made Maple want to close her eyes and fall backward onto a soft featherbed.

Something was very clearly wrong with her. She was suffering from some sort of pie-induced hysteria. Maybe even a full nervous breakdown.

Ford tilted his head, studied her for a beat and gave her a smile that almost seemed genuine.

"Hey there, Doc."

Ford squinted at Maple's T-shirt.

Were those dogs? Drinking *martinis*? Interesting choice for a late-night visit to the children's wing of a hospital, but Ford wasn't judging. He was honestly shocked that Pam had managed to twist Maple's arm into bringing Lady Bird to visit Oliver at all.

Shocked, but relieved—so relieved that he'd have happily chauffeured Maple to the hospital in her PJs, if necessary.

"What are you doing here?" Maple asked, blinking rapidly, and Ford's relief took a serious hit.

"I'm giving you and Lady Bird a ride to County General," Ford said. Why else would he be on her doorstep in the middle of the night, dressed in scrubs with his truck still running at the curb?

He wasn't sure why she couldn't drive herself. Percy's

truck was newer than his, and as far as Ford knew, it remained parked right in the garage, where he'd left it. But Ford was happy to give Maple and the dog a ride, if needed. He just wanted to get Lady Bird to the hospital by any means necessary.

"There's been a misunderstanding." Maple shook her head. "Lady Bird isn't feeling up to it."

At the mention of her name, Lady Bird made herself visible by nudging the front door open wider with her snout. The dog wiggled past Maple to offer Ford a proper golden-retriever greeting, complete with tail wags and copious amounts of drool.

Ford dropped to a knee to let Lady Bird plant her paws on his shoulders and lick the side of his face. The dog's wagging tail crashed into Maple's shins. When Ford looked up at her, a deep flush was making its way up her neck.

Liar, liar, pants on fire, he thought.

"I'm no vet, but it seems to me if this dog was feeling under the weather earlier, she's suddenly made a miraculous recovery." Ford stood, and Lady Bird added an exclamation point to his observation by continuing to prance around him like he was hiding bacon in the pockets of his scrubs.

For the record, he was not. The only thing in Ford's pocket was his cell phone, which pinged at least once an hour with a text from Gram. The last missive had been a photo of Coco lying at the foot of her bed watching *Jeopardy* on the small television in Gram's room at the senior center.

"Thank you for the pie. It was heavenly," Maple said, and Ford was pretty sure he spotted a crumb from the crust of said pie in her hair, but he thought it best not to mention it. "But this day has been a real doozie. Pam kind of strong-armed me into the whole pet-visit thing, and I just...can't."

Ford crossed his arms. After this morning, he shouldn't have been surprised. This was a kid they were talking about, though. Was she really saying no?

"Don't look at me like that." Maple scowled.

"How am I looking at you?"

"Like I'm evil incarnate." She gave her chin a jaunty upward tilt. "I told you I wasn't a people person."

Ford narrowed his gaze at her. "Is that what I should say to the eight-year-old little kid who's been puking all night after his most recent chemo treatment when he asks why he can't see Lady Bird?"

She recoiled as if she'd been hit.

"Sorry. That was probably too harsh." Ford held up his hands. He wasn't in the business of guilting people into doing good deeds, all evidence to the contrary.

And he certainly didn't think Maple was evil incarnate. Lost, maybe. Overwhelmed, certainly. Bluebonnet was a small town, and, of course, Ford had heard about Percy's last will and testament. As hard as it was to believe, Maple was Percy Walker's daughter.

The way she wrapped her arms around herself told Ford that no one found it more impossible to believe than she did.

Time to start over. "Look, Oliver is a sweet kid. His mom works nights. He's tired, and he's very sick, or else I wouldn't be standing here on your porch at two in the morning asking for this small favor."

It wasn't small to the average person—especially a person who seemed to have at least a dash of social anxiety. Ford knew this. He just really, *really* wanted Oliver to get a few minutes with Lady Bird. Once the kid set eyes on that dog, he'd sleep like a baby for the rest of the night. Happened every time.

"Lady Bird will do all the work. Oliver will hardly even

look at you, I promise. The dog is the star of the show. I'd take her there myself, but I can't. I could get called away, and hospital rules say I can't leave a patient alone with a therapy dog." Ford shifted from one foot to the other. He needed to get back to work. "Please?"

"You can't leave a patient alone with a therapy dog, but you *can* leave them with someone you don't really know? Someone who isn't even the therapy dog's owner?" She chewed on her bottom lip.

"Aren't you, though?" Ford glanced down at Lady Bird, who'd planted herself directly between them with one big paw resting on Maple's toe. Her impractical stilettos had been replaced with an oversize pair of house slippers. Brown corduroy and large enough to look like they'd come from the men's department. Ford realized he hardly knew Maple, but the shoes definitely seemed out of character.

Then it hit him: the shoes belonged to Percy.

"I'm not staying," Maple said with a shake of her head. She gestured to the house, the dog, and the town in general. "I'll figure out what to do with all of this later, but I can't stay here. I'm going back to New York in the morning."

Ford bristled, even though he couldn't help but think the slippers told a different story. Maple Walker Leighton was more curious about her birth father than she wanted to admit.

But that wasn't any of Ford's business. As for why the sight of her in those slippers filled his chest with warmth, he really couldn't say.

"Please," Ford said again and then reached to pluck the crumb from her hair. He just couldn't help it. Maple's lips parted ever so slightly at his closeness, but she didn't move a muscle. He held up the crumb between his thumb and forefinger. "What if I promised you more pie?"

Her expression softened. Just a bit—just enough for the

warmth in Ford's chest to bloom and expand into something that felt far too much like longing.

No, he told himself. *Don't even think about it.*

This was a business transaction, not a flirtation. He was offering pie in exchange for her dog-handling services. That was it. Come tomorrow, Ford would never set eyes on Maple again.

He swiveled his gaze toward Lady Bird. "Tell Maple there's nothing to be afraid of. She might even have fun."

"I'm not afraid," she sputtered.

"I beg your pardon, I'm not talking to you. This is a conversation between me and the dog." Ford flashed her a wink, and then fixed his gaze with Lady Bird's again. "Go on, tell her."

Lady Bird tossed back her head and let out a *woo-woo* noise somewhere between a howl and a whine.

Maple laughed, and the sound was as light and lovely as church bells. She should really let her guard down more often. "This is *craziness.* Have you two practiced this routine?"

No, but Lady Bird had a wide array of tricks in her repertoire. Percy had trained the dog well, and Ford had seen the golden in action enough times to have committed some of her commands to memory.

Ford didn't tell Maple that, though. He just waggled his eyebrows and shot her one last questioning glance.

"Okay, fine. I'll do it." She thrust two fingers in the air. "Under two conditions."

"Done." Ford nodded, turned toward his truck and whistled at Lady Bird to follow.

"Wait!" Maple shuffled after them in her too-big slippers. "You don't know what the conditions are."

Ford swung open the passenger-side door of his truck

and Lady Bird hopped inside. "I'm guessing the first one is pie."

She crossed her arms, all business. "Accurate."

Ford wondered what, if anything, could make this woman relax. Not that it mattered since she was so dead set on leaving, but it might have been fun to try and find out. "And the second?"

"You've got to promise to get me home in plenty of time to meet my car service for my ride to the airport in the morning."

"No problem, Doc," he said and gave her a curious look, which Maple either didn't notice or chose to ignore.

"I'll be right back. I need to put on some shoes and grab my purse," she said.

"We'll be waiting right here." Ford banged his hand on the hood of his truck and felt his mouth hitch into a grin as she disappeared back into the house.

You've got to promise to get me home, she'd said. Not *back here* or *back to Percy's house.*

Whether or not she'd realized it, Maple had just called this place home.

Chapter Five

After they'd arrived at the hospital, Maple tried to hang back and linger in the doorway to Oliver's room so Ford could check and make sure the little boy wasn't asleep, but Lady Bird had other ideas. The golden hustled right inside, dragging Maple behind her as if they'd been issued a personal invitation. Which she supposed they had, basically.

If the child was disappointed to find Maple on the other end of Lady Bird's leash instead of Percy, he didn't show it. His entire face lit up the second he spotted the dog.

"Lady Bird. You're here!" Oliver scrambled to push himself up in his hospital bed for a better view.

"Hold up, there. I've got you," Ford said as he reached for the call-button remote and pressed the appropriate arrow to raise the head of Oliver's bed.

Maple wondered if the mechanical sounds or the moving piece of furniture might spook Lady Bird, but she handled it like a pro. She shimmied right up to the edge of the bed and gently planted her chin on the edge of the mattress, easily within Oliver's reach.

The boy laid a hand on the golden retriever's head and moved his thumb in gentle circles over Lady Bird's soft, cold fur. "I knew you'd come."

If Maple had still been harboring any doubts about caving and letting Ford take her to County General, they melted away right then and there. A lump formed in her throat. *I knew you'd come.* Even at his young age, Oliver already knew what made dogs so special. They were loyalty and unconditional love, all wrapped up in a warm, furry package. The very idea of Lady Bird failing to show up to comfort him in the dead of night was inconceivable.

The ball of tension in Maple's chest loosened a bit. Even if Oliver ended up despising the sight of her, like everyone else in this town, at least she'd done one thing right. She'd gotten the dog here and managed to help preserve the child's belief in the goodness and loyalty of man's best friend. It felt good, despite the fact that she was still doing her best to blend into the beige hospital walls.

"Oliver, bud. I want you to meet a friend of mine." Ford smiled at her, and for reasons she really didn't want to think about, her heart went pitter-patter. "This is Maple. She's taking care of Lady Bird for now."

Maple held up a hand and took a step closer to Oliver's bed. "Hi."

"Hey," Oliver said without tearing his gaze away from the dog. Lady Bird had nudged her head so it fully rested in the boy's lap, and her eyes were trained on his pale face.

"I've got to go check on something, okay?" Ford glanced at the smart watch on his wrist. "I'll be back in about fifteen minutes. Twenty, max."

He was leaving? Already?

Ford shot her a reassuring wink. “Oliver, take it easy on Maple, okay? She’s shy.”

Maple’s face went warm. “I’m sure we’ll be fine.”

She was sure of nothing of the sort. So far, the people she’d met in Bluebonnet weren’t at all like the people she knew back home. She’d been in town for a day, and already everyone seemed to know more about her personal business than she typically shared with friends, much less strangers. There were no walls here. No barriers to hide behind. No *crowds.* She felt wholly exposed, which was especially nerve-racking considering she was trying to adjust to a whole new version of herself as a person.

You’re still Maple Leighton. Absolutely nothing about your life has to change.

But what if she wanted it to?

She didn’t, though. Of course not. Maple had a plan—a plan that she’d worked long and hard for. Grover had given her full permission to skip the first wasted year of that plan and move full steam ahead toward her dreams. Her dad had already paved the way for her to walk right into her perfectly planned future. Now wasn’t the time to entertain change.

Something about the quiet intimacy of a hospital room in the middle of the night was making her question everything, though. Time seemed to stand still in places like this. The outside world felt very far away.

Maple took a deep breath and moved to sit in the chair that Ford had dragged too close to Oliver’s bedside for her. This was crazy. She had no clue what to say or do, and panic was already blossoming in her chest as Ford sauntered out of the room in his blue hospital scrubs.

“You like dogs, huh?” she said quietly after Ford was gone.

Oliver nodded but didn’t say anything. He just kept

toying with Lady's Bird's ears, running them through his small fingers. The dog's eyes slowly drifted closed.

"She really likes that." Maple smiled. "I love dogs, too."

"My mom says when I'm better, I can get a dog of my own." Oliver's gaze finally swiveled in her direction. The dark circles under his eyes made her heart twist. *When I'm better...* She prayed that would happen and it would be soon. "When I do, I want one just like Lady Bird."

"She's quite special." Maple's throat went thick, and she wondered what would happen to the dog once she'd gone. She'd been staying with June since Percy's passing, but the older woman hadn't said anything about keeping Lady Bird and giving her a permanent home.

Why would she? This dog is supposed to be yours *now.*

Maple's grip on the leash tightened.

"Do you want to see some pictures I drew of her?" Oliver asked with a yawn.

Maple nodded. "I'd love to."

Oliver pointed at his bedside table. "They're in the top drawer. You can get them out if you want to."

"Are you sure?" Maple hesitated. She wasn't sure rummaging through a patient's nightstand was proper protocol.

But Oliver seemed determined. He nodded. "There's a whole bunch of drawings in there, right on top of the chocolate bars I'm not supposed to know about. My mom keeps them for me. She's going to make a whole book out of my drawings for me when I leave the hospital."

"That's a great idea," Maple said, biting back a smile at the mention of secret chocolate. Something told her nothing got past Oliver.

She pulled open the drawer and sure enough, there was a neat stack of papers covered in bold strokes of crayon nestled inside.

"These are amazing, Oliver." Maple slowly flipped

through the drawings, which seemed to chronicle Oliver's stay in the hospital.

In the first few, the little boy in the pictures had a mop of curly brown hair. Soon, the child in the drawings had a smooth, bald head, just like Oliver's.

"That's Ford," Oliver said when her gaze landed on a rendering of a man in familiar-looking blue scrubs with a stethoscope slung around his neck.

Maple grinned. "It looks just like him."

Except the kid had forgotten to add a yellow halo above Ford's head. Maple still wasn't sure what, exactly, Ford did around here, but she had a feeling that escorting therapy dogs and their handlers to the hospital wasn't part of his official job description.

He was almost too wholesome to be real—like the humble, flannel-wearing, small-town love interest in a Hallmark movie. Whereas Maple was the big-city villainess who always ended up getting dumped for a cupcake baker in those sticky-sweet movies. It happened every time. How many cupcake bakers did the world *actually* need, anyway?

"And here's Lady Bird." Maple held up the next drawing, which featured a big yellow dog sprawled across Oliver's hospital bed, definitely a case of art imitating life. "I'd know that big golden anywhere. I really love your artwork, Oliver."

The child gave her a sleepy grin. "There's lots more."

"There sure is." Maple sifted through page after page of colorful renderings of Lady Bird, and she felt herself going all gooey inside. Not full-on cupcake-baker-gooey, but definitely softer than she normally allowed herself to feel around people she'd only just met.

Then she flipped to the next page, and her entire body tensed.

"That's Lady Bird with Mr. Percy." Oliver lifted one hand

from the dog's ear just long enough to point to a crayon-sketched figure with gray hair and an oversize pair of glasses perched on his round face.

Mr. Percy. Maple's *father.*

She wasn't sure why his likeness caught her so off guard. She knew good and well that Lady Bird was Percy's dog, and he'd been the one to take the dog on her pet-therapy visits. But something about seeing him drawn in Oliver's young hand brought back the feeling she'd had just hours ago when she'd toed off her stilettos and slid her feet into his slippers.

She still wasn't quite sure why she'd done it. The shoes had been placed right next to the bed in the small home's master bedroom, as if Percy was expected to climb out of bed and slip them on just like any other day. Before she'd known what she was doing, she'd put them on and tried to imagine what it might be like to follow in her birth father's footsteps. Was it just a coincidence that she'd become a veterinarian, just like him, or was there a part of him still living inside her? Perhaps there had been, all along.

Maple wasn't sure what to believe anymore. All she knew was that somewhere deep down, she was beginning to feel a flicker of connection to a man she'd never met before.

And it scared the life out of her.

"Ford said Mr. Percy is in heaven now," Oliver said.

Maple's heart squeezed into a tight fist. She knew next to nothing about her birth father, but heaven seemed like just the right place for the kind man in Oliver's drawing.

"Ford's right," she heard herself say.

Oliver's eyes drifted shut, then he blinked hard, jolting himself awake.

"Oliver, it's okay if you fall asleep. Lady Bird and I will be here when you wake up. I promise," Maple said.

"Really?" the little boy asked, eyes wide as he buried a small hand in the ruff of fur around the dog's thick neck.

"Really." Maple nodded.

What was she saying? She had a plane to catch and a whole life waiting for her back in New York. Her *real* life, as opposed to the one here in Bluebonnet that was rapidly beginning to feel like some kind of alternate universe.

But try as she might, Maple couldn't think of a more important place she needed to be at the moment than this hospital room. For once in her life, she was right where she belonged.

"You *do* realize what time it is, don't you?" Ford narrowed his gaze at Maple, still sitting at Oliver's bedside mere minutes before the deadline she'd given him when he'd picked her up earlier and all but dragged her to the hospital against her will.

"Not precisely, but I have a good idea," she said, gaze flitting toward the window, where the first rays of sun bathed the room in a soft golden glow.

Ford crossed his arms. "You made me promise to get you home in time for your rideshare to Austin. That means we need to go now, or all bets are off."

"I guess all bets are off, then." Maple reached over the guardrail of the hospital bed and rested a hand on Lady Bird's back. The big dog was stretched out alongside Oliver, paws twitching in her sleep.

Ford didn't know what to make of this unexpected turn of events. The dog's part in the impromptu sleepover was no surprise whatsoever. He'd seen Lady Bird sleep anywhere and everywhere, and the golden seemed especially fond of Oliver.

Maple, on the other hand…

Ford felt himself frown. Every time he thought he had

this woman figured out, she threw him for a loop. It almost made her fun to be around.

"Why are you looking at me like that?" she asked.

"How am I looking at you?" Ford crossed the room to drag the other armchair closer to the recliner, where Maple had her feet tucked up under her legs. He raked a hand through his hair and sat down.

She gave him a sidelong glance. "Like you don't believe me when I say all bets are off."

"Probably because I don't. You seemed awfully sure about catching that rideshare."

She shrugged, but the way she averted her gaze told him her decision hadn't been as casual as she wanted him to believe. "I promised Oliver that Lady Bird would be here when he woke up."

Ford nudged her knee with his. "Careful there, Doc. You almost sound like a people person."

She turned to glare at him, but he could tell her heart wasn't in it. "I'm sure it's just a phase. I'll get it over it soon enough."

"If you say so." He bit back a smile.

"Can I ask you a question?" she asked, deftly changing the subject.

He leaned back in the chair and stretched his legs out in front of him. "Shoot. I'm an open book."

"What exactly do you do here?" She eyed his scrubs, and a cute little furrow formed in her brow. "Are you a nurse?"

"I'm a pediatrician. I have a solo practice in Bluebonnet, but I've got privileges here at County General. Oliver is one of my patients." Ford had, in fact, been Oliver's doctor since the day he'd been born. He loved that kid. Sometimes being a small-town doctor meant you got a little too close to your patients, although Ford usually didn't consider that a problem.

Oliver's case was different, though. *Special.* He would've moved heaven and earth to see that child healthy again.

The furrow in Maple's brow deepened, and Ford had the nonsensical urge to smooth it out with a brush of his fingertips. "Please tell me you're joking. You can't be a doctor."

"Not a joke. I assure you." A smile tugged at his lips. He was enjoying her befuddlement a little too much. "What's wrong, Doc? Have you got a thing against physicians like you do against robotic animals?"

She regarded him with what could only be described as abject horror. "I do when said physician intentionally let me believe he wasn't a doctor."

Ford shook his head. "I never intentionally misled you. Name one time I did that."

"How about every single time you've called me Doc?" She was blushing again, and Ford wasn't sure if it was embarrassment or rage. Probably some combination of the two, if he had to guess.

"But you *are* a doctor—a doctor of veterinary medicine. As I recall, you seem especially proud of the title." Okay, so maybe the nickname had been somewhat of a taunt. Ford hadn't been able to resist.

She gasped as if she'd just remembered something, and then she covered her face with her hands. "Oh, my gosh. You let me go on and on about the two types of doctors, didn't you?"

"You mean general-practice physicians who are driven by their innate need to help people and specialists who relate more to the scientific part of medicine?" Ford said with his tongue firmly planted in his cheek as he parroted her own words back to her.

"I guess we know which one you are, Mr. Hometown Hero." She snorted.

She had him pegged, that was for sure. Ford had made it his mission to become a pediatrician back in the fifth grade when his best friend, Bobby Jackson, had died from acute myelogenous leukemia. Over the course of a single little league season, Bobby had gone from being the star pitcher for the Bluebonnet Bears to being bedridden with the disease. By Christmas, he was gone. Ford's small world had crumbled down around him, and in a way, he'd been trying to put it back together ever since.

So, yeah, he'd gone into medicine to help people. Was that really such a bad thing?

Lately, he'd begun to wonder. If he'd become a specialist instead of a pediatrician, he could've done more for Oliver and other children like him.

Children like Bobby, he thought as the memory of his best friend floated to the forefront of his mind. It had been years since Ford had spent the night at Bobby's ranch, tucked into their matching Spider-Man sleeping bags in the treehouse in Bobby's shady backyard. Two and a half decades, in fact. But he still remembered those nights like they'd happened yesterday—the shimmering stars overhead, the swishing of the horses' tails as they grazed in the pasture just beyond the barbed-wire fence, the feeling that Bluebonnet was the safest place in the world and nothing bad could ever happen there...

Ford knew better now, obviously. But that didn't stop him from doing his level best to make it true. He'd moved away once, and that had been a terrible mistake. Now, he was home for good and still trying to hold things together, as if it was possible to carry the entire town on his back. At least that's what his sister always said.

Maple resumed glaring at Ford, a welcome distraction from his spiraling thoughts. Why did things always seem so much more hopeless in the dead of night?

"You're impossible. I can't believe you didn't tell me," Maple said.

Ford arched an eyebrow. "You didn't ask."

She sure as heck hadn't. She'd barreled into town like a tornado, all too ready to flatten everything and everyone in her wake.

That had certainly backfired.

Ford had heard all about Percy's last will and testament. There were no secrets in Bluebonnet. By now, everyone in town knew that Maple Leighton was Percy Walker's long-lost daughter.

She'd had quite a day. Ford should probably go easy on her, but where was the fun in that? Besides, Maple didn't seem like the type who wanted to be treated with kid gloves. Everything Ford knew about her thus far screamed the opposite.

He slid his attention away from Oliver and Lady Bird, still sleeping soundly in the hospital bed, and found Maple watching him, eyes glittering in the darkened room. Their gazes met and held, until her bow-shaped lips curved into a knowing smile.

A delicious heat coursed through Ford, like wildflower honey warmed by the summer sun. "What's the grin for? I thought I was impossible."

"Oh, you definitely are." Her eyes narrowed, ever so slightly. "And that just made me realize something."

"What's that, Doc?"

She looked away, focusing on the boy and the dog. But Ford could still spy a ghost of a smile dancing on her lips. "You're not quite as nice as you seem, Ford Bishop."

Chapter Six

"What are we doing here?" Maple peered out the windshield of Ford's pickup as he pulled into one of the prime parking spots along Bluebonnet's town square.

He shifted the truck into Park and nodded at Cherry on Top Bakery, situated directly in front of them. "I promised you pie. Or have you decided to forgo that condition, too?"

Maple's heart thumped at the mention of her conditions. Missing her rideshare had seemed like a perfectly logical decision an hour ago, when she'd been sitting at Oliver's bedside with Lady Bird. Now, not so much.

She swallowed. Oliver had woken up shortly after she'd learned Ford was the boy's doctor. Maple had seen his eyes flutter open and then slam shut when he realized the adults were still there. Oliver made a valiant attempt at faking it, no doubt to prolong saying goodbye to Lady Bird. But as soon as Ford told Maple in a loud whisper that the hospital breakfast for the day would include sweet-potato, hashbrown egg nests—Oliver's favorite, apparently—the child sat up, bright-eyed and bushy-tailed.

Ford had escorted Maple and Lady Bird out of Oliver's room just as his breakfast arrived. Approximately two seconds later, panic settled in the pit of Maple's stomach.

What was she *doing*? She was supposed to be halfway to Austin right now, not sitting in close proximity to an actual gazebo beside Ford in his charming, vintage pickup truck. He had one of those classic turquoise Fords from the 1960s, and naturally, it was in perfect, shiny mint condition. What else would Dr. Small Town Charm drive?

"The condition absolutely still stands." Maple was starving. She hadn't eaten a thing since diving head-first into the peach pie Ford had left on her front porch the night before. "But look, they're not open yet."

She waved toward the Sorry, We're Closed sign hanging in the bakery's front window. The rest of the town square was deserted, as well. Maple wasn't sure what time sleepy small towns like this typically woke up, but apparently it was sometime after 6:42 a.m.

Ford shrugged and flashed her a smile worthy of a toothpaste commercial. "I know the owner."

"Of course you do." Maple rolled her eyes.

Ford climbed down from the driver's seat and Lady Bird, who'd been nestled between them on the bench seat during the ride back to Bluebonnet from County General, bounded after him.

Maple paused, wondering how fast she could get to Austin if she went straight back to Percy's house to pack her things and summon another hired car. Why was this state so darn big?

Lady Bird gazed up at her with an expectant wag of her fluffy gold tail. *Are you coming or what?*

Maple's stomach growled, right on cue. There had to be

other flights from Austin to New York today, right? They were both huge, metropolitan cities. Just because she'd missed the early morning flight didn't mean she was stuck here indefinitely. Surely, there was time for a tiny bite of pie.

She slid out of the passenger seat and headed toward the bakery, where Ford swung the door open like he owned the place. Lady Bird pranced straight inside while Maple lingered on the threshold.

She glanced at Ford as he held the door open for her. "Are dogs allowed in here?"

"What dog?" A woman with a high blond ponytail juggled pies in each hand and winked at them from behind the counter. "I don't see any dog, just my sweet nurse friend Lady Bird."

Lady Bird immediately got an extra spring in her step at the sound of her name. She trotted toward the counter, nose twitching in the general direction of the pies, which smelled like they'd just come straight from the oven.

"Hi, there. I'm Adaline." She slid the pies onto the counter and waved at Maple with an oven mitt decorated with the same whimsical cherry print as her ruffle-trimmed apron.

"I'm Maple."

"Maple is new in town," Ford said as he lowered himself onto one of the barstools at the counter. He gave the stool next to him a pat. "Come on, scaredy cat."

Adaline lifted an eyebrow.

"Maple is a tad shy," Ford said. "Right, Lady Bird?"

Maple *really* wished he'd stop staying that, although she supposed it was preferable to Ford broadcasting the fact that she'd told him she wasn't a people person. Did he have to say anything at all, though? Why did it feel like the entire town was populated by oversharers?

Lady Bird woofed her agreement before collapsing in

a heap at Ford's feet. Great. Even the dog had an opinion about her social skills.

"Oh, wait." Adaline's eyes lit up. "You must be the peach pie from yesterday."

"That was me." Maple took the seat next to Ford. "It was delicious, by the way."

"So delicious that she insisted I bring her in for more." Ford pointed at one of the pies in front of Adaline. "Do I smell cherries?"

Adaline jammed her hands on her hips. "Ford Bishop, are you seriously waltzing in here less than an hour before we open, expecting to eat my inventory?"

"Yes." He nodded. "Yes, I am."

Maple glanced back and forth between them, wondering how they knew each other. The vibe between them was playful, but it didn't have a flirtatious edge.

Maple breathed a senseless sigh of relief. Lady Bird lifted her face from her paws and gave Maple a little head tilt, as if the dog could read her mind. Intuition was a valuable quality in a therapy dog, but in this case, it just seemed nosy.

And way off base. Maple didn't have a jealous bone in her body where Ford was concerned. In fact, a small-town baker was exactly the sort of person he should be with. Maple should be rooting for these two crazy kids.

Then why aren't you?

"Fine," Adaline said, relenting, then she reached for a silver cake server. "But only because Maple is new in town, like you said. She deserves a proper welcome."

"I'm not really, though—new in town, I mean." Maple protested as Adaline served up an enormous slice of cherry pie and slid the plate toward her. Her mouth was already watering. "I'm not staying in Bluebonnet. I'm leaving today, actually."

Probably, anyway. She still needed to get that figured out.

"Oh." Adaline shot Ford a loaded glance, which Maple had no idea how to interpret. "What did my brother do to scare you off so quickly?"

Maple's fork paused halfway to her mouth. "You two are brother and sister?"

That made sense. No wonder they seemed so comfortable around each other.

"We are." Adaline pulled a face, as if being related to Ford was something to be ashamed of.

Maple decided right there and then that she liked Adaline Bishop. She liked her a lot. Too bad she'd never see her again—or eat any more of her delicious baked goods—after today.

Maple swallowed a forkful of pie, and it suddenly felt like a rock in the pit of her stomach.

"I didn't do anything to scare her off. This big-city wariness you're observing is Maple's natural state. I've been nothing but welcoming." Ford cut his eyes toward her. When he looked at her like that—as if his dreamy blue eyes could see straight into her soul—she sometimes forgot how to breathe. It was beyond annoying.

Maple focused intently on the rich red cherries on her plate. "Except for the part where you tricked me into examining a fake dog. And then dragged me to the hospital in the middle of the night. And then lied about being a doctor."

A bark of laughter burst out of Adaline. "Oh, this is getting good. She's got your number, Ford."

"She also has quite a flair for exaggeration," Ford countered. "Where's *my* pie, by the way? You just gave her a supersized slice, and I'm still sitting here empty-handed."

"Hold your horses. I was just getting to know my new bestie." Adaline shot Maple a wink as she cut a significantly smaller piece of pie for her brother. "Too bad you're not staying, Maple. I have a feeling we'd be great friends."

"Yeah," Maple said quietly. "I think we would, too."

A heaviness came over Maple that she wanted to attribute to lack of sleep, but it felt more like regret. Aside from her study group in vet school, she didn't have many friends in New York.

"Are you sure you have to go so soon?" Adaline picked up a mixing bowl and began measuring cups of flour to dump into it.

"I actually just missed my flight. I need to try and get another one later this afternoon. Everything right now is a little—" she swallowed and didn't dare venture a glance in Ford's direction "—complicated."

Adaline nodded as if she understood, but a flicker of confusion passed through her gaze. How could she possibly understand when Maple still hadn't managed to get a handle on her current circumstances herself?

"I need—" she began, ready to rattle off a list of perfectly rational reasons why she needed to get back to Manhattan, starting with her highly coveted position at the veterinary cardiology practice. But before she could utter another syllable, her cell phone rang, piercing the awkward silence that had descended at the mention of Maple's missed flight.

She dug the phone out of her purse and nearly dropped it when she spied her mother's name flashing across the top of the display screen. Lady Bird let out a long, drawn-out sigh.

Maple's gaze darted toward the dog, but the golden's sweet, melting expression only sharpened the dull ache of regret into something much more painful. What was going to happen to Lady Bird once she was gone?

Maple gripped her phone tight. "I should probably take this."

Lady Bird was practically the mayor of this town. The dog would have no trouble whatsoever finding a good home. Maple wouldn't be surprised if there ended up being a contest of some sort. She just needed to keep her eye on the prize long enough to get out of here.

The front door had barely closed behind Maple when Adaline abandoned her baking to give Ford a sisterly third degree.

"What do you think you're doing?" she said, pointing a wooden spoon at him for added emphasis.

Ford should've known this was coming. But truly, his sister was barking up the wrong tree.

"I'm eating my pie." He aimed his fork over his plate for another bite.

"Nice try." She slid the plate away from him, and his fork stabbed nothing but air. "You know what I'm talking about. What's going on between you two?"

Adaline cast a purposeful glance over his shoulder toward the town square, where Maple was now pacing back and forth as she talked on the phone. Lady Bird scrambled to her feet, trotted toward the door and proceeded to stare out the window at Maple while emitting a mournful whine.

"Nothing whatsoever is going on. Like I said, I'm just here for the pie. I'm perfectly content to mind my own business." Ford waved his fork between his sister and Lady Bird. "Unlike you two."

"Oh, please. From what Maple said, it sounds like you've spent an awful lot of time together in the past twenty-four hours." Adaline pointed her wooden spoon at him again.

Ford just wanted his pie back. Was that really too much to ask?

"For the record, Maple hasn't even been here twenty-four hours yet." He snagged his plate back while Adaline processed what he'd just said. "And she's already got one foot out the door, so I repeat—nothing whatsoever is going on."

His sister eyed him with thinly veiled skepticism. "You bought her a pie yesterday, and from the looks of things, you just spent the night together."

Ford loved his sister. He really did. He loved Bluebonnet too, with all his heart and soul...despite the fact that the general population of his hometown—Adaline, included—had never believed in the concept of privacy. Every place on earth had its downside.

"We spent the night at County General. *Working.* I had patients to attend to, and Maple brought Lady Bird for a therapy-dog visit. That's all. I promised to bring her here in exchange for coming to the hospital in the middle of the night."

Adaline's expression turned serious. "Was this for the little boy who has leukemia?"

Ford's teeth ground together. He'd already told his sister too much about Oliver. He'd never disclosed the child's name, but even talking about one of his patients in vague terms went against his ethics as a physician.

The similarities between Oliver's case and his memories of Bobby were too much, though. Same diagnosis, same age, same sickening feeling in Ford's gut. Every time he ran Oliver's blood count or checked the results of his most recent bone-marrow aspiration, Ford was plunged straight back to that awful summer when Bobby stopped showing up at the baseball diamond and his parents couldn't look him in the eye when they tried to explain what was wrong. In a moment of weakness, he'd shared only the bare basics of Oliver's story with Adaline. She'd known Bobby, too, and she'd been there when Ford's safe little world had been rocked straight off its axis. Telling her had felt right at the time, and for a moment, a bit of the weight had lifted off Ford's shoulders. He'd been able to breathe again.

It had been a mistake. He knew that much now. Things had been easier when Ford could compartmentalize his feelings and pretend everything was fine. He couldn't do that anymore now that Adaline knew the truth. It seemed Ford's sister had as much interest in his favorite patient as she did his romantic pursuits, and Ford had zero desire to discuss either.

"You know I can't talk about that," he said.

She held up her hands. "I know, I know. I just hope he's doing okay. It's sweet that Maple came up there so late, whatever the reason. Staying all night is a pretty big deal. That's all I'm saying."

Ford shot her a sardonic look. "Is it really *all* you're saying?"

That would be a first.

Adaline crossed her arms and huffed. "Fine. You bought Maple an entire pie yesterday. That seems significant, wouldn't you agree?"

Granted, Ford wasn't generally in the business of feeding women baked goods. Until recently, apparently.

"The peach pie was Gram's doing, not mine. I was simply following orders." He gave his dessert an aggressive jab with this fork. Why did he feel the need to defend himself when he was telling the truth? Nothing had happened between him and Maple, and nothing ever would. Period. "I took Gram and Coco to the vet yesterday, and Maple works there. Or she did… Clearly, that's changed."

He was getting whiplash trying to keep up with Maple's plans. Not that where she lived or worked was any of his business. He just needed to know how to get ahold of Lady Bird, that's all.

Ford choked down the last bite of his pie and pushed away his plate. He'd lost his appetite all of a sudden.

Adaline took the plate and placed it in the sink behind the counter. Then she planted her hands on the smooth Formica and fixed her gaze with his, eyes wary. Obviously, she wasn't buying what he was selling. "Do I need to remind you what happened the last time you got involved with a woman who wasn't suited for small-town life?"

She absolutely did not. Ford couldn't have forgotten that particular disaster if he'd tried. And, oh, how he'd tried—many, many times. Certain heartbreaks had a way of burrowing deep, though.

"No need," Ford said.

"Are you sure? Because Maple seems really great. I was serious when I said I thought we'd be great friends. But she's obviously not cut out for Bluebonnet."

Ford knew better than to ask his sister to elaborate, because that would mean he was taking Adaline's warning seriously. Which he wasn't. He had no interest whatsoever in history repeating itself, and Maple had been trying to escape Bluebonnet since the moment they'd first met. How could he forget?

I'm from New York City. But I live here now...temporarily.

They'd practically been Maple's first words to him, and Ford had heard them loud and clear. It wasn't possible to place a bigger emphasis on *temporarily.*

"She'll be gone by tomorrow morning, and it can't come soon enough. You can stop worrying about me." Ford jerked his head toward Lady Bird, still pining at the door while she kept track of Maple's every move. Adaline's pristine, polished glass was rapidly becoming smudged with golden-retriever nose prints. "Lady Bird over there might be a different story."

"That dog loves everyone," Adaline said.

Ford shook his head. "This is different."

Adaline's forehead scrunched. "How can you tell?"

"I just can." Ford's heart went out to the poor dog.

He wondered if the golden could tell that Maple was related to Percy. A while back, he'd read an article in a medical journal that speculated dogs could identify blood relatives purely by smell. If that was the case, Maple was now the closest thing Lady Bird had to Percy, whom she'd adored with unfettered devotion.

"Mark my words. If you're worried about anyone, it should be Lady Bird," Ford said. For once, the dog didn't respond to the sound of her name. She kept her gaze trained out the window, laser-focused on Maple's every move.

"Are you sure you're not just projecting?" Adaline cleared her throat. "From where I'm standing, you and Lady Bird have matching puppy-dog expressions. That's all I'm saying."

"That's *all* you're saying? Again?" Ford arched an eyebrow. "Is that a promise this time?"

It was too early in the morning for a deep dive into his love life. Not that he had any love life to speak of, which was purely intentional.

"For now. As for the future, I make no guarantees." Adaline wadded up her dish towel and threw it at his face.

"Duly noted," Ford said dryly.

Ever the perfect therapy dog, Lady Bird abandoned her post to shuffle back to the counter and press the bulk of her warm form against Ford's leg. Then she rested her chin on his knee with an audible sigh, leaving Ford to wonder which one of them was supposed be on the receiving end of the comfort being offered.

Man, dog…or, quite possibly, both.

Chapter Seven

The best Maple could do was get on standby for a two o'clock flight out of Austin. She'd checked all the major airlines, and there wasn't an empty seat to be found, much to the dismay of her mother. *And* her father.

Once again, the Leightons had joined forces as soon as they'd found out that Maple had missed her morning flight. She'd done her best to assure her mother she still had every intention of returning to New York as soon as humanly possible. But no sooner had she admitted to missing her rideshare than her father had jumped on the line.

What was happening? Who knew the only way to get her parents back on speaking terms was for her to go rogue, flee to Texas, and accidentally discover she'd been adopted.

Surely, Maple could get a standby seat on one of the five flights scheduled to leave between afternoon and midnight. What were the odds she'd get stuck here...*again*?

"Not going to happen," she said out loud as she folded her cupcake pajamas and placed them in her suitcase.

Lady Bird lifted her head from her paws, where she was resting on the dog bed in the corner of Percy's bedroom. She tilted her gold head in the irresistible way that dogs had been doing since the dawn of time, and a fresh wave of guilt washed over Maple. How was she going to leave this sweet dog behind? Lady Bird was the only remaining tie she had to the father she'd never known. Was she seriously going to get on a plane and let someone else take care of her when Percy had specifically left the dog in her care?

You never knew him, she reminded herself. Things would be different if she'd known she'd been adopted before Percy passed away. It was too late to get to know her birth father, and it was definitely too late to build a life in a place like Bluebonnet. She'd spent a full year as an intern for her cardiology specialty. Small towns didn't need veterinary cardiologists. Even if she wanted to stay and follow in Percy's footsteps at his charming little pet clinic—which she didn't—doing so would mean wasting a large chunk of her education.

And then there was the matter of Dr. Grover Hayes. If she stayed, he would be her *partner*. Maple didn't know which one of them would find that prospect more horrifying. It would be a disaster, full stop.

"Why am I even thinking about any of this? I'm not staying." She slammed her suitcase closed and zipped it shut. Then her gaze fell to Percy's bedroom slippers sitting neatly beside the bed, where Maple had returned them to their proper place.

Her eyes immediately filled with unshed tears, and she squeezed them closed tight, determined not to get weepy about a total stranger who just so happened to share her DNA. What was wrong with her? She never let her emotions get the best of her like this. No wonder her parents were concerned.

Maple sniffed and squared her shoulders. Then she opened her eyes and found Lady Bird sitting at her feet, holding Percy's slippers in her mouth.

You've got to be kidding me, dog.

Maple stared as her throat squeezed closed.

"Fine." She gently snatched the shoes from the retriever's jaws. "I'm taking these with me. Happy now?"

Lady Bird's mouth stretched into a wide doggy grin as her tail swished back and forth on the bedroom's smooth wood floor.

"You're really something, you know that?" Maple whispered. She shook her head, unzipped her bag, and carefully placed the slippers inside.

The vintage rotary phone in the kitchen trilled, causing her to jump. It was a good thing she wasn't staying, because she'd never grow accustomed to that sound.

"We're not answering that," she said, but before the words left her mouth, Lady Bird was already trotting toward the source of the noise.

Maple followed, keenly aware of which party seemed to be in charge in this relationship. Spoiler alert: it wasn't Maple. But that was fine for now. So long as the dog was bossing Maple around, she didn't have much time to think about a certain pediatrician who seemed to possess a warm and wonderful center that was as soft and gooey and perfect as a cinnamon roll fresh out of the oven.

He healed sick children. He frequented his sister's pie shop. He pretended his grandmother's robot dog was real. Was Ford even a real human being?

She eyed Lady Bird while the phone continued to ring. "I already told you we're not answering that."

But what if it was County General again? What if something had happened to sweet little Oliver?

Maple plucked the receiver from its hook, all the while

telling herself that answering the call had nothing whatsoever to do with Ford Bishop, even though a teeny tiny part of her heart did a backflip at the thought of seeing him one more time before she left Bluebonnet for good. "Hello?"

"Oh, good morning! So happy you picked up. Is this Maple Walker?"

Maple's entire body gave a jolt. *Walker.* Percy's last name, not hers.

Was there a single soul in all of Bluebonnet who hadn't heard that Maple was his long-lost daughter? Apparently not—yet another reason to get back to Manhattan, where the details of her birth certificate weren't front-page news.

Maple "Um. Yes, but—"

"Thank heavens," the caller said before Maple could point out that her last name was actually Leighton, despite whatever she might have heard via the town rumor mill. "Technically, I'm calling for Lady Bird, but she's yours now, right?"

Once again, Maple had no idea what to say. This time, she didn't even try to come up with a response. She just kept her mouth shut and frowned down at Lady Bird.

I told you we shouldn't answer the phone.

The dog's plumed tail wagged even harder.

"This is Virginia Roberts over at Bluebonnet Senior Living. We were expecting Lady Bird fifteen minutes ago for her regular weekly visit. Can you let me know when she might arrive?"

"Oh." Maple's stomach churned. She couldn't allow herself to get roped into another pet-therapy visit. No way, no how. "Well…"

"We have about a dozen residents gathered in the lobby, ready and waiting. I'd hate to have to disappoint them." Virginia cleared her throat.

Maple gritted her teeth and counted to ten, steadying

herself to say no. Granted, she technically had time to squeeze in a pet visit since her ride wasn't coming for another three hours.

But still…

No.

Just say it, she told herself. *Sorry, but no.*

Then she made the mistake of glancing back down at Lady Bird. She blinked up at Maple with such trust and devotion in her soft brown eyes that Maple's resistance crumbled on the spot.

"We'll be there as soon as we can."

Luckily, the senior center was located just off the town square, a short two-block walk from Percy's house. Maple followed the walking directions on her iPhone's GPS, but she could've simply allowed Lady Bird to guide her there, because the golden clearly knew where they were headed. She tugged gently at the end of her leash, making the left at the town square, followed by an immediate right, without any guidance whatsoever from Maple. The closer they came, the harder Lady Bird's tail wagged. When the sign for Bluebonnet Senior Living came into view, Maple could barely keep up.

It was a blessing, really. Maple's social anxiety didn't have time to kick in before Lady Bird dragged her through the door.

The young man who worked at the front desk lit up like a Christmas tree the instant they crossed the threshold. "Lady Bird! It's so good to see you! We've got a big crowd waiting for you, as usual."

The dog's tail swung back and forth, but her overall demeanor instantly changed. A steady calmness came over her, as if she knew she was here to work, just like it had at the hospital.

Maple couldn't help but swell with pride, even though

she had nothing whatsoever to do with Lady Bird's training. That had been Percy's doing. Was it strange that she felt connected to them both, somehow?

"Hi, I'm Maple." She lifted a hand to wave at the young man stationed at the reception desk while he pulled a box of dog biscuits out of his bottom desk drawer. "Sorry we're late. I didn't realize Lady Bird had a visit scheduled for today."

"No worries," he said as Lady Bird rose up onto her hind legs and planted her front paws on the desk to politely take the treat he offered her. "We're just glad you were able to make it. Her visit is every Tuesday morning at eleven, just so you know. We always have it listed on the social calendar."

He tipped his head toward a wall calendar covered with colorful stickers and handwritten activities like bingo and movie night listed in bright magic marker. A paw print featured prominently on every Tuesday square beside Lady Bird's name.

Now would be the time to mention that Lady Bird's future visits were up in the air, but when Maple glanced beyond the reception desk and saw a large group of residents sitting in wheelchairs and peering toward her and Lady Bird in anticipation, she just couldn't do it.

She took a deep breath as the first tingle of nerves skittered down her spine. This wasn't like the calm, quiet visit with Oliver. This was an entire group of people who would all be focused on Maple and the dog.

More the dog, she reminded herself.

They could do this. *She* could do this, so long as Lady Bird was on the other end of the leash.

Finished with her biscuit, the dog licked her chops and hopped back down to all fours. She dropped into a perfect sit position and gazed up at Maple expectantly.

Maple stared back, unsure what the dog was waiting for.

"Go visit," a deep voice rumbled from just beyond the reception desk.

"Excuse me?" Maple leaned to the left, and that's when she spotted him. *Again.*

Maple's heart did a rebellious little flutter.

She swallowed hard. "You."

"You," Ford echoed, narrowing his gaze at Maple.

He hadn't expected to see her again, well…*ever.* Once she'd ended her call earlier at Cherry on Top and come back inside the bakery, she'd been all business. She'd been in such a hurry to get back to Percy's house so she could pack and make new travel arrangements that, much to Adaline's consternation, she hadn't even finished her pie.

Their goodbye had been strained and awkward, and all the while, Ford had told himself it was for the best. Life could go back to normal around here.

Never mind that the prospect of normal suddenly felt a little dull. A little predictable.

A little lonely.

Ford gritted his teeth and reminded himself he didn't have any romantic interest in this woman. She was going to leave skid marks in her wake when she finally left town.

"What are you doing here? I thought you had a plane to catch," he said bluntly.

"I did." She blinked her wide doe eyes, a deer caught in headlights. "I mean I do. It's not until later this afternoon."

Ford dropped his gaze to the dog sitting at her feet, wagging her little gold heart out. A pang of…something hit him dead in the center of his chest. As much as he wanted to believe it was pity for the poor animal, it felt more like empathy. "If Lady Bird and I didn't know better, we might think you didn't really want to go."

"Good thing you both know better, then," Maple said, but she suddenly couldn't seem to meet his gaze. She seemed to be staring intently at his forearms, visible below the rolled-up sleeves of his denim shirt. Then she gave her head a little shake and aimed those wary eyes of hers back on his face. "What are *you* doing here? You're a pediatrician. Shouldn't you be passing out lollipops somewhere?"

Ah, there she was—the mouthy outsider that seemed to love nothing more than getting under his skin.

The joke was on Maple, though. Ford could see right through the arrogant little act of hers. It was simply a way of keeping people at arm's length, like the armored shell on an armadillo.

"I'm off today. Once a week I do an overnight at County General, and my office is always closed the following day. I was here to play bingo with my gram." He gave the pocket of his denim shirt a pat. "But if you have a hankering for a lollipop, I might have one on me."

"Thanks, but I'm good." She held up her hand to stop him, which was just as well since he was only teasing. "What did you say a minute ago, though? I'm not sure I caught it."

"The part about you having a plane to catch?"

"No." Her forehead puckered. "It was something about a visit."

"Ah. 'Go visit.'" Ford cast a glance at the dog. "That's what Lady Bird is waiting for you to say. Percy always gave her that command at the start of a therapy-dog visit."

Maple's gaze flitted toward the golden. "Go visit, Lady Bird."

The dog immediately stood and started trotting toward her senior fan club, already assembled in the living room area of the lobby.

Maple flashed Ford a grin over her shoulder. "It worked! Thank you."

"You've got this, Maple," he said with a wink.

"Wait." She stumbled to a halt. "You're not leaving, are you?"

He'd planned on it. Visiting Gram had provided him with a welcome distraction from work, but Ford had other things to do on his day off. Bingo had ended a good twenty minutes ago, yet here he stood.

"Why? Do you want me to stay?" Ford shifted his weight from one booted foot to the other. The words had fallen out of his mouth before he could stop them. Of course, that's not what Maple wanted.

"Yes." She nodded vigorously, eyes pleading with him. "I mean, if you don't mind, that would be great. I really don't know what I'm doing, and you've clearly been around Lady Bird and Percy on their visits."

"There's really not much to it. That dog is a natural." He had no business staying and spending more time with her. Hadn't he just promised his sister earlier that he wasn't getting emotionally involved?

Good luck with that. A bitter taste rose up the back of his throat. Ford's emotions had been running roughshod over him for months now. What he needed to do now was lock the horse back in the barn.

"You're right. Sorry, it was just a thought." Maple cast a panicked glance toward the senior citizens, and Ford did his best to pretend he wasn't intrigued.

The woman was a study in contradictions. Why was she here when she so clearly wanted to be anyplace else?

"I'll stay," he said, telling himself he was simply doing her a favor, just like he would anyone else in town.

Her pretty mouth curved into a smile. "You will?" Ford

ignored the telltale thump of his heart as relief flooded her features. Tried to, anyway.

He tipped his head toward the common area. "Yep, but you should probably go ahead and get started. Gram and her friends don't like to be kept waiting. They're going to eat you two alive."

Maple's face fell.

"I'm kidding, Doc." He leaned closer and gave her nose a playful tap. "Relax. Everyone's just happy you and Lady Bird are here. Trust me, you've got nothing to worry about."

"Except that I'm not certified to be doing this and everyone here has most likely been gossiping about me nonstop for the past twenty-four hours," she said with a wince.

She wasn't wrong, but dwelling on either of those things wasn't going to get her through the next half hour.

"Get through this visit, and I'll feed you more pie." Ford held up a finger. "Or better yet, barbecue. You can't leave Texas without a visit to Smokin' Joes."

Her nose wrinkled. "Why do I feel like now isn't the right time to admit that I don't like barbecue?"

That was downright blasphemous, but Ford had to cut her some slack. She'd obviously never had proper barbecue before. "That settles it. It would be a crime for you to leave Texas without giving our brisket a fair try. If you don't like it, fine. But you at least have to taste it."

She blew out a breath. "Okay, but only because you're saying."

"It's a d—" Ford swallowed the word *date* just in the nick of time "Deal."

"It's a deal," she repeated. Then she took a deep inhale and turned her attention toward Lady Bird. "Come on, Lady Bird. Let's go visit."

Chapter Eight

Maple really shouldn't have been so worried. Lady Bird knew exactly what to do, and as her handler, Maple was pretty much just along for the ride.

The dog moved deftly between wheelchairs, resting her head on the arm handles and allowing easy access for pats and scratches behind her ears. She didn't miss a beat, padding from one resident to the next, greeting everyone with happy tail wags and a wide doggy grin. Just a few minutes into the visit, Maple found herself relaxing into her role as Lady Bird's human sidekick.

Most of the seniors reminisced about dogs they'd known or shared stories about their childhood pets while Lady Bird worked her golden magic. A few residents even grew teary-eyed as they interacted with the dog, and Maple realized she shouldn't have worried so much about what to say. She didn't need to talk at all, really. Mostly, the retirees just wanted someone to listen.

Maple could do that. She liked hearing about the dogs

that had meant so much to the seniors in years past, and it warmed her heart to see how simply petting Lady Bird for a few minutes could bring back such fond memories.

"Here you are again, you sweetheart," a woman with short salt-and-pepper hair and dressed in a colorful muumuu said as Maple and the dog approached her wheelchair. "Oh, Lady Bird, I know I tell you this every week, but you remind me so much of my precious Toby."

The woman hugged Lady Bird's neck, closed her eyes and rocked back and forth for several long moments. Then she offered Maple a watery smile. "I had to give my dog up a few months ago. He lives with my granddaughter now."

"I'm so sorry to hear that." Maple pressed a hand to her heart.

"These visits help, you know. I never miss seeing Lady Bird. It's the highlight of my week." The woman cupped the dog's face with trembling hands. "Isn't that right, darling?"

Lady Bird made a snuffling sound and nodded her big gold head.

And so it went, from one bittersweet exchange to the next, until Maple's gaze landed on a familiar face.

"Hi, there," she said as they reached Ford's grandmother, sitting at the end of a floral sofa with her walker parked in front of her. The infamous Coco sat propped in a basket attached to the front of the mobility device. "It's good to see you again."

Lady Bird touched noses with the stuffed animal as if they were old friends.

"I remember you." Gram's face split into a wide grin as she gazed up at Maple. "You're the pretty new veterinarian."

"That's right." Maple kneeled beside Lady Bird so she and the older woman were on eye level with one another. "How is your little dog feeling today?"

"Much better, thanks to you." Gram reached shaky fingertips toward Lady Bird and rested her palm on the dog's smooth head.

"I'm glad to hear it. Treating her was my pleasure," Maple said, and the tug in her heart told her that she meant it. She ran her hand along Coco's synthetic fur and the dog's mechanical head swiveled toward her. It blinked a few times, and then its mouth dropped open and the toy dog made a few panting sounds, followed by a sharp yip.

"Coco likes you," Gram said.

"I'm glad. I like her too." Maple smiled. She could feel Ford's gaze on her, and when she snuck a glance at him, he was watching her with unmistakable warmth in his eyes.

Maple's heart leaped straight to her throat, and she forced herself to look away.

"Next time, we're bringing Coco to you instead of Grover." Gram leaned closer, like she wanted to tell Maple a secret. "He won't like that, but he'll get over it."

Maple couldn't help but laugh, and for a second, she let herself believe that there really would be a next time. Would that seriously be so bad?

Lady Bird nudged her way between Gram and her walker, plopped her head on the older woman's lap and peered up at her with melting eyes. Gram placed her hands on either side of the dog's face and told her she was a good girl, just like Coco.

"It's so nice that you brought Lady Bird here today. Your daddy would be so proud of you, you know," Gram said, eyes twinkling.

For a disorienting second, Charles Leighton's face flashed in Maple's mind. Her dad had never been much of a dog person. Neither of her parents really understood her affinity for animals, but she liked the thought of making her family proud.

When Maple had been a little girl, before her parents'

marriage had broken down for good, she'd often thought if she could just be good enough, she could make things better for her family. Looking back, that was certainly when her anxiety had started. She'd foolishly thought that if she could behave perfectly, she could fix whatever had gone wrong between her mom and dad. She'd tried her best in school, but no amount of straight A's on her report card or gushing reviews from her teachers about her polite classroom demeanor changed things. Her parents' relationship kept spiraling out of control, and the only other thing Maple could do was try and make herself smaller so she wouldn't get caught in the crossfire.

That was all a very long time ago, obviously. But old habits died hard. Maple loved her parents, as imperfect as they were. She still wanted them to be proud of her—maybe even more so than if she'd followed in their footsteps and gone to law school. All during veterinary school, she'd waited for one of them to realize how wrong they'd been. Surely, they'd noticed how passionate she felt about helping pets...how *right* it seemed. She'd found her purpose. Shouldn't that make any parent proud?

Her mom and dad still didn't fully understand, but that was okay. Maple was a fully grown adult. Now she chose to believe that somewhere deep down, they really were proud of her, even if they didn't share her love for animals. And even if they didn't show it. Still, she couldn't help thinking that even the Leightons might appreciate the power of a dog's unconditional love if they could see Lady Bird in action.

But then, as Maple was reminding herself that the golden would be the absolute last thing Charles and Meredith Leighton would care about here in Bluebonnet, the true meaning of Gram's words sank in.

Your daddy would be so proud of you, you know.

Maple's smile felt wooden all of a sudden. "Oh, you mean Percy."

"Of course, I do." Gram nodded. "You're so much like him it's uncanny."

"I—" Maple shook her head, all too ready to disagree. She was nothing like her biological father. Clearly, Percy had been deeply devoted to his community. Lady Bird had a busier volunteer schedule than any human she'd ever met, but the dog couldn't spread joy and happiness without a handler. Their therapy-dog work had been Percy's doing. He'd lived in a quaint town in a tiny pink house with fanciful gingerbread trim. He'd paid for her entire education, despite the fact that she didn't have the first clue who he was.

Percy Walker had left behind some very large shoes to fill, and those shoes had nothing to do with the slippers Maple had so hastily shoved into her bag.

"I think Lady Bird's hour is up."

Maple blinked and dragged her attention back to the present. Ford must've picked up on her sudden feeling of unease, because there he was, swooping in to save her from the conversation. She wasn't prepared to talk about Percy. It hurt, and she wasn't altogether sure why.

This, she thought. *This is why I asked Ford to stay.*

Thank goodness she had. She'd choke down an entire plate full of barbecue in gratitude, if necessary.

"Gram, isn't it just about time for arts-and-crafts hour?" he prompted with a glance toward the activities calendar.

"We're making crepe paper flowers today—dogwood blossoms, just like in the town square," Gram said.

"That sounds nice." Maple gave Lady Bird's leash a gentle tug to guide the dog out of the way while Ford helped his grandmother to a standing position behind her walker.

The woman in the muumuu who'd told her about Toby

tugged on the sleeve of Maple's lemon-print Kate Spade dress. "You and Lady Bird are welcome to stay and make flowers with us."

"I'd love to, but I'm afraid Lady Bird and I already have plans this afternoon." Plans involving a food truck and a certain do-gooder who'd just rescued her right when she'd begun to feel out of her depth.

Oh, and catching a plane. She couldn't forget that crucial item on her agenda.

"Maybe another time," Gram said as she gripped the handles of her walker.

Maple didn't have the heart to admit that she and Lady Bird wouldn't be coming back. Instead, she simply smiled and said, "I'd like that very much."

Maple wasn't a thing like Percy Walker, but there was a certain type of magic about Lady Bird's therapy-dog sessions. Maple could feel it from the other end of the leash. She wasn't a patient, and these visits weren't about her, but accompanying the dog and seeing the effect she had on people filled her with hope. Joy. Peace…

And along with those precious feelings, the idea that perhaps it was okay that she wasn't just like her biological father. Maybe, just maybe, simply wanting to be like him was enough.

Ford cupped a hand around his ear and leaned closer to Maple, who sat opposite him at one of the picnic tables in Bluebonnet's town square. "I'm sorry, Doc. I'm going to need you to repeat what you just said. I'm not sure I heard correctly."

Maple's pupils flared. "You heard me the first time."

"Naw." Ford shook his head and offered Lady Bird a small bite of brisket, which she gobbled down with tail-wagging enthusiasm. "I don't think I did."

"Fine, you win." She pointed at the empty paper plate in front of her. "That was the most delicious meal I've ever eaten. Happy now?"

He winked. "Kinda."

"You're impossible." She reached to snag a Tater Tot from his plate.

He gave her hand a playful swat, but it didn't deter her in the slightest. "So I've heard."

After Lady Bird's visit to the senior center, Ford had made good on his promise to take her to Smokin' Joes. She'd hardly said a word during the short walk to the food truck, other than a quiet thank-you for intervening when Gram had brought up Percy. He'd swiftly changed the subject, poking fun of the fact that Maple continued to walk all over town in her fancy high heels, but she hadn't taken the bait. Not even when he promised her free medical services when she eventually twisted an ankle on the cobblestones in the town square.

It wasn't until she'd taken her first bite that she'd seemed to get out of her head. The second Joe's brisket passed her lips, she'd visibly relaxed. Within minutes, her eyes had drifted closed and the sigh she let out bordered on obscene. Ford had never been so jealous of a slab of beef, but there was a first time for everything, apparently.

"Seriously, where has real Texas barbecue been all my life?" Maple dabbed at the corners of her cherry-red mouth with her napkin.

"Right here in the Lone Star State, darlin'," Ford said.

Was he *flirting* with City Mouse?

It certainly appeared that way. Ford probably needed to reel that in. This wasn't a date, even though it sort of felt like one. It shouldn't, but it did. Or maybe Ford was just so rusty in the romance department that he'd forgotten what a real date felt like.

Probably that.

"Clearly, I should've made my way to Texas before now." Maple laughed, and then her forehead puckered like it always did when she was overthinking something. "Other than when I was a newborn, I guess."

She glanced around the town square, gaze softening ever so slightly as she took in the gazebo, the picnic tables surrounding Smokin' Joe's silver Airstream trailer and the dogwood blossoms swaying overhead. "I feel like I should remember this place. I know that's weird, but I can't help it. This could've been my home."

It still could.

He didn't dare say it. He shouldn't even be thinking it.

"There's so much I don't know about Bluebonnet…about my very own father." Maple swallowed, and then her voice went soft and breathy, as if she was telling him a deep, dark secret. "I wish I'd known him. Or, at the very least, that I knew a little bit more about him. Everyone in town seems to have known Percy, and I never got the chance to meet him."

"Maybe I can help. What do you want to know?" Ford didn't realize his fingertips had crept across the table toward Maple's until their hands were somehow fully intertwined. He told himself he was simply offering up moral support, pointedly ignoring the electricity that skittered over his skin at the softness of her touch.

"Everything." She shook her head and let out a laugh that was more than just a little bit sad around the edges. "Honestly, I don't even know where to start. He was a whole person with a whole life. It's easier to think of him as a stranger, but then someone will say something about him that resonates, and it catches me so off guard that I feel like the wind has just been knocked out of me."

Which is exactly what had happened at the senior center.

He'd seen the pain wash over her face the second it happened, and in that fleeting moment, Maple's eyes had brimmed with a loneliness that had grabbed him by the throat.

He couldn't remember making a conscious decision to try and extricate her from the exchange with Gram. It had been pure instinct. He'd wanted to protect her, which was patently ridiculous. Maple was perfectly capable of taking care of herself. She'd made that much clear since day one.

But Ford knew there was more to Maple than the prickly image she seemed so hell-bent on showing to the world. She kept insisting she wasn't a people person, but last night when he'd seen her with her dainty feet swimming in Percy Walker's bedroom slippers, a hidden truth had shimmered between them. Maple wasn't a people person because she'd never had anyone in her life who she could fully trust with her innermost thoughts and feelings. She was hungry for connection, whether she wanted to admit it or not.

Against his better judgment, Ford wanted to help her find it. Adaline liked to say he was a fixer, and maybe she was right. He spent the better part of his time setting broken bones, mending scraped knees, and stitching childhood accidents back together. But bodies were like souls. No matter how tenderly they were cared for, they still bore the scars of yesteryear.

Just because he wanted to help her didn't mean he was in danger of developing feelings for her. And even if he was, he'd survive. Nothing would come of it. By this time tomorrow, she'd probably be busy examining a Park Avenue purse dog.

"What if we start small? That might feel less overwhelming. If you could ask me one thing about Percy, what would it be?" Ford gave Maple's hand an encouraging squeeze.

"Oh." Her bottom lip slipped between her teeth, and

Ford was momentarily spellbound. "Just one thing. Let me think for a second..."

She glanced around as if searching for inspiration until her gaze landed on Lady Bird. The big golden panted with glee, and Maple instantly brightened.

"Oh, I know." She sat up straighter on the picnic bench, and Ford could feel her excitement like little sparks dancing along the soft skin of her hand. "He was so into pet therapy. I'd love to hear how that started...how he first got involved with that kind of volunteer work. You don't happen to know, do you?"

"As a matter of fact, I do," Ford said.

"So..." Maple leaned closer, until Ford could see tiny flecks of gold in her warm brown irises. Hidden treasure. "Tell me."

"Okay." Ford nodded.

This was going to be rough at first, but if she could stick with him until the end, he had a feeling it was a story she'd like. It would definitely give her a bit of insight into the type of man her biological father had been.

"About five years ago, Percy's mother was diagnosed with an aggressive form of breast cancer," he said, only mildly aware that he'd begun to move his thumb in soothing circles over the back of Maple's hand.

"His mother." Her breath caught. "That would be my grandmother."

Ford nodded. She'd found a family and lost it, all in one fell swoop. Percy Walker had died without a single living heir besides Maple. "She taught first grade at Bluebonnet Elementary when I was a kid. I wasn't in her class, but Adaline was. She could probably tell you stories about her sometime if you were ever interested. Miss Walker was a big dog lover. Never met a stray she didn't love, if word around town was to be believed."

"That must be why Percy loved animals so much." Maple grinned and shook off a bit of her melancholy. "Maybe even why he wanted to be a veterinarian."

"No doubt," Ford said. And that love—that passion—had found its way to Maple, too. Against all odds. The good Lord really did work in mysterious ways sometimes.

"Go on. Tell me more," Maple prompted.

"Miss Walker entered hospice care within just a few weeks of her diagnosis. Bluebonnet Senior Living has a skilled nursing unit, in addition to assisted-living and memory-care wings. They made space for Miss Walker in a private room once it became clear she was in her final days and needed around-the-clock care. From what I remember about that time, Percy would work in the clinic all day then head straight to the senior center and sit by her bedside for hours, long into the night. Like most late-stage-cancer patients, she slept a lot and drifted in and out of consciousness." Ford cleared his throat.

Maple was gripping his hand fiercely now, bracing herself for whatever came next. A bittersweet smile tipped her lips when Lady Bird moved to lean against her leg. That dog was more intuitive than any human being Ford had ever met.

"While Percy's mom was in hospice care at the senior center, one of his patients gave birth to a litter of puppies. There were some mild complications, so the mama dog stayed at the pet clinic for a few weeks so Percy and Grover could keep an eye on her. One day, Percy piled all the puppies into a big wicker basket and took them with him on his visit to see his mom." Ford shrugged. "That probably wasn't technically allowed, but everyone knew how much Miss Walker loved dogs."

"So the staff at the senior center looked the other way?" Maple asked.

"Pretty much. She was dying. I'm guessing everyone just wanted her to have one last puppy cuddle, even if she might not have been lucid enough to realize it was happening," Ford said.

Maple shook her head, her brown doe eyes huge in her porcelain face. "That is both the saddest and sweetest thing I've ever heard. Please tell me she woke up long enough to see the puppies."

"She did. In the eulogy he gave at his mom's funeral, Percy said he placed the basket of puppies on her bed. Then he took her hand and ran her fingertips along one of the tiny dog's soft fur. He called what happened next a miracle." Ford had been at the funeral and heard Percy tell the story himself. When he spoke, the look on his face had been so full of wonder that there hadn't been a dry eye in the church.

"A miracle?" Maple tilted her head, and Lady Bird did the same in a perfect mirror image. Ford hadn't seen anything so cute in, well…ever.

Don't get attached to either of these two. Alarm bells clanged in the back of his head. *Ding, ding, ding.* Too late.

He swallowed. "Yeah. A bona fide miracle. Miss Walker opened her eyes, and as soon as her gaze landed on the basket, she broke into a glorious smile. Percy said for the first time in days, he had his mom back. She was herself again. She spent hours cradling those pups, cooing at them and laughing as tears ran down Percy's cheeks."

"Oh…" Maple's fingertips slipped out Ford's grasp and fluttered to her throat. "Wow."

"Yeah, wow." Ford's hands suddenly felt as if they had no purpose. He slid them into his lap. "Miss Walker passed away the following morning."

"Seeing her so happy with those puppies was Percy's last memory of his mom, and that's why he got involved with pet therapy. That's just...*incredible*." Maple's eyes went liquid.

"'There's no better medicine than a basketful of puppies,' your dad used to say. You want to hear something even more incredible?" Ford tipped his head toward Lady Bird. "This goofy dog who seems to have fallen head over heels in love with you was one of those puppies."

Maple gasped. "Lady Bird? Seriously?"

"Seriously." Ford's eyes flashed back to Maple, and he felt the corners of his mouth curl. He'd underestimated how good it would feel to help her put a piece of her family puzzle in place. He could've sat at that picnic table and kept talking and talking until he ran out of words.

If only she didn't have a plane to catch.

"Good girl, Lady Bird," Maple whispered against the soft gold fur of Lady Bird's ear.

The dog swiped Maple's cheek with her pink tongue, tail thumping happily against the square's emerald-green grass. Maple gave her a fierce hug, and for reasons Ford really didn't want to contemplate, an ache burrowed its way deep into his chest...all the way down to the place where he held his greatest hopes.

And his greatest hurts.

Ford shifted on the picnic bench. He needed space... just a little breathing room. But then Maple sat up and met his gaze, and he couldn't seem to move a muscle. She was looking at him in a way she'd never beheld him before—with eyes and heart open wide. Then her focus moved slowly, *purposefully*, toward his mouth.

Ford's breath grew shallow as Maple stood and leaned all the way across the picnic table. She came to a stop mere millimeters away from his face, lips curving into an uncharacteristically bashful grin.

"Yes?" she whispered.

"Yes," Ford said quietly. He couldn't get the word out fast enough.

Then she gave him what was undoubtedly the most tender, reverent kiss of his life. Just a gentle brush of her perfect lips, and Ford was consumed with a kind of yearning he'd never known before.

More. The blood in his veins pumped hard and fast. *More. More. More.*

She pulled back just far enough to smile into his eyes. "Thank you."

"For?" he asked, incapable of forming more than a single, strangled syllable.

"For telling me that story about Percy and the puppies. It might be the best gift anyone has ever given me."

Ford really hoped that wasn't true. Maple deserved better than that. She deserved a lifetime of birthdays with cake piled high with pink frosting and blazing candles, Easters with baskets full of chocolate bunnies and painted eggs, a puppy with a red satin ribbon tied in a bow around its furry little neck on Christmas morning. She deserved the perfect kind of love she seemed so hungry for. Yesterday, today...always.

He reached and tucked a lock of dark hair behind her ear. "There are more stories where that one came from."

But to hear them all, you'd have to stay.

Maple's gaze bore into his, and neither of them said another word. Bluebonnet could've burned to the ground around them, and Ford would've scarcely noticed. Then she kissed him one last time, and her lips tasted of honey and barbecue. Of soft Texas sunshine. Of the slow, sweet dog days of summer.

And only just a little bit of goodbye.

Chapter Nine

"Good morning, Maple." June looked up from the receptionist desk as Maple walked into the pet clinic the following morning with Lady Bird prancing at her heels. "Good morning to you, too, Lady Bird."

Lady Bird's tail swung back and forth. Maple shifted the bakery box and coffee carrier she held in her arms and breathed a little easier. She thought she'd braced herself for anything. Not this, though. The last thing she'd expected was a friendly morning greeting delivered with a smile.

"Good morning, June." She handed the older woman a steaming cup of coffee in a paper cup with the Cherry on Top logo printed on its side. A peace offering, since Maple hadn't exactly been the easiest person to get along with the last time she'd breezed through the door.

"Oh, my. Thank you." June accepted the coffee and took a small sip. "Is this Cherry on Top's famous Texas pecan blend?"

"It sure is," Maple said. Points to Adaline for suggesting her house signature blend.

Maple had been nervous about showing up here again today, especially since everyone in town thought she'd gone back to New York yesterday, as planned. She'd walked to the bakery as soon as they'd opened and picked up treats for the office, figuring they couldn't try and turn her away again if she came bearing pie and coffee. Mission accomplished.

The funny thing was, Adaline hadn't been surprised to see her, either. She'd even invited Maple to a book-club meeting later tonight, and despite the fact that spending an evening with a new group of total strangers would ordinarily be an automatic no-go, Maple had found herself saying yes. If she was going to stay in town for a while, she might as well try and make some friends. Get a little involved.

It's what Percy would have done.

"You know we have one of those fancy K-Cup machines here, right?" June nodded toward the area behind the reception counter. "You don't have to walk all the way to the town square just for coffee."

"I figured. I just wanted to do something nice for you and Dr. Hayes." Maple felt her determined smile wobble a bit.

A fresh wave of dread washed over her at the thought of facing that man again, even though he was technically her partner. They were *equals*. There was no reason for her to be intimidated by him…

Except for his overall grumpy demeanor, along with the fact that this was his home turf and he clearly considered Maple an unwelcome interloper. Other than that, things between them should be just peachy.

June's face creased into a sympathetic smile. "Do you want to hear a little secret, sweetheart?"

"Um, okay."

"Grover's bark is a lot worse than his bite," June said in a mock whisper. Then she winked and shifted her gaze over Maple's shoulder as the bells on the front door chimed. "Good morning, Grover. Maple is here for work, and she's brought us coffee and pie. Isn't that sweet?"

Great. He was already in the office. Any second now, he'd be standing right behind her.

Maple had hoped for a few minutes to get her bearings before her grump of a partner showed up. At the very least, she'd wanted to put her things down and slip a white lab coat over her flippy black-and-white polka-dot dress. No such luck.

She straightened her shoulders, pasted a smile on her face and turned around to face her partner.

"Hi there, Grover." She shoved one of the coffees at him and pretended she belonged there. Because she *did* belong. This practice was half hers now, whether he liked it or not.

Maple really needed Grover to get on board, though. The ink on her veterinary school diploma was barely dry. Last night, she'd made the decision to stay in Bluebonnet and work at the clinic…at least for a while. She just couldn't go back yet, and she certainly couldn't leave Lady Bird. *Ever.* Now that she knew the dog's backstory, keeping her was one-hundred-percent nonnegotiable. Maple had informed her adoptive parents of her decision via text and then she'd turned off her mobile phone like a complete and total coward.

But at least she'd done it. She'd made her own decision about her own life, and she was sticking by it. So far, Maple's plan consisted of little more than staying in Bluebonnet for a bit and learning more about her birth father and the place he'd called home all his life…plus working alongside Grover Hayes.

All she needed now was his cooperation.

He plucked the coffee from her hand with a harrumph. "I hope this is decaf."

"Totally," she lied.

Note to self: no more caffeinated beverages for Grumpy McGrumperson. Maybe he needed to rethink that position. If anyone stood to benefit from a little caffeinated pick-me-up, it was Grover.

He took a gulp from his cup and glared at Maple for what felt like an eternity. Lady Bird started to drift off.

When Grover finally deigned to speak to her again, the dog's head jerked up with a start. "There's a kitten coming in at nine o'clock this morning for a routine checkup and her first round of shots. Do you think you can handle that, Dr. Leighton?"

Dr. Leighton.

He'd called her *Doctor*!

"Absolutely," she said, beaming.

Grover sighed mightily, but Maple couldn't have cared less. She'd take what she could get. At least he was willing to acknowledge her place at the clinic and give her a chance.

"Any questions or problems at all and you come find me. Understood?" He waved his coffee cup at her, and a drop sloshed out of the hole in the plastic lid. Lady Bird licked it up the second it hit the floor.

Grover sighed even harder.

Maple bit back a smile. "Understood."

After a cursory greeting aimed at June, Grover stalked past the reception area, headed for his office.

The instant the door slammed behind him, Maple shifted her gaze shifted toward the receptionist. "You're right. His bark really is worse than his bite, isn't it?"

"Told you," June said with a chuckle.

Maple glanced at the old-timey clock hanging beside the felt letter board that still listed Percy's name alongside Grover's in the reception area. Her feline patient was due in forty-five minutes—just enough time to locate the archaic file and familiarize herself with the kitty's history. How old was she? Where had the client gotten the cat? Was this their only pet?

But Maple lingered in the lobby, not quite ready to get to work.

"Can I do anything for you, Maple? Is everything okay?" June's forehead creased with concern. "Percy's office is yours now. Don't hesitate to get settled in there. If you need help clearing things out, I'd be happy to assist."

Maple shook her head. She wasn't ready to get rid of Percy's things yet. Not here, and not at home. She wanted to study them first. Who knew what sort of hidden treasures she might find?

"It's not that, but thank you for the offer." Maple cast a curious glance in Grover's wake. "He didn't seem all that surprised to see me here this morning. Come to think of it, neither did you."

At Cherry on Top, Adaline hadn't been fazed. She'd greeted Maple like an old friend, and now Maple had an entire novel to read before the book-club meeting tonight.

June peered at Maple over the top of her reading glasses. "Come on now. You've been in Bluebonnet long enough to know that nothing stays secret here for long."

"But I didn't tell anyone I'd decided to stay," Maple countered. Not even Ford.

Especially not Ford, lest he think that her decision had anything to do with him. Because it didn't.

Not much, anyway.

"You didn't have to, sweetheart. You kissed Ford Bishop right in the middle of the town square yesterday." June tutted, but her lips twitched with amusement. "Did you really think that would go unnoticed in a place like Bluebonnet?"

Maple hadn't been thinking at all. She'd acted with her heart, not her head, which was something that had always terrified her. She knew all too well what happened when people threw caution to the wind and let their feelings go straight to their heads. A year or three later, they ended up sitting in her mom or dad's law office, fighting tooth and nail over everything under the sun. There was an awfully thin line between love and hate. *Razor* thin, honestly. After everything Maple had seen and heard, particularly within the walls of her own childhood home, she preferred to stay as far away from that line as possible. Besides, she liked being in control of her emotions. Things were safer that way…more predictable.

But after Ford told her the story about Percy and Lady Bird, she'd hadn't been able to stop herself.

Who even was she anymore?

All her life she'd been Maple Maribelle Leighton—dog lover, introvert, perpetual good girl and overachiever extraordinaire. Now she was starting to think she might be another person entirely. The trouble was, she had no idea what Maple Maribelle Walker was really like. The more Maple got to know her alter ego, the more dangerous she seemed. This new version of Maple had a penchant for straying far, *far* outside her comfort zone. She did things like purposefully miss flights, defy her family's expectations without thought to the consequences, and willingly throw away a shot at her dream job—not just once, but twice.

Oh, and she also kissed the local Hallmark hunk in the middle of the town square for all the world to see.

"That wasn't a regular kiss," Maple said primly. "That was a thank-you kiss. There's a difference."

"Oh, honey. Not from where I'm standing," June said with a knowing gleam in her eye. "I'm not sure how these things work up in New York, but here in Texas, a kiss is a kiss. Plain and simple."

There was nothing simple about it, though. Quite the opposite, in fact. Maple's feelings for Ford were growing more complicated by the hour, especially considering she shouldn't be having any feelings for him at all.

She blamed Bluebonnet for this entire mess. Everyone here seemed to think Maple was someone that she wasn't, and now she'd jumped right on the bandwagon and begun to believe it herself.

Even worse, she *liked* it.

Maple Maribelle Walker might be dangerous, but she was a heck of a lot of fun.

"Ford!" Oliver's hospital gown dipped off the child's bony shoulder as he struggled to sit up. "You're here! On a Wednesday!"

"I'm here. How's it going, bud?" Ford held up a hand for a high five.

Oliver gave it a weak slap. "Things are great now that you're here. Mom's at work again."

"I heard." Ford nodded.

He'd also heard that the child wasn't feeling well. Ordinarily, that wouldn't have been too much cause for concern. Chemotherapy treatment could be brutal, but according to the call Ford had gotten earlier in the day from Nurse Pam, Oliver had started running a fever after undergoing a bone-marrow biopsy early this morning.

Fever was always a concern for cancer patients. Chemo weakened the immune system, which sometimes led to infections. Oliver's fever had been running right around 100 degrees all day, and as long as it stayed low-grade, things would probably be just fine.

But a constant low-grade fever had also been one of Oliver's first symptoms when he'd been diagnosed with leukemia. His mom had brought him into Ford's office worried he might have an ear infection. Ford had assured her his ears were fine, but looking at the child's pale skin and the smattering of bruises on his extremities had sent a cold chill up and down his spine. He'd known something was wrong—something far worse than a simple childhood ear infection.

He'd been devastated to find out he'd been right.

"I also heard you weren't feeling so great." Ford glanced at the beeping monitor at the head of the bed. The body temperature reading flashed 99.3, and he breathed a little easier.

As soon as they got the bone-marrow biopsy results back, he could relax. Oliver was midway through treatment, and the test had been a routine check to monitor the effectiveness of the chemo. His oncologist expected good news, and Ford had taken the specialist at his word. Oliver was going to live a long and healthy life.

"I'm fine." Oliver's face spread into a hopeful grin. "Fine enough to play a board game."

"You got it." Ford nodded. An evening of board games with his favorite patient sounded great. Maybe it would help get his mind off the fact that Maple had kissed him silly yesterday afternoon.

He'd been busy all day today with back-to-back appointments and a quick lunch at the senior center with Gram. Adaline had called, but he'd ignored her voice mail. Knowing his sister, she'd heard about the kiss and wanted a thorough debrief…with a side of lecture about not letting himself fall for City Mouse.

Ford just wasn't in the mood. What difference did it make, now that Maple had gone back to New York? She'd kissed him, and then she'd fled.

Did she really, though?

He gritted his teeth. Nope, he wasn't going to let his thoughts go down that troublesome road. She'd missed one flight already. The odds weren't great that she'd willingly missed another. Besides, he had more important things to worry about.

Namely, keeping Oliver company.

"What's it going to be?" Ford scanned the collection of games, puzzles, and stuffed animals piled on the shelf below the window overlooking the rolling landscape of the Texas Hill Country. The sun was just beginning to dip below the horizon, spilling liquid amber over the hills and setting the wildflowers aflame. *"Apples to Apples? Candy Land?"*

Oliver groaned. "*Candy Land* is for kids."

"Noted." Ford swallowed a laugh. "My sincerest apologies. How about *Yahtzee*?"

"Yes!" Oliver punched the air.

See? The child is fine.

"*Yahtzee* it is, then." He grinned, feeling just a little bit lighter, a little bit more hopeful as he got the game set up on the bedside tray.

Then Ford noticed a small, greenish bruise on the child's forearm, and a weight settled on his chest.

He frowned at the tender spot on Oliver's arm and wondered where it had come from...how long it had been there. Why hadn't he noticed it before?

It's just a bruise. Kids get them all the time. A bruise doesn't have to mean anything.

Oliver spilled the dice onto the table, and the clatter pulled Ford back into the moment.

"Look, I got three fives already." The boy's eyes lit up as he pointed to the dice. "I'm so lucky. Right, Ford?"

Ford tensed at the choice of words, but he pushed down his worry and flashed Oliver a smile and a thumbs-up, even as his throat constricted, making a response almost impossible.

"You sure are, kiddo. The luckiest."

Chapter Ten

"Maple!" Adaline held her front door open wide and beckoned Maple inside. "I'm so glad you could make it. Come on in and meet the rest of the girls."

Maple hesitated for a beat. Here she was again, about to dive headlong into an uncomfortable social situation, and this time, Dr. Small Town Charm wasn't there for backup. But the smell of freshly baked pies wafted from the inside of Adaline's house, and Maple had spent every stolen moment today speed-reading her way through the book club's chosen novel. She'd never missed a homework assignment in her life, and she wasn't about to start now. Not even for a recreational reading club.

So in between administering kitten vaccines and removing porcupine quills from an understandably traumatized chocolate Labrador retriever—a task that veterinary school in New York City had in no way prepared her for—she'd snuck into Percy's old office for a few stolen moments and plopped into his chair with her nose in the book. She'd had to resort to speed-reading as the day wore on, but she was here.

And she was ready. Mostly, anyway.

"I hope it's okay that I brought Lady Bird with me," she said as she followed Adaline past the entryway toward the living room, where it sounded like a group of women were talking over one another with happy chatter.

Maple hadn't asked if the dog could tag along, but something told her that if Lady Bird was welcome at Adaline's bakery, her new friend wouldn't have a problem with the golden attending a book-club meeting. Also, the novel was part of a romance series that centered around an animal rescue called Furever Yours. Maple had a feeling she'd stumbled upon a group of pet lovers, which had only made her more excited about tonight. These were her kind of people. Maybe she'd make some genuine friends.

"Are you kidding?" Adaline cast an affectionate glance at the dog. "Lady Bird is practically a local celebrity. Everyone is going to love that you brought her."

Sure enough, the instant they crossed the threshold of the cozy living space, the animated conversation came to an abrupt halt as every head turned toward the dog.

"Lady Bird!" the other two women scattered about the room cried in unison.

A more timid dog probably would've turned tail and hid beneath the closest end table at the effusive greeting. Not Lady Bird. The dog thrived at being the center of attention. Tail swinging, she pranced toward the closest human and sat politely at her feet, waiting to be petted.

Adaline gave Maple a knowing grin. "Told you."

"You must be Maple." A woman with blond hair twisted into an artful bun stood and extended a graceful hand toward Maple. "Hi. I'm Jenna. I own the dance studio on Main Street, just around the corner from the town square."

"It's a pleasure to meet you," Maple said as she shook her hand.

A ballerina, she thought. That made perfect sense. Jenna definitely looked the part.

"We've all heard so much about you. I'm Belle," the woman sitting beside Jenna on the sofa said with a wave. "I'm the librarian at Bluebonnet Elementary School."

"Wait." Maple blinked. "You're a librarian, and your name is Belle?"

"I know, right? With a name like mine, I guess I didn't have much of a choice." The corners of Belle's mouth turned up. "It's a good thing I love books."

And so it went. The women chatted while Lady Bird shuffled from person to person and wagged her tail with such zeal that she nearly took out the wineglasses scattered atop the coffee table in the center of the room.

"Lady Bird, I would lay down my life for you, but if you knock over my cabernet, we're going to have a serious problem," Belle said with a mock glare in the dog's direction.

"I'm so sorry." Maple attempted to lure the dog back to her side, but she was too busy playing social butterfly to pay attention.

"Don't worry. There's more wine where this came from. I promise." Adaline handed her a glass.

"There's also pie. Adaline makes a new creation for every book-club meeting," Jenna said.

"I like to test out new recipes on our little group before I add them to the bakery menu. I hope you don't mind being a guinea pig." Adaline gave Maple a questioning glance.

"For pie? How is that even a question? Of course, I don't mind."

The conversation grew more boisterous over the next two hours, and the wine flowed while the women discussed the book. It didn't take long for Belle to ask Maple if Lady Bird might have time in her schedule to visit the school library and help struggling readers with their skills. She'd read an article online recently about therapy pets acting as reading education assistance dogs. Jenna piped up to see if Lady Bird could come to the first day of her toddler pre-ballet class in the fall and mentioned that a teacher friend of hers thought that having a therapy dog at Bluebonnet Elementary's back-to-school events would help ease nerves for new students.

Maple loved their enthusiasm, even as it quickly became apparent that she and Lady Bird would never be able to keep up with all the community requests for pet therapy. And so far, all the requests were the result of word of mouth. There was no telling what might happen if Maple put actual effort into building a comprehensive therapy-dog program. The possibilities were endless. Hospitals, nursing homes, schools, airports, courtrooms, crisis response…

During vet school, Maple had read extensively about therapy pets working in all these settings and more. She'd just never imagined she'd have one. There was no question that Lady Bird could help spread love and joy anywhere there were people who needed a little comfort, affection, and support.

But Lady Bird was just one dog. Not to mention the spectacular mess that was Maple's personal life. She didn't know how she was going to keep up with Lady Bird's commitments, as it was.

"Thank you so much for inviting me tonight," Maple said as she helped Adaline get the dessert ready in the kitchen once the book discussion was finished. "Your friends are really great."

"They're your friends now, too." Adaline waggled her eyebrows. "That's how things work around here."

Maple smiled to herself. She had a house, a job, and the best dog on the planet. Now, she even had friends here in Bluebonnet. Somehow, in a matter of days, she'd built more of a life here in this small town than she'd ever had back in New York. If she wasn't careful, she might end up staying for good.

"Don't let them pressure you and Lady Bird, though." Adaline snuck a nibble of piecrust to the dog, who'd been staring intently at the kitchen counter, nose twitching. "You're just getting your footing here, and they know that. But you've also got an amazing dog."

Maple's heart swelled. "I do, don't I?"

"Should I thank her for convincing you to stay, or did that decision have to do with something else?" Adaline's smile faltered ever so slightly as she slid a slice of pie onto a china plate with a pretty rose pattern and handed it to Maple. "Some*one* else, maybe?"

"Oh, you mean Percy?"

"No, not quite." Adaline gave her a sideways glance as she plated another slice of pie. "Here's another fun fact about small towns—there's only one way to stop people from talking about the latest hot gossip. Do you know what it is?"

I wish. Maple shook her head, riveted. As one of the most recent subjects of the Bluebonnet grapevine, this seemed like valuable information. "I don't, but really I'm hoping you're about to tell me."

"You wait it out, because sooner or later something else scandalous will happen, and everyone will start talking about that instead. People have notoriously short attention spans."

"So you're saying eventually everyone will lose interest in my family situation." Maple couldn't wait. Whatever the new scandal might be, she was ready for it.

Adaline's forehead creased. "Oh, honey. Didn't you know? They already have."

"What's the new scandal?" Maple couldn't believe she'd missed it.

Adaline pointed the pie slicer at her. "You kissing my brother in the middle of the town square, obviously."

Oh.

Oh.

Maple's cheeks burned with the heat of a true Texas summer. "That wasn't what it looked like."

Adaline's eyebrows shot clear to her hairline. "So you didn't lock lips with Ford at a picnic table by Smokin' Joes?"

"It was a thank-you kiss," Maple countered.

"That's not a thing," Adaline said flatly.

Why did people keep saying that?

Because it's not, and you know it.

Maple longed for the floor of Adaline's kitchen to open up and swallow her whole. This wasn't a conversation she wanted to have with Ford's sister, of all people.

Of course, Maple found Ford attractive. Very, *very* attractive. And, yes, she might even have feelings for him.

But how was she supposed to make sense of those feelings when her entire life had so recently been turned upside down?

"Look, I like you, Maple. A lot. I hope you stay in Bluebonnet forever. Not just because I worry about my brother, but because I want us to be friends. Real friends." Adaline put down the pie cutter and took both of Maple's hands in hers. Lady Bird's furry eyebrows lifted as her gaze darted back and forth between them. "When you live in a town as small as Bluebonnet, new friends aren't very easy to come by. I'm so glad you're here."

"I am, too," Maple said, breathing a little easier. "But can I ask why you're worried about Ford?"

"That was probably an exaggeration. Ford is a grown man, and he can obviously take care of himself. Goodness knows, he takes care of practically everyone else in this town."

"So I've noticed," Maple said. It was one of his most endearing qualities.

Adaline paused, as if weighing her next words carefully. "Did he tell you he left once…just a few years ago?"

"Ford left Bluebonnet?" Maple couldn't wrap her head around it. She couldn't imagine him living anyplace else. He seemed as deeply ingrained in this community as Lady Bird was.

Adaline nodded. "He took a job up in Dallas at a state-of-the-art children's hospital there. I could tell straight away he didn't love it like he loves Bluebonnet, but Ford is very serious about his work. He was excited about the many opportunities to help kids up there. Then he met someone—another doctor, whose father happened to be chief of staff at the hospital. After dating for about six months, Ford asked her to marry him."

Maple's stomach instantly hardened. Spots floated in her vision as a wave of jealousy washed over her so hard and fast that she swayed on her feet.

Ford had been *engaged*?

It shouldn't have come as a surprise. Ford Bishop was clearly the marrying type. He doted on his grandmother, frequented his sister's bakery and devoted his life's work to caring for sick children. If that wasn't the very definition of *family man*, Maple didn't know what was.

Still, the revelation came as a shock. Maple didn't want to think about Ford slipping a diamond on another woman's finger or, heaven forbid, watching someone else walk toward him down the aisle of some cute country church. Someone vastly unlike Maple, obviously. Someone who belonged by his side. Someone gentler, sweeter…kinder. Someone who'd fit right in someplace like Bluebonnet, Texas.

Then again, maybe not, because Adaline's expression turned decidedly sour as she prepared to finish recounting the story. She took a deep breath and seemed to make an effort to neutralize her expression, but the smile on her face didn't come close to reaching her eyes.

"I was so happy for him. I missed seeing him nearly every day, obviously. Our parents retired and moved to Florida right about the time Ford and I graduated from college, so other than Gram, my brother was all the family I had in Bluebonnet." Adaline blew out a breath. "Then one day Gram had a bad fall. She'd been having some mild memory issues up until then, but the fall changed things. Gram just didn't bounce back. Ford rushed home as soon as it happened. He was only supposed to be here for a few days, but then…"

Adaline's voice drifted off, and Maple could guess what came next.

"He decided to stay, didn't he?" She knew it, because that's the kind of person Ford was. He valued things like family and community and responsibility. He would want to be here with his grandmother when she was at her most vulnerable, no matter how capable Adaline and Gram's caregivers at the senior living center might be.

"He did." Adaline nodded, and her smile turned bittersweet. "I can't say I was disappointed. It was so nice to have him back, and I could tell straightaway that Ford was happy to be home, despite the circumstances. His voice had taken on a certain edge whenever I spoke to him on the phone. Once he came back, he was like his old self again. Even when Charlotte postponed her plans to join him, he seemed unfazed. I don't think it ever crossed his mind that she'd never come here."

Maple swallowed. *Charlotte.* Putting a name to Ford's ex made the woman all the more real, and a fresh stab of envy jabbed Maple right in the heart. Ridiculous, considering they'd very clearly broken up. Somehow, that didn't make her feel any better.

"Never?" Maple asked. "You mean she didn't even give Bluebonnet a chance?"

She wasn't sure why she felt so indignant on behalf of a town she'd first set foot in only a few days ago. It wasn't as if Maple had been thrilled at the prospect of spending one measly year in Bluebonnet.

But here you are, even after getting handed a get-out-of-jail-free card.

"Charlotte kept putting it off, over and over again. Her parents put a lot of pressure on her, especially her dad. Since he was head of the hospital up there, he thought moving to a place like Bluebonnet was akin to career suicide," Adaline said.

Maple shifted her gaze to the countertop as shame settled in the pit of her stomach. She'd had the exact same thought...more than once. How could she not, when there was a prestigious cardiac practice in New York ready and willing to give her a job?

"There's more to life than work, you know?" Adaline said, as if she could see straight inside Maple's head. "Even when your work is something vitally important, like looking after children's physical and emotional health."

That's right. They were talking about Ford's work, not Maple's. Still, she couldn't shake the feeling that this conversation had more to do with her than she wanted to admit.

"Anyway, like I said, I want us to be friends. I really like you, Maple." Adaline handed her the last slice of pie, neatly plated and topped with whipped cream. "But until you're sure that you want to stay in Bluebonnet for good, I hope you'll think twice about giving Ford any more 'thank-you kisses.'"

And there it was.

Adaline was calling her bluff on the entire concept of a thank-you kiss, and Maple didn't blame her one bit. Who was she kidding? She hadn't kissed Ford simply because she'd been grateful. She'd kissed him because the longer she stayed in Bluebonnet, the more she wanted to know what it felt like to press her lips against his… To feel his strong hands cradle her face with a gentleness that made her forget how to breathe… To open her heart just a crack to the possibility of not spending the rest of her life alone…

"You can see why it might get confusing, don't you?" Adaline said with a kindness in her tone that Maple didn't deserve.

"I do." Maple nodded. Boy, did she ever. She'd never been so confused about things in her life.

What happened to the carefully orchestrated plan she'd made for herself? In less than a week, all her dreams had completely fallen by the wayside. Just because she'd discovered she'd been adopted didn't mean she had to change her entire life.

But what if you want to change, a voice whispered in the back of her head. *And what if your dreams change, too? A new life is possible, and so are new dreams.*

Maple blinked hard. She felt like crying all of a sudden, and she absolutely refused to get weepy in Adaline's kitchen over the prospect of something silly like not kissing Ford Bishop again.

It didn't feel silly, though. It felt like another heartbreak, another loss—the loss of yet a different life she'd never experience.

"Don't worry." The effort it took to smile was monumental. "You have my word. It won't happen again."

She wanted to reel the words back in the very second they left her mouth. Maple knew better than to make promises when she was in the midst of an existential crisis. It seemed like she'd completely lost control over rational thought, particularly when she was anywhere in the vicinity of Ford. What made her think she could exert any sort of sensible decision-making where he was concerned?

Because you care about him, and the last thing you want to do is hurt him.

And she wouldn't. *Couldn't.* The next time Maple saw Ford, she'd just turn off her feelings like a light switch. She'd simply have to learn to ignore the way his eyes crinkled in the corners, as if kindness and laughter came naturally to him… The irresistible pull she felt toward him every time he was near… The breathtaking habit he had of seeing past her frosty exterior, all the way down to her tender, aching heart.

That shouldn't be a problem, right? Maple had all sorts of practice at erecting a nice, strong wall around her innermost thoughts and emotions. She'd been doing it her whole life.

But then the back door of Adaline's quaint little kitchen swung open, and there he was—Ford, in the flesh, looking casually heroic in a pair of hospital scrubs that made his eyes sparkle bluer than ever. And the second those eyes homed in on her, they widened in surprise. Maple practically melted into a puddle as he drank in the sight of her, and the corners of his lips curved into a slow and easy grin.

"Well, look who missed her flight." He arched a single, all-too-satisfied eyebrow. "Again."

Chapter Eleven

She's still here. The tension in Ford's body began to ease the instant he spotted Maple. *Not just here in Bluebonnet, but right here in Adaline's kitchen.*

Never had there been such a sight for sore eyes.

Since he hadn't heard a word from her since their kiss the day before, he'd assumed she'd really left this time, as planned. Once he'd checked on Oliver and realized some of his initial symptoms had returned, Ford's singular focus had been on his patient. The fact that he'd missed such an important piece of local gossip was a testament to how distracted he'd been.

"I decided to stay a bit longer." Maple swallowed, clearly caught off guard by the sight of him. She crossed her arms, then uncrossed them, and recrossed then again, as fluttery and nervous as the day they'd met.

Ford tilted his head. "You okay there, Doc?"

"Fine," she said. A lie, if he'd ever heard one before.

What exactly was going on here?

Alas, Ford didn't have a chance to ask because Lady Bird had finally torn her attention away from the pie plate on the kitchen counter and registered his arrival. The dog's paws scrambled for purchase on the slick floor in her haste to get to him. Ford braced for impact as she crashed into his legs and threw herself, belly-up, at his feet.

"Hey there, sweet girl." He crouched down to give her a belly rub. "At least someone's happy to see me."

Maple let out a cough, and Ford winked at her.

"Maple is here for book club. We're finishing up soon." Adaline frowned down at her brother. "What are you doing here? And why are you in scrubs? You already did your shift at the hospital this week."

Ford straightened. "I did, but I wanted to stop by and check on a patient who wasn't feeling well. I ended up staying for a while."

After spending the evening playing *Yahtzee* with Oliver, he hadn't felt like going home to an empty house. Plus he knew that his sister always made fresh pie on book-club nights, so he'd swung by, hoping Adaline would take pity on him and let him crash the festivities. The last person he'd expected to find here was Maple.

Not that he was complaining.

"I hope everything is okay." Concern glowed in Maple's big brown eyes.

A look passed between them. She'd met Oliver and likely had a good idea how special that kid was to Ford.

He wished he could say more, but he couldn't discuss his patients. Ford's face likely said it all, though, as Maple's look of concern only deepened after their eyes met.

He gave his head a small shake, indicating they all needed to move on to a different, safer topic of conversation.

"We have pie." Adaline offered him a plate.

He took it and reached for a fork. "Thanks. I was hoping you might."

Adaline's gaze flitted toward Maple. "Come on in. You can join the rest of the book chat."

"But I haven't read the book."

Adaline shrugged. "It doesn't matter. Right now, everyone is pretty much just gushing over Lady Bird, anyway. If Maple isn't careful, that dog is going to be booked twenty-four-seven with therapy dog visits."

"Grover would love that. I'm not even joking. I think he'd actually prefer it if I was out of his hair and he could handle the pet clinic all on his own," Maple said.

"I doubt that," Ford countered as they headed toward the living room, even though he was fully aware the elder veterinarian could be a little rough around the edges.

Maple knew her stuff, though. Surely, Grover could see that, or maybe Ford just needed her to believe she was welcome at the pet clinic…welcome enough to make her stay in Bluebonnet permanent.

Maple aimed a sideways glance at Ford. "Have you met Grover Hayes?"

"Point taken." Ford laughed, but before he could offer a word of encouragement, Adaline swept between them and steered them toward chairs on opposite ends of the room from each other.

Lady Bird immediately left him in the dust to follow Maple. No big surprise there, but Ford felt lonely all the way on the other side of the living room, despite being surrounded by Adaline's friends. As the evening wore on, his gaze kept straying toward Maple. And once the pie had disappeared and the women had decided on their next book-club read, the night came to its inevitable close.

"Maple, where's your car?" Adaline peered toward the

driveway from the front porch, where everyone was saying their goodbyes. "I figured you'd be driving Percy's truck."

Maple shook her head. "We walked."

Adaline's gaze dropped to Maple's feet, once again clad in a pair of strappy high-heeled numbers that looked more appropriate for a beauty pageant than walking a dog. "In *those*?"

"My wardrobe options are limited," Maple said, and Ford could see her blushing even in the silvery moonlight.

"I need to take you shopping," Adaline said.

"Here? I didn't realize Bluebonnet had much in the way of fashion."

Adaline grinned. "Oh, you just wait."

"Meanwhile, I'm happy to give you and Lady Bird a ride home," Ford interjected before someone else could offer.

"Oh." A look of a panic flitted across Maple's face. "That's really not necessary. Lady Bird and I have been walking all over town together. We like it, don't we?"

Lady Bird wagged her tail, which meant nothing whatsoever. The dog would've agreed to anything Maple asked her in that soothing, singsong voice of hers.

"It's late." Without warning, Ford reached for Lady Bird's leash and slipped it out of Maple's hand. "And dark."

And Ford wanted to spend more time with her. Mostly, he wanted to know why she suddenly seemed keen to avoid him. He'd thought those days were over. The last time he'd seen her, she'd leaned over a picnic table in the middle of the town square and given him the most perfect kiss of his life.

"Ford, you know better than anyone that Bluebonnet is perfectly safe. If Maple wants to walk, you should let her," Adaline said with a slight edge to her voice. "She doesn't need your permission."

All at once, Ford knew exactly what was going on.

He turned toward his sister. "Adaline."

"Ford," she said with a tiny quiver in her chin.

Jenna and Belle fled toward their cars, no doubt eager to avoid a sibling squabble. Maple stayed put, and Ford knew good and well it was only because he still had Lady Bird's leash wrapped around his hand.

He knew he shouldn't be angry with Adaline. His sister loved him and didn't want to see him hurt again. She'd already said so at the bakery, but she also needed to mind her own business. He was a grown man, and if he wanted to give Maple a ride or walk her home, there wasn't a pie in the world that could stop him…

Provided Maple let him, of course.

"Maple, may I walk you home?" he asked quietly. He suddenly liked the idea of a nice quiet stroll. It would give them time to talk, which suddenly seemed quite necessary.

Lady Bird's head swiveled toward him, and she let out a booming bark at the word *walk*.

"Your dog seems to love the idea," Ford said. He owed Lady Bird a dog biscuit now…possibly three.

Maple's eyes sparked with amusement. "You truly are impossible, you know that?"

"So you've said." Ford shrugged. "Several times, in fact."

"For the record, I concur. You *are* impossible." Adaline glared at him and then turned toward Maple with an apologetic smile. "Don't let me stop you. I should probably start letting my brother live his own life."

"You really, *really* should," Ford muttered.

"Good night, Maple. I'm really glad you came tonight. I hope to see you at our next book club." Adaline gave Maple a quick hug and, with a wave at Ford, she disappeared inside the house, leaving the two of them alone on the porch.

Ford offered Maple his arm. "Well, what do you say?

It's a nice night for a walk, and we wouldn't want to disappoint Lady Bird."

"She might never forgive me, so I should probably say yes." Maple wrapped gentle fingertips around the crook of his elbow. "For Lady Bird."

"For Lady Bird," Ford echoed and smiled into the velvety darkness as the golden retriever guided them toward home.

"So tell me the truth." Ford gave Maple a sidelong glance that somehow felt as real as a caress, despite the darkness that surrounded them.

A nighttime Texas sky was nothing like the neon lights of New York City. Out here, the darkness was so thick that the stars glittered like diamonds overhead. For the first time ever, she could see the constellations. It made her feel tiny and larger than life, both at the same time.

"The truth about what?" she asked in a whisper. That was another thing about Bluebonnet after hours—the silence. There were no sirens, no honking cabs, no city noises to keep her up at night. Just a casual walk home felt intimate in a way that made goose bumps dance across her skin.

"What's the real reason you're not driving Percy's truck around town?" Ford said with a smile in his voice. "You don't have a driver's license, do you?"

She gasped in mock horror. "I beg your pardon, I certainly do. Just because I'm from Manhattan doesn't mean I don't know to drive."

"And when exactly was the last time you were behind the wheel of an automobile?"

Touché. He had her there.

"The day I got my license." She cleared her throat as Ford chuckled with self-satisfaction. "But I *do* possess one. I know how to drive—at least according to the State of New York."

"I guess I'll have to take your word for it." He gave her shoulder a little bump with his. "Yours and the State of New York's."

"Do you have any idea how much parking costs in Manhattan? Garage fees are outrageous. Plus, we've got the subway and cabs and Uber. It's just easier to take public transportation."

Ford laughed under his breath again. "Yeah, we don't have much of that here."

"So I've noticed," Maple said. And soon, she'd have the blisters on her feet to prove it.

More than that, she was beginning to worry about the heat. The temperatures were already hovering around ninety degrees at high noon, and it was only the beginning of summer. In a matter of weeks, the pavement would be too hot for Lady Bird's sensitive paws.

At least the evenings were still pleasant. Soft and fragrant with the perfume of wildflowers, almost like walking through a dream.

"I could help you practice," Ford said.

Maple narrowed her gaze at him beside her. "You seriously want to give me *driving lessons*?"

"Not lessons. You already know how to drive, Doc." His grin turned far too sardonic for Maple's liking. "I just thought you might feel more comfortable if you had a little practice. Also, if you started using Percy's truck, you could bring Lady Bird to the hospital more often."

Right. This was about Lady Bird, her therapy-dog work and, by extension, Oliver. No wonder Ford wanted to volunteer as tribute.

Even so, it was a kind offer and one that Maple would probably be wise to accept. It wasn't like she could accidentally let herself kiss him again while she was operating a moving vehicle.

Stop thinking about kissing.

She bit down hard on her bottom lip as punishment, but, of course, her gaze flitted straight toward his mouth.

"I'd like that a lot. Thanks—" she managed to squeak out the last word "—friend."

How awkward could she possibly be?

Ford looked downright puzzled. This was beyond her usual social anxiety. The way she couldn't seem to think straight around him felt like something else entirely.

Something almost like…

Don't you dare think it, Maple! Not even for a second.

Love?

She released her hold on his arm, because *whoa*. Being attracted to Ford was one thing, but thinking about the *L* word was more than she could handle. More than she'd *ever* be able to handle. In keeping with the automotive topic at hand, she needed to seriously pump the breaks.

"Maple, I'm not sure what exactly Adaline said to you tonight, but—" Ford began.

"Your sister was nothing but welcoming. Truly. I really like her," Maple said in an effort to cut him off.

She really meant it, too. She liked Adaline, and she'd had a great time meeting her friends. But even though Adaline had backed off somewhat and encouraged Maple to let Ford walk her home when he'd obviously figured out she'd been interfering in his personal life, the warning she'd given Maple still rang true.

Ford had already been hurt once by someone who'd turned her back on Bluebonnet. Maple cared too much about him to risk doing it again.

It would be different if she knew she was staying for good, but Maple couldn't make a promise like that right now…not even to herself. She'd only just recently given herself permission to take things one day at a time. Even that had been a massive leap of faith for someone who'd had an entirely different life mapped out for herself just a few short days ago.

"She told you about Charlotte," Ford said, cutting straight to the chase.

"Yes, but I don't want you to think I was trying to pry. For the record, I don't think that was Adaline's intention, either." This discussion was getting more uncomfortable by the second. How was that even possible?

"I know better than to think you'd try and interject yourself into my business, Maple. Quite the opposite, in fact. For a while there, I wondered if you were actively trying to avoid me." Ford's footsteps slowed. Maple had been so consumed by their conversation and the thoughts spinning in her head that she hadn't realized they'd reached her house until Lady Bird's tail stopped waving in front of them. The dog plopped into a down position at their feet. "Until you kissed me yesterday, that is."

"I shouldn't have done that. It's practically turned into front-page news around here. I keep telling people it was just a thank you kiss, and no one seems to think that's a real thing. Maybe it's not. I don't know. It was kind of a new experience for me. Believe it or not, that was rather out of character."

Maple was babbling. She couldn't seem to stop the stream of nonsense coming out of her mouth, and the more she said, the more tenderly Ford seemed to look at her—so tenderly that she wanted to lose herself in those kind eyes of his. Forget-me-not blue.

As if I could ever forget Ford Bishop, she thought. *Never in a million years.*

"I'm sorry," she blurted, apologizing once and for all

for the kiss heard—and more importantly, *seen*—around the world. Or at least Texas, which had begun to feel like the only place on earth.

"I'm not," Ford said in a voice so low and deep that it scraped her insides. Then he took a step closer and gazed into her eyes with such intensity that every sliver of space between them cracked with electricity. "In fact, I want you to do it again."

"You do?" Maple heard herself say. She wasn't sure how, because her heart had never pounded so hard and fast in all her life.

Ford nodded, and tipped her chin upward with a gentle touch of his fingertips until her mouth was positioned just below his. "I do. Right now, in fact."

"Right now," she repeated, as weak and small as a kitten. If she didn't give in, the longing just might kill her. So much for flipping her feelings off like a light.

He wasn't like any man she'd ever known before. He was passionate about his career, just like she was. But when he was with her, he was fully present. He made her feel like there was nowhere he'd rather be than with her. She'd shown him exactly who she was—the messy side of her that she never let anyone else see. And somehow, it only seemed to make him like her more.

How was she supposed to resist that?

She rose up on tiptoe, and just as the yearning became unbearable, her lips met his. And this time, there was no hesitation…no restraint. The warmth of his mouth on hers sent a hum through her body that made her wrap her arms around his neck and pull him closer.

Yes. It was the only semi-coherent thought in her head as his hands slid into her hair. *Oh, my, my, my. Yes, please.*

She felt her soul unfold like the petals on a flower, inviting him in. She needed him even closer—so close that she could feel every beat of his heart crashing against her rib cage. No one had ever kissed her like this before. Like she was special, like she was cherished. Maybe even adored.

Then, without warning, it was over almost as soon as it had begun.

Ford pulled back, and when Maple dragged her eyes open, she found him looking down at her with the strangest expression on his face. He was as still as stone, but his eyes were wild and dark with desire. Maple wished she could press Rewind and live the last two minutes of her life over and over again on constant repeat.

She wanted that so much it scared her a little. "What is it?"

Ford pressed a fingertip to his lips, signaling for her to be quiet.

"I think I just heard something," he whispered.

Maple blinked. *You certainly did. It was every last shred of my resistance crumbling down around me.* "Wh-what did it sound like?"

"A whimper. Or a cry, maybe. Like someone in pain." His head jerked toward the right and he peered over her shoulder. "There. I just heard it again. Did you?"

"Maybe?" She couldn't be sure. Her head was all fuzzy after that kiss, brief as it had been.

But then she glanced down at Lady Bird and snapped back to awareness.

"Ford." Maple's fingers curled around the fabric of his shirt and she balled it into a fist as a shiver coursed through her—and not the good, yummy kind of shiver she'd been experiencing just seconds before. "Look at Lady Bird."

The gentle dog's ears were pricked forward, and her hackles were raised. She'd obviously heard something, too, and whatever it was had her spooked.

"It's okay, girl." Ford rested a hand on Lady Bird's back.

The golden panted and relaxed a bit at his touch, but then a mournful cry pierced the air.

Maple's gaze immediately collided with Ford's.

"That sounds like a hurt animal," she said.

Lady Bird barked and sprang into action. She darted past Ford, dragging her leash behind her before either of them could stop her.

"Lady Bird!" Ford shouted, chasing after the dog.

Maple followed with her heart in her throat. Lady Bird was just a streak of gold in the darkness, dashing sideways across Percy's lawn toward the pet clinic next door.

Now, Maple *really* wished she'd given up on her fashionable stilettos. She could barely keep up. She finally kicked them off and ran barefoot toward the front porch of the pet clinic, where she could scarcely make out the silhouette of Ford's profile in the moonlight.

"It's a dog," he called out, and the tone of his voice alone told her it was bad. *Really* bad. "She needs help!"

Chapter Twelve

Bile rose to the back of Ford's throat as he crouched down next to the small copper-and-white dog. "It's okay, little one. Maple will get you all taken care of."

It didn't take a genius or a medical professional to see that the dog was pregnant and in active labor. Her belly was hard and swollen, but the pup was as a limp as a dishrag, stretched out on the welcome mat to the pet clinic with her eyes closed. She didn't have a collar, tags or any other type of identification. Something wasn't right, and if Ford had to guess, whoever had dumped her here knew it.

How could someone do this? He felt sick just thinking about it.

Lady Bird seemed equally upset as she gently dropped to her belly and curled her body in a protective barrier around the distressed dog. The small pup gave a weak wag of her tail at the contact.

"What is it? What's wrong?" Maple caught up with them, stumbling onto the porch barefoot. She kneeled beside Ford, and her face crumpled as she assessed the situation. "Oh, no. You poor, poor thing."

"The puppies are coming, right?" Ford asked.

"They're trying. We need to get the little mama inside so I can see what's going on, but I'm guessing it's dystocia. She can't push them out." Her hands trembled as she rooted around her purse for her keys.

"Here, let me. I'll get the door." Ford took Maple's bag, found her key ring and unlocked the clinic while she gently scooped the dog into her arms and carried her inside.

The little thing couldn't have weighed more than twenty pounds, even heavily pregnant. Ford thought it best to let Maple handle her, since she was the veterinary professional. He did what he could, turning on lights and making sure Lady Bird didn't get in the way while she carried the dog directly to a table in the clinic's operating room.

Ford winced at the streak of blood on Maple's arm as she set down the pup and slipped into a white coat. Things weren't looking good. The dog could barely keep her eyes open, and she'd started shivering. Maple spoke to her in soothing tones as she did a quick exam, checking the dog's eyes, gums, body temperature and pulse. She scanned the dog for a microchip but couldn't find one.

Then she glanced up at Ford while she gently palpitated the pup's abdomen. "She's a little Cavalier King Charles spaniel. From the looks of it, not even a year old. Dogs really shouldn't have puppies that young. Their bodies aren't mature enough to handle the strain. Plus, Cavaliers have a high incidence of mitral valve disease. No responsible breeder would breed a dog like this until at least two and half years of age, and only then if she's been health-tested and found to be heart-clear, preferably by a veterinary cardiologist."

Ford gritted his teeth. "The very fact that we found her

dumped on the welcome mat is a pretty good indication that whoever owns her isn't all that concerned with ethics."

"Owned." Maple's eyes flashed. "No collar, no microchip... Whoever had her before made sure we wouldn't be able to locate them. She belongs here now, and we're going to do everything we can to save her and her puppies. She likely came from a puppy mill, and when they realized it wasn't going to be an easy delivery, they got rid of her. At least they had the decency to drop her off at a vet clinic."

"I can't believe we found her," Ford said. If they hadn't, she wouldn't have made it until morning. That much was obvious. "What should we do now?"

Maple bit her bottom lip as she studied the dog. "Ordinarily, we'd start with a dose of oxytocin. It enhances uterine contractions. Lots of things can cause dystocia—low calcium, uterine inertia. This dog's small size doesn't help. I doubt she and her puppies have gotten proper nutrition during the pregnancy. She's probably also dehydrated."

"So you don't think the oxytocin would work?"

"It might, but we don't know how long she's been like this. The longer the labor goes on, the more dangerous this situation gets. She needs a C-section." Maple swallowed. "As soon as possible."

"Okay." Ford nodded. They were two medical professionals. They could handle this, couldn't they? "Let's do it. Tell me how I can help."

She glanced up from the dog long enough to flash him a smile. "You seriously want to assist while I do an emergency canine Cesarean section?"

"Of course, I do, but you might need to give me some instructions. We didn't cover this in med school," Ford said as Lady Bird shuffled closer to lean against his leg.

"You know what us veterinarians say, right?" Maple twisted her hair into a bun on the top of her head and miraculously secured it in place with nothing but a pencil from the pocket of her lab coat. "Real doctors treat more than one species."

It was such a Maple thing to say that he couldn't help but laugh, despite the seriousness of their circumstances.

He folded his arms. "Go on, then. Let's make a real doctor out of me."

"I take back what I said." Affection sparkled in her eyes. "You might not be so impossible, after all."

With Ford's help, Maple had the dog—whom she'd christened Ginger, because the sweet thing deserved to be called by a name—prepped for surgery within minutes. Once she'd gotten an IV catheter in place and administered the anesthesia, she got to work shaving Ginger's abdomen while Ford prepared a whelping box for the puppies. He placed a heating pad at the bottom and lined it with blankets for warmth.

With any luck, they'd be able to save Ginger's litter and actually get to use it.

"Ready?" she asked as she positioned the scalpel over the dog's abdomen for a midline incision.

"Ready, Doc." Ford nodded, eyes shining bright over his surgical mask. "You've got this."

She soaked up the much-needed encouragement. Maple had performed C-sections in vet school, but never in an emergency like this. She desperately wanted to save this dog...*and* her puppies. It might seem crazy, but finding a Cavalier in distress like this almost felt like a sign. Like Maple was in the right place at the right time. Like ending up here in Bluebonnet was meant to be, beyond the names that were printed on her birth certificate. A new Cavalier mom and her babies would certainly benefit from having a certified canine cardiologist in town.

But Maple was getting way ahead of herself. She still needed to perform the surgery. Plus, there was the matter of Grover. He was going to flip his lid when he found out about this. He'd demand to know why she hadn't called him before taking matters into her own hands, which was probably a valid question.

Except they didn't have that kind of time. Ginger's pulse was already thready. She couldn't let the dog down.

Maple pushed aside all doubts and got down to business. She held her breath as she made the incision, and then her eyes filled with tears as she caught her first glance at Ginger's moving uterus.

"We've got two puppies, and they're both alive." She pointed toward the squirming pups for Ford to see.

"Well, would you look at that?" he said in an awestruck voice.

"Get ready. I'm going to incise the uterus, and as soon as I remove the first puppy, I'm going to hand it over so you can clear its airway and stimulate breathing."

Ford stood poised with a towel in one hand and a suction bulb in the other.

Everything that happened next seemed to move in fast motion. Maple got the puppies out as quickly as she could. One of them was tiny and delicate, and the other was a downright chunk. The big pup, a boy, had likely been too large for the young mama's birth canal, contributing to her distress. The smaller puppy was a girl, and Maple had a feeling she'd end up looking just like Ginger someday. Mom and her babies all had the chestnut and pearly white markings that the Blenheim variety of Cavalier King Charles spaniels were famous for.

So whoever had unloaded Ginger on the doorstep had definitely been an unscrupulous breeder, angling to crank out a litter of purebred puppies for profit without regard to the health of the mother or her litter. Later, Maple would allow herself to feel properly enraged about that, but right now, all she felt was pure gratitude.

This was why she'd become a veterinarian. Maybe she'd lost sight of some of the reasons she'd gone to vet school in the first place after she'd become bogged down with exams and all-nighters and the extra effort it took to get a specialty certification. After her disastrous attempt at dating one of her study-group partners, she'd closed herself to other students. She'd always been a driven pupil, but she'd doubled down after Justin had taken advantage of her academic prowess.

She'd once heard her mother tell a client that the best revenge was massive success, and Maple had internalized that message without even realizing it. The one time she'd put her heart on the line, she'd gotten hurt. So somewhere deep down, she'd decided to believe all the things her bitterly unhappy parents had told her—and *shown* her—about love. She'd closed ranks around her heart even stronger than before and decided the only path forward was to be the best. Untouchable in every possible way. In the long run, she could love herself better than anyone else could.

Except for dogs.

Maple had always known they knew how to love better than humans did, which was why she'd chosen this life to begin with. It's why she'd dug her heels in and taken the grant when her mom and dad refused to fund her education. But she didn't need to work in a sleek high-rise building or cater to wealthy Upper West Siders to help animals. She could make a difference right here in Bluebonnet. Maybe that's what Percy's grant and his requirement to work for a year at the clinic had really been about.

It was a humbling thought, and it made Maple's throat close up tight as she clipped the second puppy's umbilical cord. She handed the tiny girl to Ford, and the way he looked at her nearly did her in.

He still didn't get it. They weren't alike at all. She wasn't special. She really wasn't…

But this moment certainly was. And Maple wouldn't have traded it for anything.

"Hey there, welcome to the world," Ford cooed as he massaged the puppy with a soft towel to get her breathing.

Maple couldn't wait to join in and check the new babies out from head to toe, but first she needed to get Ginger stitched up. She wouldn't be able to relax until she knew for a fact that the new mom was out of the woods.

But once Ginger was resting comfortably, Maple finally allowed herself to breathe, take a look around and bask in a happiness so bone-deep that it took her breath away.

Ford was bottle-feeding the girl puppy while the boy slept in the whelping box. Lady Bird couldn't seem to decide whether she should stand guard over the puppies or Ginger, so she alternated between all three, keeping a watchful eye over the whole furry family as best she could. And as crazy as it seemed, Maple could almost sense Percy's presence there, too…or maybe that was just wishful thinking.

One thing she knew for certain: he would've been proud, just like Ford's Gram had tried to tell her the other day at the retirement home.

"You okay, Doc?" Ford looked up from the puppy in his hands, sucking greedily at the bottle. Once Ginger was awake, they'd introduce the puppies to their mama. She'd been through a lot, but it was important for her to try and nurse so she could bond with her babies. Even so, the pups would likely need supplemental bottle-feeding for the next few weeks. "That was a lot."

"It was a lot." Maple laughed and plucked the boy puppy

from the whelping box so she could feed him. "But I'm good. I'm more than good, actually. I loved every minute of it. Tonight was..."

She shook her head and held the puppy close to her heart. "I don't think I have words for what tonight meant to me."

Ford stood, and without missing a beat of bottle-feeding duty, he walked over to Maple and kissed her cheek. "You did it, Doc."

"No." She shook her head and grinned up at him, half-delirious. Maple had no idea what time it was. The past few hours had passed in a blur, but she didn't want to close her eyes. She didn't want to miss a single, solitary second of this magical night. "*We* did it."

The magic ended early the following morning when Maple jerked awake to the sound of Grover's gravelly voice echoing throughout the pet clinic's operating room.

"What in tarnation is going on in here?"

Her eyes snapped open, and for a second, she forgot where she was. What was she doing, sleeping on the floor of the clinic, of all places? And what was *Ford* doing here, too? Other than providing her with a nice, strong shoulder to use as a pillow...

Maple sat up, blinking against the assault of the clinic's fluorescent lighting, convinced this was all a stress-induced nightmare. She'd been feeling so out of sorts lately, not to mention the calls and voice mails from her parents, which she'd been ignoring for days. A nightmare seemed par for the course at this point.

But then her gaze snagged on the whelping box beside Ford, who was just beginning to stir, and the events from the night before came rushing back to her. The abandoned dog... The surgery... Two perfect puppies.

And Ford had been there for all of it.

Magic.

"Good morning, Grover," Maple said. Even Grumpy McGrumperson couldn't spoil her mood today. Although it would be really great if he stopped looking at her like she was a teenager who'd just been caught making out with her boyfriend in a parked car. "I can explain."

Grover glanced around the room, frown deepening as he noticed Ginger resting on a soft dog bed in a kennel piled with blankets. "Please do, because for the life of me, I can't figure out if this is a slumber party or a veterinary emergency."

"Both, actually." Maple laughed. Grover, pointedly, did not.

"Hi, Grover." Ford stood and held out his hand for a shake. He had an adorable case of bed head, which probably would've look ridiculous on anyone else but somehow only made him more attractive. "You should've seen Maple last night. She saved that dog's life."

Grover accepted Ford's handshake, and eyed Maple dubiously.

"I would've called you, but there was no time. Someone abandoned Ginger on the steps of the clinic. She was in the latter stages of labor with obvious dystocia and needed an immediate C-section." She glanced at Ford. "We're lucky we even found her."

Grover regarded Ford, still dressed in the scrubs he'd worn to the hospital yesterday. "You assist with veterinary surgery now, Dr. Bishop?"

"Apparently so." Ford chuckled, and something about the deep timbre of his voice sent Maple straight back to last night and the lump that had lodged in her throat at the sight of him cradling a newborn puppy in his strong grasp. "It was fun. Maybe I can do it again someday."

He snuck a glance at Maple, and a million butterflies took flight in her belly.

I'm really in trouble now, aren't I?

Last night had changed things between them, and now there was no turning back. She knew he felt it, too. Ford held her fragile heart in his hands as surely as he'd held those puppies, and it terrified Maple to her core.

What was she going to do?

"Perhaps we shouldn't make a habit of it." Grover's eyes cut back toward Maple. "You do realize the pups will probably need supplemental bottle-feeding for the first few days, don't you?"

Maple nodded. "Yes, sir. We've already given Peaches and Fuzz two feedings, three hours apart."

"Peaches and Fuzz?" Grover's eyebrows rose. "You named them already?"

"Yes, and the mother, too. I'm calling her Ginger."

Grover's mouth twitched, as if he was trying not to smile. No way. Impossible. "So all these dogs are yours now?"

Overnight, she'd gone from owning one large dog to owning two adult dogs and two newborn puppies. It was going to take a full-size moving van to get her to New York when she finally moved back.

If she moved back.

"It's just temporary," she said, doing her best to avoid Ford's gaze. "For now, they're completely my responsibility."

"Have you introduced the pups to the mother yet?" Grover asked.

"Yes, and it went really well. But she was still drowsy from the anesthesia, and I didn't want her to accidentally roll over the puppies, so I didn't think it was best to leave them all together unsupervised."

"And you're keeping them warm?"

"Yes."

"And you offered Ginger a small amount of food and water a few hours after the birth?"

"Yes." Again, Maple nodded.

The interrogation continued, with Grover barking out question after question about the surgery, Ginger's post-op treatment, and the care and feeding of her puppies.

Finally, when he'd exhausted his long list of concerns, he waved toward Ginger's kennel, the whelping box and the pile of old blankets Maple had found in the clinic's donation closet and used for a pallet for her and Ford to get some shut-eye in between puppy feedings. "Now clean all of this up, would you? I've got a poodle coming in for a spay this morning."

He stalked out of the operating room before Maple could respond.

She sighed and glanced at Ford. "Well, that went pretty much exactly like I thought it would. That man really needs to reconsider his stance on caffeinated coffee."

Ford grinned and raked a hand through his hair. "Speaking of caffeine, why don't I run over to Cherry on Top and get us a couple of large coffees real quick? I know I could use it before my practice opens in—" he glanced at his watch and winced "—just under an hour."

"I'd *love* one of their hazelnut cream lattes, if you have time. I think Adaline calls that drink Texas Gold. I'll get all of this cleaned up. For today, I think I'll see if June can keep an eye on Ginger and her babies up front in the reception area. I'll take everyone home with me tonight," Maple said.

She started folding one of the blankets and tried not to think about what Ford's sister would say when she found out they'd spent the night together…*again*. Not that medical emergencies should count. But still…

The purely innocent sleepovers seemed to be occurring with alarming frequency.

"Sounds like a plan," Ford said, and just as he swept a lock of hair from her face and Maple thought he might be about to kiss her goodbye, Grover stormed back into the room.

"One more thing," he bellowed.

Maple's heart hammered against her rib cage as she sprang backward away from Ford. "Y-yes?"

Grover jerked his head toward Ginger and the puppies, and his expression morphed into something approximating an actual look of approval. "You did a good job here last night."

She couldn't believe her ears. Grover wasn't Percy, but he'd been his business partner for a long, long time. She'd never get the chance to hear her father utter those words, but having Grover say them was the next best thing.

"Thank you, Grover. That means a lot," she said before he could stomp off again. "Especially coming from you."

"Right. Well." He shifted his weight from one foot to the other, clearly unaccustomed to issuing such effusive praise. "Keep up the good work."

Happiness sparkled inside her, and just this once, she didn't worry about tomorrow. Or the days or weeks that followed. All that mattered was this day. This place.

This *life*.

"I will."

The text came just after Ford dropped off Maple's hazelnut cream latte with June at the front desk of the pet clinic.

He'd gotten a coffee for June as well, and the older woman had gushed about what a fine man he was to help Maple deliver the puppies. Peaches, Fuzz, and Ginger were all snuggled together in a cozy playpen-like contraption behind the reception desk. Maple had already jumped right into an appointment when a walk-in client had shown up with a lethargic hedgehog.

Ford assured June that was just fine. He needed to get going, anyway. But he'd still paused to watch Ginger and her pups for a moment. The mama Cavalier's tail wagged as soon as she caught sight of him, and Ford couldn't help but marvel at the dog's sweet and trusting disposition, after all she'd been through. Joy warmed him from within just looking at the furry little family.

Something had shifted inside Ford the night before. He'd been drawn to Maple since he'd first set eyes on her—that much was undeniable. But even when she'd kissed him—even when he'd challenged her to do it a second time—he'd thought he'd had his emotions under control. He and Maple were nothing alike. She'd been clear about that right up front. She'd never once tried to hide who she was, unlike his former fiancée, who'd never once told him she had reservations about moving to Bluebonnet. In retrospect, he should've known she was lying. The signs were all there. That relationship had always felt too much like work, unlike the time he spent with Maple. With Maple, he could be himself. He could relax. He could breathe easy, because there was no danger of losing his heart. Maple been perfectly honest about the fact that she couldn't wait to put Texas and all it contained in her rearview mirror, Ford included.

But then she'd stayed.

She'd had chance after chance to make good on her word and leave, but she'd never actually gone. And still, somehow it wasn't until Ford helped her save that dog and her puppies that he'd realized he was falling.

In truth, it had been happening all along. He knew that now. How could he not, when he'd watched her spread joy and light on her pet visits with Lady Bird, even when she insisted it didn't come naturally to her at all? Maybe that's why her commitment to it meant more. Or maybe she was more tenderhearted than she wanted to believe. Either way, it had been a sight to behold. Ford couldn't have looked away if he'd tried.

Then it had felt so nice last night when she'd fallen asleep with her head on his shoulder. So *right*. Ford had stroked her hair and stubbornly refused to move, even when his arm fell asleep. He'd told himself he was simply savoring the moment. Holding on to something—some*one*—whom he'd known from the outset was never meant to be his.

Ford had been doing the right thing his entire life. He'd come back to Bluebonnet to care for Gram. He put his family and his town and his patients first. Always. He'd never once regretted any of it. Just this once, though, he'd wanted to give in to what he really and truly wanted. And he'd never wanted anyone as badly as he wanted Maple.

So he'd let himself believe it was okay to let his guard down…to brush the hair back from her face and caress her cheek and let his fingertips linger on her soft skin while he held her and let himself fall. It might be his only chance to feel this close and connected with the enigmatic woman who'd found her way into his heart when he least expected it.

When morning came, everything had still been okay. Sure, Ford felt like he was walking around with his heart on the outside of his body, but he was good. *They* were good. Even Grover was being decent for a change.

Then Ford's phone chimed with an incoming text.

"See you later, June. Thank you for keeping an eye on the little ones for Maple," he said as he reached inside his pocket for his cell.

He was already outside on the sidewalk soaking up the first rays of the Hill Country sunshine when the message popped up on his screen. He'd half expected it to be from Maple, but instead, the name that popped up above the text bubble was Pam Hudson's from County General Hospital.

Oliver Taylor's bone-marrow biopsy results are in. It's not good news. Thought you'd want to know. I'm sorry.

Chapter Thirteen

Maple had now been in Bluebonnet long enough to expect that word about Ginger and her puppies would spread through town like wildfire. She'd actually been looking forward to it since, according to Adaline's small-town-gossip theory, the next newsworthy event would make everyone forget about the kiss in the town square. If that was the case, bring on the collective amnesia!

What she hadn't expected was the cake. Or the casseroles. Or the pair of giant wooden storks that appeared in her front yard—one pink and the other blue, holding tiny bundles in their beaks labelled Peaches and Fuzz.

Maple peered out her kitchen window at the wooden birds as she handed Adaline a bottle filled with puppy formula. "I don't get it. Can you shed any light on this?"

"You're way overthinking it. They're just yard signs, like the ones people put on their lawns when a new baby is born." Adaline nudged the tip of the bottle into Fuzz's tiny mouth, like Maple had shown her on the first day she'd brought the dogs home to Percy's charming house next door to the clinic.

The puppies had just turned five days old. Ginger was recuperating nicely from her surgery and nursing the babies every day, but because she'd been neglected during her pregnancy, Maple was concerned about her nutrition. She didn't want to exhaust the little mama, so she'd kept the puppies on a supplemental feeding schedule.

Luckily, there was no shortage of volunteers to help out. Like today, when Maple had found Adaline, Belle and Jenna waiting on her front step after work, ready for dog duty. The book-club girls had been taking shifts since she'd brought the dogs home and were still eager to help.

"We don't have yard signs in Manhattan." Maple laughed. "We don't even have *yards*. I have no idea who put those out there. They just appeared out of nowhere the other day."

Belle held Peaches close while she offered her a bottle. "You did an amazing thing. The town just wants to celebrate you."

And they certainly were. The cake had been from Adaline, naturally—a triple-layer, funfetti-flavored wonder, dotted generously throughout with rainbow sprinkles and *Bluebonnet Thinks You're Pawesome* piped in decadent frosting. Then the casseroles had started appearing, wrapped snugly in tin foil. Thankfully, most of them came with heating instructions since Maple had never cooked a casserole in her life. Yesterday, a teacher from Bluebonnet Elementary School had even stopped by the clinic with a stack of drawings of the puppies her first graders had made for Maple.

It was all so…*kind*.

And nothing at all like her job would've been like at the

cardiology practice in New York. Maple knew it wasn't fair to compare, but she couldn't help it. She'd always done her best to keep to herself and fly under the radar. That was impossible in a place like Bluebonnet, and to her surprise, she didn't mind so much anymore. It felt nice.

"Maple, are you doing therapy-dog visits with Lady Bird, or are you too busy with Ginger and the puppies?" Jenna asked.

Ginger sat in her lap while Jenna ran her hand in long, gentle strokes over the dog's back. Maple had noticed a pattern: while everyone else fawned over the puppies, Jenna seemed more drawn to the mama dog. She was glad. That poor dog needed as much love and affection as she could get.

"Are you kidding? The phone is still ringing off the hook, and it's never for me." Maple glanced at Lady Bird, glued to her legs as usual. "Is it, girl?"

Lady Bird woofed right on cue.

"I'm this dog's glorified assistant. The town might riot if I stopped taking her on visits. Why?" Maple asked.

"I have ballet camp starting at the dance studio in a few days, and I was hoping you could bring Lady Bird in for our first morning? Just to put the littlest ones at ease?" Jenna grinned. "I have a tutu Lady Bird can borrow."

"Then how could I possibly say no? Sure, we'll be there."

The answer flew out of Maple's mouth before she had a chance to feel a twinge of anxiety. Oddly, even after she'd spontaneously agreed, the twinge never came.

She buried her fingertips in the soft fur on Lady Bird's broad chest and gave the golden a good scratch. *You did this, sweet girl.* Social anxiety didn't go away overnight. Maple knew she'd probably have a lifelong struggle feeling confident in social settings. But she had the dog to thank for getting her acclimated to the pet-therapy visits and interacting with strangers—strangers who were becoming friends.

Day by day. Visit by visit.

Maple wasn't the same person she'd been two weeks ago. She'd breezed into town intent on changing things, and instead, the town had changed her.

But it wasn't all Lady Bird's doing. Someone else had been there alongside her every step of the way. And much to Maple's confusion, she hadn't set eyes on him for five straight days.

Ford had returned to the pet clinic and delivered her latte, as promised, on the morning after the pups were born. Since then…nothing.

At first, Maple had chalked up his absence to the fact that they'd both been exhausted. He had a medical practice to run, just like she did it. She figured he was simply getting caught up on things. But then one day had turned into two, two turned into three, and so on. With each passing day, Maple had started to feel more and more like a lost puppy herself.

It's for the best. You were scared to death of your feelings for him, and now you don't have to worry about that anymore.

Maple clung to that thought, just like she'd been clinging to it for the past five days. But the more she repeated the mantra, the less she believed it. Because now that he was gone, she was more terrified than ever.

She'd texted a few times and gotten nothing but short, generic responses. Even when she'd sent photos or videos of the puppies, she'd gotten nothing but a heart emoji in return. If it hadn't been for those brief missives, she would've been worried that he'd had an accident or something. But no. He was simply pulling away, just like Justin had done in college, only this was a gradual withdrawal instead of a clean break. She was beginning to realize that the latter would've been far less agonizing. This felt like death by a thousand paper cuts.

"Adaline, can I talk to you for a second?" Maple tipped her head toward the hallway.

She'd sworn to herself she wouldn't do this. Adaline had never been thrilled about Maple and Ford spending time together. She was probably the last person who'd want to shed light on why he was semi-ghosting her.

But she also knew Ford better than anyone else in Bluebonnet. They were close. So Maple had finally decided to swallow her pride and ask.

"This is about Ford, isn't it?" Adaline said as soon as they were out of earshot of the rest of the group. She didn't even give Maple time to answer before her shoulders sagged with relief. "Thank goodness. I was beginning to worry that you weren't ever going to say anything."

The ache that had taken up residence where Maple's heart used to be burrowed deeper, and deeper still. So she hadn't been imagining things. Ford wasn't just busy. Something had happened to make him stay away.

She wrapped her arms around her middle, bracing herself for whatever was to come. "I know you don't think I'm good for him, and I understand why. I happen to agree with you, but—"

"What? No, Maple." Adaline grabbed onto Maple's arm and gave it a tender squeeze. "I don't think that at all."

"But that night at book club, you told me you didn't think we should be together."

"That's not what I said. I remember distinctly telling you that I didn't think it was a good idea for you to kiss him anymore until you knew for certain you were going to stay in Bluebonnet." Adaline's eyes welled up. "I never thought you weren't good for him. You two are so alike. I think you'd make a great couple."

Maple shook her head. "No, we're really not—"

"Stop. You may seem like total opposites on the surface, but you're alike in the ways that matter most. *That's* why I was worried. My brother is head over heels for you, whether he realizes it or not. I knew if you left, he'd be heartbroken. Because you belong together, not the opposite."

Sorrow closed up Maple's throat. She'd spent the past five days trying to convince herself that she and Ford had never stood a chance, and now his sister was trying to tell her they were soul mates or something.

She wished it was true. She'd never wished for anything so hard in all her life.

"That's not what it's like between us," Maple protested.

But Adaline wasn't listening. "I promised to stay out of his business. I swore. So when I realized he'd been spending all his time at the hospital, I didn't say anything. I thought for sure you knew, and then when I realized you didn't, I knew it wasn't my place to bring it up. I figured he'd come to his senses sooner or later, but clearly he's not."

She was talking in circles, and the more she said, the more Maple realized she should've pushed harder. She should've trusted that Ford wasn't the sort of person who'd vanish from her life without good reason. He'd never given her any reason to believe that.

Maple's past had, though. All her life, she'd been taught that feelings couldn't be trusted and love never stood the test of time. Her own limited experiences with dating had confirmed everything her parents had impressed upon her, either by their words or actions. So she'd kept her heart under lock and key. The less she shared herself with other people—people who would only end up hurting her in the long run—the better. Then Ford had come along and stolen her heart when she wasn't looking. And instead of telling him how she felt, she'd held her breath and waited for the other shoe to drop.

Was it any wonder it had?

"Adaline," Maple snapped. "You're scaring me. What's going on? Why is Ford spending all his time at the hospital?"

She didn't need to ask, though. She knew, even before Adaline said it.

Oliver.

The child had been on Maple's mind ever since the teacher from the elementary school had given her the colored drawings of Peaches, Fuzz, and Ginger. She'd brought the pictures home and tacked her favorites to Percy's refrigerator with magnets, and every time her gaze landed on the strokes of bold crayon, she thought about Lady Bird's visit with Oliver.

My mom says when I'm better, I can get a dog of my own. When I do, I want one just like Lady Bird.

She could still hear the little boy's voice, so upbeat and happy, despite his circumstances, just like she could still see his tiny form, dwarfed by the hospital bed…the tired shadows beneath his eyes.

He wasn't getting better, was he? And Maple had been so wrapped up in her own messed-up life that she hadn't for a moment considered that Ford might've been experiencing a crisis of his own.

"He's got this patient." Tears shone in Adaline's eyes, and she let out a ragged breath. "Ford is very attached, and let's just say things aren't looking good. He can't tell me much, but I'm worried. My brother is a mess, and I'm not sure there's anything any of us can do to make things better."

Maple just stood there, shell-shocked, until Lady Bird pawed at her foot, pulling her out of her trance. She dragged her gaze toward the dog, eyes blurry with tears. She blinked hard, and her vision cleared a bit…

Just enough for hope to stir as she realized that maybe there was one small thing she could do to help.

It took longer than Maple would've liked to get ready to go to the hospital. She made an excuse for the book-club girls to leave and then packed things up as quickly as she could, heart pounding all the while.

Lady Bird followed her around the house with her tail hanging low between her legs. Empathy was the dog's strong suit, after all, and she could tell Maple was a jittery jumble of nerves—as evidenced by the way she nearly jumped out of her skin when there was a knock on the front door just as she was almost ready to leave.

Lady Bird, mirroring Maple's disquiet, released a sharp bark. In turn, Ginger let out a low growl in the kitchen. The sweet dog probably thought whoever was at the door must be a threat to her puppies.

"Everyone, let's just calm down," Maple said, as much to herself as to the dogs. "I'm sure that's just Adaline, Jenna, or Belle. One of them probably forgot something."

She swung the front door open without even checking the peephole. Big mistake…

Huge.

"Mom." She gaped at Meredith Leighton, unable to process what she was seeing. Then her gaze shifted to the man standing beside her mother. "And Dad?"

They'd flown clear across the country to Texas and taken a car to Bluebonnet, all the way from Austin? *Together?*

Maybe she was hallucinating. That seemed far more likely.

"Well?" Maple's mother peered past her toward Lady Bird, who'd chosen this most awkward of moments to lose her sense of decorum and bark like she'd never set eyes on a stranger before. Perhaps she'd picked up on the fact that her parents weren't dog people. Either way, it was mortifying. "Can we come in, or will that dog attack us?"

"Lady Bird wouldn't hurt a fly. She just knows I…" Maple shook her head. She couldn't tell her parents she was about to run after a man. They'd probably kidnap her and forcibly drag her out of Texas like she'd joined a cult and needed to be deprogrammed. "Never mind. We were on our way out, that's all."

"Come on in." She waved them inside, then cut her gaze toward Lady Bird. "You're fine. It's all good."

Her mother tiptoed over the threshold, sidestepping Lady Bird as if she was the star of that Stephen King story, *Cujo*.

Dad rolled his eyes at his ex-wife, but once he was inside, he scrunched his nose. "It smells like dog in here."

They still had so much in common, even after decades of trying to tear each other apart. How they couldn't see it was a mystery.

"That's because I rescued a lovely Cavalier King Charles spaniel a few days ago. She was in the late stages of labor when I found her, and I had to perform an emergency C-section. We ended up saving her and her two darling puppies." Maple gestured toward the kitchen. "Would you like to see them?"

Meredith Leighton looked at her like she'd just sprung an extra head and it was wearing a ten-gallon cowboy hat. "No, Maple. We're not here to look at puppies. We're here to take you home."

"What?" Maple shook her head, but somewhere deep inside, she felt like a naughty child who'd done something terribly, terribly wrong. The urge to smooth things over and obey was almost crushing. "If all you wanted was to try and talk me into leaving, you could've just called."

"We've been calling. You never pick up," her father said.

Yes, she'd dodged a few calls. And maybe she'd also deleted a couple voice mails without listening to them. But she knew they'd never understand why she liked it here.

For a second, when she'd first seen them standing there on Percy's doorstep, a sense of profound relief had coursed through her. She'd actually thought that now that they were here, she could show them what made Bluebonnet so special.

The Leightons weren't interested in that, though. Just like they'd never been interested in why she wanted to be a veterinarian instead of going to law school. She knew they loved her, but that love came with strings attached. Too bad they had such an aversion to dogs. Her mom and dad could've learned a thing or two about unconditional love from Lady Bird.

"I'm not going back." Maple took a deep breath and finally let herself say the words out loud that had been on her heart for days. "*Ever.* I'm staying here in Bluebonnet."

Her father's face turned an alarming shade of red.

"You've got to be kidding." Meredith threw her hands up in the air. Lady Bird's head swiveled to and fro, as if she'd just tossed an invisible ball. "You're just going to throw your entire life away for a birth father you never even met? He gave you away, Maple. Maybe let that sink in before you dig in your heels."

Maple reared back as if she'd been slapped.

No wonder she had such a hard time trusting people.

She'd been told over and over again she couldn't count on anyone. She might still believe it, if not for Ford.

Ford!

Maple turned away to grab her purse, Lady Bird's leash, and the other items she'd set aside for her trip to County General.

"What are you doing? Where are you going?" Her mother's voice was growing shriller by the second. *"We just got here."*

"I know you did, and I'm sorry. But like I told you, we were just on our way out," Maple said. She'd never spoken to her parents like this before, and she marveled at how calm she sounded.

"Let's all just settle down." Charles Leighton huffed out a sigh. "Maple, sit."

He pointed at the sofa, and even Lady Bird refused to obey.

"No," Maple said as evenly as possible. "I'm leaving now. The two of you can either stay here and wait until I get back, or you can go back to New York. Either way, I won't be going with you. I want to stay here and learn more about my birth father, but that's not the only reason. This town is special. So are its people. They've inspired me in ways that would amaze you."

Her parents exchanged a glance, and Maple could see the fight draining out of them. They were scared, that's all. They were afraid of losing their only daughter.

"I love you both. That hasn't changed, and it never will." Maple beckoned to Lady Bird and the dog sprang to her feet. "Now, like I said, we have to go. We have someplace very important to be, and it really can't wait another second."

Chapter Fourteen

Oliver grinned as he moved a red checker in a zigzag pattern of jumps, ending in the king's row on Ford's side of the playing board. "King me."

Ford then watched as the little boy plucked two more of his black checkers out of play and added them to the sizable stack of Ford's castoffs piled on the hospital bedside tray. This game was going to end just like the others had, and if things kept going at the current pace, he was about to get trounced in record time.

He placed a red checker on top of the one that had just annihilated half of his remaining pieces. "There you go, bud."

"Are you even trying to win?" Oliver cast him an accusatory glance. "You're not letting me beat you just because I'm sick, are you?"

"Absolutely not. I'm genuinely this bad at checkers." Ford made a cross-your-heart motion over the left pocket of his scrubs.

Granted, the fact that that he was preoccupied with keeping an eye on Oliver's vital signs as they flashed on the monitor beside the bed didn't help matters. He was doing his best under the circumstances, though. He could never beat Gram at board games, either—probably because she was a notorious cheat.

"You're even worse at Go Fish." Oliver snickered.

"Careful, there. Or I'll tell your mom you know where she hides the chocolate bars." Ford winked.

He'd never tell. The kid had him wrapped around his little finger. Never in his career had Ford spent every waking moment of his free time at the bedside of one of his young patients. Then again, no other child had touched his heart in the way that Oliver had.

If only he wasn't fighting the same exact disease that had claimed the life of Ford's childhood friend... If only Oliver's most recent bone-marrow test hadn't indicated that this latest round of treatment wasn't working... If only there was something more Ford could do to help...

If only.

"It's your turn again," Oliver prompted.

Ford slid one of his few remaining checkers from one square to another, and Oliver immediately jumped over it with a double-stacked red playing piece. That's right, kings could move in any direction. Ford had forgotten.

He needed sleep. He was so exhausted from trying to keep up with his regular appointments while also monitoring Oliver's progress as closely as possible that he could barely think straight. Was playing games and coloring with the child in the evenings while his mom worked the night shift doing anything to beat Oliver's cancer?

Doubtful. But Ford wasn't about to let that little boy spend his evenings alone when the odds of him beating the disease were suddenly in doubt. He hadn't been there to spend time with Bobby all those years ago. When his friend passed away, the rug had been pulled out from underneath Ford's entire life. He'd never doubted for a minute that Bobby would recover. Kids like them didn't *die*.

That's how naive he'd been back then. That's how idyllic growing up in Bluebonnet had been. Ford knew better now, and he wasn't going to let the rug get yanked out from under him again without a fight.

He hadn't been around when Oliver had his last bone-marrow test. There hadn't been a reason for him to be there since he was only the child's primary care doctor, but that was beside the point. The kid had very little in the way of a support system, hence his deep attachment to Lady Bird, even though pet-therapy visits typically only took place once a week.

The boy needed a friend, especially now, and Ford could be that friend. *That*, he could do. That much he could control.

He'd dropped the ball for a bit, that's all. Rationally speaking, he knew his feelings for Maple had nothing at all to do with Oliver's illness. But the night the puppies had been born had marked a turning point—Ford had finally let loose and given up control. He'd let himself want. He'd let himself yearn. He'd let himself love. And then, when he'd been the happiest he could remember in a long, long time, he'd gotten the text from Oliver's nurse.

It was a gut punch Ford had never seen coming.

The chemo wasn't working. *No change*, the oncologist had said. Ford didn't understand how that was possible. Oliver was handling the treatments like a champ. His spirits were up. His color looked good. Even the nausea was getting better.

The cancer, on the other hand, wasn't.

"Can we play again?" Oliver asked as he leaped over Ford's last checker. "Please?"

"I don't know, bud. It's getting late, and you have another bone-marrow test in the morning." This one would be different. It had to.

Ford scrubbed his face.

When was the last time he'd slept? He wasn't even sure. Every night when he got home from the hospital, he fell into bed, closed his eyes, and dreamed of Maple. She didn't deserve to be treated like an afterthought. Ford didn't know how to let her in anymore, though. He couldn't wrap his mind—or his heart—around allowing himself to be vulnerable and strong all at once. It was easier—*safer*—to not let himself feel anything at all.

When did you turn into such a caveman?

He wasn't. That was the problem. He couldn't turn it off. No matter how much Ford tried, he couldn't stop thinking about Maple. He had this fantasy that she'd walk through the door of Oliver's hospital room one evening and suddenly, everything would go back to feeling right and good. Ford knew it would never happen. Even if she came, she'd never look at him the same way again. How could she? His actions over the past week had been shameful. Ford knew Maple had trouble trusting people, and in the end, he'd shown her that he was the least trustworthy of them all.

"Lady Bird!" Oliver shouted, fully ignoring Ford's reminder that tomorrow was an important day and he needed to get some rest.

Ford paused from pressing his fingertips against his eyelids to slide his gaze toward the child. He'd known this was going to happen, eventually. Maybe he could get Pam to call Maple and request a visit from the therapy dog, and Ford could make himself scarce before she got there.

No, that would never work. She'd need a ride to the

hospital. He'd volunteered the last time, and Pam wouldn't hesitate to ask him again.

"How about one more game of checkers?" Ford offered. "You really need to rest up. Lady Bird can visit another time."

Oliver's face scrunched. "But she's already here."

He pointed toward the door, and Ford's chest grew so tight that he couldn't breathe as he slowly turned to look.

And there she was. Maple, just like in his fantasy—smiling, with Lady Bird wagging happily at her feet. The only difference between his dreams and the impossible reality taking place was the addition of a large wicker basket in Maple arms.

"Hi, there," she said, nodding toward the basket as she lingered in the doorway. "Lady Bird and I brought you a little surprise, Oliver. Is it okay if we come in?"

Her gaze flitted toward Ford, and his dread coiled in his gut as he waited to absorb the full blow of the inevitable hurt in her gaze—hurt that he'd put there. But when their eyes met, the only things he saw in her beautiful expression were affection and understanding and a tenderness so deep that he very nearly wept with relief.

"Yes! Come in!" Oliver demanded, then clamped a hand over his mouth as he remembered his manners. "Please?"

"Come on, Lady Bird." Maple's eyes glittered. "Let's go visit."

Maple's legs wobbled as she entered the hospital room.

She wasn't sure why she was nervous. The look on Ford's face when he'd first spotted her standing in Oliver's doorway had said more than any words of apology ever could. He'd blinked—hard—as if trying to convince himself he wasn't dreaming. And his eyes, the exact shade of blue as Texas twilight, flickered with regret.

Everything is going to be okay, she wanted to tell him. But she couldn't make that kind of promise. Maple wasn't sure exactly what was going on with Oliver, but whatever it was had sent Ford reeling. That was okay…that was *human*. They could figure out the rest later, but the important thing was she wanted to be here for him now, the same way he'd shown up for her—again and again—since the day she'd come home.

Home to Bluebonnet.

"Hi," she said as he rose from the chair beside Oliver's bed and walked toward her.

He looked exhausted to his core—much more so than the morning after they'd stayed up bottle-feeding puppies. That had been a happy sort of exhaustion. This… This was something else. This was a bone-deep weariness that made Maple worry he might break.

"Hi." Ford cleared his throat, and the smile he offered her was the saddest she'd ever seen. "Thank you. I don't how you got here or how you knew how badly Oliver needed this, but thank you. From the bottom of my heart."

"I'm not just here for Oliver," she said as Lady Bird licked Ford's hand in greeting before trotting toward the hospital bed.

Ford looked at her for a long, silent moment until, at last, the smile on his face turned more genuine.

"You could've told me, you know," Maple whispered. "You don't always have to be the strong one—the one holding up the world for everyone else. It's okay to need people. We all do from time to time. That's a lesson I only learned just recently, by the way."

His tired eyes twinkled. "Oh, yeah?"

"Yeah. From someone I've grown quite fond of." *Someone I just might love.* She took a tremulous inhale. Now wasn't the proper time or place to tell him she was in love with him, but she would…soon. "As for how I got here, let's just say there's a pickup truck taking up two spaces in the parking garage downstairs. For the life of me, I couldn't get that thing to squeeze in between the two yellow lines."

Even if she'd heard from him in the past few days, there would've been no time for driving practice. Caring for Ginger and the puppies was practically a full-time job, and Maple was busier than ever at the clinic since Grover had decided she was, in fact, competent. Just this morning, he'd surprised her by adding her name to the felt letter board in the reception area. It was listed right alongside his, where Percy's used to be. *Dr. Percy Walker* was spelled out directly beneath, along with the years of his birth and death.

"You finally drove Percy's truck?" Ford arched a disbelieving eyebrow.

"I had to do it sooner or later." A smile danced on Maple's lips. "I can't live here permanently if I don't drive, can I?"

He gave her a tentative smile that built as the news sank in that she was staying. For good.

Maple had made up her mind even before she'd told the Leightons she wasn't going back to New York with them. She'd decided a few days ago, and she'd been weaving new dreams for her future ever since. There were still a lot of things to figure out, but she was resolute.

"I just told my parents. They're here, if you can believe it." She blew out a breath. "Or they were. I left in a hurry, so I wouldn't be surprised if they're already headed for the airport in Austin."

The look in his eyes turned gentle, as if he knew how hard it was for her to tell the Leightons she wanted to start a new life here in Texas. He probably did. Ford had always seemed to understand her like no one else could.

"I don't know. From what I've seen, your family doesn't

have the greatest record when it comes to travel plans. Maybe they'll surprise you and stick around for a while," he said.

"Maybe." She took a deep breath. She might like that, actually. Bluebonnet would probably do them some good.

She'd meant it when she'd told them she loved them, just like she'd meant it when she'd said she wanted to learn more about her birth family and this town that had embraced her and made her feel like she belonged. Those two things could be true at the same time. The Leightons had loved her as best as they could. It was the only way they knew how.

"I would've been here sooner if they hadn't turned up out the blue. The only other person who knows so far is Grover." Maple shifted the basket in her arms to hide its contents from view until the big reveal. "I didn't want to tell anyone else until we had a chance to talk. I wanted you to hear it from me, not someone else."

"You're just full of surprises tonight, Doc. I haven't slept much in the past few days. If this is a dream, please don't wake me up."

"This isn't a dream." As crazy as it seemed, it was real life. And Maple was finally ready to grab on to it with all her might.

Ford shook his head and grinned like he still couldn't believe it. "So you're really standing here with a basket full of—" He mouthed the next word so Oliver wouldn't hear, although that was doubtful since the child was chattering away to Lady Bird, who'd traveled all the way to the end of her leash to plant her front paws on the edge of the bed. The boy and the dog were in their own little world. "Puppies?"

"Yes and no." At last, she thrust the basket toward him for a closer look. "Peaches and Fuzz are far too young to leave their mom for any length of time, plus they shouldn't get out and about until they're vaccinated. So I brought the next best thing."

Ford's mouth dropped open as he got a good look at the three battery-operated golden-retriever puppies nestled together inside the basket. They were robotic companion animals, just like the one his Gram had. Except these were miniature versions of Lady Bird, Bluebonnet's unofficial town mascot. As soon as Maple had discovered them on the internet, she'd known they were perfect for her new venture. She'd ordered a dozen of them on the spot.

"You're *certain* I'm not dreaming? Because for the life of me, I can't figure out why you'd have these." He shook his head in disbelief.

"I bought them for Comfort Paws." Maple bit her lip. This was the part she couldn't wait to share with him. She hadn't told a soul—the idea had begun as a passing thought at book club, and the more she saw all the good that Lady Bird did in the community, the more it had taken root.

Ford angled closer, lips curving into a slow smile, almost like he already knew. "What's Comfort Paws?"

"It's what I've decided to name the new pet-therapy organization I'm starting. I have a lot to learn, obviously, but Lady Bird has been a pretty great teacher so far. Ginger's puppies will be perfect for this type of work. Cavaliers love people and make great therapy dogs, just like goldens do. Something tells me I know a few dog lovers who'd want to help get a new group up and running." She grinned, thinking of the book-club girls.

"Oh, there's no doubt you're right about that." He looked at her with a combination of wonder and affection that left her breathless.

She could get used to Ford Bishop looking at her like that, and now she had all the time in the world to do just that.

"So you think this is all a good idea?" Maple nodded at the litter of robot companion animals. "Until we get things off the ground, I've bought some of these guys to share with patients like Oliver and your gram."

Ford pressed a hand to his heart, and she wondered if he, too, was thinking about the day they'd met and tussled over Coco and her dead batteries. She'd been so sure she had him figured out, and she'd never been so wrong in her life. She'd never seen love coming, but it had found her, anyway.

That's the way love worked sometimes—it bowled you over when you least expected it. Love could sneak up on you in the form of well-worn bedroom slippers that felt just right, in the steady presence of a dog with a heart of gold…

In the arms of a man who made you believe in yourself again, even when you hadn't fully realized how lost you were to begin with.

"It's a great idea, sweetheart. It's also rather poetic." The warmth in his gaze seemed to reach down into her soul.

"I like it when you call me *sweetheart*. It's a much better nickname than Doc."

"This might be the best dream I've ever had." His eyes crinkled in the corners. "Shall we introduce these guys to Oliver?"

"I thought you'd never ask."

"Hey, bud." Ford turned his smile on his patient. "Wait until you see what Maple and Lady Bird brought for you."

Maple followed him as he walked closer to the bed, and then she set the basket on the edge of the mattress, right next to Lady Bird's front paws. Oliver's mouth formed a perfect *O* as he peered inside. All three puppies wagged their mechanical tails, and when Lady Bird gave one of the puppies a nudge with her nose, it blinked its eyes and yipped.

Oliver gasped and let loose with a stream of giggles. "They're real! I thought they were stuffed animals, but they're *real*."

And just like that, Maple's heart lodged in her throat. It was such a small thing, but to a boy confined to a hospital bed, this trio of tail-wagging, battery-powered companions meant the world. The light in his eyes was unparalleled.

Maple prayed with all her might that he would be okay.

"Not all the way real, but as real we can get for now," Ford said.

The distinction didn't matter to Oliver. He couldn't have been happier.

"They look just like you, Lady Bird." Oliver scooped a puppy out of the basket as gently as if it was a living, breathing animal, and he held it up to Lady Bird's nose for a sniff.

"Good girl, Lady Bird." Maple massaged the golden behind her ears, praising her for playing along.

"I can feel the puppy's heartbeat!" Oliver held the stuffed animal close to his chest. "Can I keep him?"

"Of course, you can. You can keep all these pups, for as long as you want. They're all yours. Lady Bird and I wanted to make sure you had some doggy company when we're not around."

"I love them," the boy said with a yawn. "And they love me, too. I'm going to sleep with all of them in my bed tonight."

"There's no better medicine than a basketful of puppies." Maple tilted her chin up and swallowed the lump in her throat. "At least that's what my dad always used to say."

Ford caught her gaze as he took her hand in his and squeezed it tight. "Your dad was a good man."

"He sure was." Maple smiled.

And hopefully, in time, I'll learn to love the way that he did. I'll keep growing, keep dreaming, keep believing. I'll hold people dear instead of hiding my heart away.

And through it all, I'll become my father's daughter.

Epilogue

The true dog days of summer came in late August, weeks after Oliver Taylor had been found to be in full remission. On the morning the child had been declared cancer-free, Ford called Maple to tell her the good news, and later that night, after they'd celebrated with champagne and cupcakes from Cherry on Top, she'd found him with his arms around Lady Bird's thick neck, weeping quietly into the dog's soft fur.

They'd been happy tears, but they'd also been much more. Ford had told Maple about his childhood friend Bobby shortly after she'd surprised him at the hospital with the basket of puppies for Oliver, and she knew that in so many ways, their friendship had made Ford into the man he was today. Driven, responsible, fiercely protective of the people he loved. But once Oliver was released from the hospital—an occasion marked with a goodbye party, complete with cake and a real, live golden-retriever puppy that Maple had helped his mom adopt from a local rescue group—Ford seemed less wistful when he talked about his old friend. He shared good memories of their years together. Bobby's grandfather sometimes gave them sugar cubes to feed the ponies at the family ranch, and Ford smiled when he told Maple about the feel of the horses' velvety muzzles against his sticky palm. He drove her down a dusty country road to show her the ranch where Bobby's family used to live and whooped with joy when he realized the treehouse where they'd played together still stood among a cluster of live oak trees. The grief was still there and always would be, but it was less sharp than it had been before. Ford could finally let his dear friend rest in peace.

Between the pet clinic and trying to get Comfort Paws off the ground, Maple was as busy as ever—but not too busy to slow-dance in the kitchen whenever Ford's favorite country song came on. Adaline had made good on her promise to take Maple shopping for more practical footwear, but she'd instantly fallen in love with a pair of western booties so bedazzled with rhinestones that they could've doubled for a pair of disco balls. She wore them almost daily, and they glittered like crazy every time Ford spun Maple in a twirl and sang to her with his warm lips pressed against her ear.

Ginger grew healthier by the day and, with Lady Bird as their self-appointed canine Mary Poppins, the puppies had hit all their biggest milestones on the holidays that dotted the summer calendar. On Memorial Day, their bright little eyes opened. By the time Bluebonnet's annual Fourth of July parade marched through the town square, they were eight weeks old and ready to explore the big wide world outside the Sunday house. Peaches and Fuzz loved everyone they encountered, greeting strangers with an adorable wiggle that always transitioned smoothly into a sit position without any prior training. Maple knew without a doubt they'd both make perfect therapy dogs. Both pups displayed the true Cavalier King Charles spaniel temperament—gentle, affectionate and eager to please.

And now, on the Saturday of Labor Day weekend, the time had come for them to go to their new homes. Adaline was adopting Fuzz, whom she'd taken to calling Fuzzy. Belle had staked her claim on Peaches, and both women were fully invested in completing therapy-dog training. So was Jenna, who couldn't wait to bring Ginger home and give her all the love and spoiling she deserved. Comfort Paws was really happening! On Maple's birthday, her parents had surprised her with a large donation—enough to fund dog training, buy T-shirts with the new Comfort Paws logo, and purchase therapy-dog-in-training vests for the pups scheduled to start class in the fall. Charles and Meredith Leighton hadn't been back to Bluebonnet since their surprise trip a few months ago, and when she'd come home from County General that night, they'd already gone. But slowly and surely, they were coming to accept the fact that Maple had decided how she wanted to live her life and she wouldn't be swayed.

"Ford, what's going on in there? The girls are going to be here any minute," Maple called from the living room, where he'd ordered her to stay put while he got the puppies ready for one last picture with her before they left for their new homes. He'd been holed up with the dogs in the kitchen for several long minutes. She had no idea what they could possibly be doing in there.

"We're just about ready. This is a big day. Peaches and Fuzz are the foundation puppies of Comfort Paws. It seemed like they should dress up for the occasion," Ford yelled from the kitchen.

Dress up? Where had that idea come from? Maple had never once mentioned putting costumes on any of the dogs before. However, Lady Bird was going to make an awfully cute pumpkin when Halloween rolled around.

"Here they come!" Ford announced. Then, in a whisper just loud enough for Maple to overhear, he said, "Wait, Peaches. Come back here. Fuzzy was supposed to go first."

Too late. Peaches came bounding around the corner, scampering toward the living room in a Tiffany Blue sweater with white lettering that Maple couldn't quite make out.

"He dressed you in a sweater?" Maple squatted and called Peaches toward her. "Does he realize how hot it is outside?"

The little dog's tail wagged so quick and fast that it was nothing but a blur. Her paws skidded on the hard wood floor as she flung herself at Maple before landing in a clumsy sit.

She scooped up the puppy and inspected the sweater. An *M* and an *E* were positioned over the dog's back.

ME? Maple was more confused than ever. "Ford, this is super cute, but I'm not sure I get it."

Fuzz came stumbling into the room next, ears flying as he tripped over his own paws. The sweater stretched over his pudgy little body was identical to the one Peaches had on, with one notable exception.

"What does yours say, Fuzzy?" Maple set Peaches back down on the ground and tucked her hair behind her ears for a closer look.

MARRY.

She glanced back and forth between the two dogs. "Me marry?"

Ford strolled into the room behind the dogs with a sheepish grin on his face, the likes of which she'd never seen before. "Fuzz was supposed to go first."

He reached down to rearrange the puppies. "See?"

MARRY ME.

Maple's heart flew to her throat. She was so stunned that she hadn't realized Ford had dropped to one knee when he'd bent to rearrange the dogs and pulled a small velvet ring box from the pocket of his denim shirt—the same one he'd been wearing on the day they'd met, with the sleeves rolled up to reveal his forearms, just the way she liked.

"Is this a puppy proposal?" she blurted through giddy tears.

"It seemed only appropriate. How else would I propose to a woman like the love of my life? I'm not sure you realize this, but you have a thing for dogs." He flipped open the box to reveal a sparkling emerald-cut solitaire surrounded by a frame of slender baguette diamonds. Maple had never seen another ring like it before.

"I love you, sweetheart. I want to keep building this crazy, unpredictable life with you," he said as the puppies climbed all over him in their delight at having one of their favorite humans down on their level. "Me marry?"

It was the most ridiculous proposal Maple could've imagined—as ridiculous as a man bringing a robot dog into the vet's office with a dead battery and a green bean stuck in its mouth.

And that's precisely what's made it perfect.

"Yes, a thousand times *yes*."

* * * * *

A Q&A with Teri Wilson

What or who inspired you to write?

My son Cameron was the first person to really encourage me to pursue writing as a career. I've loved books my entire life, especially romance with all the swoony feels. When Cameron was in middle school, I mentioned that I wished I could a write a book and he told me to just do it. I did, and then my entire life changed. Writing for Harlequin has been the biggest blessing.

What is your daily writing routine?
I usually read a bit in the morning while I drink my coffee and then I exercise, either by walking my dogs or going to a barre class, then I get to work at my laptop. Late afternoon I usually take a little break. I try not to write late at night because when I do, I usually end up deleting it all the next day. If I get stuck, I usually change locations and that helps. I either move to a different room in the house

or pack up my laptop to go write at my favorite cupcake bakery or coffee shop.

Who are your favorite authors?

This is a fun question! I read a lot—mostly romance, romantic comedy and women's fiction. Some of my favorite authors are Michelle Major, Sophie Kinsella, Meg Cabot and Sarah Adams. I'm also a regular reader of several Harlequin series lines: Special Edition, Love Inspired Suspense and Romance.

Where do your story ideas come from?

I'm mostly inspired by experiences from real life. Little snippets from my travels, my pets and day-to-day life pop up in my books all the time. When I'm starting a new book I also like to imagine two people who make the most unlikely pairing possible, and then I throw them together. Let the cute romantic chaos ensue.

Do you have a favorite travel destination?

I love to travel! My favorite destinations are London and Paris. I would love to move to London for three to six months someday and write a book there from start to finish.

What is your most treasured possession?

My dog Charm is my most treasured possession. She is a two-and-a-half-year-old Cavalier King Charles spaniel. Total and complete marshmallow with a heart of gold, although I think of her more as my best friend than a possession.

What is your favorite movie?

This is an impossible question! I love movies, especially romantic comedies. Some of my absolute favorites are classic rom-coms like *Sleepless in Seattle*, *You've Got Mail*, *The*

Proposal and *Sweet Home Alabama*. More recent favorites are *Something from Tiffany's* and *The Hating Game*, both of which are based on fantastic books.

When did you read your first Harlequin romance? Do you remember its title?
Oh my goodness, I remember my first Harlequin with such clarity! I do not know the title, but I was about twelve years old and my family was on vacation at the beach. It was a destination romance, and I remember feeling so swept away by the emotion in the story. I was hooked, and I have never looked back. I think that's why writing for Harlequin was always my dream. Harlequin is synonymous with romance. No one does it better, and it's an honor to be part of that legacy.

How did you celebrate or treat yourself when you got your first book deal?
I went to New York to meet my editor at a conference shortly after I sold my first Harlequin, and I celebrated by buying myself a silver charm bracelet from Tiffany & Co. on 5th Avenue. It has a little silver apple charm on it (for the Big Apple), and I still wear it every day.

What are your favorite character names?
I love the name Henry so much. I have to stop myself from giving all my heroes that name! Eli is also a favorite.

Other than author, what job would you like to have?
Ballerina or princess. Somehow, romance author seemed the most realistic. I would also love to work with dogs in any capacity. My Cavalier, Charm, and I do volunteer work together as a therapy dog team.